AWAKENINGS

AN ASTOR SABBATHIEL NOVEL

AWAKENINGS

AN ASTOR SABBATHIEL NOVEL

GEORGE MANN

BLACK LIBRARY

A BLACK LIBRARY PUBLICATION

First published in 2022.
This edition published in Great Britain in 2023 by
Black Library, Games Workshop Ltd., Willow Road,
Nottingham, NG7 2WS, UK.

Represented by: Games Workshop Limited – Irish branch,
Unit 3, Lower Liffey Street, Dublin 1,
D01 K199, Ireland.

10 9 8 7 6 5 4 3 2 1

Produced by Games Workshop in Nottingham.
Cover illustration by Mauro Belfiore.

See Black Library on the internet at

blacklibrary.com

Find out more about Games Workshop
and the worlds of Warhammer at

games-workshop.com

Printed and bound in the UK.

For Tazio Bettin.

For more than a hundred centuries the Emperor has sat immobile on the Golden Throne of Earth. He is the Master of Mankind. By the might of His inexhaustible armies a million worlds stand against the dark.

Yet, He is a rotting carcass, the Carrion Lord of the Imperium held in life by marvels from the Dark Age of Technology and the thousand souls sacrificed each day so that His may continue to burn.

To be a man in such times is to be one amongst untold billions. It is to live in the cruellest and most bloody regime imaginable. It is to suffer an eternity of carnage and slaughter. It is to have cries of anguish and sorrow drowned by the thirsting laughter of dark gods.

This is a dark and terrible era where you will find little comfort or hope. Forget the power of technology and science. Forget the promise of progress and advancement. Forget any notion of common humanity or compassion.

There is no peace amongst the stars, for in the grim darkness of the far future,
there is only war.

PART ONE

MEMORY

CHAPTER ONE

'Ours is not a universe of poetry, but one of song: the sorrowful
lament of the dying, lilting on the breath of ancient gods.'
– Inquisitor Callius Marloff, *The Book of Endings*,
date unknown

THEN

Snow.

White flakes stirring on the breeze, dancing over the city spires,
occluding the view.

She walks slowly through them, feeling them patter upon her face,
catch in her hair.

There is no sound, not even the crump of her own footsteps.

Her left arm hangs limply by her side. She does not try to move it.

Her stomach aches with the hollow memory of an old wound.

Light flickers. She turns towards it, but there is nothing but the
snow.

Only the snow.

There are others here, too. She can sense it; her hindbrain crawls with agitation, but she is unable to focus – to remember. She can see nothing of them. Not here. Not now.

And so, blind and alone, she walks on through the drifting flakes, always striding forward, always heading–

Sabbathiel woke with a start.

Then she screamed.

She prised open her eyes, but the light was hot and white and blinding, so she squeezed them shut again lest it burn out the backs of her retinas.

She realised she was still screaming, and stopped.

Silence. And then:

'So, you're awake.' The voice was a metallic burr, a cacophony of pipes and whistles. Unfamiliar.

She licked her lips. Her tongue felt thick and dry. 'Where am I?'

'A predictable question,' said the voice. This time, it was tinged with a hint of wry amusement. 'A far more interesting question would be, "Where have I been?" But then, you *are* only human. One cannot expect such perspective from one so young.' Something moved – metal clacking against stone tiles. 'Do you remember?'

'I'm not sure,' she murmured. 'Not really.'

A rasping sigh. 'Then I suppose the interrogation shall have to wait. At least until you have fully regained your faculties. You are currently operating at only eighty-four point seven per cent of your anticipated cognitive capacity.'

Slowly Sabbathiel tested her movement, curling her hands into fists, stretching her neck. She was stiff but apparently unharmed. Her thoughts, though, were slow and cumbersome, as if her mind were wading through molasses... or drifts of snow. She tried to tease meaning from the other person's words.

Where have I been…

A succession of images struck her like a wall. Memories bubbled to the surface of her thoughts. And with them, pain.

She sat bolt upright, clutching at her belly, eyes wide and staring. 'I… I…'

'You are quite well,' said the voice. 'You have been… *repaired.*'

Leofric of the Grey Knights. A storm bolter. A hole…

She pawed at her midriff, but there was nothing but smooth flesh beneath the white cotton gown.

But Calaphrax, the warp storm… the betrayal…

Slowly she regained her breath, forced herself to calm. Her eyes were drawing focus. She looked at the thing that had spoken, standing beside the cot, peering down at her. She fought the urge to recoil.

It had perhaps once borne human form, but now it was a thing of nightmare. Its back was stooped, its shoulders hunched, its face little more than a mechanical skull plugged with an array of pipes and valves. Red, inhuman eyes peered out from the shadows beneath its cowl. It raised a hand, needle-like fingers of metal and ceramic clacking as they twitched in constant motion. It possessed four arms, the second pair sprouting from the misshapen brass casing of its chest. She could not see its lower half from where she was sitting, but judging by its obscene height, it was no longer carried on human legs.

'I am Metik,' it said, its face unmoving. 'And you, Inquisitor Astor Sabbathiel… well, you should be dead.'

The cool breeze on her cheek was a welcome reprieve from the clinical isolation of the old Ecclesiarchy complex in which she'd woken.

Sabbathiel had passed another day in woozy semi-consciousness, drifting in and out of awareness, before finally, that morning, she'd woken feeling more alert – more alive – than she knew she had any right to.

She'd hardly spoken to Metik. She had the sense that she'd conversed with him extensively the day before, though most of his words had become lost in the maelstrom of her fugue. A servitor had provided her with food and water, and she'd found some clothes laid out for her in an antechamber. She still wasn't entirely clear on what had happened, how she'd found herself here, at the mercy of that mechanical *thing*, but that wasn't a situation that would last. She'd get to the truth soon enough, one way or another.

Unconsciously her hand drifted to her midriff, her calloused palm tracing the line of her stomach, feeling the taut flesh beneath the loose fabric of the tunic they'd found for her to wear. She remembered nothing beyond the blistering pain, the shock of the betrayal, the ragged hole punched in her abdomen. And then swirling darkness. She shivered and moved her hand, tucking it behind her back, looking out to sea.

The Ecclesiarchy complex had been built on an island – or rather, an archipelago of smaller islands, now latticed with arched bridges and ornate walkways crafted in the same polished soapstone as the buildings. They were old, she could tell that much, but raised in the style of so many other, similar buildings she'd seen over the years, with towering, nested archways flanked by looming, sightless effigies; low lights and dressed stone, punctuated only by the occasional tapestry or tattered banner. This, Sabbathiel knew, was the aesthetic of worship, right across the galaxy. Even out here, on some insignificant world on the edge of nothingness, the trappings were the same. She supposed it made her feel comfortable, in a way.

The Order of the Empty Chalice, so Metik had told her, confined themselves to the other islands, rarely crossing the bridge to this small, outlying part of the complex, which had once been an infirmary but was now given over to Metik's work. Precisely what that work entailed, Sabbathiel was unclear, but whatever it was, he appeared to have the full sanction of the Order. More investigation, she knew, would be necessary. She'd start by exploring the island, and then seek out Metik to ask him more questions.

She walked down to the shoreline, her boots crunching on the pebble beach. The wind was stirring, whipping her hair up around her face, stinging her cheeks. It seemed only right that she should wake at a place like this. *A shoreline.* She'd heard of old, distant cultures who had once worshipped the shore, throwing offerings into the lapping, foaming waves. The shore, they maintained, was where the barriers between the land and the sea became rugged, uncertain – temporary. A place of transition, where one thing became another. A place where people could even return from the dead.

She heard footsteps on the stones behind her and turned, her hand automatically swinging to her hip, where her sword would once have been buckled. She sighed, relaxing at the sight of another servitor, which was eyeing her with a glassy, slack-faced expression. This one might still almost pass for human, if it weren't for the washed-out pallor of its flesh and the knotwork of cables erupting from the back of its skull. A diode winked above the orbit of its left eye, and its hand twitched unconsciously, like Metik's, suggesting that the tech-priest's consciousness was currently piloting the servitor's hollow frame.

'Yes?' she said, with a shrug.

The servitor remained motionless, silent.

'You want me to follow you?' It was a rhetorical question – the servitor clearly had no capacity for speech. She shrugged. 'Lead on, then. It's not as if I have anything better to do.'

* * *

Metik awaited her in a gloomy chamber that might once have been a chapel, judging by the towering window in the far wall that depicted some ancient saint in ebon power armour, carried aloft on the wings of a cherubin flock. What light did penetrate the gloaming was streaming through the coloured glass to form shifting pools upon the flagstones, designed, Sabbathiel considered, to resemble puddles of spilled blood. The air was filled with the rich tang of oil and burnt ozone.

Metik, who was settled in a nest of cables and hololith projectors, turned his head to regard her as she entered the room. The servitor remained motionless by the door. 'Inquisitor. You look well.'

'I'm alive,' she said, as she crossed the room to stand before him. 'Which in itself is… somewhat surprising. I trust I have you to thank for such fortune?'

Metik made a clicking sound that might have indicated amusement. 'In part,' he said. 'You were brought to me for treatment.'

Treatment. That was a considerable understatement. 'By whom?'

'A colleague, I presume, of the Ordo Hereticus. A man who, it seems, holds you in great regard.'

'His name?'

'Mandreth.'

Sabbathiel frowned. 'I know of no man by that name.'

Metik made a shrugging motion. His fingers clacked in a distracting rhythm. 'Then you have on your hands a mystery, inquisitor.'

'So it seems. Tell me, how long since he departed?'

'Twenty-seven days, thirteen hours and nine seconds,' replied Metik.

'And he left no word, no explanation?'

'Incorrect,' said Metik. His head twitched. He looked to the door. Sabbathiel followed his gaze to see a servo-skull hovering in the opening. It had been constructed from a bleached human skull, now appended with squirming mechadendrites and a halo of bristling antennae. One of the eye sockets had been fitted with a sensor array that glowed piercing red in the gloom.

'Greetings, ma'am,' said the skull. The voice was shot through with a burring mechanical tone but was nevertheless unmistakable.

'Fitch?' Sabbathiel peered at the skull, as if trying to give it new form, to remember the shape of the flesh and muscles that had once enclosed it. *Could it really be?*

'Aye, ma'am. Or what remains of him, anyway,' replied the grisly device.

Sabbathiel wheeled on Metik. 'What is the meaning of this?'

Metik spread three of his arms in a conciliatory gesture. 'Inquisitor Mandreth thought you would be pleased. He claimed to have recovered the remains of your former acolyte from the same warp storm where he found you, on the edge of the Calaphrax Cluster. He also reclaimed a suit of Terminator armour he believed belonged to you.'

Sabbathiel approached the servo-skull. *Fitch.* Cursed with the gift of honesty, he'd been the only one amongst her followers who'd ever freely spoken his mind. The only one who hadn't feared her. Because of that, she'd trusted his counsel above all others'. Even when she'd chosen to disregard it. And this is what had become of him. Not much of a reward for all those years of service.

She peered down at him, wondering if there was something more intrinsic in this device than a mere machine, but the skull met her gaze with blank regard. 'And the others?'

'I know nothing of any others,' said Metik.

Sabbathiel's head bowed momentarily, then came up again. 'How long? How long have I been gone? Months? *Years?*'

'Almost a century,' said Metik.

Sabbathiel opened her mouth to reply, but there were no words.

A *century.*

'Much has changed,' said Metik. He was slowly extricating himself from the nest of wires. He moved around to stand before her. 'The Imperium is not what it once was. The galaxy is torn asunder. The Adeptus Astartes prosecute a vast campaign. The Golde–'

Sabbathiel glowered at him. '*How?* How did I survive, for a century, with a wound like that?'

Metik hunched forward, so that his face was only inches from her own. 'The vagaries of the warp...' he said, but even for a machine, it sounded unconvincing. He craned his neck, regarding her from a different angle. 'What I would give to know the dreams inside that head. To understand the things that you have seen.'

'No. That's not enough. That cannot be enough. A *century...*'

Metik laughed. 'As I said, inquisitor, you should be dead.'

CHAPTER TWO

'All transformation is, at heart, born of conflict, and in turn, all wars are naught but the violent death throes of one state as it gives itself over to another.'

– Garrok the Elder, *Treatise on Warfare, Vol. IV*

NOW

The loose shale surface was covered by a foot of saltwater.

For as far as she could see, right to the clean line of the horizon, the ground was submerged, creating the somewhat alarming illusion that she was walking upon the surface of some unnaturally calm sea: glassy, serene. A sea that, she knew, hid long-buried secrets.

With every step, they walked upon the story of this broken world; the history of ancient conflicts, written in its strata, long ago drowned beneath the silent depths of that becalmed water. Sabbathiel wondered what had happened here to render the place so desolate, to utterly transform the face of the planet. The data files were scant on detail, describing only a world ravaged by ancient war. But then, weren't they all? Rare were the hidden corners of the galaxy that had not been touched by conflict.

Here, though, on Balthos, it felt somehow different. This was not a world that had been burned, or purged, or razed to oblivion. Nor had the ships come to enact Exterminatus upon the desolate remains. No, here was a planet that had been *transfigured*, its very essence altered. A world that had been drowned.

And now, the pilgrims had come. There to worship that eerie transformation. There to worship the *change*.

Sabbathiel could see their pyramidal structure, proud in the distance. It rose from the water like a glistening jewel of white and gold, shimmering in the reflected light of the bloated sun. It was the only thing that punctured the surface of the water, aside from the gnarled boughs of a handful of trees and the shell of what appeared to be the rusted hulk of a shuttle. Overhead, the silhouettes of enormous birds soared on majestic wings, but Sabbathiel could sense their reptilian glare, their hunger. Balthos was not a place that welcomed newcomers.

Especially those wearing Terminator armour, come to wreak havoc and destruction beneath its watery sun.

To Sabbathiel's left trudged Metik, his four blade-like legs making light work of the bindweed that lurked beneath the surface of the water. His servos whined with every movement, and the *click-clack* of his ceramic finger casings were a persistent annoyance. Scuttling around on his shoulders was his familiar, Nimbik – a construct he'd somehow fashioned from the skull of a large rat, adorning it with trailing mechadendrites and sensor clusters, along with three nimble legs. Sabbathiel guessed it was nothing more than a mindless shell, slaved to Metik's own mental routines – a device used for spying and surveillance – although

Metik treated the thing as if it were somehow independent of its master. She supposed she could understand that: hovering above her left shoulder was the servo-skull crafted from the remains of her erstwhile companion Fitch.

Somehow Mandreth, whoever he was, had deduced that the thing would be a comfort to her, a familiar voice in a galaxy that had changed beyond all reason while she'd slept. It had worked, too – Fitch's voice had proved something of an anchor these last few weeks, a still point in the storm. The servo-skull had calmly explained to her all that had occurred: the rending of the Imperium, the nightmares that had spilled into reality, the ensuing *silence* from Terra. There were rumours, of course, of a bright crusade of Adeptus Astartes, of ancient heroes awoken from aeons of slumber. She could have laughed at the irony of it, if she didn't already know the Space Marines for what they truly were.

Sabbathiel had once believed the Astartes to be the ultimate expression of the Imperium's might – crusading soldiers impervious to the dark imprecations of the warp. But then she'd encountered a fallen angel, an ancient, black-armoured warrior bearing the insignia of the Dark Angels, and she'd learned the bitter truth: that even these so-called scions of the Emperor could not be trusted. The traitor had killed her acolytes – had tried to kill *her* – and yet still wore the symbol of his Chapter with pride.

Since that day, she had dedicated her life to exposing the truth. To investigating the terrible secret at the heart of the Dark Angels, and many other Chapters besides. She had found evidence of traitors everywhere she looked – and more, she had watched as the Astartes closed ranks to prevent such knowledge coming to light.

And then, at the very point of her victory, as an army of

traitors had gathered in the Calaphrax Cluster and she was mere moments from exposing the truth, the Grey Knights had turned on her, too, and she had been cast into the warp and left for dead.

The galaxy was aflame with the fires of heresy, and they burned ceaselessly and without mercy.

And now here she was, playing games, wasting her time on a literal backwater to put down a few upstarts in order to prove a point.

So be it.

'If this water gets any deeper, that frecking rat-thing won't be the only thing riding someone's shoulders.'

To Sabbathiel's right, the squat, Brondel, was kicking angrily through the shallows, mumbling a string of obscene curses beneath his breath. He was half the size of Sabbathiel in her Terminator armour, and the waterline reached over his knees, sloshing around his thighs as he walked. He'd cinched his ammunition belt up high around his chest, and his red beard, which trailed almost to his waist, was spattered with scintillating beads of water. His goggles were pulled down low over his eyes. He claimed his eyes were sensitive to the harsh sunlight after so long working the prison mines of Astoria V, but Sabbathiel couldn't help wondering if it were just another form of shield. Either that, or he liked the way they looked.

The rest of her small team had split off shortly after disembarkation to approach the pyramid from a different direction. She scanned the horizon but couldn't make them out. She'd ordered them to maintain vox silence during the approach, but now she was itching to know of their progress. These new acolytes – or mercenaries, as none of them yet bore her any loyalty beyond the promise of plentiful credits – remained relatively untested. One brief excursion to take down an infestation of xenos-infected miners had been revealing, but the team was not yet forged, robust. A handful of useful individuals who had yet to learn to fight alongside one another, or to care enough to bother. Nevertheless, inexplicable as it might be, she had faith in this motley team – or at least, in the veracity of her own choices. And besides, the squat was entertaining.

'Look at it this way,' said Sabbathiel, grinning down at the diminutive figure, 'after the mission, you'll have no need of a bath.'

At this, the squat hawked up a thick gobbet of phlegm, which he spat out of the corner of his mouth in abject disgust. 'A bath? For freck's sake, why would I want a *bath?*' He shook his head in utter disdain.

'Charming,' said Metik, in his impassive, mechanical drawl.

Sabbathiel laughed, and she had to admit, it felt good. She knew it wouldn't do to let her guard down, to get attached to any of the misfits she'd assembled here, but she'd effectively been dead for a century, and Throne, she needed this – needed to feel a part of something again. She might as well enjoy it for now. At least until one of them put a foot out of line… which she knew, with the steely certainty of experience, was a sad inevitability.

Metik, though – he was another thing altogether. A creature of ambiguity, whose motives remained frustratingly opaque. Once, perhaps centuries ago, perhaps even longer, the tech-priest had been a man, and like all men he was subject to the depravations of need, desire and greed. No matter how much he'd replaced his flesh and bones with iron or clad himself in armour and augmentation – no matter how he might dress his words in the rigid strictures of logic – he remained but a man at his core. And as Sabbathiel well knew, men did *nothing* for free.

Metik had *repaired* her. He had synthesised flesh and regrown bone, fabricated organs and transfused blood. He had thought to rebuild her, to make her whole. But she was not whole. She would never be whole again.

And she was still unclear *why* he'd done it.

Mandreth had promised favours, that much was obvious, putting himself and his conclave in the tech-priest's debt. But why would Metik then choose to accompany Sabbathiel here, to Balthos, with her new team? It wasn't as if she'd extended an invitation or tried to recruit him as she had the others. She found his presence eerie, unsettling. Yet he'd insisted, claiming he wanted to see how his work held up in the field – that she might be grateful for his medical assistance if she or any of her followers were to suffer serious injury.

In the end she'd relented, rationalising that she could make use of his skills. Nevertheless, she couldn't shake the feeling that he had somehow come here with a view to protecting his investment – that he saw her as some sort of collateral that might prove valuable to him down the line. After all, those that had lived as long as he had tended to take a long view. To him, this entire mission was probably nothing but an amusing diversion.

'Any signs of activity from the pyramid?' she asked.

'Oh, they know we're here,' said Metik, his finger casings clacking with their usual flourish. 'They're just biding their time to see what we do.' He turned to regard her, his eye-lenses flaring in the reflected light.

'Then the plan remains unaltered,' she said, meeting his unnerving gaze. He gave a curt nod and turned his attention back to the horizon.

Sabbathiel sighed. Perhaps she'd be able to get rid of him when the mission was over, escort him back to his island workshop and forget he ever existed. Or put a bolt-round through his head. In the meantime, she'd just have to get used to the fact that she was stuck with this extra, unwelcome shadow, his strange mechanical eyes tracing her every movement.

Interrogator Bledheim hated the water, with a vehemence that he typically reserved for heretics or, on occasion, the pious bastards who took to judging him for his more specialised line of work. Or, as he liked to think of it – his *art*. He supposed that some people simply lacked sophistication, the ability to see the *possibilities* in what he did. Others, meanwhile, were rather more discerning.

Take the woman, Silq. She was happily trudging through the shallows as if she didn't have a care in the world, merrily soaking up – in this case quite literally – her surroundings, appraising it all with a studied technoarchaeologist's eye. Her brown skin was smooth and unblemished, her goggles pushed back upon her forehead to keep her hair out of her face. She was young. Or, at least, younger than Bledheim, by some margin. But she was observant, too: since joining Sabbathiel's entourage, she'd always shown Bledheim the respect he deserved, even if that did mean awarding him something of a wide berth. No, she had been one of Sabbathiel's better recruits. She'd even proved herself in battle, back on Lanclaw III, where the newly forged team had taken a little 'practice run' against a brood of hostile, xenos-worshipping cultists.

In the wrong company, though – he was thinking about those pious bastards again – she'd be dragged off to some austere temple to face judgement and summary execution for her reckless, heretical behaviour. All because she dared to carry a xenos weapon slung across her back.

Bledheim felt differently about such matters. If nothing else, her choice of armament was a demonstration of her strength of character, and Sabbathiel, he gathered, had always been more tolerant of such things – providing they were put to good use in the name of the true cause. He studied the rifle now, bouncing in its makeshift sling as Silq walked, the chamber of strange green light along its barrel pulsating with every movement. It was a thing of beauty.

She must have sensed him looking, for she slowed her pace, turning to glance back over her shoulder in his direction. Water stirred in ripples around her calves.

'What is it, Bledheim?' she said. She sounded exasperated, rather than angry.

'I haven't the slightest idea what you mean,' he replied, with a twitching smile. Inside the folds of his long coat, his fingertips danced, wiggling the brace of needles that capped them. 'Is there a problem?'

Silq frowned, narrowed her eyes. Then, with a sigh, she shook her head. 'No. No problem. But let's keep it that way, shall we?'

Bledheim inclined his head fractionally in acquiescence.

Silq resumed her march towards the pyramid in the distance, hoisting the overstuffed bag on her shoulder.

Bledheim, too, continued on behind. He stepped carefully to avoid a thick knot of bindweed but yanked his foot back out of the water almost as soon as he'd placed it, grimacing in disgust at the bobbing thing he felt, then saw, brushing against his leg.

'What *now?*' said Silq, sloshing once more to a halt.

Bledheim regained his footing. He felt his cheeks flush. 'Nothing. Just an old corpse, caught in the bindweed beneath the surface.'

He looked again at the blubbery, waterlogged body that had snagged his leg. It had probably once been human. The flesh was pale and bleached, and had taken on a waxy aspect, there beneath the salty water, as if it weren't quite in focus, blurred around the edges. Its head was bobbing back and forth with the motion of the water, offering some strange semblance of life, trailing hair billowing like fronds. The face was fixed in a grotesque smile, the eyes long rotted in their sockets, or else consumed by carrion creatures or any of the other nightmarish things that probably lurked beneath the surface. He wondered how long it had been there. It was utterly revolting.

'It could be the remains of a combatant from the battle that destroyed this place,' said Silq. She'd come to stand beside him and was peering down into the water. 'Although there's not much left to go on. The salt water has probably helped to preserve what remains.'

'Fascinating,' said Bledheim.

'Hardly,' said another voice from over his shoulder, the irony of his comment lost on the speaker. 'There are scores of them here. We're traipsing across a battlefield.'

Bledheim turned to see Mercy standing watching him, her arms folded across her chest, a wry smirk on her face. She was a far cry from Silq, in almost every respect: tall, muscular, and with a barrel-like torso that made a distinct whirring sound, which could only be heard when you were standing close enough – which, according to Mercy, inevitably meant you were *too* close. She carried an immense two-handed power sword, which was currently hanging from a hoop across her back. She too had a large sack slung over one shoulder.

Bledheim hadn't quite made up his mind about her yet. He didn't doubt the fact that he would rather be on her side in a fight – he'd seen her rip a cultist in half with her bare hands – but there was something just a little *vulgar* about the woman. Perhaps it was the fact she seemed to derive such satisfaction from the sheer mess of it all; that the spilling of blood to her was an act of disorder and frenzy, rather than calculation and cunning. Not that he didn't understand what it was like to watch a person die at your command – he saw the allure of that all too well – it was more that she did it with such a lack of finesse.

Still, he reflected, he was intrigued to discover more about the woman. To find out what made her tick.

Silq waded over to join Mercy. She dropped into a crouch, fishing about in the water with her hand. 'You're right. This place is littered with the dead.' She cupped her hand beneath the neck of another corpse, partially lifting it from the water. Runnels streamed from a hole in the back of its skull.

'Delightful,' said Bledheim. 'What a pleasant world we find ourselves upon.'

'It bothers you?' asked Mercy. 'Being around the dead.'

Bledheim shrugged. 'We're all just corpses in the end,' he said. 'Although given the choice, I'd rather not see them moulder.'

'Then I suggest you keep your eyes up as you walk,' said Mercy. She turned away and walked off, splashing loudly as she kicked her way through the morass of bindweed and floating dead.

Silq allowed the corpse in her grip to slip back beneath the surface, sending ripples burbling as the hollow skull once again began to fill with water. She wiped her hands on her thighs, shrugged, and went traipsing after Mercy. The bag on her shoulder clanked noisily as its contents knocked together with every step.

Sighing, Bledheim struck out after them, mindful of his footsteps.

Above, one of the flying reptiles issued a shrill cry, and he glanced up to see their numbers had increased in the last few minutes. They were circling above a particular spot, a mile or so to the east. Right where he imagined Sabbathiel and the others to be – assuming they'd kept pace with his own small group. As he watched, one of the reptiles broke formation, tucking its wings as it fell into a steep dive, jaws widening.

'Oh,' he said, to no one in particular. 'They're going to attack.'

CHAPTER THREE

'The death of worlds is carried on the perfumed breath of saints.'

— Jacobius Slint, *On the Conquest of Escher*

THEN

She was on the beach again.

These past days, she'd grown accustomed to the gentle lapping of the water against the stones, the susurration of the leaves on the bola trees, the incessant bite of the cold wind in her face. She'd found calm. Or at least, something approaching it. The nights were still plagued by creeping terror, by flitting memories – stuttering images of towering, armoured giants; the bubbling horror of the warp storm; the punch of a bolter shell rupturing her gut. Those, and the dreams of walking through the snow.

The Calaphrax Cluster was a lifetime ago, literally, and she had begun to wonder what difference it would really make if she never fully remembered what had happened in those closing moments before the warp storm rolled in, drowning everything, obscuring all that had passed. Like a wave lapping at a shore-line, ready to carry away the detritus of the past. This, then, was a new beginning, an opportunity to start again. Whoever Mandreth was – and she intended to find out – he had granted her a profound opportunity. She would not waste it.

Sabbathiel grunted, and then pivoted, swinging her sword in a wide arc, before spinning it around deftly before her, describing turning wheels in the air. Her hands moved in a blur, sweeping, dancing, diving. She pivoted again, keeping the blade moving around her as she altered her position, twisting at the waist, pushing her weight onto her front foot.

Nearby, the servo-skull – Fitch – hovered at head height, tracing her movements with apparent disinterest.

The burn in her muscles was welcome, and her head felt truly clear for the first time since she'd woken from her long sleep. It seemed her body still remembered, even if her mind refused to cooperate; she hadn't lost her ability to fight.

She planted her left foot amongst the loose stones and turned, bringing the sword around and down in a sweeping arc. It whispered through the air, slicing easily through the imagined enemies that assailed her.

If only it were that simple.

'Ma'am. There's someone coming down from the cloisters.'

Sabbathiel watched the path, narrowing her eyes as she searched for whomever Fitch had seen. 'I can't...' she started, then trailed off as the silhouette of a tall, willowy man hove into view. He was heading in Sabbathiel's direction.

'Who is it?'

'Unclear,' said Fitch, 'but he's wearing the sigil of the Ordo Hereticus on his lapel, so I'd venture he's here to talk business.'

Sabbathiel scowled at the servo-skull, and then allowed the edges of her lips to curl into a tight smile. *Yes, it was good to have Fitch back.* She returned to swinging her sword in silence.

A short while later, Sabbathiel heard boots crunching on the loose stones behind her. She turned on the spot, whipping her sword up and around, so that, as she came once more to a rest, the tip of her blade wavered mere inches from the newcomer's throat.

To his credit, the man didn't even blink. 'Inquisitor Astor Sabbathiel, I presume.' His voice was reedy and high-fluted but carried with it an air of confidence. He was clearly used to command. He ran a hand through his thinning, grey hair. He was dressed in a tanned leather greatcoat, beneath which he wore a plain black shirt and trousers. His face was thin and weather-beaten, but clean-shaven. He peered along his long nose at her with eyes the colour of ancient ice. They weren't eyes she'd encountered before.

'I hadn't expected a welcoming committee,' said Sabbathiel, lowering her sword, 'but then I hadn't expected to be alive.'

The man looked unmoved. 'I am Heldren,' he said. 'I've been charged with assessing your... well, *you.*'

Sabbathiel nodded.

Heldren glanced at Fitch, raised a quizzical eyebrow, and then shrugged. 'Might we take a walk?'

Sabbathiel scabbarded her sword. 'It's not much of a view. Unless you like water.'

Heldren indicated for her to lead the way, then fell in beside her. 'You appear in good health.'

'As good as can be expected,' said Sabbathiel, 'given the circumstances.'

'I understand your wounds were extensive,' said Heldren.

'The tech-priest keeps telling me I should be dead. Whatever he did, though – it worked.'

'Be mindful,' said Heldren. 'The tech-priest might be an ally, but he is certainly not your *friend*.'

'And you?'

'Oh, I'm no friend either,' said Heldren, with a dry laugh, 'although I suppose you have little choice but to take me at my word.'

Sabbathiel shrugged. 'Or not. You've seen what I can do with this sword.'

Heldren glanced over at her, a new appreciation in his eyes. 'It seems the stories about you are true.'

'That there are few amongst the ordo that can match my skills with a blade?'

'That you're a hard-nosed bitch.'

Sabbathiel laughed. 'Oh, the tech-priest could have told you that.'

They walked on in silence for a moment, their boots crunching on the pebbled beach. Out to sea, birds squawked noisily, diving amongst the roiling waves for prey.

'What happened to you, Sabbathiel? What did you see out there at Calaphrax? To be alone in the warp for so long... were you conscious?'

Sabbathiel sighed. 'No. I don't think so. There might have been moments, fragments of lucidity, but my memories are unclear. To be honest, I'm not sure I *want* to remember. I'm back now. That's all that matters.'

'I believe you have Inquisitor Mandreth to thank for that.'

'Indeed. I know nothing of the man. Who is he?'

Heldren shrugged. 'He's not one of ours. Hereticus, but another conclave altogether. I'd never even heard of him, until we received word that you were here.' He paused, dragged his thumb along the line of his jaw. 'The fabled Astor Sabbathiel, returned from the dead.'

'I don't know you,' said Sabbathiel, after a moment.

'And therein, we reach the nub of the problem,' said Heldren. 'The conclave is… well, let's just say that we're unsure how to proceed. You've been gone for some time. There are rumours…'

'What rumours?' snapped Sabbathiel.

'That you started a private war against the Adeptus Astartes. That you went after the Dark Angels–'

'I went after *traitors*,' said Sabbathiel. 'No more, no less. I did my duty. I sought the truth.'

'And how did that work out?' said Heldren. There was no hint of irony in his voice, but his crooked smile spoke volumes.

'I was betrayed,' hissed Sabbathiel. 'Left for dead.'

'Left to drift in the heart of a warp storm that still rages,' said Heldren. 'Over a hundred years ago. You can see my dilemma?'

'No,' she said. 'You're going to have to enlighten me.'

'Come now, surely you must understand. A feted member of our ordo sets off on a personal crusade against the Emperor's own. Her acolytes are all killed, and she, too, is presumed dead, only to reappear a century later, on an isolated outpost, having been dragged from the embrace of a terrible warp storm and rejuvenated by a tech-priest who's been put out to pasture there, himself the subject of rumours that should already have seen him executed. Not to mention the other interested parties.' Heldren let that hang for a moment, then sighed. 'It's not that you're not trusted, Sabbathiel…'

She laughed. 'I can see why they sent you, Heldren. You have a way with words.'

'You'd say the same if the situation were reversed.'

'Of course I would,' said Sabbathiel. 'But we're not talking about you. We're talking about *me*.' She stopped in her tracks and turned to meet Heldren's gaze. 'The conclave has nothing to fear from me. My dedication to the Ordo Hereticus remains unchanged. I've always been a strong voice in their ranks. I can be an asset once again.'

'For what it's worth, I don't doubt it,' said Heldren. 'Yet there remain questions.'

'Then allow me to answer them.'

Heldren smiled. 'I was hoping you'd say that. There is a way, I believe, that you might prove yourself to those who would doubt you.'

'Go on.'

'The planet Balthos. There are stories of a cult...'

'Balthos is dead, abandoned. Unless that's changed, too?'

'So much has changed that I don't even know where to start,' said Heldren. 'The galaxy has been sundered. The light of the Astronomican fades. There is much you need to know.'

'And Balthos?' she prompted.

'Not dead. Changed. And now, repurposed. The cult has taken root. They must be eradicated, like the vermin they are.'

'You want me to do your dirty work,' said Sabbathiel. 'To go to Balthos and cauterise the infection.'

'I do.'

'And then you shall speak on my behalf to the other members of the conclave?'

Heldren smiled. 'My word carries some weight. I shall add that weight to your cause.'

'And if I refuse?'

'Oh, Sabbathiel. We both know the answer to that.'

Sabbathiel's fingers played upon the hilt of her sword for a moment, before dancing away again. Heldren looked amused. 'All right. Give me a ship and the resources I'll need, and I'll start assembling a team.'

CHAPTER FOUR

'How far His spirit has wandered, how long He has dreamed. Does He not grow weary? Does He not seek the joy of rebirth, so that He might once again bring light to this galaxy of lamentable darkness?'

– Heraldus, Master of Relics,
Order of the Withered Rose

NOW

She walks in darkness.

Her ears ring with the terrifying sound of the silence; with the rushing of blood, the thump of her own heart beating in cadence with her empty footfalls.

She is not alone. She knows that. But she sees nothing. Hears... nothing. She calls out, but no words pass her lips. She shouts until her throat is raw, until her lips have split and cracked and warm blood trickles down her chin. But still, nothing.

She doesn't know where this place is. How did she get here? Where has she been?

She is trapped here, in this void, this prison. Here, with all her fears, all her doubts.

She dares not look to her left. She knows that's where they're standing, watching. Judging. She cannot bear the thought.

And then a sound: the bark of a storm bolter, firing at close range. Loud, sudden and appalling.

She staggers back, eyes wide, hands fumbling for the ragged hole in her gut...

...but there is no hole. There is no storm bolter.

The rustle of wings. Familiar. Comforting. Feathers, embracing. She wants them to furl around her, to entomb her, to keep her safe. But they do not.

And then cold darkness, and silence again.

Still, they watch. She feels their presence. Feels their eyes, burning.

There is nothing to be done. She knows she has to look. She must look. She must face her fear. Embrace its gifts.

She turns...

...but the woman who'd been watching has already turned away, is walking off into the darkness, her golden armour shining in the no-light.

She runs after her, reaching out a hand, but the woman has already gone, and she's alone once more. Alone and scared.

The creature fell from the sky like a shard of metal, a sleek silhouette against the stark glare of the blazing sun.

Sabbathiel didn't have time to think, to plan her response, but her body reacted as if it had been expecting such an attack all along, instincts driving her left – one step, two – bringing her arm up and around so that the blade of her stave swung around on an intercept course, cleaving the creature's head from its shoulders even as it came in for the kill.

The body hit the water with a spasming thrash, the sheer velocity of the impact causing the ground to tremble momentarily beneath Sabbathiel's feet. Close by, the creature's head bounced through the shallows, until the tip of its spear-like beak snagged on a clutch of bindweed and abruptly came to a halt, foul blood trailing in the murky water.

The thing was huge – the size of a man – with scissor-like jaws and a brace of eyes across the ridge of its skull. Its flesh was thick and leathery, like that of a lizard, but along its back it bore a crest of vibrant yellow and purple feathers. Its wings were similarly adorned, tipped in black, and bearing vicious-looking talons with which the beast could presumably clasp on to its prey.

Sabbathiel steadied her breath and fell into a stance, scanning the swirling mass of creatures circling overhead. 'Ready yourselves,' she said. 'That one was merely testing our defences.'

And then, as if to prove the veracity of her words, they fell as one, a hail of daggers dropping from above.

'Incoming!' bellowed Brondel. 'The frecking things are everywhere!' His plasma pistol spat repeatedly. Several of the creatures burst into flames as the plasma ignited their plumage, tumbling like fallen stars amongst their kin. They screeched as their flesh seared and bubbled and they fell, lifeless, to the ground.

Sabbathiel swept her stave in a wide arc, pivoting on one foot as she slashed at the swooping creatures, severing wings, beaks, claws as they fought to get near. They broke like a wave, fanning around her before skirling up again, circling around to come in for another attack.

She risked a glance to her left. Metik stood amongst the smoking remains of several more of the creatures, impassive and unmoved. Nimbik was clambering over the still-twitching corpse of one, lascutter boring a smoking hole in its chest.

The second wave fell, but this time they came in from all sides, swooping low, a flurry of flashing talons and snapping beaks. Sabbathiel moved smoothly, whirling her stave in a slashing circle around herself, twisting on the spot to head off the frantic reptiles as they sought to lash out for her face. Coils of spilled guts slopped into the water, blood spraying as she continued her studied movements, turning with ease despite the cumbersome bulk of her Terminator armour.

She felt something strike her from behind; felt the insistent clawing at her back as one of the beasts sought purchase. She twisted, dipping her shoulder and bringing her stave up and over, the blade narrowly missing her own head as it thrust backwards, skewering the throat of the creature that was about to puncture her skull with its beak.

Another of the beasts saw its chance and swept in, pinioning her weapon arm to the side of her chest as it sought to scramble up her armour to get to her exposed head. She turned to glower at it, saw the animal ferocity in its unblinking eyes, before pulling her dagger with her left hand and slamming it so hard into the side of the creature's head that the skull shattered and her fist sunk into the cavity. Brain matter spattered up her forearm. She yanked it loose.

Brondel was bellowing curses as he continued to ignite the beasts with well-placed shots from his plasma pistol. Right up until the moment a shot went wide, and one of the creatures, suddenly finding itself with a clear run at the squat, dived in, snagging the back of his flak armour with its talons and lifting him wholly off his feet.

Brondel's face reddened at the indignity, and he thrashed in the beast's grip as it struggled to remain airborne, dragging him several feet into the air. With a sigh, Sabbathiel flexed her neck, took aim, and tossed her stave like a javelin. The creature screeched as the weapon impaled its upper chest, crunching through ribs and organs. It gave a pitiful final flap of its wings, and then dropped like a stone, plummeting the remaining few feet to the ground, a squirming Brondel still clasped tightly in its talons. They struck the shallows with an enormous splash, dislodging whatever macabre remnants were lurking beneath the surface, so that both Brondel and the attached corpse disappeared below the waterline.

Sabbathiel strode over to where the bubbles were still rippling the surface, each footstep snapping the bones of fallen beasts. She searched the water for a moment, and then reached down, her hand emerging a moment later grasping Brondel by the arm. He gasped, scowling fiercely at her.

'Put me down, for Throne's sake! There's more of them need killing, yet.'

Sabbathiel dropped him back into the water, where he bobbed for a moment on his back, before scrambling awkwardly to his feet. He was still clutching his pistol, but the birds were already in full retreat. He shook his head in annoyance, scattering droplets of water from his beard.

She retrieved her stave from the dead beast's chest. Once, she might have killed one of her followers for such a blatant show of disrespect, but the squat amused her, and during the last few months they'd come to something of an understanding. Brondel's caustic manner *was* a demonstration of his respect; the day he acted with deference would be the day to start worrying.

Metik was finishing up the last of the diabolical flock as Sabbathiel joined him, tracking the creatures with the nose of a bizarre gun that, when fired, caused the reptiles to thrash uncontrollably, before their torsos exploded from within. She watched one of the creatures detonate in a bloom of misted blood and bone, before, apparently satisfied, Metik lowered the ornately adorned weapon, tucking it away deep inside his robes.

'I estimate a ninety-seven point two per cent probability that the remaining creatures will retreat to safe ground, following the eradication of their kin.'

'The creatures, yes,' agreed Sabbathiel, surveying the horizon. 'But that was merely the opening salvo. You might as well keep your weapons to hand. The rest of them will be along any moment.'

Bledheim was beginning to wonder just how accurate their assumptions about the age of the corpses had been. While it was clear that many of them had been here for some time – preserved in a stomach-churning state of semi-decay by something in the water – as he drew closer to the flank of the pyramid, he'd noticed there were bodies bobbing beneath the surface that looked distinctly more... *fresh*.

He knocked one with the edge of his knee and set it drifting from his path: the remains of a man, a ragged hole punched through his chest. Air bubbles burbled through the wound as the corpse bobbed and rolled, the bloated face surfacing momentarily as if coming up for air. Streaming water spilled from his open mouth, revealing the yellow stubs of teeth, before he ducked under once again, completing his roll, so that he ended the manoeuvre face down amongst the bindweed.

Bledheim shuddered. He'd never been squeamish – even as a child he'd been fascinated by the notion that people had *inner workings* like machines; that there were things that made them tick, organs that pumped and filtered and oxygenated. Later, he'd dedicated his life to studying these strange biological systems, to manipulating and interrupting their function, using such methods to extract what his masters required from whichever still-living subjects they sent his way.

There was an art to what he did. The body was a canvas, and he wielded his tools with subtlety. *Delicacy*. A little spilled blood was an inevitability, as was the occasional dissection, but rarely would he watch as the light fled the eyes of those he interrogated. Anger, yes. Hatred. Bitterness. Even acceptance. But not death. Death marked failure. Death was Bledheim getting it wrong, and oh, how he *hated* getting it wrong.

More often than not he would discover all that was required from the subject, and more – he enjoyed encouraging them to reveal secrets that only he might come to know, personal things that meant nothing to the Inquisition, but formed part of Bledheim's personal 'collection'. He would then put them back together again, and their fate would be decreed by a higher authority. Once they left his rooms, they were all but forgotten; patients who were no longer under his care.

These drowned and bloated corpses, though… they were something entirely different. To them, he was not inured. The rudeness of their injuries, the extravagance, the sheer brutality – it offended him in ways he could not even begin to describe. The way they had been cut down was diametrically opposed to his own methods. Here, death was fast, dirty and unambiguous. Feral.

And for the bodies to be preserved in such a way… It was almost as if there were intent behind it. He'd seen the heads of traitors mounted on spikes on city walls and was coming to believe that these waterlogged corpses served the same purpose: a warning.

The thought disturbed him. Was there more to this place than Sabbathiel had been led to believe?

He nudged another body as he waded through another clump of ribboning reeds, then stopped short as its motion carried it closer to the surface, revealing the distinct markings on its chest.

'Um. I think you might want to see this,' he said. His voice sounded stark and loud, breaking the spell of silence that had fallen over them since they'd first encountered the bodies.

'What is it now, Bledheim?' said Silq, splashing over to join him. Her shoulders were bowed beneath the weight of her pack; Bledheim was thankful that he'd escaped such demeaning physical labour, even if the others had seen it as another indication of his weakness. He'd never minded being underestimated.

He waited until Mercy had trudged over to join them. 'What's this about, interrogator? We haven't time to keep stopping to listen to you moan.'

'Moan?' he said. 'Hardly.' He nudged the body again with his boot, causing the dead woman to rise to the surface again. 'What do you see?'

Mercy replied through gritted teeth. 'Another dead soldier, killed in a war I couldn't care less about.'

'You might change your mind if you look a little closer.'

Silq stooped over the body, grabbing hold of it by the scuffed flak armour it was still wearing. She hauled it up out of the water. The head hung limp, lolling from side to side with the motion. Something was moving in one of the empty eye sockets. The thin light reflected off the icon emblazoned on its chest. 'An Inquisition symbol,' said Silq.

'So?' Mercy was already starting to turn away.

'So, what does that tell you?' said Bledheim. 'Am I really the only one with any sense around here?'

'We're not the first mission that Heldren has sent here.'

Bledheim smiled. 'Precisely.'

'And?'

Bledheim sighed inwardly. 'And look at the state of her, Mercy. She's only got one leg and most of her stomach is gone.'

'People die. We knew it could be dangerous. But the mission is straightforward.'

'Yes,' said Silq, 'but Bledheim has a point.'

'He does?'

'Think of it this way – if the mission was so straightforward, why is the pyramid still standing?'

Mercy frowned.

'Because the last mission failed,' said Bledheim. 'Whoever came here before us – they're all dead.'

They stood in silence for a moment, regarding the dead woman. Then, slowly, Silq lowered the corpse back into the water. It was a surprising act of reverence for someone so used to scratching around amongst the remains of the dead.

'So, whatever they've got in there,' said Mercy, turning to peer up at the gleaming side of the pyramid, 'is capable of wiping out an entire retinue, if Bledheim is to be believed.'

'It's possible,' said Silq. 'Do you think we should warn Sabbathiel?'

Bledheim studied the horizon. The frenzied aerial attack appeared to have ended. 'No. I think we follow her orders and continue with the mission. But when we're done here, we get as far away from this pyramid as humanly possible.'

'Agreed,' said Silq.

Mercy nodded as she unhitched her pack. 'Then I think it's time we started planting these charges, don't you?'

CHAPTER FIVE

'Blood is blood. It exists to be spilled. Choosing when and where to spill it? Well, that's what separates us from the beasts.'

– Commissar Furzon Grall, during the repression
of the uprising on Jhental VII

THEN

The gentle lapping of water. The guttural squawk of a seabird.

At first, she thinks she's back at the shore, as if she's only just woken from her century-long sleep, and everything that's happened since was just a dream, just a shifting pattern of possibilities. Potential futures. Threads of chance.

But this place is different. There is no shoreline here – just an endless vista of azure blue, the wave-tips glittering in the solar glare. Further out, if she shields her eyes, she can see leviathan beasts erupting from the depths, black flesh slick and smooth as they launch

themselves skyward, before gravity asserts its inevitable hold and drags them back beneath the surface.

She realises she is in a room. It's little more than a glass box, seemingly adrift on the endless sea. A prison? Perhaps. Yet she does not feel trapped. She feels liberated. Free.

She senses a presence and turns. A man stands off to one side, peering out across the water. She can see his face reflected in the glass, like a mirage, a haunting. He's tall, imposing, dark-skinned, with greying hair. He's not looking at her, intent on tracing the motion of the beasts with his gaze, almost as if she's not there at all. But then she notices his lips are puckered and sewn shut in abject silence. And in his hand, he holds the long-dead carcass of a golden eagle. Its head lolls on a broken neck. Its wings are unfolded, but unmoving.

She opens her mouth to scream, but her lips betray her, moving of their own volition, mouthing a single word, a name: Jherek.

She does not know what it means.

Sabbathiel had always found such places distasteful: the stench of sweat, blood and foul breath; the filthy miasma given off by the baying crowd; the *noise*.

There was an art to killing, a technique to be acquired and honed over decades, tools of artifice to be deployed. The finesse was forever in the timing – knowing when to strike and from which angle; studying your enemy, allowing them to relax, to believe in their own imperviousness. And then coiling like a viper, spitting venom.

Here, though, in the fighting pits, there was no finesse, no subtlety. Here, vulgarity reigned supreme, and brute strength was the order of the day.

Sabbathiel pushed her way through the surly crowd, the fevered men and women who seemed reluctant to allow her passage to the edge of the pit. Her elbow lashed out, and a man fell away clutching his left eye. Another was left buckled over in her wake, hands pressed to his stomach where she'd driven her fist down low and hard.

People *would* get in her way...

She could have taken a viewing box up on the gantry, reserved for wealthy guests and dignitaries who didn't wish to mingle with the proletariats on the heaving floor of the arena. She could even have flashed her Inquisitorial sigil and invoked her authority to clear the place, to have one of the pit masters fetch the woman for her. Sabbathiel, though, wished to see her in her element – to see if she was everything that Metik had promised Sabbathiel she would be.

She stepped back as a broad, thickset man forced his way across her path, grunting at her to watch herself. She'd been forced to leave her sword at the door – only the pit fighters were allowed to bear weapons in here – but she still had a dagger concealed beneath the crimson plating of her new armour. It would take nothing to strike out, burying the blade deep in the man's kidney, twisting away into the crowd again. *Striking like a viper.* But she stayed her hand. These people were not the enemy. They were simply in her way.

A cheer went up around her, jostling as people threw their hands into the air. Sabbathiel frowned, aware of the faint pulse of a headache forming in the back of her skull. They'd become more frequent during the last few weeks – a symptom, she supposed, of whatever Metik had done to repair her body... or else the time she'd lost to the warp.

The nightmares had continued, unrelenting, filled with roiling images of events she could no longer recall. Of hooded giants in black armour, the muzzle flare of weapons fire that still left a stain upon her retinas when she woke. And the snow. Always the snow, drifting around her as she wandered, dazed and lost.

She shook her head, rolled her shoulders, and exhaled. She was here for a purpose.

She was here for Mercy.

The knot of people ahead of her had gathered around the edges of a deep, circular pit. Their faces were all downturned, their eyes flicking back and forth intently as they drank in the scene playing out below. Sabbathiel pushed her way through to the barrier at the edge of the fighting pit, peering down into the gloom.

The pit was little more than a rough walled trench, sunk into the earth at the heart of the arena – although the term 'arena' was, itself, something of a misnomer: the grubby facility had once been an air-scrubbing plant, and still bore signs of its former use, with thick, corroded pipe shafts jutting from the walls, presumably leading to other, similarly forgotten areas of the hive.

A makeshift barricade had been erected around the rim of the pit, against which people shoved and leaned as they jeered at the three figures in the pit below.

The fighters were circling one another, weapons – consisting of blunt swords and metal bars – brandished before them. Two of them, a man and a woman, Sabbathiel guessed to be local gangers, or at least, drawn from the same stock. They were huge, boosted muscles straining beneath their ill-fitting vests. They bore elaborate hairstyles, swept up and back from their faces and dyed in waves of red and black. The man's face was studded with metal piercings and his nose was missing, leaving behind an ugly, open-skull gash where it had once been. What flesh was visible was roped in silvery scars, the flesh puckered where it had been badly repaired between fights.

The woman, too, appeared to be a veteran of such matches. Her right ear had been bitten off at some point in the past, and, from what Sabbathiel could tell, she appeared to be missing three fingers on her left hand. She bore a thick, black tattoo around her throat and breastbone, which only partially managed to disguise the damaged flesh beneath. Her face was drawn in a fierce snarl as she glanced from the man to the remaining fighter.

This, Sabbathiel recognised, was Mercy, the woman she had come to see.

Mercy was tall and as heavyset as the male ganger, with powerful, muscular arms and broad shoulders. She was dressed in loose-fitting tunic and trousers, and her hair was cropped short and wild. She moved with a kind of lumbering grace, each movement considered, bristling with power. She carried a cumbersome sword, the iron blade notched and scored from a hundred battles. As she circled the other fighters, her boots stirred the blood-soaked sand, leaving a trail in her wake.

Sabbathiel placed her hands on the barricade and leaned forward, watching with interest. Nearby, a man was taking bets from an audience stoked with bloodlust, his spindly fingers dancing over the clacking mechanical levers of his tallying device.

A horn sounded, and the crowd bellowed in response. There was movement below – the slow dance, the mesmerising circling, was at an end, and Sabbathiel realised the three fighters had simply been sizing each other up while they waited for the fight to begin. Now, they moved in earnest, edging back and forth, testing each other's reactions.

The male ganger was the first to break, launching an attack on Mercy, spiked metal bar whipping back and forth before him, seeking an opening in her defence. Her sword met the bar with a ringing *clang*, and she lurched forward, her elbow coming down hard on the man's jaw. He staggered back, spitting blood and broken teeth, shaking his head from side to side like a woozy dog.

The other woman, seeking to take advantage, rushed Mercy, swinging her sword low and ducking her head beneath where she expected Mercy's blade to sweep across in a wide, defensive arc. Instead, Mercy dropped to one knee, lowering the pommel of her weapon almost to the ground, so that the woman, unable to halt her forward momentum, eyes widening in horrified real-isation, speared herself upon Mercy's sword. She slid forward until the hilt of the blade was pressing against her gut. Her own sword wavered and dropped to the sand. Blood bubbled from her lips.

Mercy stood, pushed the dying woman back, and then wrenched her sword free – up through the woman's ribcage and out the top of her left shoulder.

Blood sheeted across the pit wall. The corpse slid twitching to the ground.

The male ganger had recovered his senses now, and was circling around Mercy, clearly intending to come at her from behind while she was distracted. He hadn't moved quickly enough. Slowly Mercy turned, gore dripping from her blade, her hands, her tunic. Her eyes were wide with fury, her jaw set firm.

The man rushed in, swinging the spiked bar wide with his left hand, drawing Mercy's blade out to parry and leaving her upper torso exposed to his right hand. He jabbed it forward, and Sabbathiel saw the glint of a dagger clutched in the fist. Mercy twisted, putting her weight on her back foot, but it was too late, and the dagger blade struck true, just beneath her left armpit.

The blade should have punctured her heart, but instead, it simply skittered off what sounded like metal plating beneath her tunic. The ganger winced, dropped the dagger and staggered back, the fingers of his right hand mangled from the impact.

Mercy twisted on the spot, looking up at her audience.

Sabbathiel could see where the knife had torn the fabric of her tunic, and beneath, the glint of something brassy and metallic. Was the woman wearing plate armour beneath her clothes?

The crowd roared. The man ran at her again, and without even looking, she snapped out her left fist, connecting hard with his jaw, dropping him to his knees in the bloody sand. Around Sabbathiel, the crowd went wild.

Mercy turned back to the ganger, on his knees before her, swaying unsteadily, his iron bar lost somewhere in the dust. He met her gaze, eyes pleading. Mercy lifted her sword, placed the tip of the blade against the soft hollow at the base of his throat, and gave the weapon a final, decisive thrust.

The man's head lifted from his shoulders with a grotesque sucking sound. Mercy watched as the headless torso toppled slowly to the ground, and then turned and looked up, meeting Sabbathiel's gaze with a look of cool detachment.

'I thought she was called Mercy,' said a gruff voice from beside her. Sabbathiel glanced down to see Brondel standing at the barricade, peering down with a mixture of awe and disdain. 'Frecking Krull, there was little mercy on display tonight.'

Sabbathiel pursed her lips. 'I'm told she picked the name herself, as a reminder never to show it.'

Mercy was now wiping her bloodied blade on the corpse of the male ganger, while around Sabbathiel, the bookkeepers were under siege from people demanding their winnings.

Brondel spat on the floor, then ground the phlegm under his boot. 'I can think of better places to recruit followers than this hive of half-brained scum. You really mean for *her* to join your little entourage? Even after seeing *that*?'

Sabbathiel shot him a warning look. 'She comes highly recommended. Metik believes she'll be a great asset to the team. And besides, I can offer her something more meaningful than *this.*'

Brondel shrugged. 'Death in a filthy pit or death on a distant world. It's all the same. Blood is blood, after all.'

'I'll remind you of that when she saves your life.'

The squat spat again, then heaved a heavy sigh. 'Aye. I'm sure you will.'

CHAPTER SIX

*'What is memory but the fashioning of a deep and personal
fiction? In memory, we shape the world around ourselves,
as if to prove our own existence, to demonstrate the mark
we have left upon the universe. We become heralds of
something better; the guiding light by which we believe
all others might navigate. This, then, is the comfort we
award ourselves for the act of living, for to comprehend the
truth – that the universe is cold and ambivalent at best,
and at worst despises our very existence – is to contemplate
madness. So it is that we grow to love the lie.'*

– Paracles Ghent, excerpted from *The Deathbed Confessions
of Sister Superior Kellora, Escher VI*

NOW

'Fitch. Tell me what you see.'

'I no longer see *anything*, ma'am. I have been dead for over
one hundred years.'

Sabbathiel ground her teeth. She looked up at the hovering servo-skull, eyes narrowed. *Was it trying to be funny?* Red light played out from a sensor cluster at the base of the skull, sweeping over her shoulder like a velvet drape.

'You know full well what I mean,' she said. 'Scan the pyramid for signs of activity.'

The servo-skull seemed to hesitate. For a moment she wondered if it was going to demand she say 'please'. 'Long-range sensors indicate an energy build-up around the base of the structure and–' It stopped short. 'Ah, yes. An opening has appeared.' Fitch turned in the air, mechadendrites curling. 'It seems you were right, ma'am. We're about to have company.'

Sabbathiel stared at the horizon. There was nothing but the glassy water, stretching into the distance, and the pyramid, glinting in the reflected light. She was about to ask Fitch if he was certain, when Metik spoke, hefting his rifle and laying the barrel across another outstretched arm. 'Here they come.'

She heard them before she saw them – the thunder of scores of feet, displacing the shallow water as they charged. Then the whooping and chirping, the chittering and indecipherable high-pitched calls.

And then there was a line of them, breaching the horizon, coming on at a headlong rush, the blue and pink tones of their flesh stark against the empty sky. They were men and women – humans, but mutated beyond any sense, touched by the sickness of a deranged god. Some wore plumes of downy feathers, others strange masks fashioned from the skulls of the lizard-birds that had attacked them earlier. Some carried staves, others laspistols and sickle-shaped blades. And several of them–

'They've got frecking *beaks!*' bellowed Brondel. 'Beaks!' He hawked up a gobbet of phlegm and spat it into the water by his feet, his face wrinkling in disgust.

'Mutants,' said Metik. His back was stooped as he hunched over the barrel of his weapon, lining up a shot. 'Fascinating, really. How a human being has the capacity to believe in something so wholeheartedly that their physiology actually alters to reflect those beliefs. That they change their bodies and minds to accommodate their madness.'

'You mean they get cursed by their false gods,' spat Brondel.

'Precisely,' said Metik. He pulled the trigger, and in the distance one of the cultists exploded. Around it, several others skidded to a sudden halt, wiping gore from their eyes. Metik pulled the trigger again, and another went the same way, blooming into a dark red mist. This time, the others kept on coming.

'I suggest you prepare yourselves,' said Metik. 'These creatures may have weak souls, but the same is unlikely of their bite.'

'Peck,' muttered Brondel.

'I'm sorry?'

'Beaks! They've got *beaks*.'

'I was speaking metaphorically,' said Metik.

'Well, you can keep your frecki–'

Sabbathiel silenced their bickering with a burst from her wrist-mounted storm bolter, which chattered like the roar of vengeance itself as it chewed holes in the entire front line of charging cultists.

And then they were on them, breaking like a chittering wave, talons flashing, pistols barking, hideous beaked jaws yawning to reveal lines of serrated teeth. Light flared in Sabbathiel's peripheral vision as Brondel ignited three of them with his plasma pistol, their shrill cries echoing across the empty landscape as they burned to a cinder. The foul stench of singed feathers filled Sabbathiel's nostrils.

She turned on the spot, her storm bolter firing percussive rounds into the clamouring horde, each shell detonating with a *whomp*, spraying water and Emperor only knew what else high into the air.

Swords and staves clattered against her armour, but she ignored them, swinging her own stave down to cleave the skull of a chattering female before bringing it round in a wide arc, gutting at least five of the idiotic things that were too slow to get out of the way. The blade hummed with power, hissing and spitting as spilled blood bubbled on its energy-encased surface.

She sensed movement to her left and spun, only to see Metik's pet, Nimbik, leaping from head to head amongst the press, punching small but effective holes in the backs of the cultists' skulls. They dropped like sacks to the ground, sliding beneath the surface of the water, only to be trodden on by their kin as more and more of the things piled in.

Metik himself was deep in the thick of the fighting, his mechanical arms darting to and fro at incredible speed, stabbing, crushing, searing and gutting. Yet still the cultists threw themselves at him with violent abandon, falling in their droves.

Sabbathiel wheeled, arcing her stave up, slicing a male cultist from hip to neck, then twisting her arm to lop off the head of another, then another. Blood spattered her white armour in dark blotches.

'For the Emperor!'

Nearby, Brondel's beard seemed to be on fire, but he hardly appeared to care as he kicked a cultist's legs out from beneath them, before caving their skull in with his bare fists. All around him, heaps of them smouldered, burned to ash by the fiery roar of his plasma pistol.

Sabbathiel heard something scrape behind her head, as one of the cultists tried frantically to jab at her neck with a jagged knife blade, but it rebounded harmlessly from her armoured hood. She reached behind her, grabbing hold of the frenzied cultist in her ceramite-clad fist. She dragged him around, hoisting him so that his head trailed beneath him in the water and his feet kicked frantically at the air. She raised her foot and stamped down on his head, feeling it pop like an eggshell beneath her heavy boot, then hoisted the corpse and tossed it into a line of his charging brethren. They toppled back, staring down in horror at the site of their murdered kin. A brief burst from her storm bolter and they were gone.

'Traitorous bastards,' she muttered.

As quickly as it had started, it was over. The few survivors had already turned on their heels and were splashing hastily through the shallows as they charged back towards the safety of their pyramid. Metik, still swinging a near-dead cultist by the head from one of his mechadendrite claws, unslung his rifle, lined up a shot and detonated one, then another, as they ran.

Sabbathiel heard laughing and turned to see Brondel standing atop a heap of steaming corpses, patting out the flames in his beard while he watched the last few stragglers weave as they failed to avoid Metik's meticulous aim.

'You were right,' Brondel said, still chuckling, 'this mission *was* too easy.' He was bleeding from a gash on his forehead, but otherwise seemed unharmed. It was the happiest Sabbathiel had ever seen him.

'It is not over yet,' said Metik. His mechadendrite curled like a gleaming serpent, swinging the dying cultist around before him. He regarded it for a moment, cocking his head slightly to one side. The cultist was trembling, peering back at him with black, beady eyes which sat above a pronounced nose that had not yet finished transforming into a beak. It had lost its weapon, and it squirmed pitifully in Metik's iron grip, trying to prise itself free.

'The blessed one is coming,' it said. Its voice was fluting, unnatural, like a chord played on scores of dissonant pipes.

It hurt Sabbathiel's ears, itching like a worm worrying at the inside of her skull. 'The blessed Angel will smite the unworthy! The blesse–'

Metik scissored the claw shut and the man's mutated head collapsed in on itself, before the limp body slopped into the water below, dripping ichor. 'Look to the horizon,' Metik continued matter-of-factly. 'This, I presume, is their "blessed one".'

Sabbathiel glanced up. A new silhouette had appeared against the skyline, lumbering towards them from the direction of the pyramid – the hulking shape of an Astartes Dreadnought.

'Freck,' said Brondel.

'Mercy, I do think you might want to consider what I have to say.'

The woman didn't look up from where she was setting a charge on a metal spike she'd thrust into the ground – one of a series of such charges she and Silq had set as they'd slowly circumnavigated the pyramid. This one had skewered one of the floating corpses, and the wet, meaty sound it had made as it went in had almost been enough to turn Bledheim's stomach. *Almost.*

Mercy gave an impatient *tsk.* 'Instead of prattling on, you might lend a hand, *interrogator,*' she said, once again delivering the last word like it was some sort of insult.

'I hardly think now–'

'I don't much care what you think. To be honest, at the moment, I'm having a hard time understanding why you're even here.'

Bledheim glared sourly at the back of her head. He could hear the strange ticking emanating from inside the metal casing of her chest, the result of whatever Metik had done to her at some point in the past. He wondered what she would look like opened up on a table. 'Well, I had agreed to stand lookout...'

'Why aren't you doing it, then?' said Mercy, the antagonism evident in her tone.

'I *was*. I am. That's what I'm trying to tell you. There's a group of cultists coming this way.'

Mercy looked round and caught sight of the group of five cultists that had rounded the rear of the pyramid and were coming directly for them, weapons drawn. She turned to Bledheim and narrowed her eyes. 'Why didn't you bloody well say so?'

'I *tried*,' said Bledheim.

From close by, where she was crouching in the midst of affixing another charge to an identical metal spike, Silq sighed. She pressed a button on the device, then unslung the xenos rifle from across her back. 'Leave it to me,' she said, getting to her feet. The green chamber on the gun began to glow as she cradled it in both hands, drawing a bead on the onrushing targets.

'No,' said Mercy, crossing to where Silq stood and placing her hand on the barrel of the weapon. 'Fire that thing now and they'll all know we're here. It's not exactly subtle. We haven't time to be dealing with any more of them. There are more charges to be set. Sabbathiel is supposed to be the distraction, remember.'

Silq shrugged and lowered the gun.

'Ummm...' started Bledheim. The cultists were almost upon them. They were chittering insanely, screeching war cries that sounded more animalistic than human. He supposed that was only to be expected, given that most of them had feathers and beaks. All the same, he didn't much like the look of those sickle-shaped blades, or the gleam of fanaticism in their glassy eyes. He reached inside his robes, his fingers closing around the hilt of his knife.

'Stand aside,' said Mercy, and Bledheim breathed a sigh of relief. She waded forward into the path of the cultists, dragging her massive sword from the hoop at her belt. Its ancient, notched edge gleamed – not from polish, but from the strange patina that marred its pitted surface. The thing *looked* blunt and damaged, but when she swung it – as she did now, whirling it over her head to build momentum – it cut like it had just been forged in the foundry.

Mercy seemed to erupt into a violent scream, her entire body twisting like a vengeful storm as she launched into the morass of cultists, spinning as she moved, her sword whispering through the air. It was like nothing Bledheim had seen before, a raw, primal dance, as the blade whipped in circles all around her, seeming to leap from hand to hand, dipping and arcing, twisting and turning. Spilled blood showered into the air like a red mist, pattering softly onto the surface of the water all around her.

Finally, her guttural scream subsided, and with a final flourish of her blade, she came to a rest. Five dead cultists lay about her like the shed petals of a flower, their wounds still burbling as the last of their blood seeped into the water, glistening like spilled oil.

At the centre of it, Mercy, the eye of the storm, stood panting, her entire body covered in a sheen of bright blood. It was as if she'd painted herself in the stuff; that, by performing her strange, hypnotic dance, she had somehow enacted some uncivilised tribal ritual from her distant home world, dousing herself in the lifeblood of her enemies.

Her eyes – bright white, staring out from the spattered red face – fixed on Bledheim, and he shuddered.

Silq edged past her, sidestepping to avoid the heap of quivering corpses, a fresh metal spike in her fist. 'I thought you were going for subtle,' she said.

CHAPTER SEVEN

'When there is nothing else, there is the Emperor.'

– Origin unknown

THEN

'It's a motley team you've assembled, Sabbathiel. Are you certain they're ready? That *you're* ready?' Heldren paced before the tall window, peering out upon the blizzard of lights shimmering from the spires of the faraway hives. The sky was bruised, thunder clouds rumbling with distant fury. Water drops spattered the pane before Heldren's face. She could see his reflection in the glass, half obscured by the lashing rain. He looked serious, dour. Plagued, perhaps, by doubts. 'I mean, I don't think I'd be prepared to go to war with nothing but a band of miscreants at my side.'

'They're ready,' said Sabbathiel.

They were standing in Heldren's chambers: a sombre, austere

set of rooms in the upper levels of a hive on the moon of Garabon. Somehow, the setting didn't seem to fit with the impression of the man Sabbathiel had so far constructed. On the beach, back when he'd first come to see her, she'd decided he was an active sort – the kind of man who ached to be in the field, following up leads, rooting out the heretics with his boots and the barrel of his gun. Here, though, in these rooms, she saw a man who appeared to have withdrawn from that kind of straightforward work. A man who preferred philosophising to combat, who preferred to get others to do his dirty work, so that he only had to worry about the consequences and not the spilled blood, the mess.

Perhaps he'd once been that other man, and being out there, on the beach, she'd seen a hint of who he had been before. Now, though, surrounded by his books, his every whim attended to by hooded servants, he appeared as much a politician as an inquisitor.

He turned slightly, watching her in the reflected light of the window. 'Of course, I *could* choose to see it as a sign that you've yet to make a full recovery from your ordeal. That your judgement has been impaired. It would be understandable if you wanted more time…'

'They're *ready*,' repeated Sabbathiel, this time more emphatically. 'As am I. You're going to have to trust me.'

Heldren turned, the corner of his mouth twitching in amusement. 'Trust? Don't for a minute assume that I, or anybody else, *trusts* you, Sabbathiel. Therein lies the path to madness. Or death, at least.'

'Isn't that what this whole sordid little enterprise is about?' said Sabbathiel. 'Winning back the trust of the conclave?'

'Don't be naïve,' said Heldren, turning back to the view. 'There's a gulf between trust and tolerance. Do this, and you prove your usefulness. You demonstrate that you can take commands. That you're still a viable tool of the Inquisition. It's enough to protect you... for a while.'

'And what will it cost me, this protection?' said Sabbathiel. 'I shall owe you a debt?'

'Of course,' said Heldren. 'Things might have changed, Sabbathiel, but much remains the same. Wheels within wheels. It suits me for you to be alive. At present, I'm the only option you have.'

Sabbathiel swallowed, constricting her left hand into a fist behind her back. He was right, of course. What choice did she have? She no longer knew the other members of the conclave. All she had was Heldren's word. One point of contact. The others were working through Heldren to protect themselves. Of course, they wouldn't want her to know their identities. Not yet. Not until they were certain.

Just as Heldren said, the more things change...

She'd just have to get on with it. Deal with this upstart cult on Balthos and buy herself some more time. Knowledge was power, and at the moment, her insights were sorely lacking. The web she'd spent so long weaving – informants, allies, enemies, followers – it had all dissolved. She'd been gone for too long. All she had now was her reputation, and even that was diminished.

For now.

'Look, I can allow you to requisition some of the security forces here on Garabon. A platoon or two might make all the difference,' said Heldren. He left his place by the window and walked to his desk. He sat down, leaned back in his chair. He was frowning.

'My thanks,' said Sabbathiel, 'but I prefer to work light. My acolytes will prove more than sufficient.'

Heldren sighed, the air whistling between his clenched teeth.

'Very well. If one thing has become more than clear to me in recent weeks, it's that you know your own mind. No wonder you have such a formidable reputation.'

'I do?' said Sabbathiel, feigning innocence.

Heldren laughed. Behind him, a servo-skull hove into view. The traceries of its bionic eye played across the front of Sabbathiel's red armour plating. She'd had the new suit crafted by Heldren's private artificers, much to his exasperation. It fit her perfectly: lightweight, flexible and strong.

Heldren waved the servo-skull away. Sabbathiel watched it drift into the corner of the room, sliding into the shadows beside a bookcase. Only the glowing pinprick of its eye implant remained visible, blood red and steady, an ever-present reminder that they were not alone. She wondered who else was reviewing the footage from that lonesome eye.

'You'll come, of course?' said Sabbathiel. 'To Balthos.'

Heldren peered at her, confused.

'I presume you're anxious to see first-hand how I perform in the field?'

She could see that, for a moment, Heldren was tempted. A flash of the old spirit returned, perhaps?

'While I'm sure that would be an… experience, Sabbathiel, I fear I have more pressing matters to attend to. There are issues that require my attention, both here and on Hulth.' He shrugged, as if to underline his words.

Hulth was the main hub of the system, the planet that, even now, Sabbathiel could see through the window, hanging like an enormous orb in the night sky, its surface pitted and gnarled by the footprint of civilisation. Cities rose like mountain ranges to the south, and to the north, a blood sea shone in the reflected light of the distant twin suns.

Beyond the planet, in the deep reaches of the void, the twisted finger of the Cicatrix Maledictum reached like a scar, suffocating the light from the nearby stars. It was a wound at the very heart of the galaxy, a suppurating gash that wept with the very essence of corruption. How the Imperium had allowed it to happen, she could not fathom. The warp storms in the Calaphrax Cluster had been bad enough. To allow such a maleficent portal to manifest in the very heart of the Emperor's domain…

She'd been away for too long.

Heldren had returned his attention to the window and was staring out at the spectre of the planet, now partially eclipsed by storm clouds. It occurred to her that that was what he must have been pondering when she'd first entered the room – not the hives, or the bristling industrial landscape below. The planet.

What is there on Hulth that has you so interested, Heldren?

Sabbathiel had never heard of the place – nor Garabon, for that matter – but she would find out more, soon enough.

After Balthos. After I prove my loyalty.

'Very well,' she said. 'If there is nothing else, I shall be on my way.'

Heldren nodded, without turning to look at her. 'There's only one other thing, Sabbathiel.'

'And what is that?'

She could see he'd returned to watching her reflection in the glass. 'Whatever else you do – watch your back.'

CHAPTER EIGHT

'Emperor knows, there are a dozen ways to win a war. But a man must be mindful – as billions of souls will attest, there are a thousand ways to die in the process.'

– From the diaries of Commander Rudolf van Este

NOW

'What are you doing?'

She felt Brondel's eyes on her as she readied herself, planting her feet, raising her stave before her in a defensive posture. 'Giving it a target.'

'Oh, good idea,' said Brondel. 'Great.'

'We're supposed to be creating a diversion, in case you'd forgotten,' she said, allowing a note of caution to creep into her tone. While she enjoyed the squat's occasional irreverence, it was important that he didn't forget exactly who was in charge.

'It's got a frecking assault cannon,' he replied. 'That's quite a diversion you're planning.'

Sabbathiel shook her head. 'Look at it. That thing's nearly as old as the Emperor Himself. I'd wager that assault cannon hasn't seen any ammunition for centuries.'

'Yet it remains a considerable foe,' said Metik.

'Aye. With a fist the size of a small shuttle,' spat Brondel.

'I calculate there is now a seventy-eight point four-five per cent chance of mission failure,' added Metik.

'I've faced worse odds,' said Sabbathiel.

'You've also had your lower torso and spinal column rebuilt after spending more than a century drifting in the grip of an unstable warp storm,' said Metik.

Sabbathiel glowered at him. 'Your point?'

'Merely that your confidence seems somewhat misplaced.'

'Well, that's reassuring, Metik. Thank you.'

'You are most welcome.'

The ground was trembling now with every lumbering step of the massive walker, sending rippling waves through the churning water. It was a thing of nightmare, a hulking remnant of the distant past, designed for one thing alone: delivering death.

Its ceramite armour had once been a rich, deep blue, trimmed with elaborate filigrees of gold, but now it was faded and battle-scarred, tinged with verdigris and pink mould. A huge hole had been punched in its domed chest at some point, and now, bizarrely, weeds sprouted from the jagged enclosure, a riot of lush green leaves and pink and blue flowers. Its left leg seemed to judder with every step, like a soldier struggling with an old wound, and its four-toed feet tore up huge clumps of bindweed as it walked. Its assault cannon hung limply from its right arm, but its left was an immense power fist, the fingers of which twitched nervously as it approached. The sarcophagus at the heart of the machine appeared to be largely intact.

Once, the Dreadnought had been the resting place of a

venerable member of the Adeptus Astartes, wounded in battle and given new life inside the shell of this ancient machine – the means by which the Space Marine could continue to serve his Chapter. Now, though, it was a symbol of pure corruption, sustained by the foul energies of the warp – the true aspect of the Emperor's Space Marines.

Sabbathiel knew them for what they were. She knew their traitorous ways; the depths to which they had sunk. The Adeptus Astartes had been lost to the Emperor's light, long before she ever went to Calaphrax. Long before she had died.

She closed her eyes. For a moment she was back there, on the Dark Angels' battle-barge, facing the Grey Knight Leofric as he raised his storm bolter and fired. As the pain lanced through her body and the darkness swept in to consume her.

A hundred years. A century, drifting in the warp storm. There was no possible way that she should still be alive.

'Sabbathiel!'

She stepped to the side. Beside her, just where she had been standing, the ground trembled under the force of an immense blow. She felt water spattering her face. Her eyes were still closed, but she knew exactly where the enemy was and what it was doing. She could *feel* it. Just as she could feel the minds of the pathetic cultists who had followed the Dreadnought here, chittering and cheering. Their thoughts were like tiny, speckled motes of light, floating in the dark. Insects, infesting her mind. If she just reached out and… The lights blinked out as one, snuffed like candles in the wind. She heard Brondel swear as he watched the cultists' bodies crumple to the ground.

Everything is calm. Everything is peace.

Sabbathiel took a step forward, swinging her stave up and around like a spear. As the Dreadnought tried clumsily to track her movement, she jabbed the stave down with both hands, deep into the gaping hole in its chest. It sank into something rank and fibrous.

Lightning crackled from the wound, pulsing out up the shaft of the stave and jolting Sabbathiel back off her feet with a percussive blast. She crashed back into the water on her back, still gripping the stave, her entire body rigid as the shock caused her muscles to spasm. Blood trickled from her nose. Her eyes flickered open.

The Dreadnought reared over her, raising its left foot from the ground...

She rolled – a near impossibility in her cumbersome armour – just as the foot crashed down beside her. She felt the thin crust beneath the water crack with the force of the blow, the surface bubbling around the breach.

Weapons fire told her that Metik and Brondel had joined the fray, and she watched as the Dreadnought swung to face the tech-priest, whose searing weapon was blistering the ceramite of its outer shell with every well-placed shot. Brondel's plasma shots were eating away at one of the machine's leg joints. He was a clever bastard, that one.

Sabbathiel took the opportunity to lever herself up out of the stinking water. Her limbs were aching with the after-effect of the shock. Her right eye was twitching, and she could smell something akin to seared hair.

She glanced at the pyramid, making a quick calculation.

'We need to drive it back,' she called to the others. 'Towards the structure.' Behind her, the surface of the water was churning where the Dreadnought's foot had punctured the rocky crust below.

'Drive it back!' bellowed Brondel. 'And how exactly are we supposed to do that?'

'Together,' said Sabbathiel, raising her arm. Her wrist-mounted storm bolter unloaded into the Dreadnought's damaged chest, and it took a step back to maintain its balance as the impact of the detonating shells made it shudder.

Metik, still firing, edged around to join her. On her right, the squat broke off for a moment, then came hurtling through the shallows, almost ramming into her leg as he skidded to a halt. The three of them fired in unison. Once again, the Dreadnought took a step back, flames licking at the mould-encrusted outer plates.

It raised its assault cannon and the weapon began to spin at tremendous speed, emitting a torturous, grating whine. Despite herself, Sabbathiel flinched – but just as she'd predicted, the weapon was long spent, and the cultists here could never have found the means to resupply it. It was a pointless gesture, an instinctive reaction, as if the controlling mind were recalling better days and battles long passed.

They pressed their advantage. Another volley. Another step back.

'What now?' said Brondel.

Sabbathiel smiled. 'It's time.'

'Bledheim?'

Sabbathiel's voice crackled over the vox, causing him to start.

'Yes, ma'am?'

'Are you ready?'

Bledheim glanced over at the two women, who were both still crouching over metal spikes, fumbling with charges. Behind them, another circle of cultists lay dead on the ground, most of them missing their heads. 'Umm, almost. Mercy and Silq are planting the final charges now. We encountered some... resistance.'

On the other end of the vox, Sabbathiel grunted. He could hear weapons fire. And something thunderous moving about.

'Is everything all right, ma'am?'

'Just get the damn charges ready,' snapped Sabbathiel. *'I need you to blow them now.'*

'Now?'

'Yes. Now!'

'Understood,' he said. 'Bledheim out.'

So much for getting back to the shuttle before the world is pitched the wrong way up.

He watched the two women finish up with the charges. They made a beeline for him.

'You were talking. On the vox,' said Silq.

'Yes.'

'And?'

'She wants us to blow it now.'

'Now?' said Mercy. 'Right now?'

Bledheim nodded.

Mercy grinned. 'Better start running then, eh?' She pulled the remote detonator from the pocket of her fatigues and held her thumb over the trigger.

Bledheim stared at her, appalled. 'No. Not yet. Just hold on a–'

She depressed the button.

Sabbathiel heard them before she saw them – a string of earth-shattering blasts that described a wide circle around the circumference of the pyramid. They erupted like a chain, detonating in sequence, filling the air with a sound like manic thunder, or the belly laugh of some malignant god.

Still locked in battle with the Dreadnought, she only had time to glance as she heard the ground give way beneath the force of the blasts, a rending crack that caused the pyramid itself to shift, listing dramatically to one side as the earth beneath it began to subside.

The Dreadnought seemed not to have noticed, still raging silently at the three combatants, its assault cannon whining pathetically as it tried to close the gap between them, only to keep being pushed back by the constant barrage of fire. They weren't going to wear it down through attrition – Sabbathiel knew that – but that had never been her plan. If they could just hold out a little longer…

Another crack rippled through the strata, closer this time. She felt a sudden drag at her feet and risked a glance down to see that the water had picked up a sudden current, rushing headlong towards the lopsided pyramid. Corpses and other detritus from past conflicts slapped against the back of her legs, pulled inexorably towards the massive hole that was opening up beneath the pyramid.

It was working. All those layers of history, of ruined cities and shattered homes, of the broken bones of the dead who had once called this place home – they had spent too long buried beneath this patina of war and false idols. The ground she now stood upon had been raised upon the shoulders of the had-beens; an accumulation of millennia, burying the lost. Now, she would tear that down. All of it. She would show the galaxy the true face of Balthos and end the foul cult that had claimed this place as their own.

And in doing so, she would prove herself to Heldren. She would show him and the rest of the conclave that the only thing they had to fear from Astor Sabbathiel was righteous zeal.

The ground beneath the pyramid emitted a piercing screech as it finally gave way. Close by, Brondel was bellowing heartfelt curses, but she couldn't hear anything over the noise of the landslide. It sounded like the end of the world.

She watched over the Dreadnought's shoulder as the pyramid suddenly *dropped*. It was as if a hand had reached up to grab it, tearing it down in one sudden gesture – like all the souls of those buried here had risen to unleash their fury.

The sinkhole was immense, and the water all around them was foaming and churning as it slid relentlessly towards it, streaming over the edges like a gushing waterfall.

Before her, the Dreadnought lurched, throwing its damaged leg forward, even as she pounded its torso with repeated rounds from her storm bolter.

Behind it, the rushing water was eroding the lip of the vast hole, and she could see chunks of debris breaking away, tumbling down into the watery ruin below.

'Push it back!' she yelled, stalking forward, unleashing a hail of bolt shells into its damaged chest. The constant barrage was having some effect on it now, and the ablative plating was pocked and cracked, fissures appearing across the ancient casement. The Dreadnought took another step back, and then stopped.

Sabbathiel roared, continuing her bombardment. The world seemed to close in around her, shrinking until there was only her and the traitor, there on the lip of a watery abyss, everything collapsing in around them.

For a moment, it looked as if the Dreadnought was going to buckle, to topple back into the gaping maw that had opened behind it, but then it lurched forward, dropped to one knee and buried the fingers of its power fist deep into the ground. Water swilled around it, pouring over the edge. A bloated corpse rolled up out of the bubbling foam, clanging against the Dreadnought's leg before disappearing from view, carried off over the edge by the current.

The Dreadnought held its ground, staring down at Sabbathiel, unflinching.

Bolt-rounds exploded across its chest, one after another, but still the Dreadnought maintained its grip, clinging to the thin crust, to the threads of fate that had sustained it for so very long. Clinging to its foul half-life, no matter the cost.

I swore I would see this place cleansed. I swore to eradicate every last stain upon its surface.

She could not fail. She had no choice. Everything depended on this.

Sabbathiel planted her stave in the ground. She drew a deep breath then let it out. And then she charged.

It was never intended as a direct assault: even clad in her Terminator armour, even as damaged as the Dreadnought was, she could not have held out for long against such a foe. But combat wasn't what she had in mind.

Sabbathiel collided with the Dreadnought with a juddering crash. She felt her shoulder shatter inside her armour – the sudden flush of pain, the wave of dizzy euphoria as her body flooded with adrenaline. She heaved, heard servos grinding and popping as her armour took the brunt of the Dreadnought's weight, rocking it back on its heels.

'Just. Die!'

Something blew in her knee. The Dreadnought tried to pivot, slamming the barrel of its assault cannon down, hard, on the carapace at her back. She shuddered under the impact, the breath leaving her lungs. But still she pushed.

I will not fail…

Something *cracked*.

And then she was pushing on air. The Dreadnought went over, a clump of grey crust still clutched in its power fist, tumbling down into the crushing depths, down amongst the broken strata of millennia, the gushing water, the cascade of debris and corpses.

Sabbathiel, on her front, inches from the crumbling edge,

watched it go, dwindling as it spun heel over head, until it was enveloped in the swirling gloom far from view.

Pain was blooming throughout her entire body, white and hot, threatening to drive her headlong towards unconsciousness. She fought against it, battling the urge to give in to it, forcing herself to move, to drag herself up to her knees, wincing with every movement.

'For the love of the Empero–'

Instinctively, Sabbathiel shot out her hand, grabbing for the squat's leg as he sailed past her on his back, dragged along, burbling and thrashing, towards the chasm's edge.

He kicked and scrabbled, dangling half over the lip, as she fought to haul him back to safety.

'Stay still, for Throne's sake!'

He scowled at her as she pulled him sharply towards her, his head dipping momentarily under the water, and then hoisted him back up onto his feet. Water streamed from his beard. He shook his head, scattering droplets like a halo. He hawked up a mouthful of phlegm and spat, watching as the gobbet disappeared over the edge.

'I told you I hated frecking water,' he said.

CHAPTER NINE

'And in such fashion do empires die. Not for lack of ambition, nor stagnation or flawed leadership – for these all might be survived – but due to blind trust in the efficacy and motivations of others. Betrayal is the greatest weapon of the heretic, far mightier than both fist and sword.'

– Excerpted from *On Betrayal*, Inquisitor Lord Jhal Imbrek, Ordo Hereticus

NOW

The mission to Balthos had been an unqualified success.

Although, Sabbathiel reflected, it had equally proved an unqualified waste of her time. She was certain now that Heldren's acolytes, or even the co-opted Garabonian security forces he'd spoken of, could have seen to the matter just as easily, if deployed in reasonable force. The cult had hardly proved taxing to eradicate.

Nevertheless, it was done, and if it wasn't yet enough to prove her outright loyalty to her former conclave, it would, at least, buy her some time to consider her position.

Besides, the conclave had yet to earn *her* loyalty. Or at the very least, her trust.

Through Heldren, they'd made their own position abundantly clear – that Sabbathiel was to be considered an outsider, a relic of a previous age, who may or may not still have a use – but they'd done nothing yet to convince her of their own standing. She'd yet to even discover their names, and whether any familiar faces had survived from the time before her unfortunate period of isolation. She presumed not; most of her former colleagues would have been too keen to gloat to remain in the shadows for long.

Still, the matter of Balthos was settled, and her wounds were already healing. The cult had been destroyed, the evidence of their very existence now sunk beneath the foetid waves. There, they would rest amongst the accumulated detritus of millennia, along with all the other secrets buried on that abysmal moon.

For all Heldren's talk about the motley nature of her team, they had proven their worth, and not one of them had lost their life – quite a novelty in Sabbathiel's experience. Of course, as acolytes they remained somewhat rough around the edges, but she would see to that easily enough. Just as soon as formalities with Heldren had come to an end and she was free to return to her own work and concerns. For a start, she was anxious to discover the truth behind the mysterious Inquisitor Mandreth, the man who had dragged her out of the warp storm in the Calaphrax Cluster, only to then melt away into the shadows before she was brought round, leaving little by way of a trail. She would seek him out and put him to the question; she didn't like the thought of being bound in someone's debt.

The thought made her think of Metik, and her lips twisted into a sour grimace. The sooner that situation was resolved, the better. She would get to the bottom of whatever it was the tech-priest wanted from her in payment for his restorative work, and deal with it swiftly. To Sabbathiel's mind, an inquisitor should carry no debts, for indebtedness left them too susceptible to temptation. Besides, the tech-priest needed to be reminded of his place. The time would come to play that particular card. For now, there were other matters to attend to.

The outer chambers of Heldren's apartments were quiet and empty, save for the stooped figure of a data serf, bent crooked from years struggling under the weight of the immense, dusty tomes in its care. The wizened old man did not even turn to regard her as she passed through the librarium, her bootsteps echoing loudly amongst the musty stacks. She wondered when Heldren had last consulted any of the esoteric works. To many in the ordo, such heretical volumes were naught but a status symbol, a signifier of their wealth and power – trophies claimed like scalps from the heretics they had slain. Others saw it as their duty to seek and contain such treasures, to restrict access to the forbidden knowledge held in their pages: echoes of the ancient times, records and rituals derived from events that had long been forgotten.

Then there were those, such as Sabbathiel, to whom such things were a tool, weapons to be carefully tamed and deployed against the enemies of the Imperium. She was yet to discern into which category Heldren fell, and as such, she had studiously kept her own predilections to herself. Better, she had decided, to keep her cards close to her chest, at least until she had a better sense of the rest of the players.

She pressed on along the silent passageway, past a small, terraced garden at the centre of a quad, and on towards Heldren's private study, where she knew she'd find him, still peering out of his window at distant Hulth, pondering the mystery that had so furrowed his brow during her previous visit. Another mystery that she intended to unravel.

The small sanctum that preceded Heldren's study was devoid of servants, save for a pallid-skinned servitor who had once been a woman, but was now clearly more machine than human. Cables trailed from the back of its skull, and its left arm had been replaced with a coiled, metallic appendage that seemed to ripple in constant motion, as if responding physically to the thrumming pulse of energy that presumably powered the machine. Both eyes had been replaced with lenses that shone with a cold, blue glow, originating somewhere deep inside the skull behind. It turned to regard her as she entered the chamber, lenses whirring noisily as it drew focus.

'Inquisitor Sabbathiel,' it burred, its voice a series of mechanical whirrs and fluting pips. 'Lord Heldren awaits you in his study.'

Sabbathiel inclined her head in acknowledgement – a futile gesture when dealing with a machine, but one she'd never quite been able to break the habit of. She took a few steps towards the door, then stopped, her hand on the lacquered surface, and turned to see the servitor still watching her. Its expression was blank, but disturbing nevertheless, in the way its gaze was utterly unflinching, even as she stared in return.

'Yes?' she said. 'Is everything as it should be?'

The servitor jerked suddenly, averting its face from her glare. 'Indeed, ma'am. Everything is precisely as it should be.'

'Very well then,' muttered Sabbathiel, pushing on through the door.

The room beyond was precisely as it had been during her previous visit, save for two stark differences: firstly, that a hovering servo-skull was projecting a vast, three-dimensional hololith of a street plan across the entire span of the room. It appeared to be a render of a mortuary site, bristling with immense, engraved stele and burial compounds. Secondly, that Inquisitor Heldren was lying sprawled on his back across his desk, two large, bloody stab wounds in his upper chest. His face seemed to jut from the surface of the hololith like a body half submerged in shallow water, and one arm was raised, curled into a loose fist.

Sabbathiel edged forward, sliding her sword from its scabbard on her hip. She glanced from side to side, scanning the room. The flickering hololith provided perfect cover, and she ducked low, dipping her head beneath the blue-tinged wash of the map to scan the ground. There was no sign that Heldren's assailant was still present. Had she only just missed them?

She glanced at the towering window, but the glass was perfectly intact. Only the light of distant Hulth shone through, brilliant and blue. They'd come and gone through the door, then.

'Are you still alive?' she said, keeping her voice low, even.

Heldren made a gurgling sound, and frothing bubbles wheezed from the puncture holes in his chest. He didn't have long. She lowered her blade, crossed to stand over him. His eyes were wide, pupils dilated. Blood flowed freely down his chin, dribbled from the corner of his mouth. She was already too late.

'Who did this?'

She glanced at the door. The servitor? Had the Mechanicus tech been somehow subverted? She had seen such things before.

She started forward but turned back when Heldren emitted a long, low groan. More blood spilled from his lips as he tried to mouth something. The urgency on his face was startling; he knew he was slipping away, and yet still he wanted to be heard.

'What? What is it?'

His eyes moved, and she followed his gaze. She realised he was gesturing with his upraised hand. Pointing towards something on the map. A tomb.

'It's connected to that tomb? That's who did this?' It didn't make any sense. 'What do you mean?'

But no answer was forthcoming. Heldren's body shifted as he expelled his final, gurgling breath. His eyes glazed. His outstretched arm dropped, thudding heavily against the side of the desk.

Sabbathiel studied the tomb for a moment. What had he been trying to tell her? There was nothing noteworthy about the edifice. A squat, columned building with a pitched roof, standing amongst scores of others, all so similar that it was near impossible to tell them apart. And where was it? She didn't even know which planet the map was supposed to represent.

And then it struck her, and she turned towards the tall, arched window at the other end of the room. The blue crescent of the planet was like an inverted smile playing across the glass, taunting her.

Hulth. Where else?

Then the door burst open, and all hell broke loose.

CHAPTER TEN

'It is a soldier's lot to die for his cause – nay, it is his duty. But we? We are an altogether different concern, for we carry with us the seal of the Ordo Hereticus, and with it, the burden of the future. For we are the guiding hand of the Imperium, the seekers of truth, the weapon that purges the unworthy. It is they who die for our cause. Our duty is not in the headlong rush towards death, but in the deliverance of it.'

– Inquisitor Lord Jhal Imbrek, from 'An Address to Initiates'

Sabbathiel's sword hummed as she swung towards the splintered door.

Framed in the opening stood a tall, lean man with the pale aspect of a human albino. He had the outward appearance of a man in his fifties, although Sabbathiel well knew that was no indicator of his actual age. His face was as smooth and white as alabaster, and his darting eyes were a bright, livid pink. His long white hair had been tied back in a taut ponytail, and his thin lips were twisted in a cruel smile. He was dressed in a knee-length black coat that, Sabbathiel surmised, probably concealed a suit of lightweight flak armour beneath. He was carrying an ebon-bladed power sword with an ornate pommel and wore an Inquisitorial seal on a chain around his neck.

Sabbathiel heard voices out in the sanctum beyond the door – the man hadn't come alone. She lowered her sword fractionally to indicate she posed no threat to the newcomer. 'It's Heldren. He's dead.'

'So, it comes to this,' said the man, edging into the room, his sword raised as if he expected Sabbathiel to charge him at any moment. He glanced at the corpse on the table.

Heldren's eyes were still open, and bright blood trickled from the corner of his mouth, stark against his lifeless cheek. Around him, the hololith flickered, as if disturbed by swirling currents in the air.

'It comes to what?' asked Sabbathiel. She took a step back as he moved closer. Something about the man felt off. The hairs on the back of her neck prickled. Was that a smirk he was concealing?

'That Heldren had to die to prove you're a traitor, Astor Sabbathiel,' he said. 'I tried to warn him, but then he always did enjoy raking up the past and sifting through whatever filth he'd dragged into the light. I presume you must have held a similar attraction.'

'I'm no traitor,' hissed Sabbathiel. 'And I'm not the one who killed him.'

The man offered her a crooked smile. 'No? Then why were you standing over his corpse with your sword drawn?'

'I drew my sword when I realised he was injured,' she replied. 'In case his attacker was still in the vicinity.' She glowered at the man. 'Who are *you*, anyway, to be questioning *me*?'

The man laughed, but it was filled with bitterness. 'Atticus Sinjan. You might say that Heldren and I are – or rather, *were* – old friends.'

'Well then, as his *friend*, perhaps you could put your damn sword away and help me to look for his killer.'

'Oh, I believe I've already found her.'

That hidden smirk again. He knows I didn't do it.

I'm being framed.

'I told you – I had nothing to do with this.' She indicated Heldren's remains. 'Why would I murder the one person among you who tried to help me? What could I possibly hope to gain? Besides, you can ask that servitor out there – I arrived just a few moments before you. I couldn't possibly have had time to kill him.'

'Servitor?' said Sinjan. 'There is no servitor.'

'Out there, in the sanctum. It told me Heldren was expecting me.'

Sinjan shrugged. 'More stories. Like the web of lies you spun for Heldren, no doubt. Obfuscations and imprecations. The weapons of a heretic. I checked the vid-feed. He was alive when you entered the room. No one else has entered since.'

The man was constructing a false narrative, weaving it out of thin air right there before her. He must have been waiting for her to arrive, setting a trap that she had unwittingly sprung. But why? What did he achieve by framing her for Heldren's murder? By conjuring this outlandish story?

'Why are you doing this?'

'Is it not my duty to mete out the Emperor's justice to all traitors? We've all heard the tales, Sabbathiel, of how you set out on some ill-fated personal crusade a hundred years ago, before disappearing into the warp. And now you're back.' He edged closer, the tip of his blade preceding him. 'Having survived, somehow. A hundred years is a very long time.'

'And it seems little has changed,' said Sabbathiel. 'I proved myself. I did everything that Heldren required of me. I took a team to Balthos–'

'And upon your return,' said Sinjan, cutting her off, 'you discovered that the mission had been entirely unsanctioned, and that Heldren had simply used you to tidy up his own sorry mess. He never had any intention of speaking to the conclave on your behalf. He meant to keep you as a pet, a tame relic of the past, someone willing to get their hands dirty so that he didn't have to. Not to mention the fact that you were a *fine* addition to his collection of esoterica – something he could wheel out whenever there was someone he really wished to impress.' He sighed dramatically. 'And so, knowing this, you killed him.'

Sabbathiel didn't like where this was heading. Not one bit. Nor did she believe it was true – at least not entirely. If Heldren really had intended to mislead her, why would he try to tell her something in his dying moments? Why would he point her at that tomb on Hulth? She recalled his final words to her as she'd left for Balthos: 'Whatever else you do – watch your back.' Was *this* what he'd been warning her about? This man, Sinjan? Could *he* be the one who had killed Heldren, and was now weaving a web of deceit to cover his tracks? A fiction intended to implicate her in Heldren's death and ensure his own supposed innocence?

'I've already *told* you,' she hissed. 'I had nothing to do with his death. Look at the evidence. Where's the murder weapon? My sword is clean. He was still alive when I got here.'

'So, you admit it, then?'

'For Emperor's sake, ask the servo-skull. It's probably recorded everything that's happened.'

'Good point,' said Sinjan. He turned, pulling a laspistol from a holster inside his coat, and fired. The servo-skull detonated in a sizzling flash. The hololith of the mausoleum complex flickered out of existence, like a memory being suddenly forgotten. The burnt shell of the servo-skull crashed to the ground, scattering ash and bionics.

'What did you–'

'You burst in, shot the servo-skull so there wouldn't be any witnesses, drew your sword and ran Heldren through. The poor man – a hero of the ordo, no less – didn't even see it coming. The sad truth was he'd trusted you, despite all the evidence to the contrary. Even carrying such a grievous wound, he fought valiantly, trying to fend you off so he could get away, so you stabbed him a second time, whereupon he collapsed across his desk and died. You were still standing there when I arrived, alerted by the sudden cry.'

Sabbathiel narrowed her eyes. This man, this *inquisitor*, had no time for the truth. In fact, he was working extremely hard to ensure the truth never came to light. It was all a ruse, a trap she'd walked straight into. 'I see what this is.'

'You do? Most perceptive,' said Sinjan. 'Do you know how the story ends, too?'

They were circling one another now, swords held ready and sparking with power. 'You'd better tell me,' she said, dropping into a defensive stance.

'There wasn't even a glimmer of remorse. When I challenged you, you simply launched yourself at me, intending for me to suffer the same fate as my dear friend and colleague. I tried to reason with you, but something in you had just snapped, and your mind had gone. I was forced to put you down. Your time in the warp had corrupted you beyond all measure. You'd become a danger to the Imperium and the Ordo Hereticus, and to allow you to live would have been tantamount to heresy. Heldren had been a fool to trust you, but then he'd already paid the price for his mistake.' He launched himself at her with a roar, his ebon blade arcing for the side of her neck. It cleaved the air with a high-pitched whistle, and she sidestepped, throwing her own blade up to parry. The two swords met in a shower of sparks, and she pushed Sinjan back, circling again, buying herself time.

She steadied her breathing.

Sinjan bared his teeth in a snarl. Again, he brought on the attack, this time changing his approach, thrusting straight for her midriff. She danced back, almost too late; the tip of his blade scored the front of her crimson armour. He laughed, swinging the blade around the back of his neck, tossing the grip from one hand to the other.

Ambidextrous, then.

Great.

There was no way she could win here. Strike him down, and the others of the conclave would come for her, accusing her of both murders. Try to run, and she'd play into Sinjan's hands, making herself out to be guilty and reinforcing his story. Not to mention the fact he'd left guards out there in the sanctum to block the exits. But she was damned if she was going down without a fight.

Sinjan lunged again, and this time she pivoted, turning to the side and flicking out her blade so that the tip of it scraped a line along his cheek, opening a long, deep gash in his pristine flesh. Blood welled, spilling down the line of his jaw, and he hissed, withdrawing to a safe distance, his sword in his left hand. He wiped the back of his right hand across the wound, smearing blood back to his ear. He licked his lips.

'You've got bite, then.'

'Come a little closer and I'll show you,' she said, leaning forward, the pommel of her sword in both hands.

Sinjan roared, coming at her fast, delivering a flurry of sharp, powerful blows. She fought to keep a grip on her sword as she parried the relentless assault, and while she was able to fend them off, she was driven back, one step, then another, under the sheer force of his attack.

Grunting, she searched for an opening, but Sinjan's assault was like a blizzard, and it was all she could do to protect herself from his slashing and stabbing blade. The man was overcommitting himself, pushing hard, and she knew that if she could just hold out, he would tire, and an opening would present itself.

He fell in and she caught his blade on her own, inches from her throat. His breathing was ragged, and she could feel his hot breath on her face as she heaved him back, their blades scraping and sparking as she levered him away.

He fell back a step, grinning wolfishly. His pale flesh, flecked with blood, gave him an almost alien aspect, but it was nothing compared to the fearsome hatred in his eyes.

Was she deserving of such passion? What had she done to inspire such animosity? Perhaps, for a man like Sinjan, the simple fact of her existence was enough. He meant to snuff her out, to erase her. To set her up for Heldren's murder. But why?

Sinjan roared again, feinting left then whipping his ebon blade around to the right. She protected her flank, blocking the blow by reversing her grip on her own blade, and then spun, kicking out at him with her left foot. The blow connected with his upper thigh, causing him to stagger back, colliding with the edge of Heldren's desk.

She brought the sword around before her again, hunching, ready.

Sinjan stared angrily at her, hawking a mouthful of bloody phlegm. He wiped his lips on his sleeve, never once taking his eyes off her. 'You're a difficult woman to kill,' he said, his breath whistling through clenched teeth.

Sabbathiel had been right. He was tired now, playing for time to recover. She had to press her advantage. She rushed him, sword humming as she went low with a slash intended to disembowel him. He was ready for her, though, parrying the attack harmlessly away, offering a desultory riposte to the neck. She'd been expecting as much, and she batted his blade away, sending his arm wide – and then reversed her own momentum, chopping down with all her strength.

Her blade bit deep, crunching through ligament and bone, severing muscle and flesh. His upper arm – his blade arm – parted from his torso at the shoulder, slumping to the floor in a shower of arterial blood. His sword skittered across the tiled floor, coming to rest against the far wall. The arm lay twitching in a puddle of oily blood.

Sinjan screamed, a sound so raw, so primal, that she felt it in her gut. He staggered back, scrambling with his good arm for the edge of the desk, attempting, futilely, to hold himself upright. His face was contorted in pain. But the look in his eyes remained one of pure, unadulterated hate.

Sabbathiel twisted her blade, bringing the point up before her, inches from his throat.

With a grunt, Sinjan slid to the ground. Blood was pumping from the meaty stump of his shoulder. The air was rich with the iron tang of it, thick and cloying in the back of Sabbathiel's throat.

She heard noises from the doorway and glanced up to see several guards swarming into the room, lasrifles raised. One of them barked a command and the others opened fire.

Sabbathiel moved, throwing herself to the ground, rolling around the other side of the desk as las-fire scorched the wall behind where she'd been standing and burned deep grooves in the floor.

There was no way out. There were too many of them. The only

way to and from the room was through the sanctum. Sinjan had her trapped.

She glanced up at the window, at the wan blue light of Hulth that hovered in the sky like the orb of an enormous eye, the only remaining witness to what had really transpired in this room. And then she saw it – the mote in that shimmering eye. A tiny, familiar form, hovering just beyond the plate glass. A fleck of hope.

Fitch. The servo-skull.

But they were near the top of a hive spire.

Sabbathiel gripped her sword. The pommel was sticky with Sinjan's blood. She could hear him now, gasping for breath and whimpering for analgesics as the guards tried to drag him to safety. All around her, the world was lit by bolts of las-fire, streaming overhead, punching smoking holes in the antique desk, misting clots of bloody meat into the air as they chewed up Heldren's corpse.

Destroying the evidence.

She looked again at the window. She wasn't imagining it – Fitch was out there, traceries of red light playing across the smooth glass… indicating the exact spot…

Time seemed to stutter. She pushed herself up, keeping her head low, and *ran*. Not in the direction of the fight, but straight at the towering plate-glass window.

Las-shots ripped the air around her. She felt something hot puncture her right shoulder, while another bolt glanced off her armour like a shove to her lower back. She didn't drop a step.

Raising her sword as she ran, she swung the blade, screaming in rage. The tip struck the glass moments before she did, right at the spot Fitch had indicated, punching a hole that fed cracks out across the entire window like the strands of a vast spiderweb.

Weakening it.

Her momentum carried her through, shards of the window spilling out around her like crystal rain. The chill air hit her like a slap to the face, and then she could hear nothing but the howling of the wind as she twisted in free fall, throwing her arms out wide, sinking into the seemingly endless abyss below.

Above, las-bolts zipped through the sky like a light show. She felt a sudden wave of peace wash over her – she'd fallen like this once before. Once, when Leofric of the Grey Knights had betrayed her, when the warp storm had rolled in.

Back then she'd drifted... drifted... just like falling asleep...

And then the air was propelled out of her lungs, and everything was on fire. Blinding white pain...

...and she was rising again, back into the air, soaring away through the velvet night.

A voice crackled over her vox. *'We've got you, ma'am.'*

Bledheim?

'Try not to move. We'll hold the ship as steady as we can until we can set her down. You're going to be fine. Metik's here. Everything is going to be all right.'

Is it?

Will it ever be all right again?

Will... it...?

Blackness closed in.

PART TWO

CONSPIRACY

CHAPTER ELEVEN

'We are but motes of dust, drifting in an endless sea; sparks that flare all too briefly. Our light does little to illuminate the fading universe, but it is in our nature to fight, to wrestle back the encroaching dark, to find a way. Thus, we open not our eyes, but our minds, and we are terrified by what it is we see.'

– Navigator Santor Bleeth, giving evidence during the aftermath of the Soltzenheim disaster

Bright blood bubbles from the ends of broken fingertips. Drool seeps from the corner of a slack-jawed mouth, pooling on the man's naked chest. The skin here is thin and translucent, and covered in inked scrawl, swirling patterns and icons that suggest arcane rites and esoteric wards, their meaning long ago lost amongst their sheer profusion. Blind eyes flicker back in their sockets, exposing their milky-white undersides. More blood dribbles from nostrils, ears, spattering the floor. And then there is the sound – the plaintive mewling of an animal in pain. He rocks back and forth on his haunches, trailing fingers scraping the rough stone floor, bringing forth eruptions of fresh blood. All around him, the walls are covered in smeared images and geometric shapes; patterns written in that bright blood, dragged straight from the depths of the warp.

Frantically, jerking as if puppeted by some unseen master, the figure shifts, twisting on the spot, raising its hands as if attempting to ward off some invisible assailant. And then the mewling grows in intensity until it becomes a scream, a hollow shriek that seems to rend the air itself. More blood, this time bubbling out of the tear ducts, streaming down the pale white cheeks, bright and stark. The man faces the wall. His arm jerks. His bloodied fingers press against the cool stone. And then he begins again, scratching out another symbol with his own lifeblood. This time the symbol is a circle or wheel, and at its heart a stylised letter 'I', broken by two small dashes across its centre. She recognises it immediately. But then, she already knew what he was going to draw. She had already felt its pull...

Sabbathiel turned her head to peer out of the viewing port, blinking her eyes to shake off the after-image of the vision. They'd been coming with increasing frequency these last few days, punctuating her waking hours as well as her dreams, and her concern at their origin was growing. Were they a symptom of the time she'd spent drifting in the warp storm? Some latent absorption of whatever existed within that horrifying bubble of the immaterium? Perhaps they were memories of things she could no longer recall, echoes of her previous life attempting to reassert themselves? Or were they somehow related to whatever Metik had done to revive her? Was she still the same as she had been, or had the process indelibly altered her in some way she was yet to understand?

Her curiosity had yet to overwhelm her revulsion enough for

her to raise the topic with the once-human *thing;* and besides, she didn't wish to pique his interest in her any more than was necessary. Or perhaps she just didn't want to face the truth.

Metik was sitting across the cabin from her now, his metal legs folded beneath him, his head lowered to his chest. His mandibles were twitching incessantly. She presumed he was carrying out some form of calculation, although she couldn't be sure – whatever went on inside that half-mechanical mind, it no longer bore any relation to what she recognised as human thought. Well, aside from the sarcasm and the creature's obvious but grotesque fascination with human physiology. His pet, the slave-drone Nimbik, perched on his left shoulder, silent and still. Unnerving.

She had hoped to leave Metik behind on Garabon, or else escort him back to his workshop on Tistus, but after her escape from Sinjan they'd not waited around to debate matters. Besides, his medical assistance had, once again, proved invaluable. She guessed she was stuck with his company, at least until she had a better handle on what was going on here on Hulth, and what it had to do with Heldren's death.

The lander banked, and she turned back to the viewing port to study the cityscape unfolding beneath them. For as far as she could see, the landscape was comprised of regimented rows of habitation blocks, punctuated only by the monolithic tower of the Gallowspire, rising from the grey morass like a towering beacon, and the spire of an immense cathedral, encrusted with all the arcane affectation of the Ecclesiarchy. A hivesprawl, vast and monumental in its ugliness.

The vessel descended, skimming over the rooftops, so that Sabbathiel could even make out the teeming masses in the gullies between the buildings: canyons of grey rockcrete, cut deep into the fabric of the city. Down in those lower levels was where the population eked out their daily lives, streaming through the packed streets like blood cells being pumped through the thudding valves and chambers of a heart.

The lander continued, skirting around the cathedral's jutting spire, before swinging left, dipping into one of the smooth-sided canyons and dropping lower still. Slanting shadows cast the interior of the cabin in oppressive gloom.

Sabbathiel massaged her temples. The after-effects of the vision had now given way to a low-level headache, leaving her feeling dulled and queasy. She fought the urge to close her eyes and rest her head against the seat back. There was too much to be done. There would be time for resting later, once she'd got to the bottom of Heldren's murder. Not to mention discovering the truth behind why Atticus Sinjan had tried to implicate her for it, and whether he was acting alone. She suspected the truth ran far deeper than it appeared. Someone was taking advantage of her return. But why? Who stood to gain by removing her from proceedings? Or rather, who stood to lose by her continued presence?

More questions that, for now, would have to remain unanswered. But she would set the record straight and restore her reputation. No matter the cost. She'd been given a second chance at life, and she was damned if she was going to see it thrown away in the name of some conspiracy.

The transport was coming in to land. Beside her, Metik unfolded himself, arachnid-like legs unfurling from beneath him in a strange parody of life. He stretched his upper torso, raising his head. On his shoulder, Nimbik stirred to life, bionic eye whirring as it drew focus. It scampered around the back of Metik's neck, hunkering down, its claws clinging tightly to his scarlet robes.

Next to Metik, Bledheim sat still and silent, his eyes closed as if in deep contemplation. His hands were tucked into the sleeves of his robe, with only the slightest glint of the protruding needle-glove that he wore on his right hand. He'd been concocting a new serum of late; Sabbathiel found it only mildly disconcerting that he was yet to reveal to her its purpose.

Mercy and Brondel sat at the rear of the cabin, deep in a heated conversation that appeared to revolve around the best way to take down an ogryn. Mercy was advocating a quick, sudden shot to the head with a bolt-round, while Brondel favoured severing the Achilles tendons, before taking a power axe to the groin. Sabbathiel gathered they must have been arguing in such fashion for hours.

'Contemplative, ma'am?'

She started at the sound of Fitch's voice above her left shoulder and twisted in her seat to observe the servo-skull, hovering close by. Its empty eye socket peered at her forlornly, while the fine red traceries from its bionic implant played across her face.

'You could say that,' she said, and then sighed, giving in to the impulse to answer the machine as if it really were her old confidant. 'Something's not right with my dreams, Fitch.'

There was a pause as the servo-skull seemed to consider her words. 'Have you considered the alternative, ma'am?'

'The alternative?'

'That there's nothing wrong with your dreams, but it's reality you should question.'

Sabbathiel smiled for the first time since leaving Garabon orbit. She glanced at Metik. 'Emperor knows how he managed it, but that tech-priest really did capture something of your twisted mind in his programming, didn't he?'

'I wouldn't know, ma'am,' replied the servo-skull. 'My reply was not intended to disconcert. Only to point out the obvious.'

'You'll have to spell it out for me.'

'You spent over one hundred years drifting inside a warp storm, ma'am. Wounded and preserved on the point of death. Only to be restored to find the universe has indelibly changed in your absence.'

'Your point?'

'Merely that, until you have adequate data, it would be advisable not to trust anyone… including yourself.'

Sabbathiel peered at the servo-skull for a moment, appraising. 'I was wrong. He didn't capture some of Fitch's mind.' She grinned. 'He captured all of it.'

'As you say, ma'am.' The red light playing on her cheek blinked out, and the servo-skull drifted away a short distance, curling its mechadendrites around a brace on the bulkhead as it took up a position for landing.

A chime from the cockpit, then Silq's voice echoing over the vox. *'Three minutes to ground fall, ma'am.'*

Around Sabbathiel, her acolytes fell silent in anticipation.

They disembarked from the lander into the waning afternoon sun.

Here, the light was tinged with hues of red, and spilled across sweeping fields of bristling funeral stele, softening the harsh gleam of the marble. The graves were irregular in both size and layout, giving the place a disordered appearance, so at odds with the regimented banks of habitation blocks they'd seen from the air. Mortuary structures, the follies of great Houses from amongst the native population, seemed to sprout from the ground as if they'd grown wild; columns and plinths, statuary and looming archways forming sanctuaries for the long dead.

Sabbathiel had not anticipated local interference – as an inquisitor of the Ordo Hereticus, her movements were rarely questioned – but following her hasty retreat from Garabon, she wouldn't have been surprised to discover she'd been trailed, or worse, that Sinjan had called ahead to stir disquiet or alert his allies on Hulth. She didn't think for one minute that he, or any of her former conclave, were done with her yet.

She still had no idea where the man had come from, or why he had attempted to frame and then kill her back on Garabon. What could he possibly have to gain from it? Had he been watching her since her return from Calaphrax? Was he the one responsible for Heldren's murder?

So many questions, and far too few answers.

There was a chance, she supposed, that she was nothing but a convenient scapegoat, a means to an end. That she'd woken to find herself a pawn in a bigger game that she couldn't yet see, let alone comprehend. She wasn't even certain of the players. She *was* certain of one thing: that whatever was going on, she was going to deal her own hand at the table.

'Mercy, Silq – guard the lander.'

The tall woman frowned at Sabbathiel, her hand closing on the hilt of her immense sword, which hung unprotected from the leather hoop on her back. 'Are you expecting trouble?'

Sabbathiel shook her head. 'No. But something about this place doesn't feel right. Sinjan saw that hololith, too. If he also discerned its location…'

'…then there could be others here,' finished Silq. She nodded. 'We'll let you know if we run into anything unexpected. Right, Mercy?'

'Mmm-hmm,' mumbled the other woman, her fingers still toying with the hilt of her sword.

Sabbathiel beckoned to Bledheim and Brondel. 'You're with me. Metik, have you identified the tomb in question?'

Metik clacked his ceramic fingertips impatiently. 'I have done what I was able to with the scarce information available to me, yes.'

'And?'

'And it's over there,' he said, using one of his mechadendrites to point out a glistening white building on the far side of a sea of stele and listing headstones.

Sabbathiel squinted. It was new, at least in comparison to the other, more-weathered monuments that surrounded it, and even in the pale light it seemed to shimmer as it caught the sun. It was ornate, too, its frontage flanked by towering statues that served as pillars to prop up a small portico, and a crenellated roof was peppered with scores of leering gargoyles that loomed down at anyone who approached.

They picked their way amongst the gravestones towards it.

It was not the tomb of a pauper. Then again, she doubted a single member of the proletariat was buried in this hallowed ground. Here was a garden in which only the rich and powerful took root, in which influence was the currency that bought the Emperor's salvation. Fitch would have called her a cynic, back when he was alive. Sabbathiel knew she was just a realist.

She glanced up to see the servo-skull trailing her, its sensor arrays bristling as its mechanical tendrils brushed the air, ever watchful for threats. In some ways, this new version of her old companion was even more useful than the original – but she would have given anything to be able to share a drink with him now.

She was lost. Adrift in a hostile universe that she no longer recognised. Stalked like a wounded beast by hunters whose motives she couldn't fathom. And in the midst of it all, she was alone, her only tether to the past a small, fragile skull that had once belonged to the closest thing she had had to a friend.

Sabbathiel heaved a heavy sigh. Surrounding herself with the bones of the dead was hardly helping her mood.

They reached the tomb. It was bigger than she'd thought from afar – about the size of a generous hab-unit. The twin statues dwarfed her, their imperious-looking faces peering off into the distance, lips pressed tight. The figures were both male, muscular and dressed in flowing robes. And both had stylised third eyes in the middle of their foreheads. The words QUINTUS BLEETH were written on a carved stone banner, hanging between the two.

'Navigators,' she said, her heart sinking. 'Just what I need.' She'd run into their kind before. All pomp and self-importance, and a tendency towards the unchecked accumulation of power and influence. Influence that, to Sabbathiel's mind, had no place in the governance of the Imperium.

Bledheim shot her an interested look. 'I've yet to interrogate a Navigator...'

'Well, I wouldn't hold your breath,' spat Brondel.

'Why not?' asked Bledheim, irritated.

'Because odds are, the one in there is well past talking.' The squat chuckled as he walked up the short flight of steps and crossed to the tomb's pressed-iron door, which was embossed with what appeared to be a stylised map of planetary orbits. The metal was still shiny, yet to oxidise. As she'd suspected, the tomb hadn't been here that long.

Brondel tested the door with the edge of his boot. It creaked open, revealing a shadowy passageway within. 'Well, these Bleeths might be well-to-do Navigators round these parts, but their security leaves a lot to be desired.'

'Or someone beat us to it,' said Metik.

'More likely,' said Sabbathiel, drawing her pistol and waving the squat out of her path. 'Come on. Let's take a look.'

The passageway inside the tomb was narrow and cramped, and they were forced to walk in single file, with Sabbathiel taking the lead. She'd left Metik loitering just inside the doorway, watching their backs. The thought made her shudder.

The only source of light was the door they'd left open in their wake, the thin sun reflecting off the polished marble blocks that formed the passage's walls. The stone was cool and dry to the touch, and the musty odour that Sabbathiel had long come to associate with such burial places – she had, in her time, breached more than she would ever have cared to – was entirely absent.

Yet the lingering sense that death had touched this place remained. It scratched at the back of her skull, like an ever-present itch. Something had happened here. Something decidedly *not good*.

Ahead, the passageway opened out into a large burial chamber, its outer edges lined with man-sized, hooded statues bearing the faces of real human skulls, each of them turned to look solemnly upon an engraved central dais. It was lit by a candle sconce that hovered just below the vaulted curve of the ceiling, throwing out a dim, sepulchral glow. A shadowy archway at the rear of the space appeared to lead on to a smaller adjoining room.

To Sabbathiel's profound surprise, there were two things of note about the chamber. The first was that there was no actual sarcophagus resting on the dais – just a stark, empty space where it should have been. The second was that an ogryn wearing thin wire spectacles was hunched over the stone platform, studying a brown stain with some interest. It looked up as she entered, its considerable brows knitting in concern. She noticed a small silver implant jutting from the base of its neck.

'Show me your hands,' said Sabbathiel, raising her pistol. She made way for the others to enter the chamber behind her, edging around amongst the forest of eerie statues.

'A frecking ogryn,' muttered Brondel. 'I'd wager you've never interrogated one of those, either.'

Bledheim cleared his throat but deigned not to reply.

'Can I help you?' said the ogryn. He peered at her myopically, before seemingly remembering something and lowering his spectacles so they perched on the end of his bulbous nose.

'You can start by telling me what you're doing here,' said Sabbathiel, 'in this tomb.'

The ogryn shrugged. 'Examining this bloodstain.' He tapped his finger on the dais to underline his point.

'And why, exactly, are you doing that?'

The ogryn was about to reply, when another voice cut across him, originating from the shadows by the archway. 'That's simple,' said the man, walking slowly forward into the globe of flickering candlelight, his hands slightly raised before him, palms out. 'Because I asked him to.'

Sabbathiel took in the tall figure. He had a gaunt face, handsome but for a scar that divided his left brow, puckering his flesh. His hair was clipped short at the sides and swept back from his forehead, and his eyes were a bright, startling blue. He was slim, and wore a faded leather trench coat, which was open at the front and trailed down around his calves. A pistol with a wooden handle and a delicately filigreed barrel was tucked into the front of his belt, and, like Atticus Sinjan before him, he wore an Inquisitorial seal on a chain around his neck. A sword was scabbarded at his side. He smiled at her, warmly.

One of Sinjan's men, then.

He'd made it here before her. She cursed herself – she should have dropped the ogryn with a shot to the head the moment she entered the chamber. In confined quarters such as this, they wouldn't stand a chance if things got up close and personal.

'And who might you be?' said Sabbathiel, swivelling to face him and tightening her grip on her pistol. Her head was buzzing. Something about the man seemed horribly familiar, although she had no recollection of ever meeting him before.

'Hello, Sabbathiel,' he said. The smile hadn't fled his lips since he'd seen her. 'My name is Mandreth. Inquisitor Rassius Mandreth.'

CHAPTER TWELVE

'You!'

Sabbathiel lowered her pistol so he wouldn't see the tremble that had crept into her hands.

Mandreth. My mysterious benefactor. The one who pulled me from the storm.

Cold prickles needled her spine. Her heart thrummed. Her palms were moist with sweat. Stuttering images flashed before her eyes: the bloom of light from the muzzle of Leofric's storm bolter; the look in Fitch's eyes the last time they had spoken; the roiling turmoil of the warp storm; the twisted, mutated forms of heretics in ancient power armour ripping through a Dark Angels battle-barge; the unfurling wings of something strange and immense, enshrouding her as her vision blurred and bled to nothing.

She gasped; held herself steady.

Mandreth. What did he know? What truths were his to share? What holes could he fill in her story of herself?

She met his gaze.

He wasn't what she'd expected – although, thinking on it, she hadn't really known *what* to expect. Someone more staid, more formal? *Older?* There was a casual irreverence about this man, in the way he held himself, the cool, calm attitude in his expression. This was not someone used to sitting behind desks shuffling papers.

'It's good to see you up and about,' said Mandreth. His tone was light and airy, conversational. It seemed incongruous given the circumstances. 'I had hoped we'd meet again in slightly more convivial surroundings.'

Sabbathiel felt unsettled, wrong-footed; unsure what to make of him. She had no notion of this man's allegiances, his motives or intentions. And what was he doing *here*, in this tomb that had been of such importance to Heldren? Could it be that he had played a part in Heldren's death?

Behind him, another figure emerged from the shadows of the adjoining chamber, moving over to stand beside Mandreth in the soft glow of the candlelight. She was young and pretty, with unblemished dark skin and close-cropped hair. She was scowling like she'd just tasted something sour. Sabbathiel sized her up. Judging by the woman's build and the unmarked black armour, she was ex-military or ex-enforcer. She was also well armed, with a rifle slung across her back, a pistol at her waist and twin daggers clutched in her fists. 'This is Heloise,' said Mandreth. He gave a crooked smile. 'Say hello, Heloise.'

The woman's scowl deepened. She regarded Sabbathiel levelly. 'Well met,' she said, although it was clear from her tone she didn't mean it. Her grip on the knives visibly relaxed, but she kept them poised ready, nonetheless.

Sabbathiel had been like that once too. Cocksure and full of herself, supremely confident in her own power, her righteousness.

And then she'd been almost murdered by a Grey Knight.

'What are you doing here? Is this supposed to be some sort of ambush?'

Mandreth frowned and made a placating gesture with his open hands. 'An ambush? No, not at all,' he said. 'More of an unexpected – but welcome – confluence. I had hoped we could be friends.'

'*Friends?* I don't even know you,' said Sabbathiel.

'No. Of course. Not yet, anyway.' He gestured for Heloise to stand down, and with a reluctant sigh, she backed away, disappearing into the gloomy antechamber from where she had come. Sabbathiel indicated to Brondel and Bledheim to relax. For now. The ogryn, bizarrely, continued to examine the bloodstains on the floor with a deep fascination.

Sabbathiel eyed Mandreth warily. 'What makes you think I'd even *want* to get to know you?'

Mandreth smiled. 'Perhaps my little gesture might go some way to standing me in good stead?'

'You're referring to the fact you dragged me out of the warp storm,' said Sabbathiel. 'Why?' It was the question she'd been wanting to ask this man for months, since the very moment Metik had first uttered his name.

Mandreth considered his answer for a moment. 'Because I could. Because it seemed the right thing to do. Because I am short of allies in this universe, and you are really quite formidable, if the stories about you are true.'

'They're true,' muttered Brondel, hawking up another gobbet of phlegm. 'Whatever they are, they're true.'

'What could you possibly know about me?' said Sabbathiel, ignoring the squat.

'I know that you went to Calaphrax hunting traitors,' said Mandreth. 'And that you found them there. I know you gave up everything trying to bring them to justice. Even your life.' He paused, met her eye. 'I saw what they did to you.'

Sabbathiel's hand drifted unconsciously to her midriff and the site of her old wound. Her every instinct was telling her this man was dangerous, that he couldn't be trusted.

But she needed to be pragmatic. She'd lost everything when she'd fallen into the warp back at Calaphrax, and she was damned if she was going to let Sinjan and his cronies take it from her again now that she was finally beginning to claw it back. 'You still haven't answered my question. What are you doing here? In this tomb, on Hulth?'

'I'm investigating the House of Bleeth. I have reason to believe they're involved in smuggling dangerous contraband – including recovered archeotech – onto Hulth. I intend to put a stop to it.'

'Archeotech?' echoed Sabbathiel. She supposed it made sense. Navigators were notorious for looking out for their own, often arcane interests, and had the money and influence to affect such an operation. 'But why visit the tomb of one of their dead?'

'I could ask you the same question,' said Mandreth.

'I'm paying my respects,' she replied, 'on behalf of a friend.' An image of Heldren flashed through her mind, dying on his wooden desk, using his final moments to point her to the tomb on the hololith. There was more to this than a simple archeotech smuggling ring. Much more. The question was whether Mandreth knew it or not.

Mandreth grinned. 'Tell me, does anything strike you as unusual about this particular tomb?'

'You mean aside from the ogryn who seems to be analysing an old bloodstain?'

Bledheim sniggered from where he had insinuated himself

amongst the skull-faced statues to her right. He was watching proceedings, taking everything in. Brondel, on the other hand, had taken up a position guarding the entrance, stroking his beard and spitting as if to punctuate every beat of Sabbathiel and Mandreth's conversation.

'Apart from Nol, yes,' said Mandreth. His tone was patient, but far from condescending. In fact, he seemed amused, as if he was enjoying their little game.

'There's no casket,' she said. 'No sarcophagus. And therefore…'

'No body,' finished Mandreth.

'But there *is* blood,' said Nol, tapping his fingertip on the stone again to underline his point.

'Something passed through here,' said Sabbathiel. 'You think they're using the tomb as a way station. A place to hide their smuggled artefacts before moving them on to other locations or buyers nearby.'

Could this be what Heldren wanted her to investigate? Could it be linked to why he was killed, and why Sinjan had framed her? It seemed tenuous, but for now, it was the only lead she had.

Mandreth nodded. 'Precisely. It's the perfect cover. Who would think to investigate a recent tomb?'

'Aside from the six of us,' said Bledheim, drily.

'And what about Quintus Bleeth?' asked Sabbathiel.

'It's all a sham,' said Bledheim. 'A front. His body was never here.'

'Then where?'

Mandreth shrugged. 'That's what we're trying to ascertain. The body could be anywhere – on the grounds of the Bleeth estate, on one of their ships, in the strata somewhere on another world. We may never know. The point is this tomb *has* been occupied. But with what, and by whom?'

'Someone who's left a mess behind them,' said Sabbathiel. She stepped up onto the dais, peering down at the ornate patterning, where thin channels had been cut into the stone to depict what looked like two planets in orbit around one another, linked by a bolt of lightning.

She dropped to her haunches before Nol – who shot her a disconcerted look – and peered at the bloodstains he'd been examining. They were extensive, but several weeks old, flaking now in the dry atmosphere of the tomb. The pattern they had made upon the stone suggested they had seeped from a stationary wounded victim or corpse. She could see no evidence of splatter marks to suggest the wounding had taken place here, inside the tomb. 'Whoever they are, it seems clear they were badly wounded when they came here,' she said. 'Are the other Bleeths all accounted for?'

'So they would have us believe,' said Mandreth, 'but of course, there are scores of others in their employ. Serfs and irregulars that help to run their operations. The family is… ubiquitous in this sector.'

'And what of Heldren?' she said. She glanced up to study Mandreth's reaction. He studied her with interest, apparently unfazed.

'Heldren?'

'An inquisitor from my former conclave.' Sabbathiel stood. 'It seems he was killed because of his interest in the contents of this tomb.'

Mandreth frowned. 'Then it seems the House of Bleeth really has stirred deep and troubled waters. Did you know him well?'

Sabbathiel shook her head. 'There wasn't time. But he was the only one amongst them who was prepared to give me a chance to prove my worth. And I believe he was onto something. The way this planet seemed to consume him… whatever is going on here, this tomb has to be just the tip of the hive.'

'Do you know who killed him?' asked Mandreth. He scratched at the skin on the back of his hand as if irritated by something.

'I can't be certain, but I believe it has something to do with a man named Atticus Sinjan.'

'Now *him* I am aware of,' said Mandreth. 'The albino with the black sword and the even blacker attitude. A dangerous enemy.'

So, he claims not to have known Heldren, and to have no fondness for Sinjan. Perhaps our trajectory isn't as misaligned as I'd feared.

Sabbathiel smiled. 'He's a little less dangerous now – he's missing an arm.'

'Ah,' said Mandreth. 'Then we must expect a reprisal. Sinjan also has interests here on Hulth and has attempted to block my investigation into the Bleeths on more than one occasion.'

'*We?*'

'Forgive my presumption,' he said, 'but it seems only prudent that we consider pooling resources. Your connections in this region must be… somewhat out of date–'

'Yet my Inquisitorial icon remains as effective a tool of persuasion as ever.'

'Indeed. Until Sinjan asserts his influence. He could make things very difficult.'

Sabbathiel turned her back on him, rejoining Brondel and Bledheim on the other side of the dais.

'Umm,' said Nol.

Sabbathiel ignored the ogryn. She turned back to Mandreth. 'You think because you "rescued" me like some sort of ancient relic that I'm just going to do as you bid? That you've earned enough of my trust that I'd throw my lot in with you so freely?'

'I'd be disappointed if you did,' said Mandreth. The man seemed utterly incapable of being flustered. 'But I do think you're a pragmatist. You wouldn't have got where you are otherwise.'

'Umm…' interjected Nol again.

'My last mission ended with me drifting for a hundred years in a warp storm.'

'Well, we all have our moments.'

Sabbathiel's lip curled. 'I don't even know you.'

'Then give me a chance to earn your trust.'

There were echoes of her own words to Heldren in what he was saying.

Could it really be that simple?

'Umm…'

'What is it, Nol?' Despite the ogryn's constant interruptions, Mandreth's tone remained infinitely patient. Sabbathiel would probably have put a bolt through the abhuman's head before now.

The ogryn pointed at the ceiling. 'There's something up there. It looks like a dead rat.'

Sabbathiel raised her eyes to the vaults overhead. Nimbik was scuttling around, agitated. 'Metik?'

Nimbik scurried around the circumference of the ceiling, and then dropped, flipping in the air and landing atop the hooded head of one of the skull-faced statues close to Nol. The ogryn flinched, stumbling back and crashing into one of the other statues, which crumbled under his immense weight. He remained seated amongst the debris, looking sheepish.

'Metik?' insisted Sabbathiel.

Nimbik pattered around on the statue's head for a moment, metal claws making ticking sounds, until it was facing Sabbathiel. Its tiny, hollow eye sockets seemed forlorn in the candlelight. A node flickered to life on its back, and suddenly a shimmering hololithic image of Metik bloomed to life in the air before it.

The tech-priest peered out at her. *'At last.'*

'What is it, Metik?' She wished she had Mandreth's patience.

Why hadn't the tech-priest just come along the passageway himself, rather than sending his minion?

'You might want to come and have a look for yourself.'

'I'm a little busy. Tell me.'

Metik clacked his fingers together in a steady rhythm. *'The lander has just exploded.'*

Sabbathiel sighed. 'I'm on my way.'

CHAPTER THIRTEEN

'In death, war finally ends.'

– Solomon Thoth, excerpted from *In a Time of Ending*

The enforcers were always going to lose. The only question was how badly.

As he emerged from the mouth of the tomb, Bledheim was forced to shield his eyes from the sudden glare of the burning lander. Black smoke curled in drifting funnels, creating a thick pall over the entire graveyard. The craft had been near obliterated, its aquila-styled wings slumped low on the ground, its passenger compartment a shredded mess of twisted metal and slag. The pilot's cockpit was still on fire. There was no sign of Silq or Mercy.

The sunlight was fading now, a sickly yellow glow as the orb dipped below the far horizon, and the black shapes of humanoid figures flitted amongst the forest of headstones and monuments, seemingly intent upon drawing a ring around the Bleeth tomb.

As if they'd ever be enough to contain her.

Behind him, the others were spilling out from the narrow door, weapons bristling. Metik stood off to one side, his antenna winking as he scanned the immediate vicinity, his mecha-dendrites shifting and coiling like restless snakes tasting the air. He was holding his strange, arcane weapon across his chest. 'Local enforcement officers,' he said, his voice a metallic burr. 'Twenty of them. Male and female. They took out the lander with grenades and are now moving to encircle our position. Their tactics are predictable and somewhat uninspired. Yet they remain effective.'

Sabbathiel nodded. 'We'll see.' She was peering off towards the blazing ship, ignoring the flitting shadows. Her lips twisted in a triumphant smile.

Bledheim followed her gaze. Another figure was walking directly towards him, this one taller than the others. A woman. She was trailing a massive sword in her wake, its tip scoring the soft loam. And she was *smouldering.*

'Mercy,' whispered Bledheim, unable to keep the admiration from creeping into his voice.

The woman's hair had been singed and her clothes were spotted with patches of soot and ash. But the look on her face was a vision of fury itself.

Two of the black-clad figures burst out of the shadows on either side of Mercy, swinging power mauls. She barely missed a step as she swung her blade up and round in a wide arc, opening the throat of one of her attackers and then chopping down through the shoulder of the other. Gore sprayed wildly into the air as the bodies collapsed on the soft ground, and Mercy continued her onward march towards the Bleeth tomb.

A few steps away from Bledheim, Mandreth was looking to the sky. He issued a shrill whistle and smiled when a huge, tawny falcon began spiralling down towards him, its wingspan broad enough to dispel even the thick smoke of the burning lander as it dipped and soared.

The others – Brondel, Heloise and Nol – stood ready, but seemed to be waiting for a signal from their respective inquisitors before moving to engage the enemy combatants.

'Ma'am?' prompted Brondel.

'Hold…' said Sabbathiel.

The shadowy figures had finished moving and had now formed a ring around the area, closing in behind Mercy. They began to push forward, stepping in time with one another; regimented, militaristic. Well trained. Their power mauls sparked, promising crushing pain. Many of them were holding raised pistols or shields. Bledheim couldn't tell which were men and which were women; they all looked the same, dressed from head to toe in black, segmented carapace armour, with black helms and tinted face visors.

'Astor Sabbathiel.' The voice was projected, tinny, female, though it was unclear which of the enforcers had spoken. 'You are hereby given notice of your arrest for heresy, murder and sedition, on the order of Inquisitor Lord Atticus Sinjan, of the Palmarian Conclave. Call off your dogs now and submit.'

Bledheim, who had taken the opportunity to creep around the side of the Bleeth tomb to watch from a much safer distance, eyed Sabbathiel, watching for a reaction. The tension was almost febrile.

This isn't going to be pretty.

Sabbathiel seemed entirely unmoved. Not even a twitching nerve blemished her studied disinterest, her calm, silent exterior. The others were looking to her too – even Mandreth, whose huge bird still circled overhead, apparently unnoticed by the ring of enforcers.

The moment stretched.

One of the enforcers cocked their head then took a step forward, breaking the formation. They straightened their arm, their pistol pointed directly at Sabbathiel's exposed head. There were only around ten yards between them now, and the woman's arm – presuming she had been the one who had spoken – was as steady as a rock. 'Inquisitor Sabbathiel. Do you underst–'

The sentence ended abruptly with the *splock* of a combat knife burying itself in the side of the woman's head. She stood for a moment, swaying slightly on the spot, before crumpling into a dead heap without making another sound. Around her, the other enforcers turned, distracted, each of them trying desperately to work out from which direction the thrown knife had come, and who could possibly have thrown it.

Bledheim chuckled quietly to himself.

Silq. Harder to kill than we all thought.

The graveyard lit up with pulses of green gauss fire, and it seemed to Bledheim a release valve had suddenly been opened and all the many nightmares of the warp broke free at once.

Nol roared – a bass rumble that seemed to shake the surrounding tombstones, rattling them like teeth in old, receding gums. He charged, thundering at surprising speed into a line of stunned enforcers, none of whom had the time or wherewithal to raise their weapons to mount a defence. Two were thrown clear, one colliding with a towering monument and breaking with a sickening crack, the other landing so awkwardly on their head that their neck shattered, and they were dead before their body had come to rest. Two more were simply trampled under the oaf's enormous, pounding feet, while a fifth was battered by his swinging backhand, sending their broken body sailing into a sixth and knocking them from their feet.

Elsewhere, Mandreth's enormous falcon dived, dropping like

a tossed spear, its beak splintering the visor of one sorry bastard as it struck. Talons rent, the beak flashed, and the man screamed, his face a bloody ruin.

Pistol fire rained, sending shards of marble and granite splintering into the air. Bledheim flinched as his face was lacerated along the line of his left cheekbone, and he dropped to the ground, edging back behind the cover of the tomb. Blood streamed down his cheek, warm and wet.

Sabbathiel, Brondel and Metik had formed a loose circle, returning fire in all directions as they moved like a turning wheel across the battlefield, a lazy spin that saw enforcers fall on all sides, disintegrated by the tech-priest's rifle, seared by the burning plasma of the squat's pistol or blown apart by the punch of the inquisitor's bolt shells.

Sabbathiel had a shard of marble embedded in her cheek, and one of Metik's mechadendrites was writhing on the ground by his feet, severed and scorched where it had been separated from somewhere above his left shoulder. The squat, as always, seemed to be escaping matters relatively unscathed, and was by turns shouting bitter curses and hooting with glee as his pistol spat more plasma at the now scattered enforcers, who appeared to have abandoned all sense of military precision – as well as the idea of taking Sabbathiel prisoner – and were now fully engaged in trying to kill as many of them as they could.

Elsewhere, Heloise had gone to work with her blades, bursting from the shadows to take down enforcers from behind, before melting away again to re-emerge somewhere else a few moments later, her swords brushing throats like a deadly kiss.

Both Mercy and Nol were employing less subtle tactics, wading through the enemy, chopping, crushing and battering the enforcers aside. Silq had slung her xenos rifle across her back – the combat was now too close quartered for her to safely deploy the weapon without risking the lives of her allies – and had reclaimed her thrown knife from the head of the dead woman. Bledheim watched as she eyed up another target from behind the protection of a listing headstone.

The scuff of a boot sounded from close by.

Too close.

Bledheim sensed movement behind him – the steady approach of a lone enemy – and turned, launching himself at the surprised man who had been attempting to sneak up on him, pistol held at the ready.

The weapon fired but the shot went wide as Bledheim scrabbled anxiously, clawing at the man's wrist, pushing him back against one of the nearby headstones. They grappled there for a moment, each of them straining desperately for the upper hand. Bledheim could smell the man's sour sweat as he leaned in, using what slight weight he had to pin the enforcer against the stone.

The man grunted and tried to push back as Bledheim bashed his wrist against the moss-encrusted monument, loosing the pistol from his grip. It thudded to the ground by their feet. Bledheim tried to kick it away but succeeded only in stamping it into the soft loam.

The enforcer heaved, shoving Bledheim back, but the momentum was such that he overbalanced and coupled with Bledheim's grip on his arm, he went over too, landing on top of the interrogator as they thrashed in the dirt. Bledheim rolled, grabbing the man by the upper arms. He swung his legs over and sat astride the enforcer's gut, holding him down.

The man kicked his legs, trying to knee Bledheim in the back, but Bledheim shifted his weight, edging forward to avoid the frantic blows.

Bledheim's breath was coming in short, shallow gasps. His

whole body sang with pain, his muscles burning with the unwelcome exertion. This was *not* how he liked to do things.

'I suppose we all have to make the best of the hand we're dealt,' he said through gritted teeth. 'Although it does seem a terrible waste.'

He released his grip on the left arm of the enforcer. The man, suddenly seeing his chance to break free, began pummelling Bledheim in the ribs. Pain blossomed, but Bledheim ignored it. Instead, he focused on trying to hold the struggling man still.

'For *Emperor's* sake…'

He jabbed the bunched fingers of his free hand up beneath the rim of the enforcer's visor, feeling the brace of needle caps dig deep into the soft flesh at the top of the man's throat. It wasn't perfect, but it would have to do.

The man was whimpering now, trying to wrench himself free, but it was far too late for all that. If he hadn't wanted to die, he should never have tried to sneak up on Bledheim in the first place.

Bledheim hit the release mechanism in his palm and waited for the multicoloured chambers affixed to the back of his hand to drain clear, pumping the cocktail of chemical compounds into the man's bloodstream.

The man jolted suddenly beneath him, his body shuddering as it went into spasm. Bledheim jumped clear, watching with interest as the man's back arched severely and his every ligament seemed to pull taut at once, contorting his limbs into positions they were never intended to achieve. The man let out a single, wheezing squeal of agony, before his spine cracked with a horrific pop and his body seemed to fold back on itself, like the corpse of a bird left to wither in the sun.

Bledheim stood for a moment, staring at the twisted, jack-knifed corpse, the remains of a once thinking, breathing man, now lying in the dirt amongst the headstones, just another tribute to this resting place of the hallowed dead.

Another bag of sodden flesh and bones to enrich the soil.

Another stupid death to add to the toll.

Bledheim straightened himself, dusted off his robes and took a moment to reset the fluid chambers on the back of his hand. He wiped the remaining gore from the needle tips on the dead man's fatigues. Then, with a brief nod of satisfaction, he returned to his vantage point by the edge of the Bleeth tomb.

The battle was coming to an end. Heloise and Silq stood back to back, hacking away at a group of four enforcers with sword and knife. The enforcers were defending themselves admirably with their sparking mauls but couldn't seem to land a single blow on either of the two women.

Nol was on the ground, apparently unconscious, but with a trail of mangled bodies in his wake. There was even one beneath him, the foot still twitching as if the owner were in the last throes of death. As Bledheim watched, it grew still.

Mandreth had recalled his falcon, which now perched proudly on his shoulder, something pink and gristly hanging from its beak. Mandreth was standing beside Sabbathiel, closely guarded by Brondel and Metik, but the threat seemed to have already passed, with no more enforcers visible amongst the wasteland of now-broken headstones.

He watched Mercy stride over to join Silq, and the final few enemy stragglers went down under three decisive swings of her blade and the sharp twist of a neck from Heloise.

For a moment they all stood in silence, catching their breath, taking in the scene of death and devastation that surrounded them. Bledheim stepped out from behind the tomb. On the ground, Nol groaned and sat up, looking around, dazed.

'Sinjan,' said Sabbathiel, with a grimace. She wiped blood

from her eyes with the back of her hand. She'd taken at least two hits during the battle, evidenced by a buckled plate on her red armour, over her left thigh, and a scorch mark on her upper torso where a power maul had slipped through her defences. Judging by the ring of corpses that surrounded her, the culprits had paid dearly for such impertinence.

'It seems you left him quite perturbed,' said Mandreth. He was stroking the head of his bird with a crooked finger. Bledheim was convinced the creature was giving him the evil eye.

Sabbathiel sighed. 'Clearly I should have taken his head as well as his arm.'

Metik clacked his fingers. 'I suggest we hasten to a new, defensible location. There is a seventy-nine point six per cent likelihood that the enforcers will have called for reinforcements.'

'With more firepower,' said Heloise, cleaning her blades on a rag as she and the other women walked over to join them. For the first time, Bledheim saw that Silq was limping, the dark, wet smear of a puncture wound on her upper thigh.

'Somewhere we can see to our wounds,' said Sabbathiel, pointedly.

'Well, if we still had a frecking lander...' muttered Brondel. He looked as if he were going to say more until he caught sight of Mercy glaring at him, her grip on the hilt of her sword tightening with every word.

'Go on,' she prompted. 'Say it.'

Brondel affected an air of innocence. 'Frecking enforcers,' he mumbled. 'Never liked them.'

Mercy grunted and slipped her sword into the hoop at her belt. Behind her, Nol was back on his feet, swaying a little unsteadily from side to side.

'I know where to go,' said Mandreth.

Sabbathiel frowned. She didn't look impressed. But then nor

did she look as if she were in a hurry to let Mandreth slip through her fingers either. She met Mandreth's eye. 'Then you'd better lead the way.'

CHAPTER FOURTEEN

Mandreth's safe house was an old stimm den, deep in one of the residential trenches on the outer rim of the nearest hive, the Gallowspire.

The stimm-heads were long gone, cleared out by either Mandreth, the enforcers or desperation, but they'd left their mark: bright paint tags swirled over the plascrete walls, shifting and altering depending on the angle from which the viewer regarded them. The abstract patterns gave Sabbathiel a stabbing headache, which – coupled with her already unquiet mind – left her feeling uncomfortable and ill at ease. Something about the clashing, foaming colours reminded her of Calaphrax and the warp storm, and she was forced to avert her eyes before her memories dragged her into a well of despair and recrimination.

One betrayal begets another.

The Dark Angels, to Leofric, to Sinjan.

An ancestry of lies.

Following the events at the graveyard, she'd considered running, conscripting a replacement vessel – assuming hers had already been blockaded in the dock by Sinjan's people – and fleeing to some other, distant world. Somewhere on the other side of that great rift in the sky.

Somewhere in the quiet darkness.

There, her Inquisitorial icon would buy her time and resources while she formulated a plan. There, her dreams might leave her be.

But Sabbathiel had never been one for running. Besides, she'd had enough of people doubting her motives and accusing her of treachery, of the hypocrisy of the *righteous.* She owed it to herself to see this through; to get to the bottom of what had really happened to Heldren and clear her name. To deliver the Emperor's justice to the real traitors of the Imperium, in whatever form they took. Even if that included Atticus Sinjan.

She knew so little of the man and his motives. Why had he framed her for Heldren's death? Why go to such trouble to attempt to track her down, to seek reprisal, when surely her flight from Heldren's chambers would be enough for him to convince others of her guilt? What was the narrative he was trying to construct, and what did he hope to gain from it? And was he really involved in the strange circumstances surrounding the missing body of the dead Navigator Quintus Bleeth?

It seemed to Sabbathiel that the answers to all of this would be found here, on Hulth.

And so, she had allowed herself to be led to this dismal pit of a safe house by a man she hardly knew – but with whom her survival, and, it seemed, her mission, had become inextricably linked.

The condition of the place didn't help her mood, of course; it stank of damp human bodies and mildew. Fungal spoores had bloomed in bone-white clusters in every conceivable corner and crevice, and what furniture there was – a few musty chairs, what had once been a reasonably comfortable-looking four-poster bed, and a single wooden table – had all served as food or bedding for rodents and Emperor knew what else. She could hear them now, skittering about beneath the floor, chattering and scratching and fighting for dominance, just like the human beings living on top of each other in the Gallowspire.

Puddles of brackish water spotted the floor where the ever-present rain had seeped through from the building above. This low down the city had its own weather front, the warm updraughts from the trenches stirring the chill air above to birth fomenting storm clouds that drenched the streets below. Sabbathiel could hear the sparking of lightning high above, the drumming of fat raindrops against the windows.

Despite the size of the structure – it had evidently once been a warehouse or storage facility rather than a residential hab-unit – there was something of an oppressive atmosphere to the place. Nol slumped against one of the walls, dozing, while Metik saw to the repairs of his ruined mechadendrite, Nimbik clambering over his shoulders, welding repairs with short, sharp bursts of flame. Silq was on the mouldering bed, resting her wounded leg now that Metik had finished patching her up, and Mercy, Brondel and Heloise were seeing to a meal for them all, raiding Mandreth's surprisingly healthy supply of provisions.

Bledheim was nowhere to be seen, but that was nothing unusual. Sabbathiel knew he'd be out there somewhere in the rain, gathering intel from the locals. He liked to remain informed and had a way of encouraging people to talk. Several, in fact – which was the main reason she kept him around.

She'd been tempted to send Fitch out to follow him, but in the end had decided against it, preferring to let the man roam. The servo-skull hovered close by, the constant drone of its presence somehow comforting.

Mandreth's bird had disappeared, too, off sailing the cross-currents high above the trench. The creature lacked the obvious bionic enhancements Sabbathiel would have expected in such a familiar, leaving her to wonder if Mandreth had some kind of latent psychic ability himself, allowing him to assert a degree of control over the bird's simple mind, or else to see the world through its sharpened senses.

It seemed everything about the man was an enigma, and one she was determined to unravel. Was it a mere coincidence that she'd found him lurking in Quintus Bleeth's tomb, or by design? And why had he been so quick to come to her aid, making himself and his team clear targets for Sinjan and the rest of her former conclave?

She watched him now as he sat cross-legged upon the floor, a long, thin clay pipe propped between his teeth. Purple smoke curled from the bowl, giving off a heady, floral scent.

'I don't know how you can smoke that stuff,' she said, wrinkling her nose.

'It helps me to concentrate,' came his measured reply.

'And what exactly are you concentrating on?'

'Our next move. Things here are escalating. We no longer have the luxury of taking our time. Sinjan will be working interference. There will be further reprisals unless we can stay one step ahead.'

'Then what do you propose?'

'That tomorrow, we pay a visit to the House of Bleeth.' His eyes, half hooded, flicked towards her, awaiting her response.

Sabbathiel nodded slowly. 'Very well. That would seem

prudent. Perhaps they can shed some light on what really passed through Quintus' tomb.'

'And where his missing body can be found,' added Mandreth.

They lapsed back into silence for a moment.

'You are troubled,' he said, allowing riffles of smoke to plume from his nostrils.

'Now you presume to know me.'

'Tell me, am I wrong?'

Sabbathiel sighed. She glanced at the others, all occupied in their own pursuits. Their conversation would not be overheard. Nevertheless, she lowered her voice. 'You are not wrong,' she said.

He nodded. 'It is the nature of what we do. As inquisitors, we choose to peer into the abyss. To seek out the darkest corners of this universe… and whatever horrors lie beyond. Finding the strength to maintain that gaze is challenging. Sometimes we flinch away.' Mandreth rubbed the back of his neck as if even the admission wore heavily upon him. 'There are times when I, too, find it almost impossible to bear – find the rigours of my calling more difficult than I ever expected.'

Sabbathiel offered him a wry smile. 'I understand all too well. And yet…'

Mandreth looked up. 'Ah. You are at sea. Disorientated and alone. A stranger in a strange land.'

'Nothing has changed. And yet everything is different.'

'It is quite a thing, to be reborn,' said Mandreth. 'To awaken to a universe that hates you and has remade itself beyond all measure.'

'You speak as though you understand.'

'Oh, I do. Perhaps not as acutely as you, Astor, but I've traversed my own awakening.'

'Tell me.'

Mandreth shrugged. 'Merely that I've learned to walk my own path. To follow my own compass and to trust no one but myself. That is what this universe demands of us. That is the only way we survive.'

'Yet you'd have *me* trust you?' said Sabbathiel.

Mandreth chuckled, thin smoke wreathing his head. 'Such is the dichotomy of our existence. Although in truth, I would counsel you against it. Trust the motives, not the man.'

Sabbathiel laughed. 'Why did you really come to Calaphrax? And don't tell me it was the "right thing to do".' She studied his face, looking for any flicker of emotion. There was none. 'What did you hope to gain?'

'Insight,' said Mandreth, after a moment. 'I wanted to know – *needed* to know – if the stories about you were true. I wanted to know what you found out there, and what had become of you.'

'And?'

'And what?'

'Did you find what you were looking for?'

Mandreth shrugged. 'I'm still deciding.'

Sabbathiel flexed a crick in her neck. She'd stripped some of the plates from her armour, stacking them neatly on the ground by her feet. The air was cool against the exposed flesh of her arms, where the ribbons of old scars formed a webwork of lines and traceries. Of memories.

'What did you find?' she said.

'Devastation. Ruin. The usual story. The war had touched Calaphrax just like it had touched the rest of this blighted galaxy.'

'The war?'

'The only war that matters. The war for the soul of humankind.' He switched his pipe from one corner of his mouth to the other, then drew deep, causing the dried leaves in the bowl to crackle and smoulder.

'The ship? The battle-barge...'

'Sundered,' said Mandreth. 'Listing in space. Nothing but an empty hulk.'

'Empty?'

'But for the long dead.'

'Traitors.'

'And Dark Angels.'

'*Traitors,*' repeated Sabbathiel. 'One and all.' She offered him a quizzical look. 'But no Grey Knights?'

Mandreth shook his head. 'Not them, no.'

Sabbathiel felt something break inside of her. Bile rose up her throat, sour against the back of her tongue. The hairs prickled at the back of her neck. She suddenly felt very cold indeed. She realised that she'd unconsciously folded her arms protectively across her stomach and the site of her wound. 'You're sure. They were on the battle-barge with me and–'

'I'm sure,' he said, his voice level. 'They weren't there. None of them.'

Sabbathiel massaged the bridge of her nose. 'Then they survived. They got away. They must have found the means by which to navigate the warp storm.'

'Or someone came for them, too,' offered Mandreth. 'Perhaps to collect their corpses.'

'No,' said Sabbathiel. She wasn't sure how, but she knew it with a fiery certainty.

Leofric is still alive. He's still out there, somewhere. Out amongst the dying stars.

'How?' she said.

'I'm sorry?'

'How did you find me? How did you navigate the warp storm?'

Mandreth offered her a sad smile. 'I waited. For over two years.'

'For what?'

'For the storms to abate. They were quite beautiful, in their own, terrible way. Crashing like rolling surf across the sector. Reality and unreality merging, and you there, at the heart of it all, drifting like flotsam in the wreckage. You weren't hard to find.'

'And I was still alive.'

'Barely. You'd been held like that, at the point of death. The storms must have preserved you somehow.'

Sabbathiel shivered. She thought she heard a sound like fluttering wings, but there was no sign of Mandreth's bird returning.

Ghosts. Memories and ghosts.

'I managed to maintain your coma on life support until I was able to deposit you with the tech-priest.'

'And my ship?'

'Another unsalvageable hulk, like the rest of them. I saved what I could – your armour and–'

'Fitch.'

Mandreth smiled. 'I'm glad it's of some comfort to you.' His eyes flitted to the hovering servo-skull.

'Why didn't you wait?'

'Hmm?'

'For Metik to wake me. For my healing to be completed.'

'Because an informant had made me aware of the Bleeths and the rumours they were smuggling dangerous contraband here on Hulth, and because I knew you'd find me when you were ready.' He laughed. 'I didn't expect you'd be investigating the same case... or that you'd cause quite as much of a stir in the process.'

'I've never been one for subtlety,' said Sabbathiel. 'Not when traitors are involved.'

'No,' said Mandreth. 'I don't doubt it for a moment.'

'So – tomorrow we visit the House of Bleeth.'

'You'll deign to work with me after all, then?' said Mandreth, with a smirk.

'I'll trust the motives,' said Sabbathiel, 'and not the man. That will have to be enough.'

Mandreth took another long draw from his pipe. 'It'll do nicely.'

CHAPTER FIFTEEN

'To engage in divination is to seek the divine, to pierce the veil between subject and God-Emperor and find a clear path through obscurity. For through the cards, His will is made manifest. Through the cards, the Emperor speaks.'

– Josiah Silverness, *The Emperor's Tarot*

Bledheim had always felt at home in the rain. The way the fat droplets burst as they struck his bald pate; the way it ran in cool runnels down the back of his neck, sought to cleanse and purify his every transgression. The rain bore no judgement, did not discriminate. The rain sought only to absolve. And Bledheim was ever a man in need of absolution.

He walked through sheets of it now, his cloak sodden and waterlogged, the shadowy depths of the trench lit by the jagged lances of lightning flashing high overhead. Here, it was easy to become anonymous, to lose himself in the crowd. To see things for what they really were.

That was his mission, his reason for stalking the dark lanes and jostling crowds; a self-appointed mission, but one of no less value for that. He would seek out all he could about the man named Mandreth, to forewarn himself – and Sabbathiel, if it became necessary – of any intended deception.

It had never been Bledheim's habit to take people at their word. He found a healthy dose of distrust was key to any successful relationship, and more than that, he credited this attitude as the reason he was still alive. It was difficult for someone to disappoint or surprise you if you always expected the worst.

Indeed, he'd spent several days investigating Sabbathiel before he'd accepted a position in her retinue, turning up all manner of salacious tales, from whispered talk of conflicts with the Adeptus Astartes to unsavoury rumours of heretical dealings with the enemy. History had not been kind to Sabbathiel, and the intervening century since her disappearance had allowed revisionists to rewrite her story in their own favour.

Yet the more Bledheim delved, the more intrigued he'd become. Sabbathiel was clearly a dangerous woman to be around. But dangerous meant *interesting*, and to Bledheim, that was a tantalising draw.

If it hadn't been for this mystery surrounding the woman, not to mention the incredible story of her long captivity in the Calaphrax warp storms and his profound interest in what it had done to her psyche, he might never have agreed to join her.

As if she'd really given him a choice.

Regardless, he'd since developed a healthy respect for Sabbathiel, and while he still didn't trust her – and probably never would – it was with some chagrin that he admitted to himself that she'd somehow managed to inspire a degree of loyalty in him, too. He supposed there was a first time for everything.

Mandreth though… he was something else entirely. Most inquisitors, in Bledheim's limited experience, were people to be avoided. Dangerous idealists, mavericks and zealots, who thought to remake the Imperium according to their own designs. Mandreth exhibited none of these qualities, at least outwardly. Yet Bledheim was convinced he was hiding something. His role as Sabbathiel's unlikely saviour, his involvement in her current case, his sudden appearance at the Bleeth tomb… to Bledheim these were nothing but warning signs pointing to a deeper, unspoken truth.

He intended to advise Sabbathiel to disentangle herself from the man at the first available opportunity, although he understood all too well the attraction his presence held for the woman. Here was someone who could answer her questions, who knew the truth about her recent history and rebirth. Who'd seen her at her most vulnerable and sought to coax her back to herself.

How could she ever resist?

Thus, it fell to Bledheim to attempt to unpick the truth from the weave of obfuscation that surrounded the man.

And yet, so far, he had failed utterly in his quest. Through less-than-salubrious drinking dens, to stimm dealers to mercenaries – he'd spent almost the entire night making enquiries… and avoiding being killed. But no one had seemingly heard of Mandreth down here, amongst the low life. Which in itself struck Bledheim as a little odd. If he really had been poking around here on Hulth for some time, the criminal elements would have identified him by now, if only to share the understanding amongst themselves to remain out of his orbit. Not so much honour amongst thieves, as the preservation of their networks and finely tuned interdependencies. A thief needed a fence, and a fence needed a buyer. A dealer needed a junky. A mercenary needed an enemy.

An inquisitor was bad for business, for everyone. Strange, then, that the web down here was not jangling, and that no one seemed to know anything at all about the fly in their midst. He'd even dragged one unfortunate into an alleyway and injected them with a cocktail of serums to encourage him to tell the truth – just in case the man was prevaricating – but he'd proved not to know anything of use. So Bledheim had left him there, slumped insensate against the wall, spattered by the streaming rain.

He'd lived amongst these sorts of people for years. He knew what buttons to press, which questions to ask, and to whom. It was a universal truth that humanity, wherever it sprung up around the galaxy, wherever it *festered*, was the same. These narrow, dirty lanes were the same as the ones he had grown up in, back on distant Kreeve; so familiar that he could navigate easily despite never having walked amongst them or seen any map. He understood these people with a familiarity so profound it had morphed into contempt. Why couldn't they see it? Why didn't they understand they were treading the same well-worn paths as a trillion souls before them, repeating the same mistakes over and over, living lives that had already been led?

To Bledheim, *this* was the true face of the Imperium. This is what they fought to protect. A future of banality. The dog end of a civilisation lurching hurriedly towards oblivion. The thought brought a sour taste to his tongue.

Onwards he went through the lashing rain, past burned-out hab-units and the shanty camps of filthy street dwellers, past foul-smelling food stalls and jittery stimm dealers, past raucous bars selling cheap liquor and gang recruiters presiding over brutal street fights, past the dead and those that didn't yet realise they were dying.

And then, finally, he saw what he was looking for: the mark of a tarot reader, painted on the boarded-up window of a hab-unit.

He crossed to it, eyeing the collection of filthy juves loitering in the adjoining doorway: gang members, judging by their matching facial scars. They bore several makeshift shanks, while one, a woman, was carrying a wooden bat hammered with vicious-looking nails. There was blood and hair on the end of several of them.

The juves scowled at him as he approached the door to the hab-unit. He smiled, baring his teeth. The woman with the bat made to step forward, but one of the others caught her wrist, holding her back. Bledheim's smile widened. He pushed on the door release. It slid open.

Inside, the hab-unit was small – a single room at the front, with a compact sleeping chamber and shower room at the rear, the sort of prefabricated hab seen the Imperium over. The sort of place that would have seemed like a palace when he'd been a child, like those youths out front, posturing to gain acceptance from the other gangers.

Now, it just seemed squalid.

Bledheim stepped over the threshold into the dimly lit room beyond. The door slid shut behind him. 'I've come for a reading,' he said.

He glanced around the room. A single table with two chairs, placed opposite one another. A set of drawers, which looked as if they'd been reclaimed from a scholam or Administratum facility. A bare lumen dangling on a cord from the ceiling, throwing out a weak, fizzing light. An open doorway leading through to the bedchamber, the room beyond cast in deep shadow.

He sensed movement in there. For a moment he wondered if he'd walked into some sort of trap, and then it occurred to him – the youths outside were the gatekeepers. Whoever lived here was paying the gang for protection. They were vetting prospective customers and dissuading those who might pose a threat.

He almost laughed out loud. How little they understood.

The figure was now standing in the doorway of the bedchamber, nothing but an indistinct silhouette.

'Credits first.' It was a woman's voice, firm, confident.

Bledheim's lip curled. They were always the same. He tossed a handful of local scrip into a chipped bowl on a stand close to the door. The coins clattered loudly against the tinted glass.

He was sodden, streams of rainwater dripping onto the bare floorboards to form puddles by his feet. He considered shrugging out of his robes – now twice as heavy as they were – but decided against it. It would leave him too exposed, too vulnerable. Instead, he pulled them tighter around his wet shoulders.

The woman stepped out from behind the door, still shrouded in shadow. She studied him for a moment, before edging forward into the light.

She was young for a crone; typically, the toll of such readings, of becoming a conduit for the Emperor's will, was enough to wizen the flesh, to prematurely age the host... if it didn't kill them outright. Most practitioners were stoop-backed and blinded, unable to control the bleeding from their eyes and ears and driven to distraction by the unspeakable pressure in their heads. This woman, though, was pretty, with dark skin apparently unblemished by the travails of her talent.

If, indeed, she even *had* talent. For every true practitioner Bledheim had found in his lifetime, there were a score or more that were nothing but cheats and frauds. Or else their abilities were so dangerous and untamed that they had to be put down.

'Sit, please,' said the woman, crossing to the small table and taking a seat.

Bledheim shook his head, scattering a shower of raindrops. 'I'll stand.'

The woman looked up, fixing him with a piercing gaze. Her eyes were mismatched – one blue and one grey – and the sight of them sent a shiver down his spine. Although it might have been the cold and the wet. 'It works much better if you're close to the cards.'

He didn't move.

The woman sighed. 'Very well.' She opened a drawer and took out a small, ornate box, which she placed on the table before her. It was carved from bone, with inlaid silver filigree. She opened the box and withdrew a thin sheaf of cards, which she shuffled carefully, before taking a deep breath and laying six of them face down on the table before her. The others were returned to the box, which was set aside.

Bledheim could see that the cards were formed from thin slivers of bone, their backs etched and inked with primitive black designs.

'Your name?'

'It doesn't matter,' said Bledheim.

The woman sat back, brushing her hair from her face. She closed her eyes.

Bledheim nearly scoffed.

Another charlatan, then.

He was about to turn back towards the door when she flipped over the first card.

'The Queen of Ruin,' said the woman.

Bledheim peered at the card on the table. It depicted the stylised image of a woman holding a sword, her once white armour now awash with bright red blood. She looked horribly familiar.

'There's no such card,' said Bledheim.

The woman shrugged. She dabbed her left eye. Her finger came away stained with oily blood. She drew another ragged breath. 'The cards reveal themselves when it is their time. They make themselves anew. I am but the vessel by which they express themselves. The nib through which the ink flows.'

Bledheim wiped water from his face. 'Nonsense. How did you know?' He took a step closer to the table.

'Know what?'

'About *her.*'

'I'm sorry. I don't understand.' The woman was frowning.

'The Queen of Ruin. Her, in the picture.'

'Ah. I see. She is known to you.' The woman rocked forward in her chair. Her bottom lip was quivering.

'Well?'

'She represents the razing of the past and the birthing of the new. The arising of a new order from the ruins of the old. She heralds destruction and rebirth.'

'Rebirth,' echoed Bledheim. He leaned forward, fascinated. He'd never seen anything of its like before. This was not the Emperor's Tarot. Not as he knew it. 'Go on.'

The woman turned over another card. She sucked in her breath. 'The Throne, inverted.'

Another bastardisation. Another card he had never seen.

'What is this?'

'Please. The cards demand to be read. Can't you hear them?'

'Hear them? No, I–'

'Shh.' The woman held her finger to her lips. Blood was trickling down her left cheek.

Silence.

If she was hearing something, it was beyond his capability to hear it too.

When she spoke again, her voice seemed to boom in the confined space of the hab-unit, rude and unwelcome. 'Death,' she said. 'The Throne, inverted. Death walks beside you. It is close.'

'When is it not?' said Bledheim.

The woman's bleeding eye twitched nervously. Bledheim wondered how she did it – had she nicked the flesh of the lower lid when she rubbed it earlier? And these cards... They were nothing but simple sheets of decorated bone.

Yes. I've allowed myself to be taken in.

Inside his robes, his needle-capped fingers wriggled restlessly. Perhaps he should end this woman for her blasphemy, perhaps...

She turned over another card. 'The Interrogator,' she said. 'He who knocks on doors in search of knowledge.'

Bledheim staggered, caught the back of the other chair. 'What did you say?'

She tapped the card with her fingertip. It showed a figure in dark robes, face cast in shadows by a broad hood. In one hand he carried a lantern, in the other a key. 'Here. The one who understands. The truth seeker. The one who shall unlock all mysteries.'

He stared down at the woman's face. Blood now streamed from both eyes. Her breathing was shallow. She met his gaze; smiled.

Bledheim lowered himself into the chair. His mind was reeling. Was this a game? Some trick of Mandreth's?

How could it be? He'd found this place himself, miles from the safe house. There was no way...

Another card.

'The Hierophant. He who leads through faith alone. The one who guards the holiest of relics.'

The image showed a man prostrating himself before a golden altar. 'A priest?' muttered Bledheim.

'Perhaps,' said the woman. 'Perhaps not. Be on your guard with this one, for his faith knows few bounds.'

Bledheim tried wiping more rainwater from his eyes, but his sleeve was so sodden that he only made matters worse.

Two cards left.

The woman was hunching forward against the table now, sucking her breath through clenched teeth. Blood pattered on the tablecloth, splashed on the surfaces of the overturned cards. The air felt heavy, oppressive. Bledheim fought the urge to run.

With monumental effort, the woman reached out and turned the penultimate card. Bledheim's eyes were stinging. His heart was kicking against his ribs. The cold trickle of water down the crease of his back felt like an anchor, rooting him to the spot, pinning him to reality itself. The world outside was near forgotten. The only things that mattered were the cards. He forced his eyes to study the newly revealed image.

It depicted a black-clad figure with a grinning skull face, holding a heart in one hand and a knife in the other, as if holding them in balance, or weighing them in judgement.

'The Assassin,' said the woman. Her words emerged as whispers, and Bledheim could hear the strain, the cost of it in her voice. 'Judge, jury and executioner. She watches, waiting. In her, all paths converge.'

An Assassin?

What in the name of Holy Terra has Sabbathiel got us into here?

'One card left,' said the woman. 'It has not been an easy draw.' Her nose was streaming with blood now too, and she was rocking gently in her chair, as if delirious.

'Do it,' said Bledheim.

The woman flipped the card.

'The Winged Serpent,' she gasped. Her right eye rolled back in its socket. Blood gushed from her nose. She moaned, her one good eye – the grey one – fixed on him, almost menacing in its intensity. 'A cuckoo in the nest. A heretic.'

And with that she folded at the waist, collapsed onto the table, and died.

The darkness is absolute.

She wears it like a blanket, draped in its clinging comfort, its womb-like intensity.

All is quiet. All is still.

There is nothing but her and the void. The cool kiss of salvation. The silence of eternity.

Here, she is safe.

Here, nothing matters. Not the wound in her belly nor the loss of her crew. Not the worthless traitors of the Adeptus Astartes or the bound thing she holds in her vault. Here, its vile imprecations cannot be heard. It can no longer be used against her.

Here, there is only her. A mind cut free of all tethers, adrift in the emptiness.

There is no reason to feel anything. She will never have the need to feel anything ever again.

The thought is a comfort.

And yet…

She stirs at the knowledge that she is not truly alone. Something else inhabits this realm, this distant place beyond life itself. Something at once both alien and cosily familiar.

Around her, space flutters. She becomes aware of her physicality, although it remains ephemeral, as though she has no concept of where she ends and the space around her begins.

She feels herself being drawn towards something, and yet she is unafraid. Nothing here could harm her. Nothing here has intent.

The rustle of feathers. Wings spreading, welcoming her in.

They fold around her, tight, enclosing.

Entombing.

Suffocating.

And she recognises for the first time she was wrong.

This is not a place of sanctuary.

It is a prison.

She screams, but this soundless vacuum does not hear her.

She fights against her internment, but this wall-less place does not feel her.

She weeps, but this empty, soulless realm does not care for her.

And she knows that her future has already been determined. She is powerless. She has no choice but to submit.

The feathers bristle and pull tighter around her.

Sabbathiel screamed.

She stuttered awake, her throat already raw. She was thrashing, as if still trying to fight her way loose from her dream.

Or is it a memory?

She sat up, gulping for air.

The room was dark. It was still night. Recent memories came swimming back to her. She'd found a quiet side room – an old office – and retreated there to rest, away from her retinue. Away from Mandreth and his followers. Away from everything.

But life had a way of intruding on her plans. As did the unwelcome tech-priest. She could hear his clacking footsteps now, approaching.

She wiped the threads of spittle away from her mouth with the back of her hand and fought to steady her trembling.

Pinpricks of red light pierced the gloom. The footsteps clattered to a halt.

'Metik,' she said.

'Bad dreams, Astor Sabbathiel.' His burring, metallic voice seemed harsher than usual in the close darkness.

'I'm fine,' she snapped.

'Your heart rate is elevated, and you are perspiring at twelve per cent above normal for this ambient temperature. Your oxygen levels are reduced by–'

'I said I was *fine.*' Her voice was firm, dogmatic.

'I merely mean to enquire after your well-being, madame inquisitor.'

'You mean to protect your *investment.*'

The tech-priest cocked his head inquisitively. 'Are the two things considered mutually exclusive?'

'So, you admit it – you have a vested interest in my continued survival?'

Metik's reply was delivered in his usual dispassionate monotone. 'You might say that I have *invested* interest in you, Astor Sabbathiel, and that I hope someday that you might be prepared to repay that investment and confidence.'

Sabbathiel laughed, unamused. She wiped a bead of sweat from her brow. 'And how, exactly, do you anticipate this debt will be paid?'

Metik clacked his porcelain fingertips in that gratingly familiar rhythm. 'I shall be sure to inform you the moment it becomes clear.'

'Go away, Metik,' she said, and was disgusted with the resignation she could hear in her tone. 'Leave me to my memories and my misery.'

Metik stood unmoving for a moment, then turned away. 'I wish you respite, Sabbathiel, from the horrors of your past. But I do not think you shall find your peace here. Be mindful of what is important as you rush headlong towards the next stage of your investigation here on Hulth.'

Sabbathiel stared after him into the darkness.

CHAPTER SIXTEEN

'Walk easy into the night, dear friend,
Walk easy into the night.
For the darkness holds naught but the dreams of the sleeping,
And in dreams we are unmade,
And so unburdened, we live on.
Walk easy into the night, brave soldier,
For in the misty haze of morning,
The horrors of the day do reveal themselves,
And the soft churn of the earth shall drag us down,
And the dead shall curse and holler,
With milky-eyed wisdom,
And show us all they have learned of war.
Walk easy into the night, dear friend,
And hold that the dawn will never come,
For with it we are broken,
And all dreams extinguished for another day.'

– Unknown, fragment found in a trench after the
Battle of Tintafell IV

The silence was deafening, but Sabbathiel would not be the one to break it.

Mandreth, walking along beside her with an infuriatingly calm, measured gait, his hands clasped behind his back and his face averted, was either studiously choosing to avoid conversation or else was lost in some deep contemplation of his own.

Hadn't he heard her screaming outburst during the night? It seemed inconceivable that it had passed unnoticed by anyone but Metik. Was he, then, attempting to save her embarrassment? Some misguided notion of chivalry? He was wrong if he thought she had anything to be ashamed of. No, she wore her scars, not with pride, exactly, but with honesty. She refused to feel any chagrin.

Or perhaps she was misjudging him. Perhaps he understood all too well, and that was why he hadn't mentioned it. The man was damned near unreadable.

Bledheim, on the other hand, was an open book. He walked hunched, as if futilely attempting to stave off a non-existent downpour. He'd barely spoken since returning from his late-night haunting of the slums – not even to conjure a witty riposte over their measly breakfast, or to mutter a snide remark beneath his breath at the expense of the squat. Nor had he met her eye. Whatever it was he'd been up to, whatever he'd been seeking amongst those dank alleyways, it seemed he hadn't found it.

She'd decided to bide her time for now. She could press him for answers, threaten him with consequences if he failed to report his activities, but she believed she had the measure of him now; that undue pressure at this stage might cause him to clam up or cease whatever clandestine activities had taken him off into the dark streets, and in doing so, she might well cut off an avenue of investigation that she had so far failed to see.

No. Better that she wait and see what materialised in due course.

And so, the three of them walked on in silence, trudging up the gravelled path, and Sabbathiel was left to stew in her own thoughts.

She couldn't help but turn over the events of her recent dreams – the silent figure in golden armour, wandering off into the no-light; the screaming astropath scratching vainly at the walls; the half-imagined, half-forgotten memories of her other life.

That was how she'd come to think of it now, that time before her reawakening – an old life, an old *her*, a different woman who happened to share some of her memories and goals. She had been *interrupted* by her time in the warp storm, not just in years, but in mind, in spirit. In *herself*. And in her mission. A setback beyond imagining.

And now, these unquiet dreams.

She had always had a measure of latent psychic ability, a gut instinct that she had learned to trust, a gift of insight that had informed her every judgement. But the warp storm had awoken something else within her, a mind's eye that was not entirely her own, that offered her stuttering glimpses of... something. Whether they were truly insightful, she did not know. Perhaps they were mere figments of the century she had passed inside her own head; images and dreams that had poured forth from her sleeping mind, and were now resurfacing, just as she had. Memories of things that had never existed or never would.

She wished she could believe that. But the immediacy of those visions, the stark, emotional brunt of them – her every instinct screamed that they were real. Moments snatched from other people's heads. Unwanted gifts.

And the memories... what if they were real, too?

She glanced up at the servo-skull hovering above her left shoulder. Fitch would have understood. She wondered what he would counsel now, if he really was still with them. Would he have told her to run?

'...impressive.'

She realised Mandreth was talking and looked round. 'I'm sorry?'

Mandreth offered her a wan smile. 'I said the house is really quite impressive, don't you think?'

Sabbathiel laughed. It was something of an understatement – this regional seat of the House of Bleeth was perhaps the most grandiose structure Sabbathiel had ever seen, a towering edifice of dressed stone, three storeys high and with a footprint the size of a governor's palace. It seemed deeply incongruous on such an overburdened hive world; a glittering jewel set in the crumbling, decaying mount of a rusted brooch. With a pillared portico, symmetrical rows of tall windows and flickering hololiths of ancient, extinct plant life playing over its surface, it was exuberance incarnate. It even had a shuttle landing pad on its roof. And this was just a territorial outpost – the Bleeths' main holdings were no doubt in the Navigator's Quarter on Terra.

'I think the Bleeths have been afforded too much autonomy,' said Sabbathiel, in answer to Mandreth's question. 'And their arrogance has led them to take liberties.'

'Their history reaches back into the deep ancestry of the Navis Nobilite. The Bleeths have served the Imperium for millennia. They are the most respected Navigator House in this sector,' said Mandreth.

'Precisely my point. They forget themselves. They are subjects of the Emperor, just as we all are.'

Mandreth laughed, now. 'You'll be sure to remind them of that.'

Sabbathiel smiled. 'Oh, I will.'

The house was not the only extravagance – the building sat in several acres of lawned and wooded grounds, estates that, had they been co-opted by the governor on behalf of the Imperium, would have provided habitation space for tens of thousands. Such was the esteem in which the Bleeths were held, then, that the land was allowed to remain under their exclusive jurisdiction, despite the chronic overpopulation of the nearby Gallowspire. Or rather – such was the power the Navigators asserted.

To Sabbathiel's mind, the balance in this relationship was deeply off-kilter. As essential as they were to warp transits, it was her belief that Navigators should be conscripted in military service, not enabled to extort fortunes from those who required their talents to ensure the defence of the Imperium.

But then, no one was above the justice of the Inquisition. She'd remind them of that, too, given half a chance.

They continued up the long avenue of trees towards the house. Slack-jawed servitors tilled the soil and sculpted the trees and hedgerows to either side, their dead eyes lifting from their work as Sabbathiel and the others passed. High above, Mandreth's bird wheeled, startling flocks of vibrantly plumed local species that had taken roost in the willowy treetops.

They'd left the others guarding the safe house, all save Metik, who had insisted on venturing out for supplies. Following the blockading of her ship, which the tech-priest had been able to confirm after accessing and interrogating the local data systems, they'd been left with precious little in the way of equipment, and she was without her Terminator armour and stave. Metik, though, was growing twitchy and needed to affect repairs after the battle at the mausoleum complex, and besides, she was unsure how much sway she really held over the machine man anyway.

The others had orders to remain out of sight; irrespective of her Inquisitorial authority, Sinjan had evidently set the enforcers on her tail, and she needed time and space to work. A tech-priest, an ogryn and a squat were likely to draw attention.

All-out war on the streets would have to wait.

Bledheim, though – he had a way of passing unnoticed. When he wasn't brooding, that was.

'Should I be worried, interrogator?'

He looked up at her, startled. His eyes narrowed. 'Your pardon, ma'am?'

'Should I be worried?' she repeated.

Bledheim swallowed. 'About what, exactly?'

'About whatever it is that's set your teeth so on edge.'

He looked miserable, nervous, like a starving mouse circling a trap, knowing that at some point it was going to have to risk the food. 'I…' She could see him reaching for the right words. 'I'll be sure to tell you if you should.'

'Then that will have to suffice. For now.'

'Ma'am.' Bledheim looked as if he'd dodged a bolt-round.

They were approaching the building now, and as they drew near, a small assemblage of guards marched out from the portico to greet them.

There were six in all, half of them men, half of them women. They wore a deep blue livery, trimmed with gold thread, with matching golden helms and arcane-looking rifles that resembled ceremonial arquebuses more than anything that would hold up in a serious fight. They were crisp and impeccable, both in appearance and the manner in which they comported themselves.

One of them, a stern-faced woman with a pronounced jaw, stepped forward as the three newcomers approached. She held her weapon across her chest, neither threatening nor particularly welcoming. But then, judging by the reaction of the guards on the outer gates when they'd flashed their Inquisitorial icons a short while earlier, they were hardly expecting a welcoming committee.

'We'll need to see your identification.' Her accent was thick and unfamiliar – presumably some local inflection from amongst the upper classes.

Sabbathiel stepped forward. 'Your men at the gate did not forewarn you of our arrival?'

'Only that there were unscheduled visitors,' said the woman, levelly.

Sabbathiel sighed.

They wouldn't even invoke our names. Superstitious fools.

She held out her Inquisitorial icon. It glinted in the late morning sun. The woman's face drained of colour.

Mandreth held open his long coat, revealing the identical sigil hanging around his neck. Bledheim shuffled awkwardly from foot to foot and refused to meet anyone's eye.

'I… um…' stuttered the woman. She swallowed, then seemed to compose herself. 'How can we be of service, inquisitors?'

'We would speak with representatives of the House of Bleeth,' said Mandreth.

'But… the master…' The woman faltered. She glanced back at one of the men. Swallowed. 'Grael, run and inform the master immediately.'

The man looked horrified. '*Now?*'

'That's what immediately tends to mean,' said Sabbathiel. 'Please tell him that Inquisitors Sabbathiel and Mandreth of the Ordo Hereticus shall be waiting to speak with him and the rest of his family in…?' She glanced at the woman.

'In the… umm… botanical room,' said the woman.

Sabbathiel nodded. 'In the botanical room.'

The man, Grael, snapped a hasty salute, and then turned on his heel and hurried off into the house.

The woman gave him a moment's head start, and then stood to one side and beckoned the small party forward. Sabbathiel inclined her head and then led the way, Fitch trailing a short way behind her.

Inside, the building was as palatial as it had appeared on their approach across the grounds. A vast hallway was enclosed by a majestic upper gallery, reached via a huge staircase that swept up and around in the twisting form of a double helix, two flights of steps intertwining and kissing at various points to enable a variety of paths for ascent and descent. Huge marble urns contained leafy green plants that may or may not have been native to Hulth, and servo-skulls flitted through the air like a flock of birds, their red and blue lights flickering like bizarre feathers. Above, an enormous stained-glass dome cast an eerie, purplish light upon proceedings. More guards stood to attention at the foot of the stairs. Several passageways branched off from this central hub, wending deeper into the fascinating house.

Sabbathiel heard Bledheim give a low whistle and flicked him a glance. He took her meaning immediately, clearing his throat and tucking his hands behind his back.

The very picture of innocence.

Hardly.

The female guard who'd shown them in came around to stand before them. 'Welcome,' she said. 'If you'd like to follow me.'

She set out, two of the other guards falling in behind her. The others waited to bring up the rear.

No, I wouldn't trust us either.

They passed along the side of the immense staircase, where huge tapestries hung from the smooth stone walls, depicting scenes that appeared to be derived from some strange mythology that Sabbathiel was unfamiliar with. In one image, a Navigator stood on a precipice clutching a staff, their third eye open and shining. They appeared to be about to lead a pack of huge wolves into the gaping void beyond. In another, a second

Navigator smote a large serpent with her staff, while around her the upturned faces of a score of Battle Sisters seemed to bask in her glow. In a third, a vessel fled the outstretched hand of some unseen leviathan beast as it whisked through the tumultuous warp, colours and shapes swirling all around it.

These, Sabbathiel realised, were most likely the legends that the House of Bleeth had accumulated across the centuries – tall tales of bravery and derring-do, encoded with just enough truth that they might resonate, accreting around them as if gravity itself were drawing them in, like space hulks mashing into one another and fusing over spans of thousands of years.

The old guard, dressed in the faded finery of their forefathers, clinging on to power and relevance in an age that sees them only as a commodity.

She'd seen their type a hundred times before.

Through more passages, lined with austere portraits and ancient star charts, and then out through a huge ballroom that finally delivered them into a vast, glass-walled room at the very rear of the complex, filled with raised beds of leafy plants and exotic, colourful blooms. The plants were everywhere, filling the space, towering over their heads, crowding their legs, brushing their faces as they tried to find a place to stand.

'If you'd wait here just a moment,' said the woman, 'Master Bleeth will, I am sure, be with you shortly.' She beckoned to her fellow guards and they took up positions by the entrance, weapons held across their chests. None of them would make eye contact with Sabbathiel.

She studied the room they'd been shepherded to. It had been carefully chosen to both impress and intimidate – the air was thick, hot and uncomfortable, and more servo-skulls buzzed around the upper reaches of the imposing plants, misting water onto the petals and fronds and lending the air a cloying, humid quality. It was an impressive collection, evidently drawn from many different planets across the Imperium; a biological museum or gallery, built either for the love of a passionate collector, or curated to underline a point: that the Imperium was nothing without the Navigators, who wove the fragile web between worlds. It was a point that was not missed by Sabbathiel.

She felt Mandreth nudge her elbow and turned to see him pointing out an icon carved into the floor by their feet: two planets tracing orbital rings around one another, connected via a bolt of lightning or electricity. The same image that had been incised into the dais in Quintus Bleeth's empty tomb.

Footsteps approached. She looked up to see two newcomers, a man and a woman, enter the room.

The man's face was wizened with age – the flesh leathery and liver-spotted, creased with deep lines – yet his body looked firm and healthy, if somewhat stooped. The crease at the centre of his forehead denoted the presence of the mutation common to all Navigators: the third eye. It was hidden now behind a plain silver headband, but the very thought of it made Sabbathiel shudder. The man's human eyes were glazed and yellowed, thick with cataracts, and he leaned heavily on a staff, similar to the ones Sabbathiel had glimpsed in the tapestries. He wore flowing blue robes with gold trim, reminiscent in many ways of the livery worn by the guards, but more elaborate in just about every way.

Beside him, the woman bore a familial resemblance, and while clearly of some age, she wore her years better than the man, having perhaps indulged in recent rejuve technology. She, too, had obscured her third eye with a silver band, but her human eyes were bright and sharp, and alighted upon Sabbathiel as she came to a stop before the small group.

'What is the meaning of this intrusion?' demanded the woman. Her voice was shrill and grating, and she was clearly furious.

'I am Inquisitor Astor Sabbathiel of the Ordo Hereticus, and this is my associate, Inquisitor Rassius Mandreth. We have some questions regarding a recently deceased member of this household, Quintus Bleeth.'

'Brother Quintus?' said the man. His eyes, although half blinded, flitted in Sabbathiel's direction. He leaned a little closer, peering at her. 'What about him?'

'He was your brother?' said Mandreth. 'Then you are...?'

'Jolas. Jolas Bleeth. And this is my wife – and sister – Nemedia.'

Sabbathiel nodded. Such things were typical of Navigator families who wished to ensure their progeny maintained the family mutation – and thus stranglehold on warp travel – for future generations.

'Jolas is the present head of House Bleeth,' added Nemedia.

'Quintus died recently, I believe,' said Mandreth.

'Several months ago,' said Jolas. His voice was like piping reeds, thin and breathless.

'Almost a year,' corrected Nemedia. 'But what has this got to do with the Inquisition?'

'We have reason to believe Quintus was involved in smuggling contraband onto Hulth from restricted worlds,' said Mandreth.

'Nonsense,' spat Nemedia, a little too quickly.

Sabbathiel glanced at Bledheim, who gave the slightest shake of his head. He thought she was lying, too. This was why she'd brought the interrogator along – not to deploy his professional skills so much as to canvass his opinion. He'd spent many years learning how to decipher the unspoken cues of the human body. Both inside and out. 'You're saying you were unaware that Quintus was involved in anything illicit, or that you know for a fact that he never brought illegal goods back to Hulth?' she said.

Nemedia frowned. 'Well, I can't be *certain*, of course. Quintus didn't involve either of us in the details of his chosen operations. But I can't believe for a moment he would jeopardise the standing of the House in such a way. He was almost four hundred years old. The family meant everything to him.'

Jolas gave a wracking, phlegmy cough. Nemedia went to beckon for a guard, but he waved her still. When the fit had passed, he wiped his lips with a handkerchief he produced from a pocket in his robes and looked from Sabbathiel to Mandreth. 'I think I know what this is about,' he said.

'You do?' Nemedia looked confused.

'Come with me.' Jolas beckoned with his staff, leading them deeper into the wild overgrowth of the botanical samples. After a few moments, he came to a stop. 'Here.' He indicated a row of bright pink flowers, their thorny stems erupting from the well-tended soil. '*Rosa damascena*. Roses from Terra.'

'You're saying *this* is the contraband Quintus was bringing in?' said Mandreth, incredulous. '*Flowers.*'

Jolas nodded. 'He did it for me. For my collection. Flowers from Terra.' He shrugged. 'It was only once or twice. Nothing that should trouble the *Inquisition*, for Emperor's sake.'

Nemedia put a hand on his arm. 'Jolas, you don't have to–'

'They're *inquisitors*, my love. Of course, I must.'

Mandreth shot Sabbathiel a look.

'How did Quintus die?' she asked.

'Same way we all die, in the end, our kind. The warp. It does things to the mind, after a time. Erodes you from the inside out. You start seeing ghosts…' He trailed off, and his yellowed eyes took on a haunted glaze.

Sabbathiel swallowed.

Ghosts.

'Since the light of the Astronomican dimmed, we've lost so many,' said Nemedia. 'Quintus was just the most recent. It is the curse of our people.'

Just like the big house and estate.

Sabbathiel met the woman's piercing gaze. 'Where is he now?'

'Quintus? Why, he's dead, just like we said. We buried him.'

'We've been to his tomb,' said Mandreth. 'It's empty.'

'Empty? No, no…' said Jolas. 'I watched them put him there myself.' He shook his head, emphatic.

'There was no body, no sarcophagus,' continued Mandreth. 'Can you explain the bloodstains we found on the floor?'

Nemedia's hand went to her mouth in apparent shock. 'Bloodstains?'

'You mean to say his body has been stolen?' said Jolas. There was a rising inflection of anger in his voice. 'What's going on here? What's all this about?'

'That's what we're trying to establish,' said Sabbathiel. 'A senior member of your household has been accused of smuggling contraband–'

'I told you–'

'Yes, yes. The *flowers*. Nevertheless, his body is now missing and there are unexplained signs of conflict in his tomb. Do you have any notion of who might have reason to remove his corpse?'

Nemedia shook her head. 'No. No one.' She frowned. 'Why is this even a matter for the Inquisition?'

'We do not have to explain ourselves,' said Mandreth, levelly. 'Even to a respected House such as yours.'

'Well, I don't see how we can help you, then,' said Nemedia. An edge of impatience had crept into her voice.

Sabbathiel ground her teeth. 'You've no reason to believe anyone means your family harm?'

'*Everyone* means our family harm,' spat Jolas. 'We'd be foolish to think otherwise. We're *Navigators*. We're rich. We have influence. Of course we're hated.' He paused, studying his Terran roses. '*You* understand that, of all people. You're damned inquisitors.' He paused, but neither Sabbathiel nor Mandreth deemed it necessary to reply. 'If his body has been stolen, it's probably some twisted attempt to "send us a message". Some foul desecration by some jumped-up locals.'

'You have a lot of trouble with the locals?' said Mandreth, glancing at the guards. 'Gangers from the hives?'

Nemedia shrugged. 'From time to time. Once you've killed a few and put their heads on spikes outside the walls, people tend to get the message. At least for a while.'

'Tell me, why didn't you bury Quintus on your own land? You have enough of it. Surely his body would have been better protected within the walls of your compound?'

'We buried him according to his wishes,' said Jolas. The fight had gone out of him now, and his voice was heavy with resignation. 'He bought that plot at the mausoleum himself. Even had the tomb built to his own specifications.'

Sabbathiel nodded. 'Why? Surely family tradition would have dictated he be buried here, on the estate?'

Nemedia laughed, and it was a cruel, cold sneer. 'Quintus was never one to uphold family tradition. In fact, I'm certain half the things he did were calculated to cause as much upset to the family as possible. If you're looking for a reason, it's as likely that as anything – an ironic salute to the history and protocols of the House.'

'So, Quintus had a rebellious streak?' said Mandreth.

'He always came through for the family in the end,' said Jolas. 'That's what really counts. No matter his quarrelsome ways.'

'Is that what got him killed?' said Mandreth. 'These "quarrelsome ways"?'

Jolas fixed him with a baffled stare. 'Of course not. As I explained, it is the curse of our people that our talents may eventually become too much of a burden for our bodies to bear. Quintus died from a ruptured mind. A terrible, terrible waste.'

Nemedia nodded. 'A meaningless death. Like so many the universe over.' She shrugged, as if it were of no real consequence. 'And now someone has stolen his body. Ours is not to reason why.'

Sabbathiel wondered at the woman's heartlessness. For all her talk of family, she didn't seem to be particularly moved by Quintus' loss. More that she was relieved to have had a troublesome thorn removed from her side. Clearly, she was more concerned with the reputation of her great House than the wellbeing of its members. Meaning that, if there was more to be said about the circumstances of Quintus' death, Nemedia Bleeth was unlikely to say it.

'Just one final question,' Sabbathiel said. 'That symbol on the floor back there. The two planets connected by the lightning bolt.'

'Yes?' said Nemedia.

'It was inside the tomb, too. What does it mean?'

The woman looked uncomfortable. 'Nothing. It's just an old family crest. A symbol from our distant past. Quintus liked it, that's all.'

'He liked it enough to have it cut into the floor of his tomb,' said Mandreth. 'His final resting place.'

Nemedia sighed. 'Quintus knew what he wanted. That doesn't mean it had to make any sense to the rest of us.'

'Very well. We'll be back if we have any further questions,' said Mandreth. He cocked a crooked smile. 'I'm sorry for your loss.'

'My wh... ah, yes. Thank you,' replied Jolas, cupping one of his roses between his fingers. 'Thank you for your concern.'

'She was lying,' said Bledheim as soon as they were out of earshot of the guards and back amongst the clamouring hivesprawl of the city.

The Gallowspire loomed vast on the horizon, occluding the sun from view. In its shadow, the accumulated structures along the uppermost edge of the nearby trench were cast in perpetual night. And night was when Bledheim truly came alive.

'I could get the truth out of her, if you wanted,' he went on, wiggling his needle-capped fingers inside his robes. 'It would be a small matter…'

'No,' said Sabbathiel. 'Not yet. We've made enough enemies here already. Better that we don't draw any more attention to ourselves than necessary.'

'Agreed,' said Mandreth.

'What about *him?*' said Sabbathiel.

Bledheim's eyes seemed to light up. 'Mandreth? He's standing right there, you know.'

'Not Mandreth,' Sabbathiel hissed. 'Jolas Bleeth.'

Bledheim shrugged. 'Hard to say. If he knows something, he's hiding it better than she is.'

'Interesting,' said Sabbathiel. 'But what has it all got to do with the murder of Inquisitor Heldren? I can't see the connection.'

'Layer upon layer of obfuscation,' said Mandreth. 'Did you believe that story about the flowers?'

'I believe that Quintus procured them for the self-entitled fool. But do I think that's what passed through that empty tomb? Not for a minute. There's something much deeper at work here on Hulth, and just as Bledheim says, it seems Jolas Bleeth doesn't know the half of it.'

Mandreth nodded. 'Then I suggest it's time we put another cat amongst the pigeons.'

'How so?'

'We pay a visit to Hulth's governor, Lord Rasmuth, and see what *he* has to say about his good friends the Bleeths.'

CHAPTER SEVENTEEN

'*Time is its own delusion.*'
  – Solomon Thoth, *On the Breaking of Nixis III*

Through labyrinthine tunnels and waif-encrusted streets; through dank passages and clanging manufactoria where workers toiled until their fingers were reduced to bloody stumps; through ancient, crumbling byways and long-forgotten halls, they trod.

Where the streets of the lowest levels of the trench felt familiar to Bledheim, the confines of the Gallowspire were claustro-phobic and bleak – an oppressive, unending warren on a scale never meant to be comprehended by man.

These were the lower levels of the hive, the domain of the walking dead, the fodder of humanity. Here, the daily grind was literal. Workers were thrown into appalling regimes of agonising repetition: stoking the vast engines that fed power to the upper levels, boiling vats of nutrients to feed the masses, stooping over unceasing feeder belts in the manufactoria, churning out components for machines they would never use or understand. Thousands died each day, only for their brothers, sisters, children to step up and take their places. A never-ending cycle.

The grind of humanity.

This was the grand machine of the Imperium, the dark heart that fed the corpulent body of the Administratum, that kept the High Lords in their finery, that fuelled the vast engines of war. Replicated a billion times over, in every hive, on every Imperial world across the galaxy. Or at least most of those that Bledheim had been unfortunate enough to visit.

Keep the hands busy and the mind won't wander.

He supposed that, in many ways, it was a graceful solution. Glorious, even, in its monstrosity, its elegance. A necessity. A *need*.

That didn't mean he had to enjoy seeing it, though. Better that it remained buried down here, at the base of the hives, out of sight and out of mind.

Why they couldn't have taken a shuttle to the top, he didn't know – Sabbathiel had insisted that they search out one of the core elevators that would take them to the uppermost levels, where Lord Governor Rasmuth kept his chambers. She'd given no reason for the decision, but Bledheim surmised it was in order to keep their presence as low-key as possible, so as not to draw attention. It couldn't be that she *wanted* to take a stroll through these malodorous districts, after all.

Bledheim watched Sabbathiel's back as she walked ahead of him through the narrow, enclosed street. Litter had gathered against the walls – the only litter down here that wasn't recycled or reclaimed: human bones. *Children's bones.*

A solitary dog loped along through the shadows, head low, eyeing them warily. Its ribs were visible beneath its mangy flanks.

It flinched at the sound of their every footstep. Electrical cables hung from prised-open panels in the ceiling. People peered out from window-slits in the walls, hiding away inside their tiny living cells, their eyes dulled and empty of dreams. They watched the little party as if they expected violence to erupt from the inquisitors at any moment, as if that were simply the natural order of things down here, and they no longer knew how to expect anything better.

And through it all, Sabbathiel strode, taking it all in, her expression impassive.

The Queen of Ruin.

Was such a title a gift or a curse? Bledheim didn't know.

But it fits, doesn't it, ma'am? It fits all too well.

He couldn't stop thinking about the sight of the dead tarot reader, sprawled across her table, blood seeping from her mouth to stain the spread of cards laid out before her.

What had really happened there? A charlatan who was suddenly blessed with a moment of true sight? Or a talent who looked too closely at something they shouldn't have? Did something infinitely more powerful turn to meet her gaze, setting her mind alight, burning her up from the inside like some brilliant, incandescent candle?

Sending him a message he was yet to fully understand.

He'd been forced to kill the gangers he'd encountered on her doorstep, luring them inside the hab-unit with cries for help, taking them down with a laspistol and a sharp knife: cold, efficient and calculated. It was regrettable, but he couldn't risk anyone linking him to the woman and her death. And besides, if they were so easy to lure to their deaths, they wouldn't have survived much longer out there in the streets. Perhaps it was even a kindness. He'd saved them from something more brutal, more drawn-out.

At least, that's what he told himself as he trailed behind Sabbathiel and Mandreth, through dank, puddle-strewn ducts and up flights of piss-stained steps, across gantries and galleries over feeble, bustling markets where every customer haggled with a knife in their hand and every transaction ended with the promise of spilled blood. Where brightly adorned gangers crowded at lonely intersections, lying in wait to mug the unwary or ambush their asinine enemies, who looked just the same as they did. Where everyone was in a hurry to get out of the way of two sigil-bearing inquisitors who didn't look as though they were in the mood for playing games.

No one had spoken for some time. Even Sabbathiel's servo-skull, Fitch, seemed unnaturally quiet, whispering along over her shoulder, traceries of red sensor light playing on the dull metal of the walkways ahead of them.

Bledheim couldn't see the attraction of the thing. As a tool, it certainly had its uses, but he'd heard Sabbathiel talking to it in hushed tones back in the shuttle and at Mandreth's safe house, and he couldn't help but wonder if she was labouring under some misapprehension about the nature of the thing's mind. Clinging to the remembrance of things that had long passed.

He supposed he couldn't blame her for that.

His thoughts strayed back to the tarot reader's final words, the haunted look on her pretty face.

A cuckoo in the nest.

Someone who didn't belong. Someone with an ulterior motive.

But who?

It had to be Metik, surely – the machine man was clearly working to his own agenda. Bledheim despised the tech-priest's implacability, his cold logic, his burring, robotic voice. But most of all, he despised the fact he couldn't get a read on the man.

Bledheim had spent most of his life learning how to read people – it was what made him so good at his job – but Metik displayed little in the way of emotion, save for his particular brand of sarcastic, superior humour. Bledheim wondered how much of the tech-priest had been cut away, and what cool, unnatural intellect lay beneath.

No, Metik was clearly plotting *something*, and it was going to take all of Bledheim's considerable skills to find out what. But find out he would. Both for his sake, and for Sabbathiel's.

'Here.'

Bledheim looked up, dragged from his reverie by the echoing voice. They'd come to a large, circular chamber with two exits. The floor had once been inlaid with what he presumed were colourful marble tiles, judging by the few that were left intact – but most had long ago been prised free and removed, leaving a broken, uneven surface underfoot. The domed ceiling showed the faded remnants of an ancient frieze, depicting towering, blue-armoured heroes from myth. He could see Sabbathiel bristling at the sight of them, her lip curling in distaste.

There had been a conflict here, at some point. Perhaps more than one. The walls were scorched with black streaks and patterned chaotically by fist-sized pockmarks. More bones lay scattered across the floor, describing the final resting place of several adults, although the skulls and whatever apparel or equipment the victims had once carried were long gone.

Mandreth was standing before a door-sized iron grille on the back wall, which was bound shut with heavy chains. The links were old and rusted. 'The macro hoist is out of order,' he said, with a wry smirk. 'It looks as though someone doesn't want the undesirables of these lower levels gaining access to the upper spire.'

'Can you blame them?' said Bledheim.

Mandreth shrugged. He seemed amused by the notion.

Sabbathiel gestured at the servo-skull. 'Fitch.'

The machine buzzed over to the grille. Mandreth stepped back. A las-tool hummed. Bledheim watched with interest as the rust on three of the chain links began to smoulder and blacken, emitting a foul-smelling odour. One of the links began to take on a deep, reddish hue, then grew suddenly bright, before snapping with a metallic *ping*. The two threads of the broken chain dropped clanging to the floor.

'The way is clear,' said Fitch, backing away as Mandreth dragged the severed chain clear, 'although I am duty bound to forewarn you, mistress, that the macro hoist mechanism itself may yet be in a state of disrepair.'

Mandreth hauled the grille aside, revealing the interior of the carriage beyond. The carriage itself was listing slightly to the right, and only one lumen strip was working, casting a thin, weak light on the rust-streaked panels.

'Are you sure about this, ma'am?' said Bledheim, turning to Sabbathiel. 'It seems there's every chance that we might plummet to our doom if we set foot on that thing.'

Sabbathiel simply stepped up into the carriage, which swayed slightly under her weight. She looked at Bledheim expectantly, raising an eyebrow.

Bledheim sighed. 'Very well.'

He stepped up to join her, trying not to think about his impending death.

He leaned against the balustrade, fingers gripping the stone as he gasped at the cool air, trying to fight back the nausea.

The ride up had been one of the most disconcerting experiences of his life – worse than the time his lander's wing had been clipped by ground-to-air artillery fire and the pilot had

been forced to make a spiralling crash landing amongst a wasteland of toxic ammonia ice. Worse than the first time he'd seen
a human body opened up like a shining purse at the age of
six, blood gurgling out from amongst the glistening organs and
peeled-back flesh. Worse than–

He vomited over the edge of the balcony. The high crosswinds
caught the effluvia and whipped it away, blowing at least some
of it back up into his face. He groaned and sought out a rag
from the pocket of his robes.

'Bledheim?'

'Just a moment.'

He sucked at the air, fighting the urge to vomit again.

They were standing on a vast balcony that jutted like a spur
from the uppermost levels of the Gallowspire. The pinnacle of
the enormous structure loomed over him now, wavering and
oppressive. Beneath, the twinkling lights of the city fell away,
disappearing into the murk of smog that hugged the lower
levels. From ground level, what had looked like the sloping
sides of a great pyramidal structure were now shown to be
jagged conglomerations of angular structures – walls, balconies,
platforms, walkways. The hive city *had* no sides, not in the strict-
est sense, instead being an almost organic set of mismatched
strata, one piled on top of another ad infinitum, reaching right
up here, to seemingly scrape the underside of the sky itself.

Much like the strata that lay beneath the shallow seas of Balthos.
Might this world one day be drowned, too?

The thought made Bledheim shudder.

He steadied himself, looking out. Shuttles and landers flitted
about like fireflies, buzzing through the steel-grey skies. Bledheim watched as one descended smoothly into the gloom,
stirring the smog around it in ripples, as if breaking surface
tension.

Footsteps sounded behind him. He turned to where Sabbathiel and Mandreth were facing the towering plasteel doors of the lord governor's residence.

The guards had been waiting for them – of course they had – when the macro hoist finally creaked to a juddering halt at the top of the immense shaft. Evidently, the hoist had once been used to carry supplies, and possibly servants, up to the lord governor's residence from the factory levels below, but hadn't seen use in some time, chained off and abandoned, presumably as a precautionary measure.

Rasmuth, it seemed, was a cautious man – judging by the professional appearance of his personal guards. Clad in black carapace armour, they lacked the sartorial finesse of the Bleeths' militia, but more than made up for it with sheer efficiency.

If it hadn't been for Sabbathiel already brandishing her Inquisitorial icon, Bledheim had no doubt they'd have been mowed down before they ever set foot outside of the carriage. As it was, the guard who appeared to be in charge of the small force – a hirsute man with a knotted grey beard and silvery hair swept back from his face – had escorted them out here to the balcony, to await further instruction. Two of the guards stood watching them now, motionless at either side of the arched doorway, fingers balanced lightly on the triggers of their rifles. Bledheim could see that, despite their best efforts, they were both trembling in fear.

Yes. She has a way of doing that, doesn't she?

If Sabbathiel wished it, they'd all be dead by now. Mandreth, too, could have executed them without a second thought. After seeing the way he'd handled himself at the mausoleum complex, Bledheim was developing a healthy respect for the man. And his falcon, for that matter. He wondered if it was watching over them now, perched somewhere far above, then decided they were probably too high for the creature to be able to navigate the air currents with any certainty.

A newcomer stepped out from between the two guards. She was dressed in elegant grey robes, adorned simply with a small brass clasp in the form of two interlocking snakes. Dark hair, pinned up in an elaborate chignon, accentuated her exceedingly pale skin. One of her eyes had been replaced with a bionic implant, which whirred as it focused on Sabbathiel and Mandreth. She was carrying a large, leather-bound book under her arm, and the fingertips of her right hand were stained black with ingrained ink.

Bledheim decided to hang back and watch things unfold.

'Inquisitors. This is most… unexpected. My name is Chandra Mol,' said the woman, bowing her head in formal greeting. She looked nervous. 'I am chief acolyte to Lord Rasmuth, responsible for all his many, busy schedules. I am here to be of service. I understand you are seeking an audience with Lord Rasmuth? If you would like to arrange an appointment, the governor would be delighted to grant you time.'

'We would like to speak with him *now*,' said Sabbathiel. 'It is a matter of some importance to the Inquisition.'

The woman swallowed. Her eyes widened, and she took an involuntary step back at the force of Sabbathiel's words. 'I… I'm afraid that won't be possible today. He's… umm… *indisposed.*' Her eyes flicked to meet Sabbathiel's, before glancing away. Under normal circumstances, when dealing with normal civilians, the woman would clearly have been quite formidable. Someone who was used to saying no. But faced with two inquisitors…

Sabbathiel took a step forward. Her eyes didn't lift from the other woman's face, but her fingers danced threateningly over the hilt of the power sword scabbarded at her hip. 'You misunderstand. I *insist.*'

Chandra Mol took a moment to steady her breathing. 'I really am very sorry, inquisitor. It's simply not possible.'

Bledheim was impressed. The woman was either brave, or incredibly foolish.

'Whatever it is, interrupt him,' said Sabbathiel.

The woman shook her head. Her mouth opened and then closed again, as if she were unable to find the words. 'I... I can't.'

'And why not?' asked Mandreth. His tone remained airy, as if he were simply having a pleasant chat with an acquaintance. Yet there was an underlying hardness there, too. A confidence that demanded a response.

The woman faltered. 'Because he's undergoing treatment. The medicae is in with him now. He's sedated.'

'Treatment?' said Mandreth, concern creasing his brow. 'For what?'

Chandra Mol lowered her gaze. Her bionic eye whirred as it refocused. 'I shouldn't...'

Sabbathiel cleared her throat.

The woman nodded in acquiescence. 'A contagion. Highly infectious. Lord Rasmuth has been quarantined.' She raised her head. 'Even if he were awake, an audience would be... *unadvisable*. He sees no one but the medicae charged with his care. The risk of infection is simply too great.'

Sabbathiel sniffed, then glanced at Mandreth.

'How did someone of Lord Rasmuth's standing become exposed to such a contagion? Aren't there *procedures*?' he asked.

'Of course,' said Chandra Mol. 'There is some concern that it might have been an attack. An assassination attempt.'

'By whom?' said Sabbathiel.

'The governor has many enemies, inquisitor, both political and, well...'

'Disgruntled civilians,' said Mandreth. 'Any one of whom could be harbouring a murderous grudge.'

'Precisely.'

'And the vector? How was this weaponised contagion administered?'

The woman looked flustered at her inability to do what was being commanded of her. 'Forgive me. Please. I do not know. No one here does. If you wish to know more, perhaps you should speak with Lord Sinjan. Presumably you're working under his jurisdiction?'

Bledheim saw Sabbathiel stiffen.

Oh, now this is interesting.

'He's here, then? On Hulth? Atticus Sinjan?' Sabbathiel did a remarkable job of keeping her voice level.

The woman nodded. 'Of course. That's why your arrival was so unexpected. Lord Sinjan is already looking into the situation.'

'I see,' said Sabbathiel.

Yes. All too clearly. Bledheim chewed his lip thoughtfully. *Sinjan's fingerprints are all over this.*

'Who governs in Lord Rasmuth's absence?' asked Mandreth. He was running his finger down the line of his jaw. His frown had deepened.

'Duke Kreel.'

'And...?'

'He's with Lord Sinjan,' said Chandra Mol. 'In the governor's library on the next level.' She gestured at one of the guards. 'Should I send word? I could make them aware of your presence?'

Sabbathiel seemed to consider for a moment. 'No. No. If Lord Sinjan has concerned himself with the matter, then I'm confident that things will soon be resolved. It seems we've troubled you unnecessarily.'

Chandra Mol bowed her head. 'Not at all. As I said, I am here to be of service.' She looked from Sabbathiel to Mandreth. 'If that will be all...?'

'One last thing,' said Sabbathiel. 'What is the nature of Lord Rasmuth's relationship with Quintus Bleeth, of the House of Bleeth?'

Chandra Mol cocked her head to one side. She frowned, as if she didn't understand the question. 'Quintus Bleeth is dead, inquisitor.'

'Ah. I'm sorry,' said Sabbathiel. 'I wasn't aware. You knew him well?'

'Not well, no. I am just a humble acolyte, after all. But I spoke with him on occasion when he visited Lord Rasmuth, and I was sad to hear of his death.'

'He came here regularly, then?'

Chandra Mol's frown deepened. 'He and the governor had a great deal of business to discuss.' She met Sabbathiel's gaze, but Bledheim could see the tiny bead of sweat trickling down the side of her face. She was clearly terrified. 'Is there any other way I may be of service to you today?'

Sabbathiel smiled. 'No. We'll be on our way.'

'The guards will send for transport.'

Bledheim's spirits soared... only to be dashed a moment later.

'No, thank you,' said Sabbathiel. 'We'd prefer to walk.' And then Bledheim saw the look on her face – the set jaw, the concentration.

She doesn't trust them.

Chandra Mol looked confused, but clearly anxious to extract herself from the inquisitors' presence. She bowed her head, smiled, and then turned and hurried off back through the door, clutching the massive tome to her like a shield.

She's going straight to Sinjan.

'Ma'am,' said Bledheim. She turned to glance at him. 'The macro hoist?' Sabbathiel nodded once. She'd understood his meaning. Getting back inside that horrific carriage was the last thing he wanted to do, so if he was suggesting it...

The two guards stepped forward. 'We'll show you the way,' said the one on the left, a young man with chiselled cheekbones and sharp green eyes. Beside him, the other guard, a raven-haired woman, was clutching her rifle just a little too tight.

'We remember the way,' said Sabbathiel.

'It's the very least we can do for such esteemed guests.' The guard indicated the exit with a wave of his trembling hand, and Sabbathiel fell in.

Oh, this is going to be messy, thought Bledheim.

CHAPTER EIGHTEEN

'From the moment we erupt violently into this universe, we are dying. It is the one, clear certainty for us all. Surely, then, if we are to accept our fate, our singular aim must be to die well, for the measure of our worth comes not in the gratification of a life well lived, but in the reflection of our truth at the instance of our death.'

– Solomon Thoth, *Reflections on War*

Sabbathiel waited until they were at the mouth of the macro hoist shaft before she killed the guards.

It was an almost trivial thing, a moment of fierce brutality born out of necessity, and it was over as soon as it had started.

She waited until she had a single foot on the lip of the carriage, before wheeling around, drawing her power sword in the process, and finishing the action with a downward, diagonal slice that parted the male's head from his shoulders before he'd even had a chance to realise what had happened.

Blood sprayed. The woman screamed. Sabbathiel silenced her with her blade, rammed through the woman's open mouth and out the back of her skull. Brain matter and blood fragments spattered Sabbathiel's boots. She raised one leg, placed her foot against the dead woman's chest and pushed her backwards. The corpse slid free from the crackling blade of the power sword and crumpled to the ground.

Quick and proficient. And a little messy.

She looked up to see Mandreth watching her, an amused gleam in his eye. Bledheim was giving the corpses a wide berth, trying not to get blood on his shoes. Fitch was hovering above her left shoulder.

'When I suggested setting a cat amongst the pigeons...' Mandreth gestured at the body of the male guard. The artery in the severed neck was still gushing, dark blood sliding across the tiles in a syrupy tide.

'They worked for Sinjan,' said Sabbathiel. 'They would have tried to kill us as soon as we stepped into the carriage.'

Mandreth nodded. 'For a moment back there, I thought you might take her up on her offer.'

'For transport? We'd already be dead.'

'No. To take you to Sinjan. It might have been a simple way to resolve matters.'

'Perhaps,' replied Sabbathiel, 'but until I know more about what's going on here on Hulth, I'm not ready to see him dead.' She sniffed. 'That'll come later. First, we need to let him operate with complete discretion. To allow him to think he has us – or *me*, at least – cornered and on the run. Only then will he show his hand.'

'It's a dangerous web you're weaving, Astor,' said Mandreth. He stepped up into the carriage, which rocked wildly for a moment before settling into a gentle sway. Mandreth braced his hands against the sides, but otherwise seemed unfazed. 'And I admire your resolve. I only hope you don't come to regret letting this moment pass.'

Sabbathiel hesitated. Was he right? Should she go back, storm the library complex on the next level and put a sword through Sinjan's chest? Finish what she'd started back in Heldren's study?

The idea certainly held some appeal. But would it truly put an end to matters? Sinjan was simply the spokesperson for her old conclave. Kill him, and another would step up in his place. Perhaps more than one. They weren't about to simply change their mind about her, after declaring her a traitor and framing her for the murder of Heldren. Indeed, killing Sinjan would only help to further the case against her.

No, her first instinct had been right. She had to see this through. Find out the reason Heldren was killed, and what connected his death with Sinjan, Rasmuth and the Bleeths. Only then would she have any chance of clearing her name.

Only then would she have any chance of peace.

She almost laughed at the notion.

Peace? In this universe? Maybe when I'm dead...

She gestured towards the macro hoist carriage. 'We carry on as planned. Bledheim, as you were so eager...'

Bledheim already looked green. 'If I must.'

'You must.'

He stepped over, grabbing for Mandreth's arm as the carriage swung out wildly to the left.

'Vomit on me and I'll kill you myself,' said Mandreth. Bledheim nodded and made a whimpering sound, and, after a moment, let go of Mandreth's sleeve. He pressed his hands, palms flat, against the rear wall and spaced his feet apart in an attempt to hold himself steady.

Stifling a grin, Sabbathiel stepped up to join them. She thumbed the switch.

The carriage began its juddering descent.

'Touch him again and I'll remove what's left of your brain from inside that tin can you call a skull.'

Heloise tapped the nose of her pistol against the side of Metik's head to underline her point. The metal made a ringing *ting*.

The tech-priest turned his head to fix his eerie bionic eyes on the woman standing over him. 'It would be unwise of you to continue with your present course of action.' He sounded testy, which, Brondel considered, was really quite impressive, given that his voice was a dry, monotone burr.

The squat watched Metik's mechadendrites curl, their tiny finger-like blades snapping open and closed like hungry mouths. On his shoulder, Nimbik shifted nervously, a tiny light winking on one of its antennae.

Definitely testy.

'Leave the frecking thing alone, tech-priest. You're making everyone nervous.'

A wave of murmured agreement rippled through the others. Or at least Silq, who was sitting cross-legged on the floor across the other side of the room, her xenos rifle balanced across her thighs. She was drawing deeply on a smoke stick while she looked on with interest.

Mercy, on the other hand, couldn't have cared less. She was pacing back and forth before the door like a caged predator, growing more fractious by the second.

Metik himself was crouching over the insensate form of Nol, the latter of whom was lying face down on the ground and seemed to be happily dozing – if the thunderous snoring was anything to go by. The tech-priest had opened the metal implant on the side of Nol's thick neck and was busily digging around inside, sending the occasional shower of brilliant blue sparks streaming into the air. Along with the odd geyser of dark blood.

'You'll kill him,' said Heloise, still clutching her pistol.

'The chance of expiration is a mere eighteen point one-seven per cent,' countered Metik, returning his attention to the ogryn's neural implant. 'And the likelihood of total brain death only thirty-six point four-five per cent. It is far more likely that your ogryn friend will wake with a mild headache and a greatly increased intelligence quotient and new-found capacity for elaborate thought.'

'Thirty-six per cent,' said Heloise, through gritted teeth.

'Thirty-six point *four-five*,' corrected Metik. One of the needle-like implements in his hand set off another plume of bright sparks. The ogryn grunted in his sleep and tried to roll over. Metik steadied him with his snake-like appendages, pinning him to the ground.

After a moment, Nol sunk back into the same unflattering pose he'd been in before. Strings of drool danced on his bottom lip with every exhalation. His expression was serene.

Like a giant frecking babe in arms.

'It is illogical that you should threaten me,' said Metik, addressing Heloise, whose snub-nosed pistol was still hovering inches from his head. 'Even setting aside the clear probability that my ministrations shall greatly improve your companion's quality of life, to attempt to wound or kill me now would be counter to your stated aim.'

'What stated aim?' said Heloise, exasperated.

'That you wish to protect Nol from harm. If I were to die with my work only partially complete – well, the likelihood of the ogryn's death becomes a much more significant proposi–'

'All right. I get the point.' Heloise shook her head, lowered her pistol and backed a few steps away from the tech-priest, but continued to shoot daggers at him with her eyes.

'A wise choice,' said Metik. 'I shall be finished presently. The benefits will be objectively clear.'

'You mean he might actually recognise himself if he looks in a mirror?' said Brondel.

Heloise turned her back on Metik, glowering at Brondel. 'Why don't you just shut your mouth, hmm?'

Brondel snorted. 'There's no frecking helping some people.'

Heloise studied him for a moment, and then called back over her shoulder to the tech-priest. 'What happens to Nol's chances if I shoot the squat?'

Metik cocked his head, considering. 'Even allowing for the momentary distraction, as well as the fact that I should wish to preserve what was left of the body – squats are a rare commodity, you understand – the additional risk to your companion's survival would be negligible.'

Heloise smiled and raised her pistol again, this time lining up a shot down the barrel at Brondel. 'Did you hear that? *Negligible.*'

Brondel hawked up a gobbet of phlegm. He spat, and then ground it underfoot. Heloise pulled a face. 'You'd get one shot,' he said, tugging on his beard. 'One shot. And then it'd be over, and not in the way you think. So, if you honestly believe you can put me down and keep me down with that single shot, you're welcome to try.'

Heloise laughed, but she couldn't disguise the nervousness that crept into the shrill sound.

'He's right, you know,' said Mercy, who'd finally stopped pacing and was looking over. 'One shot. And even if you did put him down, do you think you could stop *me* from cleaving you in half with *this* before his body even hit the ground?' She hefted her massive sword in one fist, staring pointedly at Heloise, as if daring her to try.

'I didn't know you cared,' said Brondel.

'I don't. But it's the principle,' replied Mercy, with a toothy smile.

Heloise lowered the gun. 'Look, I was only messing.' She gave another shrill laugh, as if joining in with the others' banter. 'It's just, what he's doing to Nol. It's got me all on edge. That's all.'

Brondel spat again. 'It's got us all on frecking edge.' He nodded at Heloise, indicating that all was well between them. 'I don't like it, being cooped up like this.'

'None of us do,' said Mercy, sheathing her sword.

Heloise breathed a visible sigh of relief.

'It's the waiting,' said Silq, blowing smoke from the corner of her mouth. 'It gets to you. Like something crawling under the skin, something that can't be scratched.'

There was a moment of silence.

'Perhaps I can be of some assistance with that,' offered Metik. On the ground, the ogryn groaned.

'You can keep your filthy knives away from me, tech-priest,' retorted Silq. 'If I wanted an extra arm or two, I'd ask. Otherwise, you can assume I like everything exactly where it already is.'

Metik gave a metallic *tut*.

Brondel laughed. 'Now you've offended him.'

Heloise crossed to the far side of the room, rested her back against the wall, and then slid to the ground. All the fight had gone out of her now. 'I'd just rather be out there, *doing* something, instead of hiding here in this rat hole waiting for the enemy to come to us.'

'Inquisitors Sabbathiel and Mandreth are wise to avoid unnecessary conflict while they further their investigation,' said Metik. 'Your time will come.'

'Hmm,' said Mercy. 'If the boredom doesn't kill us all first.'

Brondel glanced round at the sound of low, wordless murmuring. Nol was shifting about on the ground, slowly coming around. With a flourish, Metik finished with his tinkering, withdrew his needle-like probes, and closed the hatch on the neural implant. Servos whined as he retreated a few steps to observe the rousing ogryn.

'Or an angry ogryn, when he finds out what Metik's been doing inside his head,' said Brondel, rubbing his palms together in glee.

Nol grunted loudly, snorting himself back to wakefulness. He sat up, rubbed his eyes, then with a frown, sought out his eyeglasses, which he'd stored in a pocket of his shirt. He perched them on the end of his nose, looked blearily around at the blank faces staring at him, and then shrugged.

'Anyone know what's for dinner?' he said.

The cables holding the macro hoist carriage whined in distress as their descent gathered speed, dropping them down the near-bottomless shaft at a rate fast approaching free fall.

Or at least, that was how it felt to Bledheim, as he pressed his palms flat against the plasteel walls, slowly reciting the names of all the bones in the human body beneath his breath, trying desperately to calm his fraying nerves.

'Metacarpal, proximal phalange, distal phalange...'

It had always worked before.

Not today.

His stomach heaved and sour bile rose in his gullet. Grimacing, he fought it back down, remembering Mandreth's earlier words.

He wouldn't really kill me, would he?

The trouble was, Bledheim had seen acolytes killed for less.

Much less. He was damned if he was going to survive this hellish plummet only to be murdered by a supposed ally for spilling ejecta on the man's coat.

He turned to face the other way, just to be sure. The world seemed to list violently beneath him. He gasped for breath, steadied himself.

'Lateral cuneiform, talus, calcaneus...'

'What was that, Bledheim?'

He looked up to see Sabbathiel peering down at him. How had she grown so tall? He frowned, glanced down. Realised that he was on his knees.

When had that happened?

'Nothing, ma'am,' he stammered, conscious that even opening his mouth felt like a risk. He swallowed back another mouthful of rising bile. The caustic stomach acid burned his throat.

A *thud* from above. The carriage rocked wildly. Sabbathiel looked up. The ceiling exploded.

Bledheim heard Mandreth bellow a warning, but the words were lost amongst the screech of rending metal and the sudden punch of a bolt pistol going off somewhere too close to his head.

Ears ringing, the world slewing left and right with wild abandon, Bledheim twisted, following Sabbathiel's gaze. She was circling, her bolt pistol tracing the edges of a ragged hole in the carriage roof. Her sword was drawn and held loosely in her other hand.

Mandreth, too, had drawn his antique pistol and was standing back to back with Sabbathiel as they readied themselves for whatever was coming next.

The carriage shifted again. Someone was up there, on the roof. Even as the elevator continued its long, downward plunge into the depths of the hive.

Are they mad? They'll kill us all.

He supposed that was probably the point.

He turned and heaved what remained in his stomach into the corner.

'Sorry,' he croaked, wiping the stringy vomit from his mouth with the back of his sleeve.

'Where are they...?' muttered Sabbathiel, her voice a low growl. 'Where–'

A silver blade burst through the roof, plunging down so sharply, so precisely, that Sabbathiel barely had time to move. She twisted to the left, ducking forward. The blade speared her shoulder, biting easily through the crimson pauldron of her armour and deep into the flesh, bone and muscle beneath, narrowly missing the intended target of the spinal column at the back of her neck. Blood sprayed as the blade was wrenched free, crunching bone.

'Clavicle,' muttered Bledheim beneath his breath.

The blade slid out of sight, and Sabbathiel grunted in pain.

Mandreth opened up, blasting a series of fist-sized holes in the roof as his pistol spat gobbets of searing plasma. There was no sign of their assailant, no telltale thud or scream to suggest Mandreth had found his mark.

Fitch was circling around the hole in the ceiling, red lights tracking for any visible signs of movement.

Sabbathiel dropped to one knee, grimacing at the severity of her wound. Bright blood had speckled the pale flesh of her cheek. She glared at Bledheim. 'Cover me!'

Bledheim nodded meekly. More than ever, he wanted to be out of that damn carriage. It couldn't be long now, could it, until they reached the lower levels? It seemed as if they'd been riding the abominable thing for an eternity already.

He flung open his robe and drew his laspistol. His hand was

shaking. The carriage continued to slew from side to side as it fell, grating against the sheer walls of the shaft, drowning all other sound. Or perhaps that was still the muffled ringing in his ears. He trained his pistol on the ragged holes in the ceiling, narrowing his eyes in concentration.

He could see nothing but the taut iron suspension cables, which sang as they slipped through the ancient caddy. The occasional flickering glimpse of some distant light, deep in the belly of the hive. And then a woman's face, peering down from above. Her skin was smooth and ebon black, unnaturally glossy, and her features soft and strangely unfocused, almost as if she only resembled the shape and form of a real woman. Her eyes were red, like burning embers. She smiled.

An Assassin.

An Emperor-damned Callidus Assassin.

Death's own shadow.

The last thing you were likely to see on this or any other world.

Just like the tarot warned.

Bledheim whimpered. They were all going to die, and there was nothing at all he could do about it.

Shrieking, he pulled the trigger of his laspistol. Energy beams hissed, kissing the metal canopy, bursting through to trace threads of light back up the shaft. But the face had already gone.

Bledheim carried on shooting, perforating the roof as he tried to anticipate the Assassin's movements.

'Careful, man! If the roof gives in, you'll bring it down here with us, and then we're all done for.' Mandreth was standing over Sabbathiel protectively as she finished securing the pauldron of her damaged shoulder. Mandreth could see blood running freely into her palm from beneath her vambrace.

'It's a Throne-spurned *Assassin*,' spat Bledheim, his voice croaking.

'Just keep that pistol pointed up there and only shoot if you see it.'

'And what if I do–'

The rest of his sentence was lost as the floor beside Mandreth disintegrated in a sudden burst, and the carriage lurched dramatically to one side, rebounding off the wall and twisting on its cable, which protested with a grinding shriek.

Mandreth slid, his footing gone, slamming against the wall and going down, skidding towards the now gaping hole of shredded, smoking metal and the chasm-like shaft below.

Bledheim, thrown back against the opposite wall, watched with horror, knowing there was nothing he could do to reach the man in time.

And then Sabbathiel was there, grabbing Mandreth's arm with her own bloodied fist, hauling him back up onto the carriage floor, where he scrabbled a moment for purchase, using his heels to push himself back away from the hole. 'Seems I'm making a habit of this,' she said, through gritted teeth.

Mandreth reclaimed his pistol from the floor nearby, raised it, and took another potshot through the ceiling. The Assassin shifted, her weight tipping the carriage into another sideways swing.

And then they were finally slowing, the cables protesting loudly as the automatic mechanism applied the friction brakes and the carriage juddered.

Bledheim, breathless, looked up, just in time to see the lithe body of the Assassin swing down through the ruined ceiling, landing gracefully less than a yard from where he was standing. Her hair was a long, tight plait that fell down between her shoulders, and she was wearing what appeared to be a small canister upon her back.

The carriage came to a final, shuddering stop.

The Assassin staggered back as both bolt and plasma pistols unloaded into her chest. Her body seemed to *subsume* the detonating, burning rounds, morphing like oozing molasses around the site of each impact. She raised the shimmering blade that protruded from the top of her wrist and took a determined step forward, fighting against the force of the percussive blasts, like someone wading through a viscous swamp. Her eyes were fixed on Sabbathiel with malign intent.

Sabbathiel, still firing, rose slowly to her feet. She snarled at the Assassin, tried to raise her sword, but the wound in her shoulder was too severe, and she faltered, the tip of the sword falling to scrape the floor.

The Assassin took another step forward, ignoring the splash of a plasma shot across her right shoulder.

First she kills her target, then she kills the rest of us.

Sabbathiel took a step back, thudding against the carriage wall.

The Assassin pulled her arm back...

'No!' bellowed Bledheim, taking a step forward, his laspistol raised. 'No.'

The Assassin turned her head towards him. He watched in horror as her shape began to morph, like syrupy liquid, remaking itself before his very eyes. The glossy black seemed to drain away, replaced instead by a familiar pale pink. The whole shape of the woman's head was changing in front of him – nose becoming more aquiline, eyes closer together, chin more pronounced and chiselled...

Oh, Emperor. Not that...

The Assassin, now wearing a perfect image of Bledheim's countenance, sneered at him derisively, upper lip curling in imitation of his own smirk.

No one really wants to look themselves in the eye...

Bledheim pulled the trigger and shot himself in the face.

The Assassin staggered to one side, its features now twisted into a bizarre parody of Bledheim's face, as if someone had reached over and smeared it like wet paint.

Mandreth hauled the door open. 'Now! While we have chance.'

They spilled out into the lobby area with the illuminated ceiling, back down in the lowest levels of the hive, Sabbathiel staggering but still moving. She'd lost a lot of blood, but she was strong – stronger than anyone Bledheim had ever met – and where the wound might have felled a lesser mortal, it seemed to have the opposite effect on Sabbathiel, driving her on as they hurried across the tiled floor, the still-reeling Assassin behind them in the ruined carriage.

'We can lose it in the warren,' called Mandreth, breathless, covering their retreat with his wavering pistol. He was clearly shaken.

Throne, we all are.

Bledheim couldn't shake the image of his own face, contorted in pain, lurching back away from his laspistol, one eye blackened and the other still staring at him with abject hate.

I shot myself in the face.

He supposed in some ways it was quite cathartic. After all, it was only what others claimed to have been wanting to do for some time. And yet...

The image stuttered through his mind again, twisting a knot in his guts as he staggered along beside Sabbathiel.

Fitch flitted ahead of them, guiding their flight.

'Come on!' bellowed Mandreth. 'It'll be on us at any momen–'

Bledheim twisted in time to see the Assassin come hurtling through the air, twisting into a graceful, balletic dive. Its sword arm snapped out, blade chopping down as it soared, aimed directly at the back of Sabbathiel's exposed neck.

There was nothing Bledheim could do. He started to raise his pistol, but he already knew he was too slow. The Assassin was perfect, sublime – a killing machine without flaws. And this was its killing blow, the moment it had been waiting for all along.

He squeezed his eyes shut, expecting to hear the horrific sound of Sabbathiel's head being parted from her shoulders. The dull thud as it hit the ground. The vile spurt of arterial blood. The spasmodic death throes of her fallen corpse. To feel the sharp lance of pain through the gut as the Assassin stuck him, too.

Instead, he heard the blade *clang* loudly against another.

He opened his eyes.

The Assassin stood over Sabbathiel, its blade an inch from the back of the inquisitor's neck. Holding it there was another large silver blade, this one gripped in the hands of a slim woman dressed entirely in ornate golden armour.

He turned and belched a final stream of gaudy vomit.

CHAPTER NINETEEN

'Only in silence might one hear the true voice of the Emperor, for He speaks to us not with words, but with stillness. For silence is the absence of rage. It is the eye of the storm, the moment of hesitation before a fall. It is the dreams of mankind made manifest and pure. Yes, silence is a soundless scream of victory in a universe that drowns in the bitter cries of the dying. Silence is the sound of a soul railing against the injustice of life itself. When the final tally is counted, silence is all we have left to give.'
– The final testament of Hieronymus Treach

Blades flashed. The Assassin and the woman danced: black and gold, dark and light.

Sabbathiel could feel nothing but a dull, aching buzz in the back of her skull, an emptiness, a void where something should have been – as if someone had reached inside her head and released an overwhelming knot of pressure that had always been there, a discomfort that she had learned to live with throughout every single day of her life.

She felt light. Free.

She wondered if it was the blood loss, a euphoria brought on by giddiness and pain; if everyone felt like this in the moments before their death.

And then she remembered.

She'd died before.

It hadn't been so easy, then. Just cold darkness closing in from all sides, a bleak sense of slipping away, of losing herself in a sea of agony.

But *this?* No, this was like a gift. Like a reclamation. A breaking of old chains. This was something new, something different.

She watched the two figures as they matched one another step for step, blades singing and sparking as they clashed. The Assassin clearly had the edge – through sheer ferocity of will, through speed – but the serenity of this newcomer, her poise… it was as if she moved in effortless slow motion, out of step with time. As if she had attained such acute control over her physical form that it countered and parried, strafed and counter-attacked without the need for conscious thought. As if she were a figment of will alone.

Guided by the Emperor's light.

Sabbathiel had never seen anything like her. She'd heard stories, of course – women dressed in shining gold, suits of ancient armour passed down through millennia of service. Women who carried huge two-handed swords and wielded them with astounding proficiency, who wore their hair in topknots and hid their mouths behind armoured grilles. Who never spoke a single word, and whose sheer presence could cause raptures of disgust in the many, and calming peace in the few. Women who sailed the Black Ships across the gulf of stars, seeking out abominations to quell.

A scion of the Silent Sisterhood.

A null maiden.

Here, on Hulth. Interceding in Sabbathiel's fate.

A woman in golden armour, just like the one in my dreams...

Things were about to get a lot more complicated.

The Assassin leapt, pirouetting through the air, its blade darting for the other woman's eye. The Sister of Silence feinted left, as if leaning into the attack, but then went low, ducking the blade, before twisting at the waist as she came back up, the tip of her sword grazing the Assassin's stomach as she passed overhead. The Assassin landed, turned, and darted forward, trying to get in close, but the null maiden's blade swept up to protect her flank, battering her attacker away.

Beside Sabbathiel, Mandreth had finally righted himself, overcoming the wave of revulsion that had caused him to stagger drunkenly in the wake of the null maiden's appearance. Bledheim, too, was picking himself up off the floor.

'Kill the bitch,' she said, hefting her pistol in her good arm, sighting along the barrel and loosing a shot at the Assassin. The bolt-round clipped the Assassin's shoulder and it wheeled, momentarily distracted. The null maiden took the opportunity to come in fast and low, her sword blade biting deep into the Assassin's left thigh on the downswing. The Assassin grunted, pulled back, raising its blade in time to stave off another swing from the null maiden – but catching another shot from Bledheim's laspistol in the arm.

Another grunt.

Another sweeping attack from the null maiden, her blade chopping down into the Assassin's upper arm, almost severing it below the shoulder. The Assassin fell back, its shoulder re-forming around the injury.

Another blast, this time directly in the chest, burning plasma searing that strange, amorphous flesh.

The null maiden lurched, spearing the Assassin through the gut, her massive blade erupting from the Assassin's back in a fountain of blood.

The Assassin screamed – a sharp, piercing cry that echoed off the domed ceiling – and then launched itself backwards, allowing the embedded blade to slide up and out through its chest as it flipped heel over head, its wound parting like a gaping mouth.

It finished its manoeuvre standing upright on its feet, facing Sabbathiel. Its body seemed to squirm, rippling as it re-formed along the site of the wound, sealing like pursed lips, which, after a moment, seemed to sink away until its torso was whole once again.

Sabbathiel raised her pistol. Flanking her, the two men did the same. The null maiden adopted a defensive stance, sword ready.

The Assassin lifted its head fractionally, as if in acknowledgement of some agreed debt, and then turned and ran, back towards the waiting macro hoist carriage.

Sabbathiel pulled the trigger. Beside her, Mandreth and Bledheim's weapons ignited.

The shots struck the back of the carriage, but the Assassin was already gone, bounding up the shaft like some crazed acrobat.

They stood for a moment in silence, each of them drawing breath.

The macro hoist carriage finally collapsed with a rending *screech.*

'Good riddance,' said Bledheim, and Sabbathiel couldn't tell if he was more pleased about the retreating Assassin, or the heap of contorted metal now resting at the bottom of the shaft.

She turned to the null maiden, who was watching her with cautious eyes. 'Who are you?'

The null maiden slung her blade across her back, and, still holding Sabbathiel's gaze, made a series of short, precise gestures with her hands: a complex sign language that was familiar to Sabbathiel – although her recollection was somewhat rusty – from her time as an acolyte, when her then master, a mute, had insisted on the use of thoughtmark amongst his followers.

I am Aethesia of the Silent Sisterhood, signed the woman, *and I am here to offer you my protection.*

'Oh, good,' said Sabbathiel, before crumpling into a heap on the ground.

The stitches hurt like the abyss itself.

'Does it have to smart so much?' said Sabbathiel, wincing. She was prostrate on the rotten old bed, back at the safe house. The tech-priest was stooping over her, his mechadendrites flitting as they manipulated a series of miniscule needles and threads, weaving a webwork of stitches across the top of her shoulder. Candles flickered in iron holders on either side of the bed.

'Might I remind you, inquisitor, that you were the one who ventured out into a city swarming with known hostiles and engaged in a battle with an Assassin of the Callidus Temple? With, I might add, minimal support from your acolytes.'

Sabbathiel rolled her eyes, then grunted as the needles marched over the top of her shoulder, biting deep into the underlying flesh. She was still covered in blood, which had now become sticky and uncomfortable as it began to coagulate and dry. There were no working washing facilities at the safe house – she cursed Mandreth again under her breath for his lack of foresight – but Silq was arranging some clean water and towels.

'It was a lucky escape, ma'am,' said Fitch. He was hovering in the corner of the room, observing, the ever-vigilant companion. 'If it hadn't been for Sister Aethesia…'

'Yes, yes,' said Sabbathiel. 'I'm not so far gone that I don't understand that, Fitch. She saved us all.'

Metik cocked his head. His mechadendrites continued to duck and weave as they stitched. 'Yes. The one from the Silent Sisterhood. I am... most intrigued,' he said. 'Are you certain it was wise to bring her here?'

'No,' said Sabbathiel. She was unable to stop a tiny whimper of pain inflecting the word as she spoke. The needles were now criss-crossing down the back of her shoulder, where the muscles were still taut. 'But then, it's not as if I had much of a say in the matter.'

It seemed that following her collapse, Bledheim and Mandreth had staunched her wound and hurried her back here from the industrial sprawl of the Gallowspire's undercity, abandoning the agreed protocol and making use of hired transport to relocate her so that Metik could carry out the very procedure he was now undertaking. He'd evidently pumped her bloodstream full of analgesics, too, for her head was swimming and she was feeling strangely light-headed. Although it hadn't seemed to have done much to alleviate the pain of the actual surgery.

'No, I do not suppose you did,' said Metik.

'Where is she now?'

'Sister Aethesia has adopted a position of vigil, outside this very room. It seems she is most concerned with your wellbeing.'

'Hmm,' said Sabbathiel.

The stitching had come to an end.

Thank the Emperor that's *over.*

Metik stood back, appraising his work. He rapped his porcelain fingertips against the side of his head but didn't say anything. Sabbathiel couldn't tell whether he was pleased or disgusted with himself.

She flexed her shoulder, winced at the stabbing pain, then sat forward. She opened and closed her hand. Everything appeared to be working. It might slow her down for a while, but she'd recover.

'I advise caution, Astor Sabbathiel. Your wound is severe, and you have lost approximately twenty-one per cent of your total blood capacity. I have done what I can with the equipment available to me, but meagre tools make for meagre work. You must rest.'

Sabbathiel smiled and swung her legs off the side of the bed, looking down at her blood-stained hands. 'You've worked miracles, Metik. As usual.'

The tech-priest inclined his head. 'Most kind of you to say.'

'I'm certain that you'll add it to the bill.'

Metik's fingers clicked out a stuttering rhythm. 'Bill?' he said, a little querulously.

Ah. So, the knife finds its target.

'What is it you want from me, tech-priest?' Sabbathiel winced as she shrugged on her undershirt. 'What would you have me do?'

'Ah, I see,' said Metik. 'You think of *payment*. You think of indebtedness.'

'I don't like owing people,' said Sabbathiel. 'It can lead to dangerous compromises. And compromises can lead to a fall.'

'With respect, inquisitor, I am unsure how much further there is left for you to fall.'

Sabbathiel laughed. 'Oh, in some ways you're right, Metik. But in others...' She rolled her neck, stretching life back into the muscles. 'I've seen the true meaning of that word,' she said. 'The *fallen*. The lost.' She met his red-eyed gaze. 'I've seen where that path leads. It is not a path I shall ever tread. So, I ask again – what is it you want from me? I would understand now what you would have me do.'

Metik considered for a moment. 'Nothing. For now. Your concerns are… most pressing, and I am a creature of patience. We have both of us haunted this universe for longer than we ever thought we would.'

'But?'

'But there shall come a time when I shall require your assistance with an undertaking. The retrieval of an object that was taken from me long ago.'

'An object?'

'Quite so. And so, you see, inquisitor, that your indebtedness is not quite so grave a prospect as you feared. A single mission, when the time is appropriate. That is all I ask. To help me to reclaim that which I have lost.'

Sabbathiel searched his implacable face.

What depths are concealed behind those unfathomable eyes? This creature has lost more than an object could contain, no matter the nature of the thing.

Sabbathiel sighed.

We are all of us the same, here. Clutching desperately at memories in search of the anchors of the past.

Her eyes flicked to Fitch, to the yellowed bone of his skull, the orbit of his hollow, empty eye.

We seek to define ourselves by who we were. But the truth is that we need to understand who we are. *To leave the past behind and embrace the future.*

If only it were that easy.

'Does that answer not suffice, inquisitor?'

'No, Metik. I fear it is the mission that will not suffice.'

The tech-priest gave her a curious look. 'I do not understand.'

Sabbathiel offered him a wan smile. 'No, I don't suppose you do.' She pulled the collar of the undershirt away and glanced down at her shoulder. The wound was like a puckered seam running up and over, around the base of her neck. The black web of stitches was stark and violent against her pale flesh. 'Are we done here?'

Metik took a step back. 'Yes. I shall inform Silq that you shall be requiring cleaning materials presently.'

'Thank you, Metik.'

The tech-priest inclined his head, and then turned and left, his pneumatic steps retreating into the other room.

'You can come in now, Sister Aethesia,' said Sabbathiel. She turned to face the open doorway.

Something shifted in the opening. And then the weak light of the candles seemed to catch on the polished gold of the newcomer's armour, as if setting her suddenly aflame. Her bright eyes – a vivid blue – seemed to come alive, too, peering at Sabbathiel over the top of the censoring grille covering the woman's mouth and nose.

Sabbathiel waved her forward impatiently. Underneath the wave of nausea, she felt that same low-grade buzz at the back of her skull, the same easing of pressure; the same sense of overwhelming peace in this woman's presence.

But I am not to be fooled. The woman cannot be trusted – not until I understand her motives.

I am pleased to see you are well, signed Aethesia, coming to stand by the foot of the bed. *For a time, the tech-priest thought he might lose you. I feared I had failed in my duty.*

'And what duty is that?' said Sabbathiel.

To protect you while you carry out your investigation.

Sabbathiel appraised the woman properly for the first time. She was tall, slim, but powerfully built. A grey fur cloak was draped over her shoulders, falling almost to her calves, and her armour, while impressive, was obviously old – like a relic from another time, an ancient time, when the Imperium was still young and breathless with enthusiasm. Her massive sword – rivalling even

Mercy's blade – was slung from a hoop on the woman's back, and her expression, or at least, what Sabbathiel could see of it behind the grille, was fixed and serious. This was a woman who had taken a vow; an elite warrior spoken of only in the language of myths, or glimpsed in the strange and disturbing dreams that had plagued Sabbathiel since her return from Calaphrax.

What in the name of the Emperor was she doing *here?*

'And what makes you think I need your protection?' said Sabbathiel, but the question failed to carry the spite she had intended. It was obvious, sitting there gravely injured, that Sabbathiel could do with all the help she could get.

There are grave and powerful enemies arrayed against you, inquisitor, signed Aethesia. *An Assassin of the Callidus Temple...*

'I know, I know,' muttered Sabbathiel. 'It nearly killed me.'

The woman nodded.

'Who sent you?'

Someone who has taken an interest in your case.

'You'll have to do better than that,' said Sabbathiel.

I cannot, for I do not know, replied Aethesia. *I was despatched by my knight-commander on the understanding that the request had come from within the highest ranks of the Order.*

'And you didn't question her further?'

It is not my place to question, signed Aethesia. *It is my privilege to serve.*

Sabbathiel wanted to scream in frustration. *Wheels within wheels,* she thought. *Mystery layered upon mystery. Like the stratified levels of the Gallowspire, with the rich and entitled perched somewhere at the top, looking down upon the rest of them.* Whose game was she really playing? Were Heldren and Sinjan just pawns, too, in some greater gambit? She felt as if she were playing with one arm tied behind her back.

'How do I know I can trust you?' she said.

The null maiden frowned as her fingers moved, as if the answer were obvious. *I have taken a vow.*

'And that is enough? What if you do not agree with my cause?'

Your cause is the cause of the Emperor. That is enough.

'And Atticus Sinjan?'

It seems he has lost his way.

Well, now… Whoever was behind this really *was* paying attention.

'You believe he was the one who sent the Assassin?' asked Sabbathiel.

I do not know. Yet it seems likely, does it not?

Did this woman know more than she was letting on? It was impossible to be sure.

Regardless, Aethesia continued, *the Assassin shall make a further attempt on your life. It shall keep on coming, again and again, until it is slain. That is the nature of these predators.*

'And you shall stand in its way?'

I shall. Until I fall.

Sabbathiel suppressed a snort. *Reassuring…*

'Very well. It seems I owe you my gratitude,' she said.

The woman shook her head as she signed. *No. Gratitude is not necessary. I do the Emperor's work.*

Sabbathiel nodded. 'Help me up.'

Aethesia frowned. *You must rest.*

'And I shall. But first I must show my acolytes what it is to be strong.' *They're going to need it,* she thought.

Aethesia came around the side of the bed and offered her arm. Sabbathiel took it gratefully, hauling herself up. Then, standing, she shook the other woman off and straightened herself, biting down on the flaring pain in her shoulder.

Together, the two women walked through into the other room.

* * *

'For freck's sake. She's back.'

Brondel clutched at his stomach and turned away as the two women entered the room. Sabbathiel felt the others bristle. At first, she thought it was the sight of her wound that had caused them to blanch – the red sleeve of her undershirt, the blood spattered across her face – but these were all veterans of death and bloodshed. Even Bledheim, who was presently slumping against a wall, eyes closed as if trying unsuccessfully to sleep. She was about to say something reassuring, but then recognised their revulsion was not a response to her present condition, but to the presence of the null maiden at her side.

She noticed Mandreth by the window, looking out into the silent street, his hands clasped behind his back, lost in thought. He hadn't turned to greet her. Close to him, Heloise had laid out all of her blades on the ground and was going through some sort of well-rehearsed ritual, cleaning each of them in turn. Her eyes flicked up to take in Sabbathiel, before returning to the combat knife in her hands. Metik, as usual, had disappeared, following his own path.

'This is Sister Aethesia,' said Sabbathiel.

'We've met,' said Mercy, cursorily. The woman had finally stopped pacing and was now scrolling through the contents of a data-slate. Sabbathiel couldn't see what was on it.

Nol, slumped on the ground beside Brondel, was holding his ample belly in both hands. 'I think that stew might have disagreed with me.'

'It's not the stew, you frecking idiot,' spat the squat. 'It's *her*.'

Nol frowned, then turned to peer over the top of his spectacles at Aethesia. 'She hasn't disagreed with me,' he said. 'She's not spoken a word since she arrived.'

Brondel turned his head and spat. 'Precisely.'

I am well aware of the ill-effects my presence has on others, signed Aethesia. *It is a burden of my kind. I shall take first watch.* She drew her sword from the hoop on her back – also freshly cleaned, Sabbathiel noted – and cut a beeline for the door. After a moment, she was gone.

'There's something *not right* about her,' said Brondel. He was caressing a small globe-like object in his hands which, Sabbathiel realised, looked disconcertingly like a grenade. She decided not to ask.

'Rarely has a truer word been uttered,' said Bledheim, from across the room. His eyes were still pressed shut, but as Sabbathiel had suspected, he was aware of everything going on around him.

Shrewd, that one.

The squat grunted.

'Ma'am.' Sabbathiel turned to see Silq standing behind her, holding a towel. 'I've done what I can.'

Sabbathiel nodded. 'My thanks.' She reached out and took the towel from the other woman.

I can see this is going to be a long night...

CHAPTER TWENTY

'The unquiet mind of the psyker is a landscape filled with
sorrow, madness and waking dreams. It is a dangerous
world in which reality and unreality clash in a constant
duel for supremacy, in which the whims and passions of
the dreamer might be made manifest through sheer will
alone. It is a world inhabited by the echoes of the living and
dead, and by the gravest sins of the universe given form.
In short, it is an abomination, and it must be destroyed.'
— Horace de Clareth, *On the Annihilation of the Mutant*

Shimmering birds – golden eagles – *circling around the spire of a
vast cathedral. Three of them, gliding on outstretched wings, feathers
ruffled by the fierce crosswinds. They open their beaks, but their
squawking is stolen by that same current, whisked away across the
rooftops of the surrounding buildings.*

*Lower they soar, lower, still circling that immense tower, where the
banner of the Ecclesiarchy hangs proud, barely stirring in the breeze.*

This is a peaceful scene. Serene.

But then, one by one, the eagles burst into flames.

The act is sudden, appalling, grotesque. The birds scream, flapping wildly, but the fire has already ignited their feathers, climbing up their wings, the vivid plumes of their chests, searing their eyes, driving them to frenzy.

From the sky they fall, like tiny bombs dropped upon a dying world, shining heralds of destruction against the frigid, unyielding night.

One burns up as it tries hopelessly to climb higher, a dead husk, trailing naught but ash as it plummets towards the streets far below. No one will ever know its awful fate, for there will be nothing left of it by the time it hits the ground.

Another collides with the spire of the cathedral – so familiar now. This place is known to her. The bird, already dead, smashes into the rippling Ecclesiarchy banner, igniting the flag, so that plumes of smoke billow off on the wind, and the whole of the spire seems to be on fire, just for a moment, as the cloth is hastily consumed, leaving nothing but a black, sooty stain where it had once been, so proud and true.

The final bird, hardier than its brethren, skirls across the sky like a beacon, trailing gleaming light.

She watches it describe frantic circles, the last, fading glimmer of its will to live, and then, still burning, it drops like a stone: down, down towards the city; down, down towards that burgeoning nest of washed-up humanity; down, down until it collides with the rattling tin roof of a crumbling hab-unit, a mile from the cathedral, on the teetering edge of the trench, until, at last, it is still.

It fizzles in sudden, driving rain, steam curling from its ashen husk.

Inside the hab-unit, a man screams. A man with blood for eyes. A man covered in scrawled tattoos that seem to writhe across his pallid flesh like living things. He claws at his temples with the nubs of bloodied, broken fingers. And then, weeping tears of bright blood, he turns and begins scratching again on the wall. Scratching a–

This time, she didn't scream.

Sabbathiel sat up, feeling the pull of the wound in her shoulder, hissing with pain. It was dark. She waited for her eyes to adjust to the gloom, the stain of those burning eagles still bright upon her retinas.

But how can that be? I didn't really see them. Not with my eyes…

She caught her breath. Tried to remember.

She was still on that miserable old mattress in the safe house. And she was alone…

No.

She sensed them, then. That tiny shift in the air currents, that sense of being watched…

Someone's there.

She scrabbled for the pistol she'd hidden beneath her pillow, brought it around before her, glanced from right to–

Golden armour, glinting in the near darkness.

The woman who makes no sound.

Sabbathiel felt it now, that unmistakable, calming presence in her mind. That *silence.* That was why her dream had ended so abruptly. Her *vision.*

'What are you doing here?' she asked, lowering the pistol to her lap.

Aethesia dropped to one knee beside the bed. She leaned closer so that Sabbathiel might see her eyes in the gloom. Her hands flashed a series of signals: *I've come to quieten your dreams.*

To quieten my dreams, Sabbathiel thought. *Yes. So that I might finally rest.*

She nodded. 'Thank you,' she said, collapsing back onto the damp sheets. 'Thank you.'

She allowed her eyes to flutter closed again.

And everything was quiet.

Bledheim couldn't eat. Not with that woman still hanging about, curdling what remained in his guts every time he sensed her near. He watched her now, emerging from the small side room where Sabbathiel had been sleeping. She looked resplendent in her shining gold armour. Like a hero from some mythical age, ready to stand in the face of whatever darkness the universe could throw at her. More a hero than he, or any of these others, would ever be. She glanced over, met his eye, nodded in greeting.

Bledheim returned the nod. He supposed she might even be considered beautiful – at least as far as he could tell behind the metal grille which hid the lower half of her face – but something about her inspired such an upwelling of revulsion, of sheer disgust, that he longed to get as far away from her presence as he could. He hoped that whatever Sabbathiel had in mind for him next, the null maiden wouldn't be a part of it.

Sabbathiel herself emerged from the side room a few moments later, looking more rested than she had in days, despite still obviously carrying a severe injury. She was dressed in her crimson armour, and it appeared that the work Nol had carried out the previous evening, hammering out the damage around her pierced and buckled shoulder pauldron, had sufficed to make it wearable again.

She glanced around until her eyes settled on Mandreth, and then crossed the room to where he was standing with Heloise, who offered Sabbathiel a reluctant nod in greeting and then backed away to give the two inquisitors space.

Bledheim, on the other hand, shuffled closer so that he could overhear their conversation.

'The Ecclesiarchy,' said Sabbathiel. 'They have a role to play in this.'

'Good morning to you, too,' countered Mandreth, with a wry smile. 'I trust you're feeling better?' He took a draw from his pipe. The embers crackled pleasantly.

Sabbathiel's expression was impatient. 'I am much improved. But I–' She stumbled over her words, as if unsure how to give voice to something.

'You've seen something,' offered Mandreth. 'In your dreams.' He shrugged. 'I've heard you calling out.'

'I've… seen something,' agreed Sabbathiel. She heaved a sigh of relief. 'A vision, during the night.'

Mandreth nodded, looking thoughtful. 'And?'

'And as I said, I believe the Ecclesiarchy have a role to play in unravelling this mystery.'

'Tell me.'

Sabbathiel swallowed. Bledheim had never seen her this unsettled. Not even after she'd been wounded or was facing down the enemy on the field of battle. Not even when the Callidus Assassin had come for her in the macro hoist. Something about these visions had shaken her, left her feeling exposed, vulnerable. Either that, or the simple act of admitting them to the other inquisitor was troubling her in some deep-seated way, as if she were giving up some small part of herself, her *truth*.

'Golden eagles,' she said, after a moment. 'Burning up as they circled the spire of the great cathedral here on Hulth. Blistering to ash, their remains crashing into the walls. It's an omen. A message of some sort. And yet… I can't decipher what it means.'

'Eagles,' echoed Mandreth. He frowned. 'It could mean anything. Or nothing. You believe they were pointing you at the cathedral?'

'I can't be certain,' said Sabbathiel. 'But I think it's worth investigating. At the very least, we can establish whether the Ecclesiarchy here has any links to the Bleeths.'

'Yes,' said Mandreth. 'You're right. A priest must have officiated over Quintus Bleeth's interment. At the very least, we might be able to establish who else was there.'

'Which in turn might present us with some fresh leads.'

Mandreth nodded. 'We should pay a visit to the cathedral today.'

'You go. This morning. See what you can uncover.'

'You're planning to wait here, rest?' asked Mandreth. He looked sceptical. Clearly, he was getting to know Sabbathiel as well as Bledheim did – there was no version of this in which Sabbathiel spent the day resting while sending others out to do her work. She thrived on being out there, in the thick of things, even if it wasn't in her own best interest to do so.

'No. There's something else. A man. An astropath. A recurring figure in my visions. One of the burning eagles showed me where to find him.'

'Very well. We split up. I'll head to the cathedral, while you and your team seek out this astropath.'

'I'll take Aethesia,' said Sabbathiel. 'Bledheim, you go with Mandreth to the cathedral.' She turned to glower at him, and for a moment he thought he might wither beneath her oppressive stare.

Emperor, but she's a sharp one.

'Yes, ma'am,' he managed to stutter.

'Mercy and Silq will carry out surveillance on the Bleeth estate. Brondel shall remain here to ensure the place isn't compromised.'

'And your tech-priest?' said Mandreth.

'Metik is not *my* anything,' replied Sabbathiel, 'but I shall encourage him to remain here, too.'

'As shall Heloise and Nol,' said Mandreth. 'We'll draw less attention if we work in small teams.'

'Precisely. The last thing we need at the moment is another run-in with Sinjan's pet enforcers.'

'Or his pet Assassin,' said Mandreth, blowing smoke from the corner of his mouth. 'He really has taken a grave dislike to you.'

Sabbathiel smiled wryly at the man's understatement. 'First, he frames me for Heldren's murder, then he sends an army of enforcers to attack us at the mortuary complex. Now a Throne-damned Imperial Assassin. You're not wrong. Yet the question remains – *why*? What does he hope to gain from it all?'

'And how does it connect to Quintus Bleeth's missing corpse and whatever it was the Bleeths were smuggling in from off-world?' said Mandreth.

'It seems obvious to me that Heldren was getting close to something,' said Sabbathiel. 'That he was investigating the Bleeths and that tomb, and that someone – possibly Sinjan himself – killed him for it. A secret with links to both a Navigator House and a lord governor. And possibly the Ecclesiarchy. Something far more sinister than a simple smuggling operation.'

'But what could they possibly want with a Navigator's dead body?'

Sabbathiel shrugged. 'Aethesia believes Sinjan has lost his way. That others within the ordo are watching. It could be–'

'That he's a traitor?' finished Mandreth. 'That's he's planning to use the corpse in some sort of bizarre rite? That's a bold claim, Astor. A lord inquisitor, of Sinjan's standing? And all those others, too?'

'I've seen it before. The web of treachery ever grows.'

'Nevertheless…'

Sabbathiel nodded. 'We must maintain an open mind and deal in facts. Yes. And we must dig until we uncover the truth, no matter what it might be.' She nodded to Aethesia, then turned to leave.

'Watch your back, Sabbathiel,' said Mandreth. 'Even with the null maiden by your side…'

'I understand all too well. Time is against us. Whatever is going on here, however it links to Heldren's murder – we must get to the bottom of it soon.'

Mandreth took another long draw from his pipe and let the smoke play out from his nostrils, wreathing his head before fragmenting and billowing away. 'Well, Bledheim. Something else to make you nauseous – it seems we're off to pay a visit to a priest.'

Bledheim stifled his groan.

Perfect.

Just perfect.

CHAPTER TWENTY-ONE

'What is the Imperium, but the dream of the Emperor
made manifest? A vast empire carved from the will of that
one man, a stage upon which the drama of humanity might
play out across the millennia. The Imperium is the theatre
of the Emperor's mind, and in that theatre the legends of
great heroes are born. For what is a play without heroes?
What is a narrative without tragedy? What is a life without
conflict? We all of us have a part to play in this greatest
of tales – we are all bound by the Emperor's great script.'

– Cardinal Acorus Meddius, *The Emperor's Dream*

The Cathedral of Saint Euphrades was a towering edifice, as
impressive in its way as the Gallowspire itself. Its immense single
spire dominated the hivesprawl for miles in every direction,
erupting from the jumbled horizon like a warning, the shaft
of a huge spear thrust into the world, unwavering and precise
in its intent.

The building itself was like every chapel Bledheim had ever seen the galaxy over: encrusted with parapets and castellations, ancient stonemasonry in the facet of leering gargoyles and hissing serpents, towering arched windows and glittering stained glass. Only, the scale of this particular place of worship beggared all belief. It was like a city unto itself, a monument raised to the God-Emperor, designed to show the inhabitants of Hulth precisely how small and insignificant their lives were when held against the majesty of the Imperium at large.

A big place to make people feel small.

Bledheim knew it was heresy, but he had never placed much faith in the strictures of the Ecclesiarchy. The Emperor – now, that was another matter entirely. Bledheim's faith in His guiding light was undiminished. In fact, had he not seen the will of the Emperor just recently, in the reading of the tarot cards? That insight, that warning, had that not been the Emperor's way of reaching out a hand across the darkness?

No, his faith in the Emperor was as strong as it had ever been, and he believed wholeheartedly that Sabbathiel served as an instrument of His will. There was a reason she suffered the torment of her nightly visions: the Emperor Himself walked in her dreams, leading her by the hand, guiding her along His path.

The Ecclesiarchy, though? To Bledheim's mind, it was an organisation dominated by those who would line their own pockets in the Emperor's name, who worshipped power above saintliness, who sought to put themselves above those to whom they would preach salvation.

He supposed in many ways he was just envious – the Ecclesiarchy had perfected the art of manipulation. After all, they always got what they wanted in the end. Even Bledheim couldn't manage that, despite the years he'd spent honing his interrogation skills. Perhaps he should have thought to become a priest?

'Brace yourself, interrogator,' said Mandreth from beside him. Bledheim realised he'd allowed his attention to wander, and the crowds around them had thickened as they'd walked. Within moments, pilgrims, worshippers and petitioners were pressing in from all sides, dressed in rough woollen cloaks, their rancid breath hot in his face.

'Praise the Emperor!'

'In His name!'

Bledheim shuddered.

The forum leading up to the cathedral entrance was at least two miles in every direction, and flanked by a veritable village of supporting buildings, including dormitories, libraries and smaller chapels.

'Do you think there's a garrison here?' he asked Mandreth, who nodded.

'Adepta Sororitas. The Order of the Broken Key.'

Bledheim pulled his robes closer around him, as if trying to make himself smaller. 'Best that we don't cause too much of a stir, then. The last thing we need is Battle Sisters joining forces with the enforcers to hunt us down.'

If he heard, Mandreth didn't seem concerned in the least. He just continued his insouciant stroll towards the cathedral, the people in the crowd seeming to part for him like a wave.

The Inquisitorial sigil. No one wants to stand in the way of an inquisitor. At least no one who is even half sane.

Preachers stood in pulpits around the edges of the forum, reading to the crowd from great tomes, their voices sonorous and impassioned, inspiring the crowds towards ever-increasing fervour. Bledheim elbowed his way through, ignoring the raft of angry complaints he left in his wake.

And then they were at the bottom of the steps leading up to the gaping entrance to the cathedral.

Huge, banded wooden doors had been propped open, each one at least five times Bledheim's full height. The peak of the arched opening was so high that it wavered dizzily when Bledheim glanced up at it, leaving him feeling somewhat unsteady on his feet. He decided to keep his eyes on the ground before him as they crossed the threshold and into the surprisingly well-lit interior of the building.

Acolytes in dull brown robes and moccasins hurried about the place, feet scuffing on flagstones, heads bowed within shadowy cowls. Above the huge central nave, a vast brass orrery was suspended from the ceiling, describing the slow, concentric orbits of several globes around a glowing central sun. Occasional flashes of bright electrical light, like miniature bursts of lightning, flickered and spat between several of the globes, deepening the shadows below and lighting Mandreth's upturned face with their stark radiance.

Along the aisles to either side, shirtless flagellants shuffled in long columns, the constant lashing of their whips like the thunder of distant drums. Bledheim could see the lacerations they'd opened in their own backs, the sheen of sweat and fresh blood, the ropey scars of previous ministrations. Scores of them – hundreds, even – walked in this dull, monotonous procession, shedding their lifeblood as penance for whatever crimes they believed themselves to have committed in the eyes of their Emperor.

In the distance, Bledheim could see the brilliant glare of an enormous stained-glass window, but it was too far off to be able to discern its imagery in any detail. Beneath it, a pyre was burning, black smoke curling up towards the distant roof of the spire, spiralling as it rose.

Like burning eagles.

A man in red-and-black robes was approaching them from

further along the nave. A priest, Bledheim presumed. The man wore his age: his hair was a shock of silver-grey, swept back from a receding hairline. His forehead was large, as was his nose, and his eyes, when he drew close enough for Bledheim to see them, were a dull steel blue. He smiled toothily at Mandreth, and barely paid Bledheim any heed.

Just as I like it.

'Blessing of the Emperor be upon you… Inquisitor?'

'Mandreth, of the Ordo Hereticus. And this is my acolyte, Bledheim.'

His acolyte? Now who's taking liberties?

The priest gave Bledheim a cursory glance, then returned his attention to Mandreth. 'I presume you are here for more than mere devotional purposes?'

'I would speak with the priest who officiated over Quintus Bleeth's interment,' said Mandreth.

The priest blinked, obviously taken aback. He recovered himself quickly. 'Quintus Bleeth? You're nothing to do with that rogue inquisitor who caused such terrible destruction at the mausoleum complex, are you?'

'Of course n–'

'No,' said Bledheim, cutting Mandreth off. 'But we understand she's taken an interest in this matter. It's likely she might come here seeking information. And she has a reputation for getting what she wants…' He let that hang for a moment as the priest's jowly face paled. 'Unless, of course, we're able to resolve matters beforehand. Which would clearly be in all of our best interests, as I'm sure you agree. It wouldn't do for that rogue inquisitor to bring any… *trouble* here, to this holiest of places, would it?'

'Oh, no,' said the priest. 'Perish the thought.' He shuddered.

'So…?' prompted Mandreth.

'Yes, yes. Of course. The person you're looking for is Father

Rand. I'll take you to him now.' He turned back the way he had come, towards the far end of the nave. 'If you'd care to follow me.'

They fell into step behind him.

To either side, the march of the flagellants continued, and Bledheim realised there were even more of them than he'd at first imagined, their bloody processions curling back on themselves like the coils of a snake, slithering up and down the aisles in constant, harrowing motion.

Above, the crackle and hiss of the bizarre orrery caused the fine hairs on the nape of Bledheim's neck to stand on end, the static like an aura, giving him the sense that he was standing in the presence of something of immense power.

He supposed that was the point.

As they drew closer to the far end of the nave, the design of the towering window hove into focus. It depicted a man in simple red robes, adorned with rose-like purity seals, striding forward, a human skull held in one hand and a papyrus scroll in the other. Around his neck was a broken lock on a heavy chain, hanging down at his knees.

This, Bledheim presumed, was Saint Euphrades, the ancient preacher to whom the cathedral was dedicated. Behind the figure of the man, the panes were decorated with images of colourful planets, against the backdrop of the black void of space.

He heard Mandreth mutter something beneath his breath, but when he turned to ask the man to repeat himself, Bledheim saw that Mandreth's eyes were fixed upon the burning pyre at the foot of the nave.

Bledheim wrinkled his nose. The stench was appalling. Almost like... charred meat.

A figure was on his knees before the conflagration, dressed in near-identical robes to their guide, his hands splayed out before him so that his forehead was almost touching the marble floor.

'Father Rand?' said the priest, coming to a stop a few yards from the prostrate man. 'I apologise for interrupting your devotions, but there is an inquisitor here to speak with you.'

The other man made no sound of acknowledgement, but slowly straightened his back, before rising steadily to his knees. He stared up at the burning pyre for a moment longer, and then turned towards them, his smiling face half lit by the glow of the dancing flames, half cast in shadow.

'It is of no consequence, Father Crucias. The Emperor's work manifests in many different ways, and thus we show our devotion with each small act of our lives in pursuit of such duties. Now, how can I be of service?' He clasped his hands before him in supplication.

Bledheim stifled a cough. The reek of the pyre was near overwhelming, coating the back of his throat in thick, oily mucus.

'This is Inquisitor Mandreth, of the Ordo Hereticus. He wishes to speak with you regarding Quintus Bleeth.'

Father Rand didn't miss a beat. 'Ordo Hereticus?' He sounded overjoyed by the very prospect. 'Then you must be made aware of the great work we are doing here on Hulth! Indeed, this very day, we have committed eleven heretics to the purifying flames.' He gestured expansively in the direction of the pyre.

Bledheim narrowed his eyes, cupping his hands around his face to ward off the glare.

Was that...?

People. He's burning people.

There were several husks bound to the central post at the heart of the flames – blackened and ashen, their bones cracking from the severity of the heat. Dead for hours.

One still writhed and twitched, but the act was mindless now, the result of superheated muscles and ligaments contracting before they burned. Melted fat ran from the corpse, mingling with the ashes below. It had been a woman, and she'd died screaming.

Bledheim was just pleased they'd arrived too late for the start of the show. Mandreth had been right – something else to make him feel nauseous.

'I'm sure your work is of great service to the people of Hulth,' said Mandreth, diplomatically.

Father Rand beamed. 'Kind of you to say. If you so desired, I could show you some of the other means by which we're identifying and purging heretics. Indeed, in the lower levels we have a wooden wheel that…' He trailed off, studying Mandreth's expression. 'Forgive me. I share my order's tendency towards zealotry.'

'Not at all. It's merely that time is ever against us,' said Mandreth.

'Ah, the cruellest of mistresses,' said Rand. He waved his hand, and the other priest, Crucias, backed away, leaving the three of them alone before the roaring pyre. Bledheim could feel beads of sweat trickling down the crease of his spine. 'You wished to speak with me about poor Quintus Bleeth?'

'That's right,' confirmed Mandreth. 'I understand you officiated his interment.'

'Indeed,' said Rand, puffing out his chest. 'The brothers of this cathedral have long served the House of Bleeth.'

'Was the funeral well attended?' asked Mandreth.

Rand shrugged. 'No. It was a small affair. Private. What I mean to say is that Quintus had left very clear instructions regarding how he wished to be laid to rest. No mourners. None of the household staff or so-called friends and business associates. Just the immediate family, myself and Lord Rasmuth.'

Rasmuth.

Another connection.

'The governor was there?' said Mandreth.

'Of course. The Bleeths are a cornerstone of Hulth's society,' said Rand. 'Lord Rasmuth was anxious to pay his respects.'

So, the funeral had taken place before Rasmuth fell ill.

'And did you see the body yourself?' pressed Mandreth.

Rand frowned. 'Yes. I did. I blessed his earthly remains before they were committed to the tomb.'

'Earthly remains that are now missing,' said Mandreth.

'Yes, I heard about that. Something to do with a rogue inquisitor, I understand? Broke into the tomb and stole the body clean away. That poor family. I told Jolas that I expected the woman to hold the corpse to ransom – a means to extort credits or favours from the family – but in truth I suspect she has already disposed of it in some blasphemous ritual. When inquisitors fall, in my experience, they do so very hard indeed.' He met Mandreth's gaze. 'Forgive me – was she known to you?'

'Only by name,' said Mandreth levelly.

Bledheim didn't know how the man was maintaining his calm. Personally, he was fantasising about jabbing one of his needle-capped fingers into the priest's left eye, watching him stagger back, blinded, into the roaring flames. Bledheim wondered how long it would take for the man's robes to catch fire. Perhaps his fine, blond hair would go up first – a fiery halo, a crown of pain for this most regal of men. And then his fat, rosy cheeks would split and crack and blacken, and he'd throw his head back and scream like a stuck pig as his eyes bubbled and burst.

Bledheim sighed.

If only.

'Ah well, probably for the best,' said Rand. 'A heretic such as her... well, you wouldn't want to be implicated by association, would you now?'

Mandreth seemed not to acknowledge the priest's veiled

threat, smiling dismissively and tapping his chin with the tip of his index finger. 'Leaving said inquisitor aside, you can think of no one else who might bear a grudge against Quintus or the Bleeths?'

Rand laughed. 'My dear inquisitor, there are dozens, scores, hundreds! One does not forge a dynasty as successful and powerful as the House of Bleeth without making enemies, here on Hulth, back on Terra and probably out there amongst the stars themselves.' He waved his hand in a bold, all-encompassing flourish. 'Quintus was an excellent man, you understand, but he was a *Navigator*. A *mutant*. From a family of mutants.' He nudged the side of his nose with the tip of his finger and leaned closer, as if inviting them to participate in some closely guarded secret. 'What's more, he and Jolas controlled what amounts to a monopoly in warp travel in this sector, with Hulth being the hub of their operation. The credits flowed freely into their coffers. Thus, there are probably even those within the extended Bleeth family who were glad to see Quintus bound for the grave.'

'So, Quintus wasn't popular?'

'No, no. You misunderstand, inquisitor. Quite the opposite. Quintus was popular in the way only those with wealth and power can be. It is that same popularity that made him a target.'

'You're saying that any number of people might have held a grudge against him?'

'Quite so.' The priest sighed. 'Although the whole discussion is rather moot, given that we know the perpetrator responsible for the theft of his remains. What other possible reason would that inquisitor have for breaking into his tomb, if it weren't to rob it of its most precious prize?'

'And what of the blood that had been spilled in the tomb? Signs of a conflict, perhaps?'

'There is no honour amongst traitors or thieves, inquisitor. You of all people should understand that. No doubt they fought between themselves in order to win a greater share of the prize.'

Bledheim watched Mandreth grinding his teeth. A tiny bead of sweat had formed just beneath his hairline, and it trickled now, tracing a jagged tributary down his temple and the side of his face. Bledheim could see the dancing flames reflected in the man's glassy eyes. He was silent for a moment.

'Perhaps you're right,' he said eventually. 'It seems we've wasted your time.'

'Not at all,' said Rand airily, offering a toothy grin. 'I ever have time for the good servants of the Emperor.'

'We shall leave you to your devotions.' Mandreth half turned towards the exit, then hesitated before turning back to face the priest. He leaned closer, so that the firelight seemed to wash his face in a bright, amber glow. 'And know this: if you ever threaten me again,' he said, his voice low, 'then even the Emperor will not be enough to protect you from my wrath.'

Rand's face visibly paled. All of his forced ebullience drained away. He sniffed, edged back a step as if Mandreth's words had carried a physical weight. 'Yes, inquisitor. Quite so.'

Bledheim allowed himself a wry smile.

Mandreth was definitely growing on him.

CHAPTER TWENTY-TWO

'To those of you who fear the future, I say to you this: you will not live to see it. The future is our gift to the generations that follow. We purchase that future with our lives. We seek the release of death, safe in the knowledge that, in doing so, we craft a better universe for our children, so that they might live an hour, a day, a week longer – so that they too might take up the fight and bring such vengeance upon the enemies of the Imperium that their death throes shall reverberate down the millennia like the footsteps of immortal gods.'

– Commissar Natalia Rostov, from 'Address to the Vostroyan
12th before the Battle of Nunessian Fields'

The hab-unit was just as it had been in the dream: decrepit, rundown and barely inhabitable. The tin roof looked as though it offered little protection from the near-constant battering of rain, and if there had once been windows, they had long ago been boarded over and sealed. There appeared to be no power, here or elsewhere in the block. There was no sign that any other people had passed this way for some time.

A scaly hive rat was scrabbling around in the mulch before what passed as the door, its whiskers twitching as it nosed through the filth in search of food. It gave up when it heard Sabbathiel approach, skittering off down the alley, paws stirring up puddles of murky rainwater in its wake.

It was a wonder even rodents could live in such abysmal filth, let alone human beings. But then, it forever surprised Sabbathiel what people were able to tolerate in order to survive. Humans were a resourceful species, if nothing else.

I'd be wise to remember that.

She drew her sword, felt the power stir in its humming blade. A quick glance over her shoulder told her that Aethesia was right behind her, guarding her back, one eye on the mouth of the alley through which they'd come, as if traipsing down the gullet of some festering, felled beast.

Elsewhere, the streets had been busy with the hustle and bustle of daily life here on Hulth. The changing over of the shifts meant that zombie-like workers trudged through the trench towards their habs in search of thoughtless sleep, while others, fresh from their beds but no more enthusiastic for the rest they'd achieved, trudged back in the opposite direction towards the manufactoria. Food stalls had sprung up selling bowls of pungent slop, and preachers, presumably from the cathedral, had taken root on various prom-enades, declaring salvation for all who would listen.

Sabbathiel herself had seemed to glide through the chaotic press, still somewhat numbed by the analgesics that Metik had given her that morning to help compensate for her wound. Despite the intense nausea she felt in Aethesia's presence, she found herself enjoying the pleasant, clarifying buzz that the null maiden's proximity brought to her mind, quelling the disturbing visions that had otherwise plagued her of late. For the first time since childhood, she felt whole, as if some malingering presence had been excised from her mind.

She understood, of course, that this was an exaggeration of the truth – that her gut instinct and psychic insight had saved her life, and those of others, on more than one occasion. Yet to be free of that burden, even just for a short while, was intoxicating.

She faced the door.

'Ready?'

Aethesia nodded.

Sabbathiel kicked the door in.

The steel panel buckled immediately, crashing loudly to the ground, hinges popping. It would have barely withstood a child, let alone an armoured inquisitor.

She dragged the remains of the door out of her way.

Inside, the single room was dark. A wretched stink, carried on a thick, rancid heat, wafted out, causing her to cover her mouth and nose with the back of her free hand. She peered in but could make out only a few humped silhouettes in the gloom.

'Fitch. Take a look.'

'Yes, ma'am.'

The servo-skull buzzed as it swept into the room ahead of her, its red lights tracing patterns on the walls, floor and ceiling as if mapping the place. Sabbathiel glimpsed a heap of rotting wooden crates, around which there appeared to be the remnants of several meals, and what she took to be a mattress on the floor made out of discarded rags and old robes.

As Fitch's light skimmed over the far wall, she saw the ghosts of hastily scrawled images and words, and the familiarity of the sight, even glimpsed so fleetingly, brought her up short. Her heart felt as if it were in her mouth. Blood roared through her ears. She felt momentarily dizzy and put her hand out, catching the door frame to support herself.

It's real.

It was all real.

She felt Aethesia's hand on her arm, looked up.

Are you well? the null maiden signed.

Sabbathiel nodded. 'I'm fine. Just give me a moment.'

Aethesia looked doubtful, but stepped back, giving Sabbathiel room. The woman probably thought it was the after-effects of her shoulder injury, but in truth, it was more like relief. Relief twisted with guilt and fear and revulsion. Relief that proved she wasn't *entirely* losing her mind.

But what about the man, the astropath she'd seen in her visions? Where was he?

Fitch had completed his sweep of the room. He hovered before her in the doorway as she straightened. 'No imminent threats detected. Several life forms, most of them vermin. There is human blood encrusted on the walls, but the patterning is unfamiliar, suggesting it was purposefully applied.'

'Hold on. What do you mean, *most* of them?'

Fitch regarded her for a moment in silence. Then: 'There is one human male present, although his vital readings suggest he is close to death.'

'Show me.' Sabbathiel moved forward, causing Fitch to jerk back to avoid a collision. Mechadendrites curling, the skull turned on its axis and slid through the air towards the back of the room. 'Lights, Fitch. Unlike you, I can't see a thing in here.'

'Apologies, ma'am.' A lumen ignited at the end of one of Fitch's curling arms. A sphere of light bloomed around him, with Sabbathiel at its heart. She heard Aethesia coming in behind her, taking a defensive posture just inside the door.

Fitch had been right – the man on the ground looked

more dead than alive. Dressed in filthy, soiled rags, he was so malnourished that he resembled a skeleton more than a human being. Paper-thin flesh was stretched over his bones like parchment, and his blind eyes were sunken in deep pits. His cheeks were hollow, and his breath wheezed from shallow lungs. Blood had poured down his face, streaming from those unseeing eyes, and was now dry and crusted upon his bared chest. His fingers had been reduced to bloodied stumps, the flesh worn down to the bones and then beyond, so that the nubs of his distal phalanges now protruded from the raw and festering meat.

Above him, the wall was covered in an array of images, sigils and disconnected words, ripped from the tumult of his mind and scratched there in his own blood.

Sabbathiel dropped to one knee before him. 'Astropath? Can you hear me?'

The man's unseeing eyes flicked towards her face. He twitched, his body juddering. His lips pursed and then cracked. He moistened his tongue on the bright blood. 'You. *You*. You came.'

'You know me?'

The astropath shook his head. He tried to pull himself up but managed only enough to prop himself on one shaky elbow. 'I see what I know, and I know what I see. You are at the heart of this.' He tapped a bloody finger against his chest, over his heart. He smiled, and Sabbathiel was appalled by the bloodstained teeth and mouldering gums.

'The heart of what? What do you see?'

He laughed – a thin, reedy laugh – and gestured at the wall. 'I see the universe unfold. The dreams of so many, the deprivations, the dying. I see beyond the flesh to the bursting light beneath, that wants to get out, to climb out, to *burn* its way through. I see what cannot be seen. I know what cannot be known.'

'He's delirious,' said Fitch. 'Starved of water and sustenance. These are the ramblings of a dying mind.'

'Quiet, Fitch,' said Sabbathiel. She turned back to the astropath. He was searching her face with his clouded eyes. 'Tell me about the eagles.'

'On golden wings they soar amongst the stars.' His voice changed timbre suddenly, becoming harsher, more insistent. 'They do not belong here. They never should have come. He should never have brought them.'

'Who?'

'The one with the all-seeing eye.'

'Quintus? Quintus Bleeth?'

The astropath reached out, tried to grab her arm. She withdrew it, leaving him flailing in the dark. 'Find him. Find the one who guides. Find him *soon.*'

'Quintus is dead,' said Sabbathiel.

The astropath laughed, blood bubbling from his lips. 'We're all dead, aren't we? We're the walking dead. Most of us just don't know it yet.'

'His heart rate is spiking,' said Fitch.

The astropath jerked spasmodically and collapsed back onto the ground. His breath was becoming increasingly shallow, and blood was now dribbling from his nose.

'Can you hear me?' said Sabbathiel. 'Astropath?'

The man jerked again, eyeballs rolling up in their sockets.

Sabbathiel stood, closed her eyes. Then she opened them again and thrust the tip of her power sword into his chest, gently piercing his heart. His body tensed suddenly, and then relaxed. He didn't even gurgle as his head lolled and his final breath whistled from his parched lips. 'Let that be an end to his misery,' she said.

She glanced over at Aethesia, still standing in the doorway, watching. There was no judgement in her eyes, only compassion.

I like this one.

Sabbathiel turned to the wall. 'Fitch, I want picts of all of this.'

'Yes, ma'am.'

She took a step back, studying the crazed, sprawling insanity of it all. It was almost impossible to decipher. Layers upon layers of bizarre imagery had been scratched on top of each other, a palimpsest of blood and pain. Here, the word REBIRTH. There, the image of an eagle's wing. Here, what looked like the crude depiction of a golden helm. And there...

She stopped for a moment and stared. Then took another step back to try to take it all in.

That's it. The whole sorry mess.

There's a master design to it all.

'Fitch, keep your light pointed at the wall.'

She backed up even further, until she was standing beside Aethesia at the door, taking in the whole of the image. Every component, every little bit of reworking, where the patterns had been remade on top of one another – it all added up to one enormous design on the far wall. A life's work painted in blood. He must have used nearly every ounce of the stuff in his veins.

She narrowed her eyes.

Two planets in orbit around one another, joined by a jagged bolt of lightning.

'Well, *that's* unexpected,' she said.

CHAPTER TWENTY-THREE

'*Competency is the surest path to a knife in the back.*'
– Garrok the Elder, *Treatise on Warfare, Vol. III*

Brondel was taking a piss up the back wall when the door inside exploded.

'Frecking Throne!' He struggled to hoist his breeches up as the sound of weapons fire erupted from the other room.

The bark of a ripper gun.

The buzz of lasrifles.

The dull thud of bodies striking plascrete.

The roar of an angry ogryn charging into the thick of a melee.

Moments ago, he'd been lounging with his back against the armchair, chewing over old war stories with Nol. He'd only stepped out for a moment to relieve himself.

Now *this.*

'Wait for me, you *bastards!*' he bellowed, tearing his plasma pistol from its holster and barrelling in through the safe house's rear door, head low. Across the adjoining room he ran, and then through into the main chamber and immediately into the thick of the fighting. Blades whipped overhead, las-fire scored the walls, and the bodies of dead enforcers crunched underfoot.

The room was thick with them, and all order had already been lost.

Glorious.

Brondel grinned, hawked up a gobbet of phlegm, and then raised his pistol and fired, punching a hole of searing plasma through the chest of an enforcer who was fumbling with his gun.

He didn't know how the enforcers had found them, but it hardly mattered – they were here now, and they were falling in their droves.

Laughing, he turned and fired again, then again, each time dropping an enforcer as his pistol emitted a satisfying *whomp* and the plasma rained burning death, chewing easily through the plasteel armour plating of the enforcers' standard-issue uniforms.

He had no idea where they'd come from, and he didn't much care; he'd been spoiling for a fight for days, and the Emperor had just answered his every prayer.

On his left, a still-helmeted head bounced heavily across the floor. He looked up to see Heloise execute a perfect backflip, her twin blades drawing ropes of dark blood from the chest of the woman in front of her. She landed behind another, punched a blade through the small of her back, and then pivoted and took the head off the shoulders of a third. She glanced at Brondel and winked.

I think I'm in love.

He twisted, stomped on the booted foot of an enforcer, who looked down in sudden surprise, only to be met with a face full of searing plasma. The man didn't have time to scream.

The enforcers were pouring into the chamber in even greater numbers. Heloise was thick in the midst of them, her blades dancing balletically, arcing up and around in smooth circles, swooping low, cutting deep, but always moving, their motion traced by threads of spilled blood, like red ribbons drifting on the wind.

The throaty punch of Nol's ripper gun tore Brondel's attention away from the woman, as he turned to see a line of four enforcers crumple, the massive, percussive shell blasting a clean line through their guts, before detonating in the belly of a fifth, showering the wall in fragments of bone and soft tissue. It lacked the finesse of Heloise's sublime dance of death, but it was just as effective in its way. Nol roared, thundering forward, using the massive gun as a bludgeon to batter swathes of enforcers out of his path.

The enforcers tried to swarm him from all sides, pulling knives, jabbing at his thick hide, but the ogryn seemed to laugh off the wounds as if they were paltry scratches, hooting loudly as he bashed in skulls and crushed throats, or shattered spines with each sweep of his meaty fist.

Brondel sensed motion and pivoted, opening up with his pistol without even a moment's thought. Two shots found an enforcer's chest, while a third shot went wide, splashing across the shoulder of a second enforcer, causing them to reel back and scream, only to detonate on the receiving end of Metik's archeotech gun.

The tech-priest, too, was at the heart of the fighting, mecha-dendrites flashing as they ducked and dived like burrowing worms, piercing armour to chew into chests and still hearts, or lash other attackers across the sides of the head, sending them sprawling to the ground, where they were promptly crushed to death underfoot. Every time an opening presented itself, Metik would take aim with his weapon and detonate another combatant from afar, all while his mechadendrites continued to fight as if utterly independent of the man at the centre of their writhing nest.

Meanwhile, Nimbik leapt from shoulder to shoulder, dropping enforcers with swift, deadly pulses from its lascutter, searing tiny but highly effective holes into the sides of their heads. As a consequence, the room was filling with the rich aroma of burning meat.

Still taking potshots into the morass of the enemy – which was now beginning to thin – Brondel slid a knife from the sheath at his belt and reversed it in his grip, so that the blade was pointed along the line of his wrist. He pushed his way into the crowd, blade flashing, and several of the enemy went down with severed hamstrings, only to find Brondel's toothy grin awaiting them as they buckled to their knees.

More plasma, more dead enforcers.

Brondel hopped up onto a heap of the dead, his boots leaving imprints in the malleable flesh of the fallen. He surveyed the scene. Heloise was by the door, finishing off the last of those trying to force ingress, while Nol was still battering a man who was clearly long dead – the enforcer's skull was cracked open and his brain matter was oozing sickeningly out of the wound. Metik had recalled Nimbik and, like Brondel, seemed to be taking in the scene of utter devastation. There had to be thirty, forty – even more – dead enforcers on the ground, or else spread halfway up the walls. It was an utter triumph: aside from a few small knife wounds on the ogryn's forearms and lower back, the four of them had seemingly emerged unscathed from the fight.

Something, though, was off. Brondel could taste it, like the stink of animal crud on the breeze. Why had the enforcers stormed the building in such numbers, and why had they abandoned all logic in the process? With all the resources at their disposal, surely it would have been more effective to set up outside and deploy superior firepower – to either force Brondel and the others to abandon the building or else bring the structure down on their heads. These weren't the tactics of–

Heloise let out a wet, rasping gurgle.

She was standing facing an enforcer. Close. *Too* close. She staggered, her blades clanging to the ground. There was something...

She slid backwards, her knees giving way beneath her, the point of a long, black power sword sliding out of the wound in her midriff. The bearer of the weapon had thrust it directly through the back of the enforcer she'd been fighting, skewering and killing the man, and catching her unawares in the process.

The wound was deep. Blood was seeping out over the top of her legs.

Heloise gurgled, blood foaming on her lips, writhing in agony atop a heap of sprawled corpses. She clutched at the wound with both hands, shot Brondel a confused, pleading look, and then fell still, her face still caught in a desperate frown.

Brondel roared, charging across the room towards where she'd fallen, but as he ran, the wielder of the black sword allowed the body of the enforcer to drop heavily to the ground, slumping forward off the blade, revealing his ghost-like visage in the doorway like some Throne-damned mirage.

Atticus Sinjan.

His pink eyes fixed on Brondel, running towards the fallen Heloise.

Something flashed – a pistol.

Brondel felt the shot like a punch in the chest, thudding into the front of his flak armour, caving in ribs and sending him wheeling back off his feet. He slammed into the wall, blood spewing from his lips like a fountain. He rolled onto his back, pain flaring in his chest, his arm, his back. He fought for breath, but every time he pulled at the air, there was nothing but a wet sucking sound and another stab of fiery pain in his chest.

Darkness limned his vision.

Oh well. At least I emptied my bladder first...

Nol's heart felt ready to burst. Like someone had grabbed it in their fist and was squeezing it as tight as they could, and soon it was going to stop working, and he'd be dead.

He stared at Heloise's crumpled body, sniffed, and then looked at the little guy too. The one whose name he could never remember, but who made him laugh. There was blood in his beard.

Blood in his beard.

This is all wrong.

He turned back to the door, bunching his fists, shaking with raw energy.

The pale man stepped into the room, flanked by a squad of black-clad enforcers wearing armour that, to Nol's eyes, looked different from that worn by all the dead ones on the ground. It was shinier. More impressive. More... black.

Like shiny ants, ready to be squashed.

'Under my boot,' he growled. 'Under my thumb.'

The pale man looked at him curiously. *'What?'* He sounded annoyed. He was dressed in ornate black armour beneath a long, flapping leather coat, and his stark white hair was pulled back from his face in a taut ponytail. One of his hands had been replaced with a bionic implant.

'Won't be so shiny *then*,' muttered Nol. All he could think about was bludgeoning the man, over and over, dashing his scrawny little head against the wall so that the gloopy stuff leaked out. Wiping that smug look off his face. Making him say sorry for what he'd done to Nol's friends.

Although he won't be able to say sorry when his brain is on the floor.

'Maybe I'll do it the other way around,' he said.

The pale man eyed Nol for a moment longer, before turning his attention to Metik. He raised his sword, pointing the tip of the weapon at the tech-priest. Now he was wearing a satisfied smile, which just made the fire in Nol's heart burn all that much hotter.

'It seems my timing is a little off,' said the man. 'Where is she?'

'Where is who?' replied Metik.

Nol frowned. 'I think he means–'

Metik waved an arm to silence him. 'Not now, Nol.'

Nol glimpsed movement out of the corner of his eye and looked over to see that Nimbik, the tech-priest's living-rat-skull-child, had scampered over to where Brondel was lying on the ground. It climbed up on top of him and started doing stuff to his chest. Something that involved knives and lasers. Confused, he looked away, back to where the pale man was still pointing his sword. He looked stupid, as if he were trying to seem threatening, but failing.

What was his name again? I should know. They told me.

The pale man...

Sin...

Si...

Nol shrugged. He supposed it didn't really matter, because the man would be dead soon anyway. He'd killed Heloise, and maybe the little man too, and that was a *bad* thing. *Very* bad. It made Nol very unhappy.

'Sabbathiel,' said the pale man. 'Tell me where she is.'

Metik did that thing with his fingers that Nol couldn't stand, tapping them all together to make a sound that felt like he was knocking repeatedly on the inside of Nol's skull. The tech-priest cocked his head. 'I think... no.'

The pale man sighed. 'Then I shall have to–'

'Squashed like an ant!'

Nol, who'd had enough of talking, bellowed as he charged at the pale man, who looked suddenly startled, as if he hadn't been expecting it. Which, even Nol knew, was stupid, because what else did ogryns do?

The pale man managed to twist just in time, his sword still raised, and Nol felt something sting as he swung his left hand down in a battering motion, as if to swat the puny human who'd made his heart hurt so badly.

Nol's hand suddenly stopped, encountering some kind of strange resistance.

He looked down.

The black sword had skewered the palm of his hand, right up to the hilt. Blood was running down his thick, ropey arm, and the blade was jutting up and out of the back of his hand. He looked at it thoughtfully for a moment.

The pale man was still holding the hilt of the sword, now in both hands, and he staggered under the downward pressure of Nol's attack.

Nol cracked a broad smile.

And then punched him with his other fist.

The pale man went sailing backwards, eyes wide, slamming into several of his guards, who scattered like felled trees, crashing to the ground.

Nol stumbled forward, picked one of them up, slammed them back onto the ground before him, and stomped on their head. The skull cracked like a broken egg. He did it again, just for good measure. His boot came away trailing something sticky.

The other guards were picking themselves up now, readying their guns. Two of them were dragging the pale man back towards the door. He looked bleary eyed, as though he needed to go to sleep.

Nol would make sure he went to sleep forever.

One of the guards fired, and Nol shifted to the left, so that the las-shot glanced his upper arm, causing the flesh to sear and blacken. He winced, looked at it, and then back at the woman who had fired.

He growled.

The woman took a step backwards, but her boot caught on the edge of one of the dead enforcers and she stumbled, dropping to one knee as if in prayer. The thought made Nol giggle.

Like she's praying for her life.

But the Emperor doesn't like bad people.

He grunted, yanked the black sword from the palm of his hand and threw it at her, blade first, like a spear.

It entered her chest with a loud *shunk*, the point exploding out of her back in a spray of blood, organ and shattered bone. Beside her, a man started screaming.

'Get back, Nol.'

He turned to see Metik lining up a shot with his old-fashioned gun and frowned. 'Don't shoot at *me!*'

'I am not shooting at you, Nol. I am shooting at *them.*'

The weapon spat. The screaming man exploded.

'Now, take cover before they have the opportunity to shoot back.'

'Ah-ha,' said Nol, understanding dawning just as the las-fire began streaking in through the shattered remnants of the doorway. He took two steps back, and then ducked behind the wall as Metik fired again, detonating another of the black-clad guards.

'I want to break the pale one,' said Nol.

'That might have to wait,' replied Metik, loosing another shot.

'Retreat!' bellowed one of the guards. Most of them had already made it back through the door, dragging the pale man out along with them. They'd taken the dead woman too, the one with the sword in her chest.

Nol looked down at his sore hand. He could see the floor through the middle of the hole. He stepped away from the wall, turned towards the door.

'Nol, no. They'll kill you if you go after them. Let them go.'

Nol crossed the room. He stood for a moment, looking down at Heloise, at the look of shock frozen on her face.

'It's not right, Metik. She's supposed to look peaceful, like she's asleep.'

'I know, Nol. I know.'

Maybe I can help. Maybe I can make her feel better.

He dropped to one knee, gathered her up in his arms and held her close to his chest, rocking her gently, like a baby.

And then the tears came.

CHAPTER TWENTY-FOUR

'What is the loss of a single life when set against a galaxy
of misery? What is the cost of a soul? How do we weigh
its worth? The truth is, we do not. We cannot. Because
to comprehend such a thing is to walk the path towards
madness. To understand all that we have lost – all that
we have yet to lose – is a burden even the strongest of us
could never hope to bear.'
– Johan Francois, *On the Eve of Exterminatus*

Sabbathiel knew there was something wrong the moment they
entered the trench. A stirring in the ether; a twisting in her guts.
Images and sounds lashing unbidden through her mind, like
the fleeting, strobing stutter of another reality encroaching on
her own.

Brondel bellowing as he throws himself at an enforcer.
Heloise pirouetting through the midst of a melee, blades flashing.
Sinjan's ebon blade sliding from its scabbard.

A scream…

Sabbathiel folded double, clutching the side of her head. She emitted a low moan.

'Astor?' Mandreth was at her side, a reassuring hand on her shoulder. They'd rendezvoused shortly after leaving the dead astropath and were now making their way back to the safe house. 'More visions?'

She shrugged him off, fighting to regain her composure. 'Sinjan. He's found us.'

Mandreth stiffened beside her, his hand straying to the hilt of his weapon. 'Where?' His eyes searched the narrow alley openings, dark and foreboding like the starved mouths of the dead. But there was nothing amongst those foetid streets but imagined phantoms.

'Not here. The safe house.'

'How?'

Sabbathiel wiped at a bead of sweat that was trickling down her temple. 'It must have been Mol. She probably set people on our trail when we left the Gallowspire. Either that, or the damned Assassin. Either way, they're all working for Sinjan.'

Mandreth nodded, drew them all to a stop. The heavens had opened again, down here in the foul microclimate of this lowliest of undercities, and the dirty rain was streaming down their faces, staining their clothes. 'Do we risk it?'

Sabbathiel glanced across at him. 'What choice do we have? Our people…'

Mandreth worked his jaw. 'You've seen them in action. They can look after themselves. It's *you* he's after, not them.'

'Nevertheless.'

'You'd really offer yourself up to him on a platter?'

'He was the one who lost an arm the last time we met,' she reminded Mandreth. 'I'd very much like to take the other one, along with his head.' She was surprised at the bitterness in her own voice. She'd always deemed the pursuit of vengeance to be unbecoming of an inquisitor of her station. But then, this business with Sinjan was more than mere payback for the trouble he'd caused her. He'd become an obstacle to her investigation. One that needed removing, and in short order. That she might also glean some vague sense of satisfaction in the process was… *incidental.*

Or is that just what I tell myself to sleep better at night?

'All the same, ma'am,' said Bledheim, shifting his weight from foot to foot as if impatient to get out of the downpour, 'perhaps caution *is* advisable. There's the Assassin to consider…'

Aethesia hefted her sword as if in answer.

Sabbathiel laughed. *'Caution?* We're hardly inconspicuous, strolling through the slums with a golden-armoured Sister of Silence in tow. We're well beyond caution now, Bledheim.' She wiped rainwater from her eyes with the back of her hand. 'We carry on. We get our people, and we get the Throne out of there.'

Bledheim's face paled. He wouldn't meet her eye.

'What is it, interrogator? Spit it out.'

'It's…' Bledheim seemed to stumble over his words, before finally changing his mind, drawing his robes tighter around his shoulders to stave off the rain. 'It's nothing, ma'am. I'm merely concerned for your safety.'

She eyed him for a moment longer, then nodded.

Not in front of the others, eh? No matter. It'll keep. But I mark your concern, interrogator. I mark it well.

She turned and resumed walking, Fitch a few yards ahead of her, his scanners winking as he probed the shadows for any lurking threat.

The others fell in behind her. Their silence spoke volumes.

We are all of us caught in this web of death and deceit, and none

of us knows which way to turn next. And so, we do the only thing
that we can: we walk on, willing ourselves to survive another day.

Mandreth had apprised her of his and Bledheim's encounter
with Father Rand at the Cathedral of Saint Euphrades. While
he'd been unable to put his finger on anything specific, it was
clear he hadn't taken to the priest, and the revelation that Lord
Rasmuth had been in attendance at Quintus Bleeth's funeral
was a sure indicator that whatever Heldren had uncovered here
on Hulth involved the very highest levels of governance and
society. Sabbathiel had no doubt that the priest was in on it too.

The Navigator. The governor. The priest.

What am I not seeing?

The significance of the golden eagles still troubled her, for a
start. She hadn't yet given voice to her fears, but the sight of that
scrawled armoured figure on the wall, coupled with the dying
birds in her vision, had conjured forth images of gold-clad
warriors with glittering plumed helms; towering, inhuman
things that were said to be cast in the very image of the Emperor
Himself. His elite bodyguard. The Adeptus Custodes.

If they are a part of this, we are all doomed.

The thought passed through her like a bolt of electricity.

The Adeptus Custodes.

Here…

She gasped, her hands straying unconsciously to clutch at her
stomach, images of her past life stuttering before her like strobing lights, obscuring her vision until she was back there, on that
ancient battle-barge, standing in the shadow of giants while the
enemy closed in from all sides.

'That which *begets* heresy might *see* only heresy.' Leofric's voice
rang with judgement, with pride, with such damned *arrogance*.

Who was he to judge *her*?

Was she not a tool of the Emperor's will?

Had she not the presence of mind, the *strength,* to control the thing in her vault? To wield the daemonhost as a weapon against the enemies of the Imperium? To understand the poison that ran through its veins, to use that same poison against it and its foul brethren? She had bound the accursed thing into flesh and blood. She had learned its true name.

Sarasti.

The spawn of the warp itself.

'You sought the counsel of daemons?' The words were like weapons, intended to sting, to flense the very flesh from her bones. But in them, she heard only wilful ignorance. The Grey Knight could not possibly understand, too blinded was he by learned truths and obfuscation. Too unwilling to accept the failings of his kind.

Under duress, Sarasti had led her to the truth.

That the Adeptus Astartes were lost to the Emperor's light.

Sabbathiel willed Leofric to understand. 'I sought the *truth.* Through whatever means proved necessary. We must root out the heresy that festers in the heart of the Imperium. We must cleanse it with *fire.* There can be no exception.'

But he was as blind as the rest of them.

She knew exactly what was coming. What that stupid bastard was about to do. And there was nothing at all she could do to stop him.

The Grey Knight raised his arm. 'Now, finally, you speak the truth.'

His storm bolter barked.

Sabbathiel's body jerked as the explosive round tore through her.

The blackness closed in.

'Sabbathiel?'

The voice cut through the darkness, like a chink of light.

She opened her eyes, realised she was still standing in the rain.

In the trench.

On Hulth.

'Is everything…?' A pause. 'Are you well?' There was a note of genuine concern in Mandreth's voice. She felt his hand on her upper arm.

Sabbathiel allowed the rain to play over her face for a few seconds, washing away the last vestiges of the memory. 'I'm well.'

'Another bad dream?'

She sighed, shook herself, brushed his hand away. 'Something like that.'

What if all of this is just a bad dream? What if I'm still back there, tumbling through the warp, a gaping hole in my stomach? What if none of this is real at all?

She glanced round, saw Aethesia watching her, her expression unreadable behind her mask.

What if Leofric was right? What if I'm not worthy?

What then?

She let the raindrops trickle down her cheeks like tears, and then, nodding her thanks to Mandreth, she walked on.

'Fitch.'

Sabbathiel beckoned the servo-skull forward with a wave of her hand.

From across the narrow street, it was obvious they were too late. Sinjan had deployed with overwhelming force, and the devastation was clear to see. The door was gone, leaving a ragged, burnt hole where it had once hung, and there were bloodstains on the plascrete out in the street, mingling with the filthy rainwater like swirling oil. There were no signs of movement from within.

Sabbathiel knew that there was every chance the others were

dead, and that Sinjan was waiting for them inside, ready to spring his trap.

That would be his second mistake.

The first was killing her people.

The servo-skull swept low, mechadendrites testing the air, before dipping up through the open doorway and disappearing inside.

Mandreth glanced over. 'Whatever happened here, he'll pay.'

Sabbathiel gave a curt nod. She studied the doorway.

Nothing.

'Fitch?'

The vox-link crackled, bursting to life in a sudden hiss of static. '...*what the freck is that thing doing? Get it away from me, tech-priest. Now.*'

Sabbathiel shot Bledheim a look. He was grinning. She pushed herself away from the wall and started walking towards the safe house, her fingers wrapped tightly around the hilt of her unsheathed sword.

'Fitch?'

The servo-skull reappeared in the doorway, hovering at around head height. 'The premises are secure, mistress.'

Thank the Throne.

'And the others?'

Fitch seemed to pause. 'Perhaps it's best you see for yourself.'

Sabbathiel frowned as she stepped through the burned-out portal...

...and into what appeared to be some sort of grisly charnel house. There were bodies everywhere: on the ground; slumped against the walls; one still standing in the corner, propped where its armour had snagged on some old, decorative protrusion. All of them – *almost* all of them, Sabbathiel corrected herself – were wearing the same enforcers' uniforms as those who had attacked them at the mausoleum. At least one of them, just inside the door, was dressed in shiny black carapace armour that set it apart from the rest.

The air reeked of spilled blood and piss. Sabbathiel could taste it on her tongue – the familiar, depressing stink of the abandoned battlefield.

There was no sign of Sinjan.

Metik crouched in the midst of this bloody apocalypse, carrying out what appeared to be an invasive medical procedure on Brondel, who was squirming on his back with his shirt and armour removed, the left side of his chest sliced open and several of the machine man's manipulator mandibles buried deep inside. The squat, evidently in intense pain, seemed determined not to admit to such, grinding his teeth and uttering ridiculous curses.

'Throne dammit, tech-priest, but your hands are *cold*.'

On the other side of the room, an entirely different scene was playing out.

Nol was sitting against the wall, his knees drawn up, cradling what appeared to be the limp body of Heloise in his massive arms. He was rocking her gently from side to side like an infant, but her head was lolling awfully with every motion, and her eyes, still open, were fixed and unresponsive.

'Nol.'

Sabbathiel stepped to one side to allow Mandreth space. He barely seemed to notice the heaped corpses, the slick puddles of blood and viscera, as he walked calmly over to Nol's side and dropped to his knees beside the ogryn.

He put his hand on Nol's shoulder. 'It's all right, Nol. I'm here.'

'The pale man stabbed her,' said Nol, his voice wavering. 'Right through the middle. And then she wasn't moving any more. She just lay there, on the ground. But she didn't look peaceful. She was supposed to look peaceful.'

Mandreth reached over and, with finger and thumb, delicately closed Heloise's eyes. 'There, Nol. She's peaceful now, see? It worked. All that rocking – you made her peaceful again. She can rest now.'

Nol turned to look at Mandreth, fixing the inquisitor with those big, staring eyes. 'I wanted to break him, for what he did. I wanted to snap him in half, but he stabbed me in the hand and got away.' The ogryn held up his left hand to show the gaping wound in his palm.

'You did well, Nol. You all did.' Mandreth stood. He held out his arms. 'Now, give me Heloise and I'll take her away from all of this mess.'

Nol nodded, and then, with a forlorn look on his face, he scooped up the body from his lap, lifting the dead woman as if she were as light as air. Mandreth took her in his arms and carried her off towards one of the adjoining chambers.

'The little guy was hurt too,' said Nol.

'I'm not. Frecking. Little,' spat Brondel from across the room. 'And I wasn't hurt. Just took a shot to the chest, is all. A few broken ribs.'

'And a collapsed lung,' added Metik. 'You almost drowned.'

'Again!' said Brondel. 'I *hate* water.'

'It was not water–' started Metik, but Brondel had already passed out.

'Will he live?' asked Sabbathiel.

'Unfortunately,' confirmed Metik. 'His chances of survival are eighty-nine point three eight per cent. I am fusing his broken ribs now. He may suffer a little residual pain, perhaps, but there will be no lasting damage.'

She turned to wave Bledheim towards the ogryn. 'The techpriest is busy. See to his hand.'

'But I'm not skilled–'

'Just do it,' said Sabbathiel, irritably. She glanced around, saw Aethesia stooped over the body of the soldier in the black carapace armour. She crossed to join her.

The man's corpse was now headless. Fragments of what was left of the errant head were spread across the plascrete in several directions, and the severed stump looked ragged and raw, with flaps of skin still attached where the head had been torn off.

Nol.

Aethesia was holding the dead man's right wrist, where a black marking marred the otherwise smooth, olive-hued flesh. The null maiden held it up so Sabbathiel could see.

It was a tattoo of familiar design: two planets in orbit around one another, linked by a bolt of lightning.

'Metik – this one. Who was he?'

The tech-priest glanced up briefly from his ministrations on the squat. 'He was with Atticus Sinjan. One would presume a member of his personal guard.'

His personal guard.

Sabbathiel sighed.

The Navigator. The governor. The priest… and the inquisitor.

Sounds like the start of a damn joke.

Of course Sinjan was in on it. Whatever *it* was. It made a terrible kind of sense. That had to be why they'd killed Heldren, because he was getting too close to the truth. And it explained why Sinjan was so intent on stopping Sabbathiel from continuing Heldren's investigation.

This wasn't about her at all. It wasn't about the conclave's lack of trust in her, or her need to prove herself innocent of Heldren's murder. It never had been. She'd simply been in the wrong place at the wrong time.

I was convenient. I got in the way.

And now I know too much.

Were the rest of the Palmarian Conclave involved, too? She had to assume so, at least for now.

What in the Emperor's name had she woken to? A galaxy rent apart, and a conspiracy in her own ranks. But to what end? She still didn't know what any of them were actually up to, what they hoped to achieve. Nor was she any closer to understanding what had happened to the body of Quintus Bleeth, and what – if anything – had been smuggled onto Hulth through his tomb.

One thing, though, was eminently clear: the conspirators were prepared to kill to keep her, and anyone else, from finding out. Which only served to make her more determined than ever to expose every single one of the corrupt bastards.

She rocked back on her haunches. The dying astropath's words were swirling around inside her skull like an echo chamber, growing louder and more urgent with each iteration.

'Find him. Find the one who guides. Find him soon.'

She looked up to see Mandreth was standing behind her, looking down at the corpse over her shoulder. His expression was grim.

Sabbathiel met his gaze. 'We have work to do,' she said.

CHAPTER TWENTY-FIVE

'And the Emperor, He shall live again.'
– Polytheminus the Last, excerpted from
The Shriven King Awakens

Bledheim was glad to be out of there, away from all those sight-less, staring corpses. There was something disconcerting about a place like that, where sudden, extreme violence had occurred – an after echo of all that had transpired, a residue hanging in the air, an unvoiced scream waiting to be heard. Like the universe had disowned the place, or a wound had been opened that could never be healed.

He knew the sensation well enough. He wished he didn't.

I carry that silent scream within me, wherever I go.

One day, I shall have to let it out.

They were on their way back to the Bleeth estate to rendez-vous with Silq and Mercy, who had been tasked with keeping watch on the place while... well, while everything else had been going on.

Brondel was back on his feet and complaining bitterly, despite the analgesics Metik had pumped into him while he'd been unconscious. His ribs had been fused, his lung reinflated, and, as far as Sabbathiel and everyone else was concerned, he was fit and ready for duty. The issue causing him the most consternation, however, seemed to be that no one had bothered bashing his armour back into shape – it still carried a large dent in the chestplate where he'd taken the hit – and he was insisting that it was unconscionable for a squat to be seen in public wearing such shoddy artifice.

'For freck's sake. I'd rather you'd left me to die than drag me out here wearing *this.*'

Bledheim had to admit, he was glad the squat had survived. He'd hardly had a chance to get to know Heloise, and if he was honest with himself, he'd found her a rather intimidating presence – but the squat's constant blathering was the only thing preventing the mood amongst them descending into something maudlin.

Bledheim wondered if Brondel knew exactly what he was doing – giving them all something else to think about. Giving *himself* something else to think about, too. He'd hardly imagined the squat to be the most compassionate amongst their small band... but all that bluster had to be covering something, didn't it? And besides, what did *he* know? He was a torturer, after all. He probably wouldn't recognise compassion if it stepped up and bashed him in the face.

Nearby, Nol walked along silently, his head hanging, that bright, childish glee now dissipated.

Reality is a harsh mistress indeed.

Mandreth seemed to have taken the woman's death more in

his stride, although his expression remained sombre. Here was
a man who had seen death before, who had faced it down and
turned the other cheek; who had been forced to live with the
consequences of his actions. Like Sabbathiel, he was blessed –
or, perhaps, cursed – with a steely, single-minded resolve. Loss
was just a simple fact of life.

In some ways, Bledheim admired that ability to compart-
mentalise, to suffocate one's own humanity, to free oneself of
pain. On the other hand, he'd seen the logical end point of that
train of thinking – the cold, calculating machine that a person
could become if they sought to excise all emotion.

At what point did a person stop being human?

Bledheim studied Metik's back as they walked through the
outskirts of the hivesprawl, as if expecting to see some outward
sign of what the implacable machine man was thinking, some
clue as to his intentions.

A cuckoo in the nest.

Could it really be that the tech-priest had betrayed them? It
was certainly possible – he could have given away their position during any one of his jaunts around the city in search
of supplies, or else sent his little pet to do it for him. Yet to
what end? If that were the case, why had Sinjan attacked when
Sabbathiel was absent? And why would Metik help defend the
safe house rather than take the opportunity to flee?

Brondel, while semi-delirious from the drugs, had praised
Metik's performance during the fight, even if he'd done nothing
but curse the tech-priest for shoddy medical work since. But
that was the thing, wasn't it – that Metik's endeavours had been
far from shoddy. He'd saved lives on a number of occasions
already, including Sabbathiel's as well as the squat's. It seemed
unlikely, then, that he was in league with Sinjan. And since
Sinjan was clearly working with the others involved in the Bleeth

conspiracy, that suggested the tech-priest was not involved with any of them, either.

What, then, was Metik's game?

He'd almost blurted out his concerns to Sabbathiel earlier, but had stopped himself, suddenly uncertain. It wouldn't pay to sow seeds of distrust if he was wrong. To leave her doubting her own team. Not until he was sure. And so, he'd studiously avoided her since they'd returned to the safe house, leaving her no opportunity to quiz him further. That wouldn't last, of course, and he supposed when the time came, he would have to tell her about the tarot reading, if not the specifics of his suspicions.

You, Sabbathiel, are the Queen of Ruin, mistress of all you survey.

Meanwhile, he would have to wait. And watch.

'What's this? Come to check up on us, ma'am?'

Silq shifted from her vantage point on the spur of a ruined building, shuffling down until it was safe to drop to ground level. She did so, her boots crunching amongst loose scree and shards of broken glass. Mercy, meanwhile, remained where she was, lying flat on an outcropping of shattered roof, watching the grounds of the massive house beyond the high wall. She didn't even glance down to acknowledge their approach.

The ruined building, Bledheim gathered, was one of a series of such former Administratum structures that had been purchased by the Bleeths back when their estate was first being planned – not for the eyesore, otherwise they would have been torn down long ago, but merely because the Bleeths of the time couldn't bear the thought of other people living and working so close to them. This, despite the fact that there was at least half a mile between the ruins and the big house. Not to mention the imposing wall that encircled the estate.

You should try growing up in the alleyways of a hivesprawl. That'll teach you to really *fear your neighbours.*

Now, the structures were overgrown and long abandoned, festooned with rodent droppings and virulent vine-like weeds, which had forced their way through cracks in the stone floors as if the natural world were extending fingers through the earth, attempting to reclaim the ruins as their own, to drag them back into the soft loam.

Nothing in this dark, entropic universe wants us to survive. Not even the weeds. In the end, we're all just fertiliser anyway.

Look at Heloise.

While the others of their motley gang took up positions around the edges of the ruins – a precaution that didn't go unnoticed by Silq – the woman stood before Sabbathiel and Mandreth, a questioning look in her eyes. Bledheim lowered himself to sit on a large hunk of rock where the foot of a staircase had once been.

'Your findings?' asked Sabbathiel, ignoring the jocular tone of Silq's earlier question.

'It's been quiet,' said Silq. 'A few servants coming and going, as you'd expect, but the Bleeths haven't left the house once. Just one visitor.'

'Go on,' urged Sabbathiel.

Silq shrugged. 'A woman, wearing plain grey robes. Dark hair tied up in some kind of fancy knot. She had pale skin and a bionic eye. Looked like an administrator.'

'Carrying a book under her arm?' asked Mandreth.

Silq frowned. 'How did you know that?'

Sabbathiel and Mandreth locked eyes. 'Chandra Mol.'

'That confirms it,' said Sabbathiel. 'Whatever's going on with these Bleeths, Rasmuth is tied up in it, too.'

'If he's even still alive,' said Mandreth.

'You think…?'

'I don't know what to think. But that Mol woman, she was certainly keen to prevent us from seeing him, wasn't she? All that stuff about him being unwell.'

'And then the Assassin. I'd thought it must have been a coincidence that Sinjan's agents had tracked us through the Gallowspire, but now I find myself wondering whether the Assassin was lying in wait all along. Like they knew we'd turn up at Rasmuth's place sooner or later if we followed the trail of crumbs.'

'A trap.'

Sabbathiel nodded. 'I'm beginning to think this whole thing is a trap. One that's closing in around us with every passing moment.'

With bloody teeth and jaws.

'They may have people watching the house,' said Mandreth. 'We should tread very carefully indeed.'

Sabbathiel nodded. 'Perhaps. But the Bleeths have their personal guards. Their arrogance is boundless. They probably think they're impervious behind those grand walls. Untouchable.'

Bledheim shifted, tapping his injector-fingers against his knee in a nervous rhythm.

The wolves are circling, and there are still too many players, too much we don't understand. We don't know which way to turn.

'We need to find the body,' he said. 'Quintus Bleeth's corpse. Find that, and we can at least start to work out why in the Emperor's name someone took it in the first place, and what transpired in that tomb.'

Sabbathiel peered at him. 'Why do you think we're here, Bledheim? This all started with the Bleeths. It'll end with them, too.'

'Then we're going in? With force?' said Silq.

'Not yet,' replied Sabbathiel. 'Not until we have a few more answers.'

'Then why are you here?' Silq glanced around to take in Nol, Brondel, Metik and Aethesia.

'The safe house,' said Sabbathiel. 'It's not so safe any more.'

'And Hel–'

'Dead,' cut in Mandreth.

Silq swallowed, nodded. 'So, more surveillance?'

'In a manner of speaking,' said Sabbathiel. 'Metik?'

'I'd be delighted, inquisitor,' came the dry, mechanical response.

Nimbik scuttled through the shadowy recesses of the house, clinging to the moulded architrave that hugged the ceilings. The transmitted picts from its bionic eye were grainy and punctuated with bursts of fizzing static, but they seemed to resolve and stabilise every time the thing was forced to remain still for more than a few seconds. Which was often, given the sheer amount of serving staff milling about the place.

So far, it had managed to remain unseen and unhindered.

Bledheim had never seen Metik parted from the thing by more than a few yards, and he had to admit, the control the tech-priest continued to assert over it was impressive. Bledheim still wasn't sure what Nimbik actually was – a servo-skull, a slave unit or something else entirely. Probably something heretical, knowing the sort of company Sabbathiel was wont to keep.

Metik was displaying the relayed images through a hololith projected from his upturned palm, and Sabbathiel, Mandreth and the others had gathered around him in a loose semicircle to follow Nimbik's progress – all save Nol and Aethesia, who were keeping watch for any signs of trouble. And Brondel, who was preparing some rations over a small campfire, seemingly indifferent to whatever was going on inside the house. The smell of roasting meat was causing Bledheim's stomach to growl.

He watched Aethesia pacing the perimeter of the ruins, her

sword drawn and held in readiness at her hip. He was glad to put a bit of distance between them – the low-level nausea her presence inspired wasn't helping his anxiety. He doubted there'd be any trouble out here, this far from the Gallowspire and the surrounding hivesprawl, although that damned Assassin was still lurking somewhere, so he supposed it paid to remain vigilant. He could feel it in his waters – they hadn't seen the last of her yet. Or Sinjan.

More's the pity.

Nimbik had passed into another of the grand chambers inside the house, only to find it empty of Bleeths.

'Try the glasshouse at the rear of the building,' said Sabbathiel. 'The botanical garden.'

Metik cocked his head to one side, as if contemplating her words. The image shifted and blurred as the creature – Bledheim was struggling to see it as anything but – scuttled off through the doorway and back up onto the ceiling. The image flipped disconcertingly, and Bledheim felt a sudden rush of vertigo. He looked away again.

'Through there,' said Mandreth. 'And then left and left again.'

A burst of static.

The image went dead.

For a moment, Bledheim wondered if Nimbik had been discovered and destroyed by one of the security personnel...

...and then the feed winked back on.

There was a collective exhalation of relief from those watching. And a grunt from Brondel, as he sniffed the dripping meat at the end of his skewer and took a healthy bite out of it, smearing his beard with grease. Suddenly, Bledheim wasn't feeling quite so hungry as before.

Nimbik hurried along a series of other passageways, following Mandreth's instructions, and then, as it slowed by the lip of an open doorway, Bledheim caught sight of a blurred image of huge, leafy fronds. The botanical garden.

'In there,' said Sabbathiel. 'And slowly.'

Nimbik crawled forward, coming up around the inside of the door frame, before hopping onto the curved branch of a tree, which it scuttled along until it was able to settle itself into a small nest amongst a bushel of leaves and flowers.

A sudden, high-pitched whine, and then the distant sound of voices, almost lost beneath the hiss of static. Bledheim strained to hear.

'...Nemedia... pass me that...'

'That's Jolas,' said Sabbathiel. 'See if you can locate him.'

The pict-feed shifted jarringly as Nimbik scanned the interior of the glasshouse. After a moment it settled again, and a pixelated image of Jolas Bleeth began to resolve. He was stooping over a raised planting bed, apparently tending to his beloved plants. As Bledheim watched, Nemedia Bleeth walked into view, standing over Jolas, holding out a small implement or tool.

Jolas looked round and took it from her. His voice crackled over the link. 'My thanks.'

'Hmm.' Nemedia remained standing there, one hand on her hip, as Jolas turned his attention back to the plants, worrying at the soil with the implement now in his hand. They remained like that for a moment, him continuing to work at the soil, her standing watching, evidentially unhappy about something.

'Jolas.'

'What's the matter now?' he snapped impatiently.

'Nothing. It's just...' She shook her head, sighed. 'Oh, it doesn't matter.'

'Let me guess.' The comment was laden with spite. Whatever this was about, it was clearly a long-running, bitter argument between them.

'All right, yes. I was thinking about poor Quintus.'

'Quintus. Always bloody Quintus. One would think you'd rather have been wedded to him.'

'Don't be ridiculous, Jolas. But don't you forget, either – Quintus is family.'

Sabbathiel glanced up. She caught Bledheim's eye. He'd heard it too – the use of tense. *Is*, rather than *was*.

A slip of the tongue?

Sabbathiel had already turned back to the hololith.

'Quintus is gone, Nemedia.'

'But that's just it, isn't it? He hasn't gone *anywhere*. He deserves better than this, Jolas.'

Jolas stood, turned from his plants to face her. 'Look, you're upsetting yourself. You know there's nothing we can do. When all of this is over, we'll welcome him back with open arms. But until then…' He crossed to her, took her in his arms. They stood for a moment, locked in an embrace.

Sabbathiel straightened. She was looking straight at Bledheim. He met her gaze as the full implication of the overheard conversation began to sink in.

So, we're not looking for a body after all.

He exhaled slowly, the air whistling through his teeth.

That changes everything.

Quintus Bleeth is alive.

PART THREE

SALVATION

CHAPTER TWENTY-SIX

'When all other options have been eliminated, sometimes even a lie might come to be accepted as the unassailable truth.'

– Prefect Kamil Khara, *On the Wisdom of Lies, Vol. IX*

'Alive? Quintus Bleeth is *alive?*'

Mercy was peering at the grainy image on the hololith as if it might yet reveal deeper truths. She'd scrunched up her eyes, causing the skin to wrinkle on the bridge of her nose, and she was bending forward at the waist, her face a couple of inches from the projection. She looked puzzled, lost. It was the most human Sabbathiel had ever seen the woman look.

There's hope for me yet, then.

Sabbathiel, too, was having difficulty processing the revelation. She was furious with herself for discounting the possibility early on in her investigation – she'd simply taken it as read that no one would go to the extreme length of erecting a wholly unnecessary tomb and faking their own death, simply to smuggle off-world contraband onto a backwater hive world.

Those hundred years in the warp have made me slow.

Metik closed his fist and the pict-feed winked out of existence. 'So it would seem.'

'But we went to his tomb,' refuted Mercy, her frown deepening.

'And saw no sign of his body,' added Mandreth.

Sabbathiel ground her teeth in frustration. The implications continued to unravel in her mind. 'All this time, we've been labouring under the assumption we were searching for a corpse,' she said. 'When it now seems, the tomb was just another part of the Bleeths' illicit smuggling operation.'

'A convenient place to store whatever it was they were bringing in from off-world,' said Silq.

Brondel, still gnawing on a hunk of meat, turned his head and hawked up a gobbet of phlegm. Then returned to his meal.

Bledheim rose from his seat on the broken steps. 'Why bother with the tomb in the first place?'

Sabbathiel studied him for a moment. It was a damn good question. 'Because it's not the sort of place people are going to go looking,' she offered.

'Yes. But it's more than that,' said Bledheim. 'The size of the Bleeths' operation in this sector – they could have hidden their contraband anywhere. Plus, it's likely they have the governor in their back pocket, too, from what we already know about their relationship. They could have used an out-of-the-way warehouse or storage silo, even this very estate, all without much fear of discovery. But instead, they chose a tomb as their hiding place, even, it seems, going so far as to pretend to the world that Quintus was dead. What does that tell you?'

'That they're frecking idiots,' said Brondel, between bites.

Mandreth was frowning. 'That whatever it was they were hiding was either too risky to leave hanging around, or…'

'Or it *was* a body,' finished Sabbathiel. 'Just not Quintus.'

Bledheim shrugged. 'It seems a logical conclusion. Where better to hide a body but in a tomb? And yes, Inquisitor Mandreth – it would also imply that they feared the repercussions of discovery, perhaps beyond even the influence of Lord Rasmuth or the local enforcers.'

Sabbathiel nodded. It did seem to make a twisted kind of sense. She had to admit, she was impressed with Bledheim's insight.

'But the tomb was empty,' said Mercy. 'There *was* no body.'

'Perhaps they'd already moved it on to its final destination,' said Silq. 'Once Quintus' supposed funeral had taken place and the way was clear for them to operate without drawing attention.'

'Then we're *still* looking for a body,' said Bledheim. 'As well as another Bleeth.'

'But *whose* body?' asked Silq. 'And what possible use could they have for a corpse, that they'd go to such lengths to procure it off-world and smuggle it back here to Hulth? There are plenty enough corpses here already. Or fresh, living bodies if it came to it. Why go to such extreme lengths?'

'That is rather the question,' said Bledheim.

Mandreth sighed. 'This is all supposition. I admit there's a certain logic to it, but as it stands it's just a story that fits our frustratingly partial view of the facts. We cannot confirm any of it.'

'That's not entirely true.' Sabbathiel looked at each of them in turn, her eyes finally settling on Mandreth. 'I think it's time Jolas and Nemedia Bleeth answered a few more of our questions, don't you?'

Behind her, Brondel emitted a loud, gaseous burp.

* * *

This time, the guards on the front entrance were a lot less obstructive – they parted without question at the sight of the two inquisitors marching up the gravelled path, weapons drawn, a mismatched army of acolytes trailing in their wake.

They can probably see which way the wind is blowing.

Either that, or they've seen the look on my face.

'Inquisitors,' murmured one of the guards, and a quick glance confirmed for Sabbathiel it was the same woman they'd spoken with during their previous visit. She nodded in nervous greeting when she saw Sabbathiel looking at her, then dipped her gaze to the floor. 'You'll find them in the botanical garden.'

'I know.'

Sabbathiel led the way under the portico, across the hallway and into the bowels of the house. Servants scattered in her path. The guards made no move to follow.

Behind her, Nol exclaimed loudly as he whacked his head against a low-hanging chandelier, causing glass shards to spill across the stone floor like frozen rain.

'You frecking oaf.'

'Be silent, little one.'

'Who are you calling *little…?*'

Sabbathiel ignored them, mirroring the route taken by Nimbik through the winding corridors, until, moments later, she stormed into the glasshouse, beads of sweat prickling her brow at the sudden backwash of warm air. The atmosphere was as thick and cloying as before.

Mandreth fell in beside her as she made a beeline straight for the astonished form of Jolas Bleeth. She sensed movement on her left and half turned towards it, raising her blade, but it was only Nimbik scurrying down the branch of a tree to rejoin its master. She turned back to the Navigators.

Jolas was still standing before Nemedia as if the conversation

Sabbathiel had observed had continued after the pict-link was cut, and now, upon setting eyes on Sabbathiel – and in particular the crackling power sword she was brandishing in her right hand – his mouth fell agape, and he took an involuntary step back, before seeming to remember himself. He stiffened, standing tall, taking a deep, rasping breath. He was unable to hide the trembling in his hands, however, clearly intimidated.

Good.

'What is the meaning of this intrusion?' he said, affecting an air of grievance. He gave a wet cough into his fist.

Nemedia had turned now, and she was scowling at Sabbathiel with evident distaste.

Bledheim and the others had taken up position just inside the door, spreading out to form a wall of bristling weapons that would stifle any attempted escape before either of the Bleeths could even consider it. All except Aethesia, who had remained outside in order to maintain her ever-constant vigil for the Assassin.

'I have some more questions for you,' said Sabbathiel, 'and this time, I suggest you answer truthfully.'

Nemedia's glare deepened. 'How dare you! How dare you storm in here with your weapons drawn and threaten us in our own home? How dare you accuse us of *lying?*'

Sabbathiel had expected this, that deep-seated streak of arrogance that inevitably manifested in the rich and powerful when they came under siege. This pathetic self-aggrandisement that allowed the Bleeths to raise themselves up above others, to believe themselves not only better, but excused from the same laws and judgement as everyone else.

Not today, you Throne-damned hypocrite.

'I dare, because I stand before you with the full authority of the Emperor's Inquisition, and because *I know you have lied to me.'*

For a moment, Nemedia looked as if she were about to

respond. Her mouth opened as if to say something, but then her shoulders sagged resignedly, and she promptly closed it again. She stood there, seething, her gaze boring holes in Sabbathiel. Jolas stepped forward, placed a hand upon her shoulder, but she flinched away, drawing her arms tightly around herself as if attempting to withdraw from the world.

'What my wife means to say,' said Jolas, 'is that we have cooperated fully with your investigation, inquisitors. We welcomed you into our home and disclosed confidential information about our family. We answered all of your questions.'

'With falsehoods and lies,' said Mandreth, his voice a low growl. Sabbathiel noted his fingers tightening around the hilt of his own sword, his knuckles turning white as he fought to contain his frustration.

'How so?' demanded Jolas defensively. 'We were open about what became of poor brother Quintus. We know nothing more about the disappearance of his body.'

'Because you know that he's actually still alive,' said Sabbathiel. The tip of her sword hovered before her, as if in warning. Jolas took another unconscious step back.

'*Alive?* You're… you're telling us that Quintus is still *alive?*'

'I'd advise you to think very carefully about your next words,' said Mandreth, his eyes tracking Jolas. 'We only require one of you alive enough to talk.' He ran his finger along the line of his jaw. 'And Interrogator Bledheim would be only too happy to ensure we get the answers we require.'

Jolas' eyes flicked to Nemedia, who remained standing to one side, withdrawn, her arms still wrapped around herself. He swallowed, looked back at Mandreth. 'But–'

'They *know*, Jolas.' Nemedia's voice was like ice; sharp and unemotive. 'There's no point getting yourself killed. We can't protect him now.'

Jolas stuttered something incomprehensible, and then all objection seemed to leave his body with a heaving sigh. He stumbled, then lowered himself slowly to sit upon the edge of one of his flowerbeds.

A sudden burst of activity overhead caused her to start, but it was nothing but a startled bird, taking wing from one of the treetops nearby. Sabbathiel slowly lowered the tip of her sword. The tension in the room seemed to ease fractionally.

Jolas was watching them, unsure what to do or say next. Nemedia, though, was slowly unfurling her arms. She straightened, raised her head, as if attempting to recapture some of her familiar, haughty poise. 'You're right, of course. Quintus is alive. But then you know that already.'

'Where?'

Nemedia shrugged. 'The last we knew, the enforcers were holding him at their central command post in the Gallowspire, mid-hive.'

'On whose authority?' asked Sabbathiel.

I know what you're going to say...

'Lord Atticus Sinjan's. For his protection.'

'Protection? From whom?'

Nemedia sneered. 'From people like *you.*'

Sabbathiel felt a flare of anger erupting in her chest. 'I think you'd better start at the beginning,' she spat. 'Why did you fake Quintus' death in the first place?'

'No, no. It wasn't like tha–'

'*We* didn't do anything of the sort,' said Nemedia, cutting her husband off. 'As we said before, this was all Quintus' idea. He was the one who got involved with...' She trailed off, shrugged.

'With *what?*' pressed Mandreth.

'With Sinjan. Don't you understand? Whatever Quintus was up to, he was doing it on the orders of the Inquisition.' Nemedia clicked her tongue against the roof of her mouth. 'Or perhaps you're simply not high-ranking enough to have been briefed?'

Sabbathiel forced herself to take a deep breath. 'I answer to no one but the Emperor,' she said. 'Atticus Sinjan represents only himself.'

And perhaps the rest of my old conclave… but that's another matter entirely.

Nemedia shrugged. 'So, the two of you don't get along. No wonder he hasn't told you about his little schemes.' The woman had found her backbone again now; the sarcasm dripped from her tongue like poison.

Sabbathiel decided to cut to the chase. 'Whose body was placed inside that tomb?'

Nemedia shook her head, glanced at Jolas. 'That's the thing. We don't know. Quintus said it was better if we didn't. That Lord Sinjan thought it might put us in danger.'

'It already has,' growled Mandreth. Sabbathiel could tell his patience was wearing thin.

'So, it *was* another body. That was the contraband. That's what Quintus brought in from off-world,' she said.

Nemedia flashed her a defiant look. But Jolas nodded. 'As far as we know.' He rubbed his hands across his face. Sabbathiel could see the line of telltale scars between the third and fourth fingers of his left hand – the result of surgery to separate them during childhood. Webbed fingers were a known mutation amongst interbred families such as the Bleeths. 'We were telling you the truth when we said we were following Quintus' wishes,' he went on. He sounded defeated. His voice was a dry rasp. 'We just went along with it. He said it was in the best interests of the House. That Sinjan had given him the opportunity to take part in something that would bring glory to our family for generations.'

And how could you resist?

Sinjan knew how to appeal to these egotists. How to buy their loyalty.

As if you don't already have enough.

'And where's the body now?'

'We've told you – he's still alive.'

'Not Quintus,' said Mandreth. 'The other body. The one that was entombed.'

Nemedia shrugged. 'How should we know? You'd have to ask Quintus. Or Sinjan for that matter, since you're on such good terms.' The point of Sabbathiel's sword rose again, until it was hovering before the woman.

'No, please…' said Jolas, rising to his feet. 'Don't. I beg you.'

Sabbathiel whirled.

Beside her, the oak tree emitted a dry, creaking sound, and then, as Jolas watched in wide-eyed horror, began to topple to the left, its trunk severed cleanly through about three feet from the ground.

'No. No, no, no…'

The tree gave a final, awful groan, and then fell, pitching to Sabbathiel's right, away from the two Navigators. It crashed down across several flowerbeds, sending them, in turn, tumbling towards the ground. Soil, leaves and broken stems spilled across the stone floor.

Then everything was still.

There were tears in Jolas' eyes. 'No… I'm sorry…'

Sabbathiel glanced at Nemedia, saw the hatred in her empty eyes.

He'd rather I'd cut down his wife.

That I didn't is punishment enough.

'Lie to us again, and I shall raze this place to the ground.' She turned her back on the two Navigators and signalled for her acolytes to file out the way they had come.

'What… what are you going to do now?' Jolas croaked pathetically as she made for the door, Mandreth beside her.

'I'm going to have overdue words with your brother,' she said.

CHAPTER TWENTY-SEVEN

*'There is nothing to be gained through subtlety. While the
enemy engages in shadow play and misdirection, we have
already punched a hole through the heart of their defences
and fed their soldiers to the gnashing maw of war.'*

– High Commander Infris Bel, *War Journals, Vol. XII*

The lander banked sharply, and Bledheim felt the contents of
his stomach cavity shift uncomfortably. He put his hand to his
mouth, fearing the worst – but the lander righted itself again a
moment later, and he sighed in relief as the sensation passed.
The nape of his neck was damp with perspiration.

Silq, it seemed, was not the subtlest of pilots. Although,
judging by the satisfied hoots originating from the cockpit,
she certainly seemed to be enjoying herself.

Bledheim leaned forward against the restraining belt and
peered out through the forward viewing port. Ahead of them,

the flank of the Gallowspire loomed large and ominous, almost organic – an accreted city that had grown upwards from the filthy crevasses below, like a flower reaching for the sun. Only, this particular flower was far from beautiful, and twice as deadly.

It was cramped inside the rear of the small lander. The ogryn was sandwiched between Mercy and Brondel, which in itself was a ridiculous sight. His thick neck was craned forward, his head bowed beneath the curved roof of the hold. None of the restraining belts had fitted around his massive shoulders, but he'd seemed content to simply wedge himself into place and hope for the best. For a while after take-off, he'd been intent on cleaning and polishing his ripper gun, but partly because he kept elbowing the angry squat in the face, and partly, Bledheim suspected, because Sabbathiel didn't trust him not to accidently fire it and punch a hole in the hull, she'd told him to put it away. Now he was sulking, chewing on his bottom lip and eyeing Mandreth plaintively as if the man might choose to reverse Sabbathiel's order.

Mandreth himself had been almost silent since they'd taken off. Now, he was leaning back against the bulkhead wearing a faraway expression, focusing on something no one else could see.

Bledheim glanced across at Sabbathiel.

Her ire was up. She was sitting opposite him, her jaw clenched tight, her gaze fixed on the plasteel sheeting behind Bledheim's head.

Just like Mandreth, gazing off into the abyss.

Or perhaps the warp.

Or maybe she was simply preparing herself for battle.

The thought hardly filled Bledheim with glee. After his encounter with the enforcer at the mausoleum, and then seeing the appalling mess they had made of the safe house – not to mention what had become of Heloise, and Brondel – Bledheim would much rather be sitting the whole thing out. After all, his moment to shine would come afterwards, surely, when Quintus Bleeth had been acquired and someone was needed to put him to the question.

He could hardly do that if he was shot up in the preceding recovery mission. Not that Sabbathiel had given him a choice.

He'd resolved to keep his head down. Let the others do what they did best: draw fire and smite the enemy. He could always help with the mopping up when things had calmed down a little and there wasn't so much las-fire zipping around. No, he would find a quiet spot and hole up until it was over. Surely Sabbathiel knew him well enough by now to expect nothing less.

He patted the laspistol in his pocket all the same, just for reassurance.

Beside him, Metik noticed the gesture and cocked his head inquisitively. He clacked his porcelain fingertips together in that ever-annoying rhythm. 'Fear not,' he said, his voice burring gently. 'You are far more likely to be killed during the impact than the ensuing battle.'

'Impact?' Bledheim shot the tech-priest a worried look. 'What do you mean, impact?'

The tech-priest made a grating sound that might have been a chuckle. He looked as if he were about to say more, but then the lander banked again, dipping momentarily lower before circling like a bird caught on an updraught, spiralling upwards and gaining speed and momentum in the process.

Bledheim's stomach lurched again.

Impact… What did he mean, impact?

They'd taken the wedge-shaped shuttle at gunpoint from the transport hub, Sabbathiel and Mandreth flashing their Inquisitorial sigils to requisition the vehicle from the terrified pilot, whose purpose, as far as Bledheim could tell, was to ferry a constant stream of officials, bureaucrats and politicians up and down the flank of the Gallowspire. This was deemed the quickest – not to mention safest – means by which to reach the mid-to-upper levels, where the offices and private dwellings of the city's elite could be found.

It had seemed like a risk, giving away their identities and location just to lay their hands on a lander. What if the pilot alerted the enforcers?

He supposed, in truth, it didn't matter. They'd know soon enough, regardless. And Sabbathiel hadn't left them time to prepare, or attempt to move Quintus Bleeth out of there, either. They were in for a rude awakening.

But what had Metik meant about an *impact*?

The lander suddenly accelerated, forcing Bledheim back against the hard, riveted hull. He groaned and tried to push himself forward, but the ship wasn't slowing, and the forces working against his body were only increasing with each passing moment.

'*Brace yourselves.*' Silq's barked command echoed over the vox.

Bledheim strained to lean forward, just enough that he could see through to the cockpit and the viewports beyond. The flank of the Gallowspire loomed large and ominous before them, growing larger with every passing moment.

We're coming in too fast. We're going to…

Oh…

The lander struck the side of the hive like a bolt fired from a crossbow, its prow shattering plasteel and plascrete as it dived through the wall of the enforcers' command station. The side of the building opened like a broken smile, sucking the lander inside with hungry abandon. Sparks showered, pillars gave way, and half of the ceiling came crashing down atop the hull of the

lander as it slid to a grating stop, all but its still-venting exhaust
ports buried inside the structure.

Bledheim, jarred and shaken, covered in a thin film of dust,
shook his head and felt something warm and damp trickling
into his ear. His skull was ringing, his vision blurred.

He lurched forward, trying to get to his feet, but something
was pulling him back, yanking him down. He fumbled, swat-
ting at thin air, until he realised it was only the seat restraints.
He released the clip and sagged forward.

Around him, the others were getting to their feet, hoisting weapons. Nol, hunched over in the confined space, was
wiping trails of blood from his nose with the back of his
hand. Sabbathiel was barking commands, but Bledheim
couldn't hear them over the shrill ringing in his ears. His
fingers brushed the side of his head, came away stained with
oily red. He'd bashed his head. He winced as pain flowered
above his right temple. He probed the wound gingerly – it
was only a shallow gash.

Slowly Bledheim's senses returned. He could hear voices from
outside the wrecked ship, someone – a man – bellowing orders.
He peered through the pall of dust, narrowing his eyes. The
lander's cockpit had crumpled in the impact, the viewports
splintering away. Silq was dragging herself out of the pilot's
cradle, fishing for her xenos weapon. Beyond that, the command station was a haze of dust and sparks.

He felt a hand clasp his shoulder and turn him roughly
around. Mercy was peering down at him, her expression
beaming. 'That woke you up, didn't it, interrogator?' She was
laughing. Actually laughing, like she was enjoying herself.

He heard Brondel mutter something angrily, and then
Sabbathiel was giving the order to deploy, and they were up
and out, shouldering him out of the way as they surged through

what was left of the cockpit and out into the command centre through the now empty viewports.

Weapons fired, lighting up the dusty space beyond like comets streaking through the void.

Someone screamed.

Bledheim sighed.

Bledheim winced as he clambered out through the twisted remains of the viewport, his palm stinging from several shallow lacerations caused by the remnants of the shattered screen that still clung to the buckled frame.

The air was filled with swirling dust, making it near impossible to discern anything beyond flitting shadows and the hulking outlines of toppled furniture – although the flare of gauss fire several yards away suggested the fighting was already concentrated towards the rear of the mangled space. Las-fire flashed in a flickering storm, each bolt igniting the dust as it zipped through the air, leaving a trail of burning sparks in its wake. Overhead lumen strips were flickering erratically, causing every movement to appear stuttering and jagged.

Bledheim ducked as a shot zipped close by, missing him by a couple of inches, and, panicked, he slid in a heap down the compacted nose of the lander, sprawling awkwardly onto the floor. He hurriedly dragged himself around the edge of the ship, pressing himself against its plasteel hull. He pulled his laspistol from his robes. His hands were shaking. His head was still throbbing, the side of his face damp with blood. His palms were slick with sweat.

Around him, the dust had cleared enough to reveal the catastrophic mess that the lander's impact had caused – the floor had partially given way beneath it, causing the wreck to sag on fractured lintels, threatening to collapse at any moment and send him, and anyone else in the vicinity, plummeting to the level below. Several enforcers had been caught beneath the vessel as it slid into the breach, and now their bodies were trapped there, smeared and broken, limbs detached and scattered like fallen twigs. One such arm was lying by his feet, sheared off just below the shoulder. Two of the fingers had been torn away leaving bloody stumps, but bizarrely, the hand was still clutching the broken lower half of a datapad.

He heard running footsteps and risked a glance. Three enforcers were charging across the room, making a break for where Bledheim presumed there must be an exit on the far side. He raised his pistol, its butt shifting in his clammy grip. He took aim and–

A red cape swirled out of the dust, like an arc of blood following a sweeping sword. Metik's gun barked – once, twice, thrice – and the three enforcers burst as they ran, misting into clouds of red vapour that mingled with the airborne dust. The red cape swept away again, enveloped by hazy smoke.

To Bledheim's left, Nol roared as he thundered into a knot of enforcers, pummelling with his meaty fists. Bones crunched. Men howled. Bledheim watched as the ogryn scooped up one of the limp men by his ankles and swung him in a wide arc, battering several others who were attempting to close on him with power mauls. They fell like bloodied skittles, necks broken, chests crushed, hips shattered. When, a moment later, Nol finally stopped swinging, all he had left in his hands were the dead man's two calves and shins. He was spattered with gore, and he was grinning.

Elsewhere, enforcers were dropping in pockets where they stood, accompanied by bright flashes of searing light and dull, throaty screams. Bledheim watched as another chain of them seemed to ignite, silhouetted by the glare, and realised it had to be Brondel, barrelling amongst the forest of legs, hamstringing them and then letting rip with his plasma pistol as they fell.

He saw Silq drop, hissing in pain as a las-shot burst through her right shoulder. Her xenos rifle skittered away across the tiled floor, and she pushed herself back with the heels of her boots, drawing ragged breath and attempting to clamp the wound with her left hand.

Bledheim chewed his lower lip. He thought about breaking cover, running to help the downed woman, but in truth, he'd only be making a target of himself. He had no means of stopping the bleeding, and while he might have been able to help with the pain, the wound would already have been cauterised by the searing las-shot. Provided she didn't take another hit, she'd survive until Metik could get to her.

He watched Mercy stride forward, her massive blade sweeping back and forth at speed, as if describing an elaborate knot. A female enforcer's head left her shoulders, striking the wall above Silq with a dull thud, before tumbling away into the murk. Another fell, his chest half opened, while a third was speared through the gut, wailing and vomiting blood as Mercy hoisted him into the air on her blade, peering up into his face with a sneer of disgust. This, Bledheim assumed, must have been the one who'd shot Silq.

As he watched, the man writhed in agony, trying to grab for Mercy's face, but she simply flicked her sword and sent him sailing into two of his compatriots, trailing streamers of blood through the speckled air.

The dust was settling now, revealing a scene of utter carnage. Sabbathiel and Aethesia stood back to back, swords flashing, one clad in crimson, the other in gold. Dead enforcers were piled at their feet, and still others came on, only to be cut down in kind. To Bledheim, the two women looked like sword mistresses from some ancient tale: holy warriors from a time long past, delivering righteous vengeance upon the enemies of mankind.

Above Sabbathiel, Fitch flitted in a wide circle, red lights tracing enemy movements in the gloom.

The fighting was beginning to abate. The shouting had given way to the slow moans of the injured and the dying, punctuated by the occasional bark of a weapon or the clang of a power sword.

Laspistol still clutched tightly in his grip, Bledheim edged slowly around the front of the crashed ship. Bodies were strewn everywhere, and the air was thick with the scent of spilled blood and burning flesh. To his left, Mandreth stood eerily still, dust still skirling around his boots. He was holding a laspistol and was calmly shooting uniformed enforcers as they broke cover, dropping each of them with a single shot to the head. His expression was as calm and unruffled as his measured movements. If anything, he looked bored.

Beside Mandreth, Metik was interrogating a data terminal, mechadendrites burrowing inside the casing as if seeking hidden treasure. Nimbik was off somewhere, ferreting out the last of the enemy survivors from wherever they'd taken root.

There was no sign of Atticus Sinjan, or any of his carapace-wearing personal guard, amongst the dead. That would strike a sour note with Sabbathiel. With Mandreth too, who no doubt wished to give answer for the murder of Heloise. But vengeance would have to wait. At least until they'd located and extracted Quintus Bleeth.

Something hot flared by Bledheim's left cheek, and he flinched away, eyes going wide as a stray las-shot – a las-shot that had passed so close to his head that it had burned his skin – struck the wreckage of the lander beside him. Frowning, his hand reaching for the seared flesh, he turned instinctively to see a male enforcer charging at him from across the room.

So, it wasn't a stray shot. The bastard was aiming *at me.*

Bledheim edged back, panic flaring in his chest. His mouth was suddenly dry. His heart was pounding.

Not again. Not again.

He raised his laspistol and fired. The weapon jerked in his grip. The shot went low – so low that it caught the charging man in the front of his right foot, and he howled in sudden pain, falling forward, reaching out for an overturned table in an attempt to stop himself from going down.

And then a bearded face leered up from below, eyes bright and white against a terrifying aspect that had seemingly been smeared in dark, red blood. The squat bared his teeth, grabbed the enforcer from behind, and pulled him roughly to the floor.

The man screamed shrilly as Brondel's plasma pistol burned a hole through the place where his heart would have been.

Bledheim eyed the squat as Brondel slipped his pistol back into his holster and dusted his hands. 'Looks like we're done here.' He hawked up a gobbet of spit and put his hands on his hips. 'Least the freckers could have done was put up a fight.'

Bledheim eyed the devastation all around them.

Put up a fight…

He shook his head, incredulous.

Brondel laughed. The sound seemed inordinately loud in the strange, silent aftermath of the battle.

'I have located Quintus Bleeth,' said Metik, his grating voice echoing through the ruined space. As if to punctuate this news, one of the plasteel spurs beneath the wrecked lander groaned as it finally gave way, and the whole floor seemed to shift dangerously, before settling again a moment later. The lander creaked as it rocked gently from side to side, threatening to topple from its precarious perch at any moment. 'If you would care to follow me, I can lead you to his cell.' Metik started for the door, his finger casings clacking. 'Preferably before we are all irreversibly crushed.'

Bledheim was first behind the tech-priest to the door.

CHAPTER TWENTY-EIGHT

'We are all of us prisoners, whether it be within the four
walls of a cell, or in the shadowy recesses of our own minds.'
– Archduke Petro Engleheard, *On the Subject of Human Frailty*

The passageways beyond the impact site were crowded with
panicked enforcers and administrators, some attempting to flee
the imminent collapse of the structure and the wave of sudden
death that had struck their colleagues, others clearly operating
under orders to secure the evacuation and slow the progress of
the invaders.

These latter were met with the same measure of hostility that
had been awarded their companions back in the main hub of
the command centre – they were cut down where they stood,
efficiently, cleanly and without comment.

Bledheim knew that it was inconceivable that *all* of these
men and women were a part of Atticus Sinjan's conspiracy.
Indeed, that dubious honour was most likely limited to the

senior officers within their command structure. Nevertheless, as an organisation they remained under Sinjan's thrall, and in following his orders and detaining the errant Navigator, they had – willingly or unwillingly – made targets of themselves.

Targets that some of us are only too keen to despatch.

Bodies dropped or slumped against walls, left to bleed out into puddles of their own piss in the wake of Sabbathiel, Mandreth and their team. It had turned into a massacre – a cruel and blatant reply to what had occurred at the safe house, echoing the charnel-house nature of what Bledheim and the others had found upon their return.

He supposed he couldn't blame his comrades. They were being hunted, after all.

And there's still a damned Assassin on the loose.

Behind Bledheim, Mercy was helping Silq to keep up. The woman's wound was severe – she would probably lose the arm – but Metik had done enough to keep her alive, packing the wound and pumping her full of analgesics. It was these, rather than the wound itself, that had left her unsteady on her feet, swaying slightly from side to side with every step. He glanced back at her.

'I could give you a shot of stimms.'

Silq looked at him with bleary eyes. 'I… I think…'

'No,' said Mercy, offering Bledheim an appraising look. 'Maybe later, if she has to defend herself. For now, let her float along in ignorant bliss.'

Bledheim shrugged. 'As you wish. The offer stands.'

Mercy clearly didn't know what to make of this. 'Why?'

'Why what?'

'Why offer her stimms?'

'Because she's struggling to walk, and they might help.'

'And *you* want to help her?'

Bledheim sighed.

Am I really that much of a monster?

'Why not?'

Mercy frowned. 'Well… it's just…' She trailed off.

'I might be a coward, but that doesn't mean I don't… well, I have my uses,' said Bledheim.

Mercy was quiet for a moment. 'You're not a coward,' she said eventually, her voice low.

Up ahead, another flurry of weapons fire marked a further knot of resistance.

Bledheim met Mercy's gaze. 'Thank you.'

There was shouting from the corridor ahead. Barked orders.

She nodded. 'Looks like you're up.'

Bledheim turned to see Metik was hunching over a control panel beside a cell door. Sparks were dancing before his face as he attempted to cycle through the various locking sequences.

Bledheim cast one final look back at Mercy and Silq, and then pushed his way to the front, past Brondel and Nol, who appeared to be deep in some obtuse conversation. He caught Sabbathiel's eye, and she offered him a small, joyless smile. He was about to be put to work.

A shiver of anticipation passed through the interrogator.

Now we get some answers.

Metik emitted a frustrated sound, like the clicking on a non-existent tongue. More sparks showered from the control panel, and the lumen strip above the door flared red. He cleared his throat and continued with his ministrations.

Bledheim noted that there were several more dead enforcers heaped in the passage ahead of them. They'd obviously attempted to form a beachhead here, to prevent them from getting to Bleeth.

And they'd failed. Miserably.

At least they would have, if Metik could open the damn door.

More sparks. Bledheim was sure he heard the tech-priest curse beneath his breath. 'I shall have the door open momentarily,' he said.

Mandreth, who was standing beside Sabbathiel with a look of growing impatience, gestured to the ogryn. 'Nol?'

Nol looked up from his conversation with the squat, blinked, and then, after a moment, seemed to finally fathom the intent behind his master's question. He grinned, showing his cracked and yellowed teeth. 'Aye, sir.'

Nol placed his hand, surprisingly gently, on Bledheim's shoulder and steered the interrogator back towards the other side of the passageway. Then, with a grunt, he rolled his shoulders, stretched his thick neck, and dropped into a crouch, preparing to launch himself at the door.

'There is really no need...' protested Metik.

Nol threw himself bodily at the door, crashing into the plasteel barrier with the flat of his immense shoulder.

To the credit of the fabricators, the door didn't give way. But the wall around it did. With a thunderous crack, the entire front wall of the cell simply *lifted*, still in one piece, and then crashed to the ground inside the cell, sending up a billowing cloud of dust and grit.

Bledheim hacked, waving his hand before his face as he tried to make sense of the scene before his eyes. Where the wall had been was now a gaping hole, and Nol – who had clearly been taken by surprise at the efficacy of his endeavour – was sprawled upon the toppled plascrete, spitting and choking and trying ineffectually to push himself back up to his feet.

'You might have killed him!' said Metik, his tone dripping with recrimination.

Killed him? More like annihilate *him.*

Sabbathiel took a step forward. She raised her hand, one thin, gloved finger pointing to a huddled shape in the far corner of the ruined cell. 'At last.'

Quintus Bleeth was cowering on the floor beside the bowl of a toilet, his once black robes now grey with the stirred-up dust and debris that was still pattering down from above. He was a thin, willowy-looking man, with greasy, pale skin. His lower lip was quivering, revealing a mouthful of splintered teeth. His eyes – the two human ones – were open and staring and a bright, clear blue, while his strange third eye was closed, the lid crusted and weeping as if concealing an open sore. Despite being younger than Jolas, to Bledheim's eye, he looked several decades older than his brother. He had clearly lived a far harsher life.

The man lifted his left arm and pointed a bony finger back at Sabbathiel. 'She has come. I warned them she would. I *warned* them!' He remained where he was, his finger pointing accusingly, his breath coming in shallow, desperate gasps.

Brondel hawked up a mouthful of phlegm.

Bledheim cleared his throat. 'Do you want me to do this here, ma'am?'

Sabbathiel stared at the Navigator for a moment longer, then shook her head. 'No. We're heading up-spire. Bring him.'

With a curt nod, Bledheim crossed the room to collect his charge.

'Tell me about Atticus Sinjan.'

Quintus Bleeth rolled his head groggily to one side, resting his chin upon his prominent collar bone. It had taken two shots just to calm him, and now Bledheim was worried that he'd overdone it. He selected another finger, reached under the man's chin and slipped the needle into the side of the Navigator's neck, probing for a vein. One of the colourful chambers strapped to the back of his hand drained with a pneumatic hiss. Bleeth groaned. His eyelids fluttered.

Bledheim stepped back and waited.

They were holed up in a disused hab-unit they'd discovered two levels up from the enforcers' command station. It had once been the domain of someone affluent – most likely a politician or Administratum official of reasonable standing – but had long been stripped and abandoned, never to be repurposed… at least not officially. Most likely it was maintained as some sort of holding cell or off-the-record meeting place, judging by the empty caff cups on the floor and the discarded stubs of several smoke sticks. Nevertheless, it would serve their purpose admirably – assuming he could get Bleeth to talk.

The Navigator emitted a strange mewling sound, and then bucked wildly for a moment against his bonds as the sudden rush of stimms elevated his heart rate and spiked his adrenal system, until he was once again wild-eyed and awake. He looked up from his chair, staring first at Bledheim, then at Sabbathiel, and finally Mandreth.

The others were spread out through the hab-unit and the corridors beyond, keeping watch. The alert would have gone out by now – soon the whole of the Gallowspire would be swarming with people who wanted them dead. Bledheim knew he was working against the clock. And he hated it. He much preferred to take his time, to draw the results out *slowly*. But that, apparently, wasn't an option.

Bleeth chewed his lip feverishly until blood was dribbling down his chin. He looked deranged, like an animal that had been caged for too long and had lost its mind.

'Don't kill him, Bledheim. Not until we have what we need,' said Sabbathiel.

'By rights I should be offended, ma'am,' said Bledheim. 'But

I'm not used to working in such conditions. He's quite well.'
Bledheim considered for a moment. 'Or rather, he's as well as
he was when we found him. He's clearly been mistreated for
some time.'

'I don't need an interrogator to tell me that,' she replied drolly.

'About Sinjan,' prompted Mandreth.

Bledheim nodded. He leaned closer to Bleeth, who was evidently having trouble trying to focus.

Good. That makes this easier.

'Quintus. Tell me about Atticus Sinjan.'

'Where is he?' said Bleeth. 'Is he here?' He looked agitated.
'I'm sorry, Atticus. I promise.'

'What do you promise?' asked Bledheim.

'To stay dead,' replied Bleeth. 'You like it when I'm dead,
don't you? You're happy when I'm dead.' The man's mind was
clearly gone, perhaps lost to the vagaries of the warp, or else
the result of whatever had been done to him in that cell. 'I
promise, no one will know. I'll be dead as long as I need to be.
I'll be dead forever.'

The poor bastard. And now I'm going to make it all so much worse.
I'm going to make him relive it all.

'Why are you dead, Quintus?'

'You *know* why I'm dead.'

'Remind me.'

Bleeth frowned. He tested his bindings again, as if he wanted
to bury his face in his hands. 'Because you told me I had to
be. You and Jolas.' The man's eyes were flitting back and forth
rapidly, as if he were dreaming.

Bledheim glanced at Sabbathiel, who nodded for him to continue. 'And what else did I tell you, Quintus? Do you remember?'

'You told me,' muttered Bleeth. 'You told me where to find it.'

'Where to find what?'

Bleeth scowled. He rocked forward as far as he could in his chair, as if taking Bledheim into his confidence. 'The *body*,' he hissed. 'You told me where to find the body. On the hulk. You knew it was there.'

'The *body*,' echoed Bledheim.

Now we're getting somewhere.

'The body that was hidden in your tomb?'

'I didn't want to do it, Atticus. You know that.' Bleeth's tone was pleading.

'Why, Quintus? Why didn't you want to do it?'

'Because of *them!*' Bleeth was getting agitated again now, rocking on his chair. A clear, viscous liquid was trickling from the gummed-up third eyelid in the centre of his forehead, running down his face like glistening tears.

Bledheim swallowed, his mouth suddenly dry.

If he opens that eye...

Hurriedly Bledheim tore a strip of fabric from Bleeth's robe, folding it to form a blindfold. He tied it around Bleeth's head, pulling it taut to bind the eye shut.

Bleeth winced. 'There've come for it, haven't they?' he said. 'I knew they would! I knew we couldn't get away with it. They'll kill us *all.*'

Bledheim reached out and grabbed Bleeth by the shoulders, holding him steady. 'Who, Quintus? Who's coming for it?'

'*Them!* The golden ones. The eagles.'

Bledheim heard Sabbathiel gasp. He squeezed Bleeth's shoulders. '*Who?*'

'The Emperor's Talons! The Adeptus Custodes!'

Bledheim felt a surge of panic. He released his grip on Bleeth. His heart was thrumming.

What is this? What have we got ourselves caught up in, here?

Trembling, he turned to Sabbathiel. 'The Adeptus Custodes...'

Sabbathiel's expression was stern. '*Ask him,*' she said, her voice level, controlled. 'Ask him about the body.'

Bledheim nodded meekly. He turned back to the Navigator, who was lolling in the chair, almost spent. 'The body. It was one of them? A... a Custodian Guard?' Bledheim couldn't quite believe what he was saying.

Bleeth laughed. It began as a low rumble, but seemed to build deep down in his chest, until it was filling the room, wracking his body, and he was sitting up again, propelled by the force of his own desperation. It was a sound born of hysteria rather than mirth. 'You know it was, Atticus. You know it was.'

'They've doomed us all,' muttered Mandreth. 'The *fools!*'

'What did they want with the body, Quintus?' said Sabbathiel, stepping forward, pushing Bledheim aside. She leaned closer, until her face was level with the Navigator's. His eyes were still rolling slackly in their sockets, lost and seeing something else, somewhere far away.

'You!' Bleeth sucked at the air, tried to drag himself away from her, as if shrinking. 'You!'

Sabbathiel stood back, the frustration clear on her face. 'Bledheim.'

'It's all right, Quintus. You have nothing to worry about. Now tell me, what did they want with the body?'

'The body?' Quintus giggled. 'No body, no.'

'What? What do you mean, no body?'

Bleeth tried to shrug, but it came across more like a nervous twitch.

'*Tell me!*'

'He was still alive. In a coma, almost gone. But still breathing.'

Throne.

Bledheim swallowed. His throat was dry.

Still alive...

'And what did they intend to do with him?'

'I don't *know*. You wouldn't tell me, would you, Atticus? You said I was asking too many questions. That you'd have to take me away to keep me safe. But I wasn't safe, was I? I wasn't safe…'

'All right. All right, Quintus. That's over now.'

'Over?' Bleeth chuckled nervously. 'It's not over. It'll never be over. Don't you understand that?'

'Who asked you to bring the Custodes here, to Hulth?'

'Jolas,' said Bleeth. 'Jolas and Nemedia.' He almost spat the woman's name.

'But you don't know why?'

'Of course I know why.'

'You do?'

Bleeth nodded. 'Because Rasmuth told them to.'

'Rasmuth,' said Mandreth. 'I *knew* he was a part of this.'

'More than we could have imagined, it seems,' said Sabbathiel. 'And the Bleeths, too. They're up to their neck in this. A damned Custodes! No wonder they wanted Quintus out of the way where he couldn't talk.'

'Then why not kill him?' said Mandreth. 'Why keep him locked up like this?'

Sabbathiel shrugged. 'Perhaps they intended to bring him back into the fold once their scheme had run its course? You heard Nemedia back at the house. She said he deserved better. Perhaps he's simply too valuable to the House?'

Quintus flinched at the sound of Sabbathiel's voice.

'What is it, Quintus? What's the matter?' asked Bledheim.

'Her!' said Bleeth. 'She's going to bring it all crashing down. All of it! That woman! The Queen of Ruin!'

Bledheim stared at the Navigator.

The Queen of Ruin. The one who will damn us all.

He risked another glance at Sabbathiel. If she was affected by the man's ramblings, she wasn't showing it. But Bledheim *knew*. He'd heard those words before.

How is this going to end?

'I…' He glanced away, unable, for a moment, to look at her, lest he betray his thoughts. 'I think we've got everything out of him we're going to, ma'am. He's broken. His mind is gone.'

'Agreed,' said Sabbathiel. 'He's given us much to consider.' She turned towards the door.

'What should I do with him? Bring him round so we can take him with us?'

'No. Leave him.'

Bledheim frowned. 'Leave him? He can hardly fend for himself.'

'Bledheim's right,' said Mandreth. He tugged his laspistol from the holster on his belt. 'The least we can do is put the poor bastard out of his misery.'

Bledheim stared at him. 'But we've spent all this time trying to find him.'

'And like you said, he's given us everything he can. Time to end his suffering.' Mandreth glanced at Sabbathiel, who inclined her head in affirmation.

The laspistol flared.

Quintus Bleeth slumped in his chair, a neat, smoking hole through the centre of his forehead, right where his third eye had once been. He wheezed a final, croaking exhalation, and was silent.

Still dead, then, Quintus.

Still dead.

CHAPTER TWENTY-NINE

'Only in death are our truest natures laid bare.'
– Attributed to Father Ramos IV of Belusia, following the fall of
Sister Auralias of the Order of the Gilded Flame

Their passage through the upper levels of the Gallowspire had become a death march, a corpse road punctuated by way markers comprising the remains of all who opposed them. Mostly, these consisted of small knots of enforcers, breakaway units sent to harry them, remnants of the force they'd obliterated on the lower level. None of them had proved more than a brief distraction.

Wasted lives, spent in the pursuit of needless games.

Sinjan will answer for this.

All of it.

Every single drop of spilled blood; every single blasted or mutilated corpse. They're on his *hands.*

Yet it wasn't the enforcers that troubled Sabbathiel as she

strode along beside Mandreth, Aethesia tracking one pace behind on her outer flank, the rest of their mismatched band bringing up the rear. She was watching the shadows, acutely aware that the last time she'd ventured into this region of Lord Rasmuth's domain, she'd come close to being cut down – permanently – by a Callidus Assassin.

Where are you lurking now?

She couldn't help but expect the Assassin to show itself at every turn. The nagging pain in her shoulder was a constant reminder of that imminent danger, of how fallible she was in the face of such refined, calculating skill. She'd sent Fitch ahead to scout every possible crevasse or nook, but she knew that wouldn't be enough – the shape-shifting Assassin could be anyone, at any time, ready to slide out of the gloom bearing death.

'If it's still here, we'll kill it,' said Mandreth, who had evidently noted her disquiet and correctly assumed what was troubling her. 'Yet it seems we have little choice but to re-enter the lion's den. Rasmuth has questions to answer.'

'Such as what in the Emperor's name does he want with a wounded Custodes?'

'Precisely,' said Mandreth. His tone was ominous. He, too, had evidently been disturbed by Quintus Bleeth's revelations.

Sabbathiel could barely begin to conceive of the foolishness that had led Rasmuth and his cronies to this point. Didn't they understand the danger they were courting? Irrespective of Sinjan's status as an inquisitor, the Adeptus Custodes would wreak bloody vengeance upon him and all of Hulth if they were to discover the truth of what he and Rasmuth had done.

To take a fallen brother…

She'd been wracking her brain trying to understand the purpose of such a thing. What were they hoping to achieve? Did they intend to *experiment* upon the wounded warrior? To carve him up and attempt to graft those inhuman organs into their own living bodies?

She needed to understand. She needed to know what had driven Sinjan to such dangerous extremes. Nor could she tolerate a man such as Rasmuth to continue in the role of planetary governor. His reign would have to be brought to a swift, sharp end – once they had extracted the pertinent answers from him. Answers that would enable her to bring Sinjan to justice. Answers that would expose this whole sorry conspiracy and allow her to resume her place amongst her conclave, or at least to be free of their perfidious insinuations.

They were approaching the entrance to Lord Rasmuth's official residence.

'Last time we were here, we left three dead guards in our wake,' said Sabbathiel, thinking back to their encounter by the macro hoist and their planned execution at the hands of those selfsame guards. 'We're hardly going to be welcomed with open arms.'

Mandreth gave a nonchalant shrug. 'I think we burned our bridges some time ago, don't you?'

Sabbathiel grinned. She hefted her sword and glanced at Aethesia, who offered her a silent nod of understanding.

Ahead, the towering doors to the complex were barred shut.

'Nol?' said Mandreth, over his shoulder.

'*Again?*' said the ogryn.

'Again.'

The floor shook with the pounding of Nol's booted feet.

Of the ten guards assigned to protect the governor's private residence that day, three were fatally crushed beneath the collapsing doors as Nol exploded through in a shower of shattered wood and plasteel.

As the other guards swarmed to form a blockade, they were

taken down first by a hail of las, plasma and bolt-rounds, and then by the flashing blades of Sabbathiel, Mandreth and Aethesia as they followed Nol into the entrance hall, despatching the last few survivors.

Within moments an eerie stillness had settled upon the scene, belied only by the evidence of the extreme violence that had taken place a few seconds before. Dead or dying, the bodies of the guards were scattered across the pristine marble floor, droplets of their spilled blood beading on the polished surface like swarming insects. One of them emitted a rattling, rasping final breath.

The *click-click* of approaching footsteps – shoes on marble – shattered the illusion of calm.

A single person, wearing heels. And judging by their nonchalant pace, they've got damned nerves of steel.

Sabbathiel raised her power sword in readiness.

The figure emerged from the side passage on the other side of the entrance hall. *Chandra Mol.*

Her hair was still perfectly coiffured, her dress smart and unblemished. Yet, instead of carrying a book beneath her arm – the leather-bound tome that had seemed to Sabbathiel to be a permanent fixture – she was carrying a snub-nosed meltagun, one hand bracing the stock, the other cupping the trigger. 'We had not thought to see you again, inquisitors.' She stepped over several of the fallen guards as if they weren't there; calm and proficient, somehow able to ignore the scene of horrific carnage all around her. She smiled, but it was a tight, unwelcoming smile. 'We'd hoped you would have heeded our warning.' She trained the nose of the meltagun on Sabbathiel. 'Still, I'm sorry about the mess. It seems you've caught us at a bad time.'

Sabbathiel squeezed the grip of her sword. 'Where is he?'

Chandra Mol shrugged, but the aim of her weapon didn't

waver. 'You can't see him. No one can. I told you before, he's *unwell.*' She stuck her chin out in a defiant gesture. 'He needs his rest.'

'What he needs,' said Sabbathiel, 'is to answ–' She was cut short by the sudden, deafening report of a pistol from close beside her.

Chandra Mol took an uncertain step forward. She lowered her gun, but then her fingers went slack, and the weapon began to slide from her grip. She was wearing a confused expression. Blood welled from a gaping hole in the centre of her forehead.

Even this hasn't ruffled her perfect hair.

The woman collapsed, dead, on the spot.

Silence again, just for a moment. And then:

'Enough,' said Mandreth. He slid the pistol back into its holster at his belt, and, like Chandra Mol before him, began picking his way through the sea of corpses towards the passageway from which the woman had emerged.

With a gesture for the others to follow, Sabbathiel continued on behind him.

The broad passage was as immaculate as the entrance hall: spotlessly clean, the walls and floor gleaming with polish and precision. Life-sized statues of robed figures lined both sides, peering out from their shadowy alcoves with blank, featureless faces, their hands clasped before them as if in prayer. Each of the figures was near identical to those beside it, aside from small, seemingly trivial details – the shape of a fold in the carved robe, a slight variation in the height of the hands, the angle and setting of the shoulders. There were seven of them in total, three on the left and four on the right. Something about them seemed deeply unsettling to Sabbathiel, but she could put her finger on nothing beyond the low-level nausea she felt in their presence.

The passageway terminated in a set of ornate double doors – white with gold filigree, depicting that same pattern Sabbathiel had seen time and again during her time on Hulth: two spheres orbiting one another on concentric tracks, a flash of lightning flickering between them. If there had been any doubt before regarding Rasmuth's connection to the Bleeths, it was now long banished.

She approached the doors, Mandreth at her side. Testing the handle, she discovered they were unlocked. She pushed one of them open on smooth hinges, revealing a darkened room beyond. The scent wafting from inside was thick and pungent, and redolent of decay.

Perhaps Rasmuth really was unwell?

She paused on the threshold, glancing at Mandreth. 'We could be exposing ourselves to a dangerous pathogen.'

Mandreth shook his head, pointing up at the ceiling. 'Listen. Air scrubbers. They're running a filtration system.'

Sabbathiel cocked her head. Sure enough, she could hear the grinding whirr of the extraction fans.

'So long as we don't get too close...' Mandreth added.

Sabbathiel looked back to Bledheim and the others, who were waiting a few steps behind her in the passageway, look-ing uncomfortable under the unwelcome gaze of the faceless statues. 'Wait here. If necessary, buy us all the time you can.'

Bledheim nodded. Beckoning Mandreth and Fitch forward, Sabbathiel slipped into the room, allowing the door to swing shut behind her.

Once inside, she paused for a few moments to allow her eyes to adjust to the gloom.

Rasmuth himself was reclining in a large bed in the centre of the chamber, covered from the neck down by a white cotton sheet. He looked a mess – his breathing was harsh and gasping, and the skin of his face was necrotic and peeling, bilious green in colour, apart from where it blackened around the orbit of his left eye. His hair, evidently once a lustrous blond, was now stringy and lank and had fallen out in huge clumps. In here, the sweet, sickly smell that Sabbathiel had noted from the passageway was more intense, headier. It was the scent of someone dying, rotting slowly but determinedly, their life being leeched away as their body betrayed them.

The man was either so weak or so beyond caring that he hadn't even turned his head to regard them as they'd entered.

Sabbathiel slid her sword into its scabbard and hefted her pistol, pointing it lazily in the direction of the bed. It was intended merely as a threat; so far as she could ascertain, Rasmuth posed no danger to anyone in his dire condition.

'Governor Rasmuth. I am Inquisitor Astor Sabb–'

She didn't get any further, as the man's eyes flickered open and he raised a hand to wave it at them with surprising deftness. 'Yes, yes. I know who you are, and why the two of you are here,' he said, his voice thin and reedy, but cut with an undercurrent of severity that spoke of years spent in positions of authority. This was a man who was used to being listened to. 'Let's not pretend any more, shall we?' he continued, repositioning himself slightly so he could look at them. His eyes were jaundiced and rheumy but fixed on her attentively.

'Good,' said Mandreth. He was watching Rasmuth keenly, with the air of a wolf eyeing its prey. 'Then you won't mind answering our questions.'

'Mind?' said Rasmuth. He croaked, and Sabbathiel thought for a moment he was struggling to breathe, before she realised he was laughing. 'Mind? Well, I don't see that I have a choice in the matter, do I?'

'I see we understand one another,' said Mandreth.

This time, Rasmuth did sputter as he tried to speak, his whole body rattling with the severity of the cough. Thick, green mucus spilled from his lower lip, dribbling down his chin in ropey strings. Sabbathiel noted it was streaked with bright blood. 'Where's Chandra Mol?' he said, after the fit had passed. He withdrew his claw-like hand from beneath the thin, white sheet and wiped his mouth on the edge of the sleeve, but much of the mucus had already pooled on the bedclothes. Sabbathiel thought she saw something moving there, beneath the sheet, but if so, it was only fleeting, for he soon settled back into his pillows, his breathing returning to the same short rattle as before.

A mutant?

It was unlikely, but far from impossible. Sabbathiel had seen it before: a mutant who had successfully hidden their affliction while rising through the ranks of governance, earning command of an entire city before finally being exposed and eradicated. But here? Could that be what Rasmuth was hiding?

Sabbathiel took a step closer. 'Chandra Mol is... indisposed,' she said.

'Ah,' said Rasmuth wistfully. 'I see.' He made a gesture that might have been a shrug. 'Too bad. She was a good girl. Always looked after me. Appreciated the cause.'

The cause. Then Chandra Mol had been a part of it all too?

'Tell us about the Custodes,' said Sabbathiel. She lowered her pistol, but only fractionally.

'So, you found Quintus then, hmm? I suppose it was only a matter of time.'

'The wounded Custodes,' pressed Mandreth. 'What did you want with him?'

'The *dying* Custodes,' corrected Rasmuth. 'The sad truth is that he has more to offer the Imperium in death than he ever did in life.'

Had the man lost his mind? Had whatever blight that had cursed his body also robbed him of his sense of reason?

'In what way?' said Sabbathiel.

Rasmuth clicked his tongue. More mucus was dribbling freely from the slack corner of his mouth. 'Well, I might as well start at the beginning, since you've come all this way.'

Mandreth made an impatient sound.

'Go on,' prompted Sabbathiel.

Rasmuth smiled, revealing the stumps of rotted teeth. 'Take a moment, if you will, to consider the plight of our beloved God-Emperor. Elevated to divinity in the moment of His near death, He has been robbed of His purpose, His freedom. For millennia, He has been trapped within the shell of a broken body, a corpse-god bound to a throne of gold, anchored in the mortal realm and unable to properly enact His divine will.'

'So, you... *pity* Him? You dare to presume that much?' said Mandreth.

'No, you do not understand,' said Rasmuth, trying and failing to prop himself up on one elbow, agitated now. 'I do not *pity* Him. I worship Him. In all His true glory.' He wiped at the drool, pulling it away with his fingers. 'Yet I understand that, in trying to preserve His physical form, humanity has shackled him. We have unknowingly made Him our prisoner, when He should be our god.'

'What has this got to do with a dying Custodes?' said Sabbathiel. She could feel her patience waning. The man was clearly some sort of fanatic.

Rasmuth held up a single bony finger. 'Everything,' he said. 'You see, while the God-Emperor's body remains in chains, His spirit wanders free, searching abroad for the means to lead us once again.'

'And you believe you've found those means,' said Mandreth, averting his gaze in disgust.

'Indeed, we have!' said Rasmuth. 'The Emperor shall be born again!'

'Born again? How, exactly?'

Rasmuth grinned. 'By decanting His wandering soul into a divine vessel so that He might walk amongst us once more.'

Sabbathiel stared at the man, appalled. She could see it now, the whole sorry plot unfolding right there before her.

Throne. The man was utterly insane.

'The Custodes. That's your so-called divine vessel.'

Rasmuth beamed. 'Ah, I see the understanding now, the gleam in your eye. You see the truth of it, don't you?' He chuckled, and it was a wet, rasping sound. 'The perfect host, is it not? A husk, soon to be discarded–'

'*Discarded?*' spat Mandreth. 'Do you know what the Adeptus Custodes will do to you, to this planet, if they discover the sick games you've been playing here with one of their own? How did you even obtain such a thing?'

Rasmuth shrugged. 'The warrior was dying when we found him on the battlefield of Zern, fatally wounded in battle with a coven of xenos witches. His mind has gone, trapped in a catatonic coma. The Adeptus Custodes have no need for his empty shell.'

'But *you* believe you can fill it?' said Mandreth, disgusted. 'Decant the Emperor's wandering spirit into a dying man's body, just like that?'

'*Just like that?* I think you underestimate the challenge and scale of this operation, inquisitor.'

'But not the depths of your madness,' said Mandreth. He looked to Sabbathiel. 'He's insane. They all are.'

She inclined her head. She'd heard tales of cults like this, even hidden within the ranks of the Inquisition – those who believed they could affect the Emperor's rebirth, if only a worthy form could be found to host His beleaguered spirit. They foresaw a day when He would return in all His glory, to lead the Imperium once more in another Great Crusade.

It was madness. Utter, unadulterated madness. Heresy. Sabbathiel had seen what was out there, beyond the veil of the warp. If the Emperor's spirit wandered there too, it was already lost to them.

'Sinjan helped you. And Jolas and Nemedia Bleeth. They were all in on it.'

'The Bleeths were useful. Their influence and control in this region are profound. They provided the means to transport and store the host vessel without arousing too much suspicion. Falsified logs. Culled data serfs,' said Rasmuth, proudly. 'They share our beliefs. They carry our hopes upon their shoulders. And they shall be rewarded when the newly born Emperor walks among us.'

'What of Quintus?' asked Sabbathiel. 'He seemed somewhat more… dubious.'

Rasmuth shook his head. 'Quintus was never a believer. But he did what was necessary, and so played his part. He understood the requirements of his family.'

'And that's why you kept him locked up,' said Mandreth, 'so that he wouldn't give away your little secret? Why not kill him? It would have been an easier way to guarantee his silence.'

'Oh, you still don't understand, do you?' said Rasmuth. He scratched at his peeling pate, shedding streamers of golden hair. Again, Sabbathiel sensed that shifting movement beneath the cotton sheet, as if there were something under there with him. 'We didn't need Quintus, not after he'd served his purpose. He was simply a distraction, a tool. A means of keeping Heldren busy chasing his tail, and then the two of you in Heldren's stead. A little run-around to keep you out of the way while we saw to what was needed.'

Mandreth took a step towards the bed, his hands balled into fists. 'Distraction or not, we'll put a stop to whatever foul ritual you're planning.'

Rasmuth laughed. 'Oh, I'm sorry, inquisitor. Don't you see? You're already too late. The ritual is underway. The Emperor *will* rise again. And Father Rand will lead our people to welcome Him.'

Sabbathiel shook her head. 'You're chasing ghosts. If what you claim was even remotely true, if the Emperor was somehow adrift and the mere shell of an Adeptus Custodes was enough to grant Him new life, don't you think it would have happened before now? You're dealing in conspiracies and legends. Myths. The Emperor is on His throne on Terra, and whatever it is you think you're doing is nothing but heresy.'

Rasmuth frowned. 'No. No, you're wrong. Wrong!' He was growing agitated now, trying to heave himself up from his bed. 'The moment has come. It has been foreseen. As Father Rand is wont to remind us, the new-born Emperor will be our salvation!'

Sabbathiel had heard it all before – the babbling of the desperate and the lost. 'There will be no salvation for you now, Rasmuth. Look at yourself. Your insane games have opened your mind to the depravations of the warp. You carry the foul stink of Chaos.'

Rasmuth glared at her, defiant. 'You're blinded by your ignorance, Sabbathiel. You couldn't possibly understand. It is merely that my love for the Emperor runs so deep, so pure, that my heart could no longer contain it…' With a jerk of his hand, he pulled aside the bedsheet, revealing a green, pulsating chest, the skin bubbled and blistered, leaking foul-smelling pus from several glistening, open sores. Worse, though, was the knot of slick grey tentacles that erupted from a fist-sized hole where the man's heart should have been. They twisted and curled, like sea anemones buffeted by an unseen current.

'See? See the gift which He has given me?' He opened his mouth and laughed, blood and mucus bubbling down the ruin of his chin.

Sabbathiel raised her pistol and squeezed the trigger – once, twice, and then a third time, the bolt-rounds detonating in the corrupted man's face and chest, spreading his foul pustulence across the wall behind him. His body slumped in the bed, maggots already festering in the rancid flesh.

Sabbathiel tasted bile rising in her gullet.

So, now we know.

A plot to rebirth the Emperor in the body of an Adeptus Custodes, led by a murderous inquisitor and a mad planetary governor who had lost himself to the imprecations of Chaos.

It didn't bode well.

'He was trying to delay us further,' said Mandreth, already heading for the door. 'Why else spin his story? He knew we were going to kill him. It was just another tactic.'

Sabbathiel nodded. 'You're right. We have to stop that ritual. Throne knows what they'll conjure if they're all as deluded as this sorry bastard.'

'But where? We don't know where they're keeping the body.'

Sabbathiel considered for a moment. 'Rand. He mentioned the priest.'

'The cathedral. That's got to be it.' Mandreth pushed open the door, and Sabbathiel was grateful for the sudden wash of cool, clean air. She saw Bledheim watching her inquisitively.

'Come,' she said, beckoning for him and the others to follow, 'we're going to need another ship.'

CHAPTER THIRTY

'I wandered lost,
'cross fields of old,
Where the souls of the dead,
Still clung to the white bones of their squalor,
And the rattle of war,
Was naught but the distant lament of birds.
Lost, I was,
Yet found again,
For upon that churned loam,
And sunk in peat bog and empty trench,
Did my own self lie,
In sad regret,
A temple to the hollow battle,
In yellowed tooth and bone,
And foul hatred raised.'

– 'Peace', unattributed

The Cathedral of Saint Euphrades looked ominous in the waning light; an edifice cleaved from the fabric of the world, sheared from the very bedrock and raised like a prison guard to stand over the hivesprawl, a warden against all thoughts of impurity.

Yet, if Sabbathiel was right, this very building, erected and dedicated in the name of the Emperor, had become home to such corruption that its entire purpose had been inverted, that the shadow it now cast upon this world writhed darkly with unseen horrors.

The wind ruffled a stray strand of hair. She tucked it behind her ear. She longed to be cocooned inside her Terminator armour and carrying her stave – to feel more prepared for what she was certain was a coming battle – but those remnants of her old life remained trapped on her blockaded ship at the void port, along with most of their other equipment.

Relics of a lost age.

She would have to do as she was. Her, and her motley gang of acolytes. She glanced at them now, each in turn: Bledheim, who blanched in the face of danger; Silq, still carrying a terrible wound in her shoulder; Mercy, wearing her confidence like a fragile mask; Brondel, tugging the end of his beard in gleeful, outlandish anticipation.

Perhaps Heldren had been right.

Did I choose wisely?

And then there were the others, accreted in her wake: Metik, whose labyrinthine mind was near unfathomable; Aethesia, implacable behind her brass gorget; Nol, chewing on his bottom lip like a nervous child; Mandreth, whose set jaw and steel gaze spoke of his determination to see this through.

No. The only mistake would be in underestimating these people.

She'd questioned them – and herself – long enough.

They mounted the steps leading up to the cathedral's main

entrance. As they neared the top, caught in the shadow of the towering doorway, Mandreth held out his arm, crooked at the elbow, and glanced to the skies. Sabbathiel followed his gaze. A dark blur spiralled out of the iron smear of the clouds, at first nothing more than a tiny spot, but then resolving as it spread its wings, describing lazy circles as it drifted down over their heads, before finally coming to settle on Mandreth's outstretched arm, head bobbing. His falcon.

Sabbathiel shuddered at the sight of it. She'd seen what it could do at close quarters, rending with its talons, gouging with its beak. It was as deadly a weapon as any power sword.

So, Mandreth's anticipating a fight, too.

Swallowing, she led the way through the door.

Inside, her footsteps rang out in the empty space. Here, she sensed, was a place haunted by the absence of life and sound, emptied now of the throng and bustle, the fire and brimstone, the contemplators and the aesthetes that would typically inhabit such a world.

An empty cathedral.

An empty vessel.

Beside her, Mandreth bristled. Footsteps approached, the soft scuff of moccasins upon stone. She looked up to see an older man in robes coming towards them along the central aisle. Above him, a great mechanism whirled and turned – an orrery, of sorts, resembling again the symbol which had now grown so familiar to her. Planetary bodies circled in their ponderous dance, and electrical currents danced and arced between the two globes, spitting and crackling as the orrery cycled.

Thanks to Rasmuth, Sabbathiel now thought she understood the significance of the design.

Two bodies in alignment, joined by a bolt of power.

One globe represented the Emperor, the other the Divine

Avatar. The electrical charge marked the passage of the soul between the two. It was the core of their philosophy, the ideology that underpinned everything that had happened here on Hulth.

The becoming of their new Emperor. Their so-called salvation.

Why didn't I see it earlier?

Sabbathiel had not even paused to consider what would happen if they were right. The notion seemed inconceivable. If the Emperor really could transfer His consciousness into a new host, then everything would be different. The Imperium – the *galaxy* – would shudder with change. The universe would be remade.

Just as it was when I awoke from my slumber. When I was remade.

But no, she'd seen what had become of Rasmuth. Blighted by the Plague God's kiss. Tainted by his own blasphemous concept of faith.

This plot, this ritual, it was not an exercise in piety; it was a dangerous game of corruption.

The robed man, a priest, had come to a halt before them. He looked tired, unshaven, with dark rings around his eyes, bruised from too many years of service and lack of sleep. Yet the way he held himself was somehow imperious, too, superior – as if he were looking down upon them from some lofty position of grace.

'Father Rand?' asked Sabbathiel.

He looked at her appraisingly. 'No. I am Father Crucias. I'm afraid Father Rand is unavailable at this time.' He glanced at Mandreth and smiled. 'Nevertheless, I welcome you back, inquisitor. And I see that, this time, you have brought along all of your friends. The pious are always to be encouraged here. Might I be of some service?'

'You can tell us where they are,' said Sabbathiel.

Crucias frowned. 'I'm sorry? I'm not sure I understand what you mean.'

'Rand, Sinjan and the others. We know they're here.'

The priest's brow furrowed. He offered her a deep frown. 'You must be mistaken, inquisitor. As I explained, Father Rand is pre-occupied with his sermons. He requires utter solitude in which to contemplate the Emperor's good word. As to the other name you mentioned – Sind-Jon, was it? – there is certainly no one here by that or any other name.'

Sabbathiel gritted her teeth. Her patience was stretched so taut that it wasn't so much threatening to snap but to rend her apart from the inside. Just as she was about to respond, she heard Mercy issue a polite cough from over her shoulder.

Curious, Sabbathiel turned to regard the towering woman.

Mercy met her eye, then glanced at the priest. She made a slight gesture as if seeking approval to approach. Sabbathiel nodded, stepping to one side to allow Mercy room.

Mandreth shot her a confused look. Sabbathiel shrugged. Mercy stepped closer to the priest.

'Yes, my dear? How might I–' He reeled back as Mercy's fist struck him hard across the jaw, sending a spray of bloody spittle high into the air. Crucias' hand started to lift towards his face… and then he toppled over, backwards, into an unconscious heap on the flagstones.

Mercy regarded her fist, before plucking free an errant tooth that had embedded itself in her knuckle. She flicked it at the insensate priest. 'The bastard *bit* me,' she said, before shrugging and returning to her position at the rear of the small group.

Sabbathiel gestured for them to fan out. 'They've got to be somewhere here. Find them.' She glanced up at the servo-skull hovering over her left shoulder. 'You too, Fitch. Tell me where they are.'

She watched him drift away into the depths of the cavernous interior, red traceries playing over every surface. Then, drawing her sword, she stepped over the unconscious priest and followed behind.

'Over here.'

Sabbathiel, who had been studying the figure in the immense stained-glass window, doused red in the refracted light of his robes as the waning sunlight spilled through from outside, turned to regard Silq. She wrinkled her nose; there was a lingering stink here of charred meat and ash, the remnants of a recent pyre. 'What is it?'

Silq motioned for Sabbathiel to join her. Elsewhere, the others were searching the other exits, passages and side chambers.

Where was everyone? The priests, officials, penitents, worshippers – the place was disturbingly empty.

She hurried over to join Silq, who was standing close to the altar, peering down at the worn flagstones beneath her feet. They carried a glossy patina from centuries of scuffing boots.

'What?'

'There, can't you hear it?' said Silq.

Sabbathiel waved her quiet, tilting her head as she strained to hear over the echoing sound of the others moving around. 'I can't–'

And then she heard it.

A sound like distant, soaring moaning, a plaintive lament, rising and falling in crescendo. A sound that felt somehow *wrong* – not quite discordant but sung at a pitch that seemed to curdle the contents of Sabbathiel's stomach. The sound of a choir, giving itself up to the taint of the unclean.

'They're down below,' she called. Her voice seemed to fill the enormous space of the nave, reflecting from every surface. She saw Mandreth making a beeline for her. The others, too, had stopped what they were doing and were watching her, waiting intently for instruction. She glanced up at Fitch, ever-present above her left shoulder. 'Fitch – find us a way down. It must be around here somewhere.'

'Yes, mistress.' She was sure she could detect a hint of irony in its tone.

The servo-skull began a slow sweep of the surrounding area, lights tickling every surface as it passed overhead. After a moment, it stopped just above the far side of the altar. 'There is a hollow space here, beneath one of the slabs.'

'Nol,' said Mandreth, nodding for the ogryn to investigate. Nol lumbered around to the other side of the altar, his footsteps so thunderous that Sabbathiel was surprised he didn't shatter the flagstones underfoot.

'Where?' said Nol. He gave the altar a light shove out of the way, which – given the ogryn's size and strength – had the effect of sending it crashing over, spilling candles, icons and the leaves of an ancient-looking book across the floor. He watched it happen with a vaguely interested, yet somewhat confused expression, before turning back to Fitch, who was playing a beam of red light back and forth across the slab in question. The stone had the size and appearance of an inlaid tombstone, but as Nol stooped down to lift it, Sabbathiel was surprised to see a concealed iron hoop embedded at one end, through which the ogryn looped a single index finger.

Nol grunted as he slid the stone aside with a grating screech, revealing a dark hollow beneath.

Sabbathiel and Mandreth moved closer. The others were circling now, too – in particular Aethesia, who had refused to stray out of eyesight of Sabbathiel during the search and had already drawn her sword.

Sabbathiel peered into the hollow. Worn stone steps descended into some form of subterranean grotto or crypt, where they disappeared into a puddle of Stygian gloom. The strange, disharmonious chanting she'd heard earlier was louder now, clearly emanating from whatever lay below.

Sabbathiel glanced around the small group, meeting each of their eyes in turn.

This is it.

This is where we bring this sorry mess to a close. This is how we purge the heretic. Nothing else matters now.

Nothing.

Each of them understood. Each of them was ready. She hadn't spoken a word.

Aethesia made a series of small, precise gestures with her hands: *I shall scout ahead and ensure the way is clear.*

Sabbathiel nodded. She stood back to allow Aethesia room to broach the opening. The null maiden paused, then glanced back at Sabbathiel. There was something there, in her eyes. Something knowing, something unsaid.

Her hands moved again. *If I do not return from this, seek out Jherek.*

Jherek.

The name from her vision. The man by the water.

Another twisted player in this bizarre game? The mysterious benefactor who had sent the Sister of Silence to her aid?

'Aethesia, wait–'

But the null maiden was already gone.

They stood for a moment, listening to Aethesia's retreating footsteps, watching the darkness for any sign, any movement, as if she had left ripples in her wake as she waded into that liquid night.

Silence.

And then:

The familiar sound of a sword sliding into flesh. A low groan. A wet thud. The clang of metal on metal.

Sabbathiel hurried down the steps after Aethesia, her own blade in her fist, power crackling along its glinting edge.

The steps opened out into a wide passage, lit warmly by a series of tallow candles mounted in small, irregular recesses in the walls. Walls that were formed from human skulls and thigh bones, neatly stacked and architecturally set – an ossuary, a repository of the lost. There must have been thousands of them in that small space alone, watching her with their mournful, fleshless smiles and empty eyes.

Ahead of her, several yards along the passage, Aethesia was carefully lowering the body of a black-clad man to the ground. He had a puncture wound through his chest, and his head was lolling back on muscles that had recently lost all sense of tension and animation. Another similarly dressed man was already dead on the ground beside him. Sabbathiel recognised the look of their armour immediately, from the corpse she'd seen back at the safe house after the attack.

Sinjan's personal guard.

'He's here, then,' said Mandreth, from behind her. She hadn't heard him follow her down the steps. His voice was tight, constrained.

Sabbathiel's only response was to heft her sword in readiness, and nod for Aethesia to continue leading them deeper towards the ominous sounds of the ritual.

Ahead, the passage wound around a dog-leg, and Sabbathiel realised they were skirting the void beneath the main nave of the cathedral. The walls here were still formed from the remains of the dead, but now they seemed older, more gnarled and yellowed, encrusted with a thin patina of grime. The floor, too, had become more like loose scree, and her boots crunched with every step. Not that they feared announcing their approach – the noise of the chanting had reached such a volume that Sabbathiel was barely able to hear herself think.

The sound continued to stir within her a deep sense of unease, and while she was in no way fearful, she was nevertheless trepidatious of what they might find at the end of this short journey. It felt to her as if they were descending into some surreal underworld; as if they'd somehow left the physical realm behind up there in the cathedral and were now trespassing on the domain of something baneful and unreal, a thing that should not exist.

Such is the nature of Chaos.

She was more certain now than ever that the cult had succumbed to the same imprecations as Rasmuth, fed, no doubt, by the man's hubris, his desperate desire to shepherd his own, peculiar version of the God-Emperor back to life, to bask in the reflected glory of that act.

But what are they really awakening in that ritual?

It looked as though she was about to find out: ahead, the passage opened up into a huge underground chamber full of people.

And there, on a raised plinth at the heart of their gathering, was the pale, unarmoured body of an Adeptus Custodes.

CHAPTER THIRTY-ONE

'To face one's past is to face one's future.'

– Sister Phelia Vengous, *On Human Endurance*

Sabbathiel sucked at the warm, stale air, trying to drag it down into her lungs, trying to steady herself.

The subterranean chamber was vast – a huge, cathedral-like space, mirroring the immensity of the edifice above. Yet the walls down here had been erected from human suffering, the net sum of a million deaths, their skulls and bones woven into some dreadful semblance of order, some grotesque temple to the oblivion of death.

Beneath a stark, vaulted ceiling, lit by the warm glow of myriad candles that floated free on suspensor platforms, people had gathered by the score. Many of them wore the same black carapace armour of Sinjan's guards – his entire personal army was here, it seemed – but others bore the hallmarks of clerks, arbiters, enforcers and minor officials.

All of them had their heads thrown back in rapturous, disharmonic song, apparently oblivious to the arrival of Sabbathiel and her team.

The worshippers had gathered around a central plinth, which in turn was surrounded by the surviving architects of this foul theatre: Jolas and Nemedia Bleeth, Father Rand and Atticus Sinjan, along with several dignitaries that Sabbathiel did not recognise.

On the plinth itself lay the thing that had sent such shock waves through Sabbathiel when she had first glimpsed it: the pale, disrobed form of the Custodes.

His eyes were closed, his inky-black hair swept back from his milky flesh. Ribbons of silver scar tissue described a map upon his body. Not a map of grids and lines, but the cartography of stories; a history of his travels, his life, his personal war. His chest fluttered with shallow breath. A gaping wound, packed with primitive bandages, was evident in his lower torso. He was near death, enveloped in a deep coma from which his mind might never emerge.

Sabbathiel forced herself to look upon him.

A Custodes. One of the Emperor's chosen, forged in His image. Just like the Astartes…

She was back there, on the battle-barge, standing in the shadow of Leofric. He towered over her, resplendent in his gleaming silver armour, this supposed knight of redemption, of purity. A symbol of all that was good and right. The very embodiment of the Emperor's will…

And yet, in truth, he was as blind and lost as the rest of them.

The Dark Angels had searched her ship, even while the enemy stormed their barges. And all the while, the Grey Knights had waited.

They had found the thing in her vault, the daemon bound in human flesh.

Sarasti.

They had killed her acolytes, obliterated everything she was, everything she could have been.

And now, here, she was living it all again:

The snarl on Leofric's face, the curl of his lip, the *disappointment…*

The punch of the bolt-round chewing into her gut, her hip, throwing her back, blinded by agony.

The kiss of the warp as the storm roiled over her.

The comfort of downy feathers, embracing her as the light faded from her eyes.

The promise of peace, of sleep…

A hand on her shoulder, dragging her back from the brink.

Lights pricking her eyes.

The roar of the chanting.

The chamber beneath the cathedral.

The dying Custodes.

'Sabbathiel?'

Mandreth.

He was right there beside her, a tether to the material world, clasping her shoulder, concern etched into the thin lines of his face. 'Sabbathiel? *Astor?*'

She nodded groggily.

'Can you fight?'

She blinked, comprehension dawning. He was holding his sword.

She turned. Sinjan's guards had peeled away from their flock, weapons raised.

They were attacking. Scores of them.

Sabbathiel nodded. 'Yes. I can fight.'

Mandreth met her eye. 'We finish this, here and now.' He twisted, his sword flickering out to decapitate an onrushing guard. And then he was gone, taken by the tide of the melee, his blade rising and falling as he disappeared into the sudden press.

All around her, Sabbathiel's team were scattering to meet the guards' attack, cutting like scythes into the first wave. Weapons fire flared, bright and stark in the gloom. Men and women screamed. She caught a glimpse of Aethesia, trying to edge closer but mired in the midst of several knots of guards. All the while, the terrible chanting continued, led by Father Rand as he gesticulated rapturously, his hands raised above his head in sheer ecstasy.

The feeling of dislocation intensified. Nothing felt real. It was as if she were a mere observer, as if she were still watching memories replaying before her eyes, and there was no recourse to affect their outcome. As if all of this had already happened, and Sabbathiel was floating free, out of time, still drifting in the warp.

She swallowed, squeezed the grip of her sword until her fingers hurt. The pain cut through the haze. She drew another breath, held it in her lungs for a moment, then exhaled.

Come on, Astor. Don't let them win.

A path was opening before her. If she could get to the Custodes and finish him, then the ritual could be stopped. He was beyond saving now, but she might yet set him free.

Mandreth was right. They would end this, here and now.

Sabbathiel threw back her head, bellowed until her throat was raw, and charged.

Bledheim ducked. The guard's shot went wide, inches from where his head had been. He was certain he could feel the heat of it, the rush of disturbed air where the las-round had passed.

Throne. I'm going to die.

His heart was thudding, his skin prickling with sweat.

We're all going to die.

He stayed down, low, watching as the faceless guards fell in droves all about them.

Silq and Mandreth have this under control. They know what they're doing.

Don't they?

He glanced down at his pistol, gripped tightly in his sweaty palm. He hadn't fired it yet, unwilling to draw attention to himself, to encourage reprisal.

What am I even doing here?

On his left, Silq stood before a sea of partially dissolved bodies, her legs braced, her shoulders hunched, her xenos rifle spitting streams of raw, green gauss fire. The weapon had the alarming effect of disintegrating any living matter that came into contact with its strange, alien discharge. That included the upper torso, limbs or heads of people. As he watched, another two guards – a man and a woman – were caught in another blast. The man staggered back, waving the bloody stumps of his arms, while the woman slumped, a strange, ragged hole where the left half of her chest had been.

Silq grunted, grimacing in pain as she shifted position. The wound in her shoulder was probably suppurating now, with only a moment's superficial treatment from Metik in the back of their second requisitioned lander, cauterising the entry and exit sites to stem any further bleeding. That she was able to operate her weapon at all was a miracle as far as Bledheim was concerned.

On his right, Mandreth was hacking at the guards with abandon, his visage locked in a wild-eyed grimace as he swung, parried, cut and thrust. Nameless men and women fell at his feet, the sounds of their death cries lost beneath the ominous chanting. Above, Mandreth's falcon swooped and dived, gouging the eyes of any who came too close to its master.

Yet still the guards came on in their droves, unrelenting, swarming, throwing themselves to their deaths in an effort to overwhelm the opposition, to mindlessly protect those who had convinced them of the sanctity of the ritual. Their grinning faces were proof positive of their belief that they were giving themselves to a just and worthy cause, dying as martyrs in the name of the reborn Emperor.

Bledheim tried to tamp down the panic that was threatening to overwhelm him.

Fanatics.

That's all we need.

Sabbathiel's sword blade trailed sheets of blood as she charged towards the stone plinth at the heart of the ritual, cutting down any and all in her way. A twist to the right eviscerated a guard who was rushing in to tackle her flank; a wheeling swing overhead decapitated another on the left.

All the while, the monotonous chanting filled her ears, as if it were trying to worm its way into her mind, infect her with its torturous simplicity. As she drew closer to the plinth, the power of the chanting grew stronger, like a febrile tension in the air, and she was forced to grit her teeth as she pushed through it.

Another guard fell, still chanting as she clutched at the stump of her arm, apparently unaware of the spraying artery in her thigh.

Sabbathiel ignored the gritty spatter of blood on her face, ignored the sting of a las-burn on her left leg, the press of the buckled armour plating against her back where someone had managed to land a blow in her wake.

The path to the body was clear. One clean strike, and it would all be over.

Three more steps.

Sabbathiel launched herself, swinging her blade overhead in an executioner's arc, aiming for the clean, soft tissue of the Custodes' neck.

Her sword swept down before her as she took her final step…

…only to be intercepted in its downward arc by the thrust of a familiar ebon blade.

The two swords clanged and sparked as they collided.

Sinjan.

Sabbathiel twisted, trying to right herself, to alter her momentum, but Sinjan was too fast and was already pressing his advantage, pushing her back with a force that made her stagger, one step, two, away from the plinth.

Sabbathiel shifted her weight, regained her footing. The crowd had parted around them, giving them space. And still the chanting continued, Rand's voice rising and falling with the awful melody of some corrupt, blasphemous sermon.

'You're a difficult woman to kill,' snarled Sinjan as he came on, his blade seeming to rise and fall in time with the makeshift choir. His pink eyes looked stark and feral in the wan light of the chamber, and his pale, unpigmented skin seemed to shine. His expression was one of arrogant satisfaction – as though he knew, with supreme confidence, that he had already won this fight, or at least had done enough to secure the success of his grand scheme, irrespective of Sabbathiel's interference.

Overhead, Fitch circled, his red lights tracking Sinjan's movements as if the man were doused in blood.

'How's the arm?' she asked, stepping into his swing, parrying, and replying with a fierce swing of her own.

In answer, he simply reached out and caught her sword on

the downswing, his metal fist closing around the sparking blade. He yanked, dragging her closer, unwilling as she was to release her own grip on the weapon.

'A considerable improvement,' he hissed, his spittle speckling her face.

Sabbathiel lashed out with her free hand, striking him hard across the side of the head with her gauntleted fist.

Sinjan reeled, releasing his grip on her sword and staggering back, his own sword momentarily lowered so that its tip raised sparks from the stone floor.

She came on, thrusting for his heart, but he managed to get his own blade back up in time, battering hers aside so that it merely scraped across his upper arm, rending the armour plating and drawing a thin line of blood.

Sinjan winced and fell back, his sword at the ready, circling like a wolf awaiting the right moment to rush in for the throat of its prey. 'Why won't you just *die?*' he spat, working his sore jaw. 'You're just like Heldren, dogged to the very last.'

'Is that why you killed him?' said Sabbathiel. 'Because he got too close to the truth?'

'He wouldn't let it go,' said Sinjan. 'And then when he took an interest in you... I couldn't allow that. You were too much of an unknown factor.' He laughed. 'But he was right, wasn't he? To put his faith in you. You got close. Closer than he ever did.'

'Close enough to stop you,' said Sabbathiel. She bellowed as she closed on him again, raining blow after blow, battering him back with sheer power and ferocity.

Grunting, Sinjan dropped to one knee, breathing hard. Sabbathiel raised her sword.

'Get the frecking Throne out. Of. My. Way.'

The *whoomph* of searing plasma followed this decree, and two more guards fell, screaming as their torsos melted into sizzling puddles on the flagstones.

'I'm trying to *see*.'

Brondel had been at the heart of the fighting since the moment the guards had attacked, and now, circling around behind Sabbathiel, he was doing his best to both cover her back and watch as she beat Sinjan into oblivion. The sight made his heart sing; after what the frecker had done to Heloise, he deserved to end up wearing his guts around his scrawny neck. Brondel had never seen Sabbathiel so ferocious. She was like a hammer, beating Sinjan back, over and over – an unrelenting, unstoppable tide.

He squeezed off another shot, hooting with laughter as the recipient, who had been trying to rush Sabbathiel from behind, tried to grab at his burning backside, before tumbling over, whimpering. Even as he died, he was still trying to chant in time with the other cultists. It was an ignominious death, but no more than he deserved – the man *had* been trying to stab someone in the back, after all.

Nearby, Metik was lining up a series of shots with his usual unerring, mechanical precision, detonating guards as they closed on the rest of the team, all the while continuing to maintain several ongoing combats around him, his snaking mechadendrites darting, swiping and slashing at any enemy combatants who risked coming too close. Nimbik was off somewhere else, most likely burning holes in cultists' skulls.

Close on Brondel's left, the null maiden was a smear of flashing gold as she moved with such grace and speed that the squat was barely able to see her amongst the carnage she wrought. She was whipping her blade around her like a spinning wheel, forcing her way through the press towards Sabbathiel, and anyone who even tried to get close staggered away with missing limbs, slit guts or cleaved faces. Brondel still couldn't bring himself to *like* the woman – the nausea she induced in him was too close to a hangover for him to ever do that – but it didn't prevent him from admiring her martial skill, or her determination.

Maybe he *was* starting to like her, after all.

Just a little.

Brondel heard a roar and glanced up to see Nol pounding past, running in the opposite direction, huge fists breaking heads, collapsing skulls into one another so that the bodies of the cultists slid to the floor in his wake, brain matter mashed and oozing.

Mercy, too, was giving no quarter, chopping and cleaving with her oversized blade, wiping gore from her face with her forearm in between each swing.

The ranks of Sinjan's army were beginning to thin. But then, the eerie chanting seemed to be reaching some sort of crescendo, too.

A shimmering wall of yellow flame had now encircled the plinth at the heart of the ritual – a blinding, ethereal light that the squat could barely look at, even seen through the polarising lenses of his goggles. Worse, though, scores of the cultists were now casting off their robes and walking willingly forward into the searing light, their faces upturned in ecstasy even as their naked bodies were utterly consumed. All the while, the priest, Rand, implored more of them to join with their brethren in the conflagration.

'Come, brothers, sisters! Give yourself to the Emperor's Holy Light! Be at one with His divinity! Walk into the flames and be reborn in His Love! Only then might He rise again to walk amongst us!'

Brondel glanced back at Sabbathiel. There was still time to stop this madness.

Sinjan was nearly finished.

* * *

Sinjan, still down on one knee, raised his blade defensively, but there was little strength left in him. Sabbathiel could see that. His sword tip was wavering, his expression tight, controlled. Blood seeped from a gash in his forehead, and his jaw had begun to swell from where she'd hammered him with her fist a few moments earlier. He knew he was going to die. She'd seen that certainty in men's eyes before – the recognition of their own end, coming up to meet them like a sudden, unexpected wall.

Sabbathiel's own muscles were burning from the constant rain of blows she'd been forced to maintain just to keep the man down, to push him back. She was close to exhaustion and her wounded shoulder pulsed with a bone-deep ache. But she could not let up. Not now. Not until it was over.

She raised her sword. It was time to end it. Sinjan *and* the ritual.

She stepped close, battering Sinjan's sword aside and then raising her arms for the killing blow. His eyes met hers, and where a moment before there had been stark resignation, now there was a flash of amusement. He smirked.

Sabbathiel hesitated, suddenly unsure. She sensed movement and glanced to her right, just in time to see one of the nearby guards – a helmeted man dressed in the same black uniform as all the others – seem to shift, as if his entire body was melting, oozing, morphing...

Throne.

Sabbathiel pivoted just in time to block the Assassin's darting attack. The force of the impact was enough to bowl her backwards, slamming her onto the ground, the air rushing from her gasping lungs.

Her vision swam as she fought to breathe, to raise her weapon to defend herself.

Close by, she could hear Sinjan's rasping laughter.

Above Sabbathiel, the slender form of the Assassin loomed.

CHAPTER THIRTY-TWO

'And in the darkness, He shall rise again.'

– Sextus Harl, *The Thorian Solution*

Sabbathiel rolled, her chest screaming as she forced air down into her resisting lungs.

The Assassin's phase sword raked the ground where Sabbathiel had lain, scoring the flagstones with a high-pitched screech. It wheeled, flipping up and over, its front morphing from its back as it came at her again, blade flashing.

So fast.

Desperately, still on her knees, Sabbathiel parried – left, right, right again – as the Assassin unleashed a flurry of targeted blows. She was already close to exhaustion from her fight with Sinjan; she didn't know how long she'd be able to hold out against an even more skilled assailant.

A blur from above.

Fitch dived, lasers flickering as he swooped in towards the

Assassin's face, burning deep furrows into its strange, amorphous flesh, and then coming about the back of its head for a second pass. The Assassin lurched back, fist swinging.

Fitch took the punch in the side of the skull, and the force of the blow sent him rocketing away, his repulsors out of control. He slammed into the back of a nearby guard, sending the woman sprawling to the ground, before crashing hard into the flagstones, splinters of bone and mechadendrite erupting into the air like shrapnel.

The move had given Sabbathiel a chance to lurch to her feet, however, and she rounded on the Assassin, power sword gripped in both hands.

The gaping wounds in the Assassin's face and neck were already closing, stitching themselves together before Sabbathiel's eyes. She risked a glance towards Sinjan, worried that he might close in on her from the other side, but he'd already returned to his place by the plinth, evidently confident that the Assassin was more than a match for Sabbathiel.

As far as Sabbathiel could tell, the others in her team were all still busy taking on multiple guards – she couldn't rely on anyone but herself to get her out of this.

Great.

The Assassin came at her again, another flurry of feints and attacks. Sabbathiel fought to hold her guard – blocking, ducking, sidestepping – but the Assassin was simply too fast, and the phase blade caught her left arm, slicing through armour, flesh and muscle before darting away again, ready for another strike.

Pain blossomed. Sabbathiel emitted a low groan. She could feel warm blood running freely down her forearm, pooling inside her gauntlet, leaving her fingers slick and greasy. But she wasn't dead yet. She raised her sword.

The Assassin lurched forward, and then suddenly left, as a

wheeling blade came sailing out of the press of the nearby melee, driving the Assassin back. Sabbathiel took a step away, staggered to see Aethesia, her golden armour streaming with rivulets of blood, rushing forward to engage the Assassin.

What was more, the null maiden's attack was actually working.

Sabbathiel breathed. Trying to ignore the strobing pain in her arm, she raised her weapon and hurried to Aethesia's side, pressing the attack against the implacable Assassin, who was now forced to defend itself on two fronts, parrying furiously as both Aethesia and Sabbathiel pressed their advantage.

'You don't have to do this,' Sabbathiel gasped, tasting sour blood on her lips. She was unsure if it was her own or someone else's. 'You've got the wrong target. This ritual' – she dragged air into her lungs, pivoted, slashed out, only for it to be blocked again – 'it's corrupt. They're not summoning the Emperor. Can't you sense it? The foul taint of Chaos.'

If the Assassin heard, it offered no acknowledgement. Its face remained blank, near featureless, unemotive. Its blade continued to dart back and forth, at such a speed Sabbathiel could barely register it.

And then Aethesia was falling back, blood fountaining from a puncture wound in her abdomen, her sword tumbling weakly from her grip.

The Assassin turned back to Sabbathiel. It wasn't even out of breath.

The guard seemed to come out of nowhere. One moment the coast was clear, the next he was rushing Silq, his eyes hungry for bloody murder.

Silq tried to whirl around, loosing another gauss blast, but the man was already too close, and the shot went wide, striking the wall on the other side of the chamber. Desperately, she swung the rifle as a club, but she didn't have room to get any real power behind the blow and the man blocked it easily with his upraised arm, launching himself forward, a curved dagger clutched in his other fist.

Bledheim fumbled for his laspistol, tried to get a bead. He fired. Once, twice, but his hand was shaking, and the shots did nothing but singe the dust on the flagstones by Silq's feet.

He watched in horror as the man closed the distance in a single bound, his dagger plunging deep into Silq's chest. She screamed, trying weakly to push the guard away, but her damaged shoulder meant she was too slow, and the man raised his fist and struck again, burying the blade up to its hilt.

'No!'

Silq gave a burbling cry, blood frothing at her lips, and toppled backwards, her head cracking against the stone floor.

The man grinned wolfishly and stooped to retrieve his dagger.

Something snapped inside Bledheim. He felt a hot rage welling up inside him, spreading up into his chest, his face, his mind.

How dare they?

How dare they do this *to his friends?*

He glanced down at Silq's unmoving form. Her eyes were still bright in the gloom, but there was nothing there behind them, no spark of the life that had once inhabited that face, that skull.

I should have stopped him.

I should have...

Bledheim's fingers closed around the stock of his pistol.

Vengeance.

He strode towards the guard, who was still grinning inanely, wiping the blade of his bloody knife on his sleeve. He turned as he saw Bledheim coming, his expression slowly turning to one of confusion as he noted the expression on the interrogator's face.

The man lifted a hand in paltry defence, but Bledheim didn't stop, didn't give it even a moment's thought. He simply raised the pistol and shot the man in the face. Then he did it again, and again, and again.

Another guard came at him then, and coolly, calmly, Bledheim turned and shot him, too. Then a third, and a fourth. He would defend Silq's body until this was over. No one would come near.

No one.

From his vantage point atop the pile of enemy corpses, Brondel, breathing heavily, watched as Mandreth tried and failed to cut a path to Sabbathiel. The remaining guards were refusing to rout, fanatical to the last, and Mandreth was effectively swarmed, boxed in on all sides, fighting desperately for his life. His bird was still providing what support it could from above, but it had taken at least one glancing shot from a laspistol and several of its feathers were blackened and still smouldering.

Things weren't going well.

Elsewhere, Nol was knee-deep in corpses, whacking guards with one hand while he used another as a shield to fend off pistol rounds and thrown knives. Metik, too, was mired in the bodies of the fallen, and had taken to moving about on his mechadendrites like some alien beast, still picking off guards with his antique rifle.

Brondel had seen Silq go down – he'd make the bastards pay for that tenfold once he'd caught his breath – and witnessed Bledheim unleash a storm of las-fire in response, wailing and gnashing his teeth as he dropped guard after guard.

With a pistol.

Hidden depths, that one.

Footsteps sounded behind him. Brondel turned, swinging his boot up and around, and catching the man who'd been sneaking up on him in the side of the head. The guard grunted and fell back, shaking his head groggily, then collapsed in a heap as a plasma round burned a clear hole through his chest. Brondel took a potshot at another while he was at it, but only managed to take off their arm as they tried to dive out of the way.

He hawked up a gobbet of phlegm and spat.

The chanting had shifted in pitch and tempo again, and the fools gathered around the plinth were still casting themselves wilfully into the flames, their bodies bursting and bubbling as they fizzled away to ash. But the light had begun to take on a different hue. Where earlier it had seared a brilliant golden-white, now there was a sickly tinge of green. The green of nausea and rot. The green of Chaos.

As Brondel watched, the last of the sacrificial worshippers threw herself into the infernal wall of flame, her body disintegrating before it had even hit the ground. The flames grew brighter, stronger, taller – *greener* – and then, as if disturbed by some otherworldly draught, began to twist and turn, circling from the base of the wall like a gathering tornado. Brondel watched, transfixed, as the flames twisted and lifted, still circling, until – with shocking urgency – they began to pour themselves into the slumbering form of the Custodes on the slab.

The body began to twitch and shudder, as though someone were passing an electrical current through its limbs.

Close by, Rand's expression had grown beatific. He threw his hands out, basking in the adoration of his remaining followers. He reached up, yanking his collar free in triumph, revealing a puckered circle of bloody, open sores around his throat. 'He comes! He comes!'

Brondel looked back at the shuddering corpse.

'Freck,' he said.

* * *

Bledheim lowered his pistol and took a heaving breath. His arm was trembling. Around him, in every direction, the dead and the dying lay in pools of their own life fluids, some already beginning to congeal. Others writhed in agony, clutching their wounds but nevertheless somehow finding the strength to continue with their disturbing, monotonous chanting, giving even their dying breaths for the sake of their illusionary saviour.

The reek of death filled his nostrils. Bile burned the back of his throat.

The remaining guards were giving him a wide berth.

What have I done?

He glanced up. On the plinth, the body of the Custodes was twitching, its arms and legs jerking with unnatural motion, as if an invisible puppeteer was plucking at its strings, attempting to instil the catatonic warrior with some strange semblance of life.

Around it, the worshippers had reached feverish intensity, and he realised that, for them, for Sinjan, the guards had served their purpose all too well – they had held the interlopers at bay long enough for the ritual to near completion. These men and women had been fooled into thinking they were a part of something greater, some sacred order, when in fact they had been nothing but fodder all along.

How could they not see it?

A deep, guttural roar sounded from across the chamber. Bledheim turned to see Mercy making a break for the plinth, her massive sword canted above her head, ready to try for a swing, to cut the revenant down before the ritual was completed.

Robed followers, unprotected now by the last few surviving guards, parted in a wave to let her pass, and for a moment Bledheim thought she was going to make it.

Until Sinjan lurched out from amongst the throng to face her, his black sword braced in both hands. Mercy's momentum was such that she couldn't stop.

With a metallic rending, the sword punctured her chest, just under where her ribs should have been. It burst out of her back, sparks raining like fireflies, as cables, cogs and Throne only knew what else Metik had installed inside her were severed, mangled, destroyed.

Mercy, shocked, came to a sudden, jolting stop. Her weapon fell from her grip, clanging loudly to the floor. She looked down at the sword hilt jutting from her chest, and then back up at Sinjan.

Then, with a look of sheer disgust, she reached out and took Sinjan by the shoulders and slowly, painfully, pushed him away, so that his sword slid free of her innards with a grating sigh. She stared at him for a moment longer, then staggered away, collapsing against a nearby pillar, where she remained, propping herself up, heaving ragged breaths.

Bledheim glanced down at Silq's body by his feet. Her eyes peered up at him, not in judgement, but in empathy, understanding, compassion. Slowly, he dropped to his knees and, with his fingertips, carefully drew them shut.

Sabbathiel grunted with pain and exertion. Her left arm had taken another hit and was now hanging limply by her side. She was certain it was broken, or worse. Her armour was scored with multiple near misses, and she hadn't managed a counter-attack for what seemed like hours. It was all she could do to hang on, to keep the Assassin at bay. And soon she would fail at that.

Aethesia was on the ground nearby, unconscious or dead. Mandreth was still battling a small army of Sinjan's guards and, as far as she could glean, the others were all either dead, dying or locked in futile combat like Mandreth. Even Fitch was unmoving on the ground.

Is this it? Is this *what I returned for?*

Better that you'd left me to fester in the warp, Mandreth.

Better that I'd stayed dead.

The Assassin swung wide. Sabbathiel shifted to counter, but the motion was too sudden, too far, and her footing went from under her, sending her crashing to the ground beside Aethesia, her sword skittering from her grip. Her left arm exploded in lancing pain.

Grimacing, she pushed herself back ineffectually with her heels. The Assassin took a step forward, towering over her. It hadn't even broken a sweat.

'Stop,' said Sabbathiel, appalled at how small, how weak, her own voice sounded. '*Listen* to me. The ritual…' She trailed off, sudden realisation dawning.

The room had grown instantly, profoundly silent.

She stared up at the Assassin; gave a small, barely perceptible shake of her head.

It seemed to hesitate.

'He *lives!*' Rand's voice was a triumphant roar. It echoed through the chamber, brutally loud in the ethereal silence that had fallen over the waiting crowd.

Oh, Throne. No…

Sabbathiel twisted, unmindful now of the Assassin, of what it might do. All eyes in the room were on the Custodes' body, still twitching ominously, spasmodically.

And then it fell still.

Before a massive knot of green, slime-covered tentacles burst from its writhing guts.

They spewed out in multitudes, sliding over the quivering pale flesh, slopping to the floor, curling and probing as if tasting the air, growing in both size and number. The stench that accompanied them was foetid and heady, thick with sweet rot.

Rand fell to his knees, wailing in insane, ecstatic triumph, tears running down his cheeks. 'He lives! He lives!'

Sabbathiel looked back at the Assassin. It was watching the scene unfolding at the plinth, its phase blade hovering above her, only a single thrust away from finishing her off. It turned and glanced down at her.

'We need to stop it,' said Sabbathiel, her voice raw. *'Now!'*

The Assassin continued to study her for a moment, as if weighing its options, and then warily took a step back, lowering its blade.

Sabbathiel allowed the breath to whistle out between her teeth.

Thank the Throne.

There was no time to wallow in relief, however. Another glance at the plinth told her the tentacles were multiplying exponentially, erupting from the dead body in size and number too great for the vessel to ever contain, as if the dying Custodes had become a mere portal, a doorway, an opening...

To the warp.

They're bringing forth a daemon.

And Sinjan must have known it all along.

Somewhere along the way, they became lost. Him, Rand, Rasmuth... perhaps even the Bleeths. So fervent in their desire to reincarnate the Emperor that they lost sight of the truth and embraced the lie. They welcomed Chaos into their midst.

They are traitors all.

Sabbathiel dragged herself up to her knees, her limp arm pulsing painfully with every movement. Beside her, Aethesia was stirring, groaning and rolling onto her side.

Still alive, then.

Emperor knows, she's a hard woman.

Shrill screaming now filled the chamber, as the true nature

of the ritual finally dawned on the remaining cultists, and the writhing tentacles began to flicker in their direction, probing now at their skin, puncturing and sliding inside, wriggling maggot-like in their flesh.

Sabbathiel saw Nemedia Bleeth stagger back as a fat tendril lashed out in her direction. She reached for her husband, clutching for his arm, but rather than dragging the slower-moving man to safety, she shoved him into the tentacle's path in her stead.

Jolas turned, making to run, but the tentacle burst out through his chest, causing his ribcage to yawn open like a blooming flower, its bony spurs unfurling like fragile petals. His exposed lungs glistened as they deflated. His haggard face wore an expression of terrible shock as he stood there, already dead, yet supported by the worming thing that still squirmed inside his flesh.

Nemedia screamed, bolting for the exit, but more tentacles flickered out to snare her around the ankle, the waist, the wrist. Struggling, crying out, whimpering, she was slowly dragged back towards the plinth, panic now overriding all sense of her usual stoic control.

Sabbathiel, who was now on her feet and reaching to reclaim her sword, watched in horror as a thinner tentacle snaked out from the morass at the heart of the plinth, coiling like a viper, sliding slowly up Nemedia's back. She screamed in abject terror, bucking wildly as it pressed against the back of her neck, before it burrowed up through the base of her skull, curling its way into her brain.

For a moment the woman slumped in the tentacles' grotesque embrace, still propped upright like her dead husband, hanging like a puppet on shifting strings. But then her third eye blinked open and her head whipped back, her mouth gaping slack and loose. The sound that emerged from her throat was utterly inhuman: a terrible, alien dirge that seemed to shake the very foundations of the cathedral and tear at Sabbathiel's soul. A thing so alien, so violent, that blood trickled from Sabbathiel's ears and nose, and she was forced to double over, hacking and spluttering as nausea overcame her in a wave.

Yet the foul dirge was spreading like a virulent infection, a plague, taken up by all in its path. Those who had not already died at the hands of the probing tentacles – Sinjan, Rand, Nol, Bledheim and Mandreth, along with a dozen more guards and cultists – were throwing their heads back in unwilling unison, the dirge now spilling from their slack-jawed mouths.

As the cacophony grew, so too did the tentacles of whatever creature was emerging into this realm through the pale form of the Custodes.

And so, too, did Sabbathiel's utter dismay.

CHAPTER THIRTY-THREE

'Purge the Unclean.'

– Traditional

Sabbathiel felt a hand on her shoulder, but it was not a hand offered in reassurance – the other person was leaning on her to prop themselves up.

The dirge had grown worse, like a vice tightening around her mind, probing, testing her defences. She fought back another wave of nausea.

Why hadn't she succumbed like the others? She peered at them now, heads aloft in a melody of corruption, bodies trembling as they fought against this violation, this twisted possession. Even the Assassin had been unable to resist the enemy's lure.

She glanced at the woman resting against her shoulder. The only other one free of the curse.

Aethesia.

The null maiden.

Aethesia's presence was diluting the efficacy of the creature's psychic attack. Her proximity to Sabbathiel was the only thing that had saved her.

Then it's down to me.

Sabbathiel raised herself to her full height, gripping her power sword in her right hand.

Beside Sabbathiel, Aethesia tested her footing, then stood, nodding, raising her own blade in both hands. The ragged wound above her hip was still seeping blood, stark and bright against her golden armour.

Sabbathiel wasn't sure how much longer either of them could last, but she had little choice – if she didn't stop this thing, here and now, she'd be dead within minutes regardless.

Fighting back the swirling blackness that limned her vision, she took a lurching step forward, towards the suspended form of Nemedia Bleeth, still hanging in the daemon's invasive embrace.

Then another.

And another.

The volume of the dirge seemed to drown out her very thoughts, washing everything away in a tide of pollution. There was a simplicity in it that seemed somehow enticing, a hidden beauty that called to her, offering to release her from the pain, to set her free.

But it was all a lie. A fallacy to encourage the weak.

The carrion call of Chaos.

Sabbathiel shook her head, as if to shake off the insidious thoughts.

One more step.

With a roar of effort, she forced herself forward, one step closer to the dead Navigator. Blood streamed from her nostrils, a warm river over her lips, her chin. She raised her sword.

And swung.

Nemedia's head parted from her unliving shoulders with a wet crack. It spun away, striking the wall with a dull thud, bloody and unrecognisable, its three eyes staring bleakly into nothingness.

The dirge ceased almost immediately.

Around Sabbathiel, people slumped as if their strings had been cut.

Before her, the corpse of Nemedia remained hanging, shifting slightly with the swaying of the sickening limbs that held her. The buds of tiny tentacles wormed from the stump of her neck, as if grasping for the air.

More of them were still bubbling out of the Custodes' guts, preceding, Sabbathiel guessed, the bulk of something even larger. She turned to Aethesia and the Assassin, the latter of whom was picking itself up from the ground, groggily shaking its head. 'We need to clear a path to the plinth. The only way to stop this now is to destroy the host body before the daemon fully manifests.'

Aethesia gave a curt nod of understanding. The Assassin's only response was to raise its phase blade and fix its gaze on the beast.

Perhaps we can still do it. Perhaps the three of us c–

She turned at the sound of running footsteps, instinctively raising her sword.

Sinjan, snarling with hatred, closed to meet her at a run.

Still crouching by Silq, Bledheim watched the tentacles slowly coiling around the kneeling form of Father Rand, who, in his madness, appeared to be welcoming the daemon's serpentine embrace, offering himself up to it like some sacrificial victim.

The creature was only too obliging, wrapping its limbs around his torso and throat, choking the life from him in the manner a python would constrict and crush its prey. Rand's eyes bulged, his face slowly turning a bright shade of cerise.

Even as the last of his breath was forced from his lungs, the fool was still burbling on about the risen Emperor and His sacred light.

Close by, the fighting was growing in intensity, as the null maiden and the Assassin – Bledheim could hardly believe that the deadly thing was now *assisting* them in taking down the daemon – fought to clear a path to the plinth where the Custodes' host body still lay. They fought like engines of war, like things born to deliver death, their whirling blades slicing and chopping tentacles in a hazy blur of ichor and blood. Where the severed tentacles fell, they seemed to disintegrate, dissolving into festering puddles of black goo that seeped away into the cracks between the flagstones.

Yet for every tendril they removed, another two would rise, hydra-like, from the stump, regenerating and swelling at alarming speed. Even without the nightmarish call of the dirge – Bledheim could still taste its lingering after-effects, like poison coating the roof of his mouth – the daemonic thing was growing in strength, dragging itself closer to reality from whatever festering bubo of surreality had born it.

Closer still, Sabbathiel was barely managing to keep Sinjan at bay. She looked weary, bloody, her left arm hanging loose by her side.

The Queen of Ruin.

The tarot reader had been right. What was left of them now?

Regardless, he knew he had to act, to help her any way he could. He staggered to his feet, raising his pistol. But Bledheim's aim was far from sure, and the two combatants were engaged in a shifting dance, back and forth, back and forth, as if swaying to the rhythm of their ringing blows. He couldn't draw a reliable bead.

Movement from the corner of his eye. He spun to see Mandreth hurtling across the chamber, sword drawn, charging to intercept Sinjan.

Thank the Throne.

Bledheim lowered his pistol. His relief was palpable.

A tentacle whipped out from the plinth, flicking over Aethesia's head. It caught Mandreth hard in the chest, reversing his momentum and lifting him bodily into the air, tossing him across the room like a broken doll. He issued a harrowing screech, before slamming into a pillar and sliding slowly to the floor.

Bledheim staggered, mouth agape. He took two steps towards where Mandreth now lay in a crumpled heap, and then paused, glancing back at Sabbathiel, torn over what to do.

And that was when he saw it.

Across the far side of the room, Metik was hunching low over his rifle, lining up a shot. Straight for Sabbathiel's back.

The cuckoo.

Bledheim ran.

He didn't have a plan – he hadn't had time for that – and he knew he was no match for the tech-priest, but all he had to do was interrupt the shot, send it careening wild instead of catching Sabbathiel in the back of the head.

Wasn't it?

Bledheim launched himself at Metik, throwing his arms up to protect his face from the whipping mechadendrites.

'What in the–'

He struck the unsuspecting tech-priest hard in the shoulder, sending them both sprawling awkwardly to the ground in a mess of squirming mechanical cables and arms. The rifle went skittering away across the flagstones, coming to rest against a heap of dead cultists.

'What in the name of the Omnissiah are you *doing?*' said Metik, somehow managing to communicate his fury despite the grating monotone of his vocoder, and the fact he was on the ground with Bledheim lying on top of him.

Bledheim rolled off the tech-priest onto the cold flagstones, wincing at the lacerations on his hands and wrists. He lay there for a moment, gasping. Then it dawned on him that Metik might be about to seek reprisal, and he hurriedly scrabbled to his feet. He'd lost his pistol somewhere during the fall, and he searched the ground for it desperately, to no avail.

'Interrogator Bledheim?' said Metik, now carefully lifting himself back to his feet by means of his mechanical arms. 'Must I repeat my question?'

'I was stopping you,' ground out Bledheim.

'From doing what, precisely?'

'From shooting Sabbathiel in the back. I saw you lining up to take the shot.'

Metik made a wheezing sound that might have been an approximation of a sigh. 'For an intelligent man, Bledheim, you lack common insight. It is a very human failing. I was going to shoot Sinjan.'

'But...' Bledheim considered for a moment. How could he trust what this machine man was saying?

'Yes?' prompted Metik.

Bledheim stared at the tech-priest, uncertain how to proceed. He knew what he'd seen. But then... could he have been mistaken? Wasn't he, himself, about to try for a shot before Mandreth made his attempted charge? How might that have looked from across the room?

He sighed.

I have no choice.

I have to let it go.

For now.

'If I had wished for her to be dead,' continued Metik, when it was clear Bledheim wasn't going to answer, 'why would I have rebuilt and resuscitated her in the first place?'

Bledheim shrugged. 'I apologise,' he ground out. The words tasted bitter, hollow. 'I thought I saw–'

'Yes, yes,' said Metik, cutting him off. 'There's no time for that. We have to help her.' He sent out a snaking mechadendrite to retrieve his rifle.

Bledheim nodded.

It'll wait.

Getting past the snapping tentacles was proving next to impossible. Shooting them, too, was almost as ineffective, since they refused to stay still while he shot at them. So, Brondel had decided, if he was going to be the one to get to the plinth and destroy the Custodes' body – and he damned well wasn't going to let anyone else beat him to it – he was simply going to have to go *through* them.

He tucked his plasma pistol into his belt and waded forward into the writhing morass, grabbing for the nearest, fattest, juiciest-looking tentacle. It squirmed in his grip as he tried to squeeze it, bend it back on itself and then, when that failed, wrestle it into submission and squash it beneath his boots.

He couldn't even break the thing's skin.

Roaring in frustration, he wrapped his arms around it and brought it close to his face. Then, with another roar for good luck, he gnashed his teeth and bit it.

Blood and foul ichor dribbled down Brondel's chin, matting his beard. He raised his head and spat a fat gobbet of putrid flesh, before going back in for a second bite.

The tentacle, however, had other ideas, and, with the end of it still pinned between Brondel's hands, it flexed along its length, lifting itself, and the squat, high into the air.

Brondel kicked his stubby legs, trying to wrap them around the girth of the fat tentacle, but to no avail, as the limb whipped him back and forth at speed. He felt his palms sliding on the oily, mucus-covered surface.

'For freck's sake,' he muttered, before – with one last flick – the appendage sent him sailing across the chamber.

Brondel, having been in a similar position once before, had the foresight to tuck his legs up beneath him and hunch his shoulders to protect his neck, so that when he struck the slab-like back of Nol a moment later, he bounced like a cannonball, thudding to the ground and rolling, before coming to a breathless stop a few strides from the ogryn's feet.

Uncurling, groaning, Brondel tried to wipe foul-tasting sputum from his lips.

Nol, still busy mashing the last of Sinjan's guards with his fists, simply turned to look down at Brondel, shrugged, and returned to what he was doing.

Brondel looked back at the pit of tentacles and narrowed his eyes.

So, I'm going to need to find another way through…

He looked up at the ogryn and smiled.

The ringing of the blades had become the ticking of a clock, a steady countdown to her impending death. Her body seemed to move of its own volition, countering attack after attack as Sinjan feverishly came at her.

The man had forsaken all sense of his humanity, so lost was he now to the depredations of Chaos.

'Is this what you wanted, Sinjan?' she ground out through gritted teeth. 'Is this the Emperor you so desired?'

Sinjan growled, his expression twisted into a visage of hate.

It mattered little. He would die here. If not by her hand, then by the daemon he had welcomed into their midst. His was a victory that could only ever be hollow.

'The path is almost clear. There is a sixty-four point two-one per cent chance of success if you strike for the host body now.'

Metik's grating voice cut through the fog of her weariness.

The path?

Aethesia. The Assassin.

They were doing it.

Sabbathiel grunted, blocked another of Sinjan's swings. The force of the blow reverberated up her arm into her aching shoulder, and she staggered back a step.

And then suddenly Metik was there beside her, his mecha-dendrites swarming, driving Sinjan back. 'Go for the plinth.'

'No...' she breathed, hardly able to emit a sound.

Metik, you fool. I'm already half-dead.

But it was too late.

It took Sinjan only seconds to recover from the initial shock of Metik's attack and – driven by some deep, animalistic rage, some warp-born fury – he pressed his attack. His ebon blade sung as it sent hunks of mechadendrite spinning, as he cut his way through the forest of flailing limbs, driving closer and closer to the tech-priest at the heart of his metal nest. Sparks rained.

Metik tried to hold the rogue inquisitor at bay, but Sinjan would not be stopped. He pushed on, ignoring a flensing gash to his cheek, a puncture wound in his belly, chopping and wheeling, thrusting and cutting, sending severed mecha-dendrites sparking to the ground.

Metik tried to back away, but Sinjan was utterly relentless.

'It seems you have me,' said Metik, matter-of-factly, the moment before Sinjan's blade slashed through his waist, sending him toppling back in a heap of broken metal and bone, gushing oil, blood and steam across the ground.

He gave a gurgling hiss and was silent.

The whole thing had taken only a matter of moments.

Sabbathiel circled, moving around the wreckage of the tech-priest, trying not to think about what it meant, pushing the loss aside, burying it.

'*See?*' spat Sinjan, matching her pacing, his sword tip slowly tracing patterns in the air between them as if he was toying with her. 'This is what Heldren could never understand. All who oppose me die in the end.'

'And all your friends too,' rasped Sabbathiel, 'if the Bleeths are anything to go by.'

Sinjan shrugged, a mad gleam in his eye. 'They weren't worthy enough. Just like you.' He lunged, and Sabbathiel moved to counter, but then he shifted his weight, altering his trajectory into a wide swing.

She saw it coming, but it was too late – one-handed, she couldn't shift her position to accommodate the blow.

His sword caught her blade just above the pommel. Pain shot up her arm, and her fingers released automatically, unable to maintain their grip on the reverberating weapon. It spun out of her hand, clanging to the ground several yards away, energy still crackling along its blade.

Sabbathiel grunted. She took a staggering step back.

Far enough?

No. Another.

She dropped back again, cringing as Sinjan lurched forward to deliver the killing blow. He was overextending himself as he had before, but it hardly mattered; she had no weapon with which to defend herself against his attack.

No weapon except my wit.

Sabbathiel waited until the very last second, until Sinjan had committed, transferring his weight to his front foot, and then propelled herself forward with every ounce of strength she had left. She dropped her shoulder, moving inside the arc of his swing, colliding with him straight-on, barging him backwards. He had no chance of maintaining his balance and, huffing as the air was expelled from his lungs, he fell back, staggering one, two, three steps before he finally overbalanced and went down, landing ignominiously on his rump.

Shaking his head, he sat there for a moment, his shoulders rocking with laughter. Then, slowly, he dragged himself up to one knee, still clutching his sword. 'You're a sly one, Astor Sabbathiel, but you're simply postponing th–'

He stopped abruptly, looking down at the tentacle that had surreptitiously snaked around his right ankle. Frowning, he raised his sword as if to hack at it, when another curled around his wrist, pinning his arm.

Sinjan pulled against it for a moment, growing increasingly frantic. 'No. No, no, no…' He looked up, peering at Sabbathiel in confusion. '*You…*'

A third tentacle burst through his midriff, rupturing his guts, driving the air from his lungs. The slimy appendage wormed at the air, dripping blood and other grimy fluids.

They came with surprising speed and ferocity after that – burrowing through the shoulder, the upper thigh; wrapping around his neck, yanking his head back and probing his mouth.

He tried to scream, but they were in his throat, questing for his eyes, his ears, his nose.

Sighing, Sabbathiel drew her pistol and put a bolt-round through his heart.

His body drooped, the fight finally gone out of him.

Another hollow victory.

Wincing, Sabbathiel crossed to where her sword had come to rest. She bent to pick it up–

And hit the floor, hard, screaming in agony as someone smashed into her broken arm, then landed heavily on top of her back, weighing her down, pressing her into the cold stone slabs.

They didn't seem to be moving.

Groaning, Sabbathiel raised her head, spitting dirt. Her arm was on fire. Throne, *all* of her was on fire.

What had just happened?

She shifted, levering herself up slowly using her good arm, heaving the dead weight off her back and sliding her legs out from beneath it. She twisted, still on the floor, looking back over her shoulder.

Golden armour glinted in the low light.

'No.'

Sabbathiel scrabbled up off the floor, onto her hands and knees. She shuffled over to Aethesia, who was lying prone on the ground, unmoving.

Not you, too.

She felt numb.

She saw immediately what had happened. The null maiden had thrown herself in the way to protect Sabbathiel – a tentacle had punched a fist-sized hole in the back of the woman's head, killing her instantly.

I hadn't even noticed…

I'm sorry…

She placed her hand on Aethesia's chest. 'Thank you… for quietening my dreams.'

Sabbathiel left the body to retrieve her sword, rising slowly to her feet.

She looked around just in time to see Brondel, launched by Nol, sailing through the air towards the plinth, clutching a grenade in his hands, a beaming smile writ large across his hairy face.

The squat landed heavily in the dead Custodes' lap, right in the centre of the nest of tentacles.

'*Freck,*' said Sabbathiel.

Everything went white.

CHAPTER THIRTY-FOUR

'All victories are hollow when the taint of Chaos yet persists.'
– Sister Evangeline of the Order of the Withered Rose,
On the Razing of Cavor City

Light. Ringing. Pain.

Sabbathiel breathed. Pain lanced through her chest with every intake. She could taste something gritty. Dust?

Where?

What…?

Images fluttered through her mind like scattered feathers.

The subterranean vault.

The Custodes.

The squat.

She opened her eyes.

She was lying on the floor, face down. She could taste blood – she'd bitten the inside of her cheek. She spat it out onto the flagstones, pushing herself up with her good arm.

Clouds of dust spiralled through the air, motes picked out by shafts of streaming red light from above.

Red?

The stained-glass window.

She glanced up. The explosion had ripped a hole in the vaulted ceiling, cracking the chamber open like an egg. Rubble was strewn all around her, great hunks of masonry and stone. Flames licked hungrily at the lip of the opening. The cathedral was on fire. The heat of the explosion had evidently vented upwards, throwing burning fragments into the building overhead.

Sabbathiel coughed and pulled herself up into a sitting position. Her ears were still ringing with a sharp, tinnitus drone. She wiped ineffectively at her streaming eyes with the back of her gauntleted hand.

The plinth had been destroyed, and with it, the corpse of the Custodes, which had served as the entity's host. What remained of the body was now buried beneath the collapsed ceiling – Sabbathiel could see nothing but a pale, lifeless hand, jutting from amongst the settling debris.

The tentacles, too, had been destroyed in the blast. Even as she watched, the remaining tendrils were blackening, dissolving into a thick, rotten mulch, seeping away into the cracks between the flagstones.

We did it.

Brondel did it.

Flakes of white ash were drifting down through the hole in the ceiling now, settling on the fallen stones, the pummelled bodies, the ground. Sabbathiel, groggy from the pain, searched the wreckage for any sign of her team. Were they all dead, like Aethesia, like Brondel… like *Fitch?*

If the Assassin had survived, it had already fled – there was no sign of the body near to where it had been fighting. Aethesia still lay close, her golden armour washed crimson like Sabbathiel's in the strange light from above.

Movement caught her eye. Mercy was dragging herself up out of a pile of stones, battered, bruised – her metallic chest punctured and partially caved in – but alive. Behind her, Nol was staggering unsteadily through the ruination, the limp form of Mandreth draped in his arms. From here, Sabbathiel couldn't tell whether her fellow inquisitor was dead or alive.

Now the dust was beginning to clear, she saw other shapes, too – mere silhouettes – pulling themselves clear of the wreckage, like ghosts peeling away from their graves to haunt the living.

She hung her head. Her eyes wanted to close. She was so weary…

Hands grabbed her roughly from behind, reaching under her arms, hauling her up to her feet. She stood shakily, her head still swimming. When she was certain she was steady enough that she wouldn't topple over, she turned to see Bledheim, his face caked in dust, staring at her in concern. His lips were moving but she could hear nothing beneath the sharp whine in her ears. He was pointing urgently in the other direction.

Unsure what else to say or do, Sabbathiel nodded, and then leaned on Bledheim's shoulder as he hurried her, as best he could, towards the exit.

The cool air was like a brisk slap to the face.

Sabbathiel stood for a moment, staring up at the sky. Behind her, the cathedral raged in a blazing inferno, but out here the air was crisp and chill, and flakes of ash rained down from the sky like fresh snow, dancing on the breeze over the city spires, occluding the view. She felt them patter upon her face, catch in her hair.

Bledheim had hurried off to help someone else, and now she

saw him dragging Metik's torso from the flaming portal of the cathedral doors, ably assisted by Nimbik.

Mercy was sitting in the ash a few feet away, hunched forward, her massive sword laid across her lap. Nol had wandered off into the night with Mandreth – presumably to seek help. Sabbathiel's head was still thick with buzzing pain, and her hearing had yet to return.

She saw Bledheim start in shock and followed his gaze. More movement – another figure emerging from the ruins. This one short and stocky, dressed in blackened rags, and patting out a lengthy red beard that appeared to be on fire.

Brondel stood for a moment at the top of the steps, the flames of the burning cathedral forming a bright halo around his head and shoulders. He turned and spat, bellowed something Sabbathiel couldn't hear at the sky, and then collapsed in a steaming heap. Bledheim hurried over.

Smiling, Sabbathiel took a step, then another, and then she was walking, striding forward into the blizzard of snowy ash. There was no sound – not even the crump of her own footsteps. Her left arm hung limply by her side.

I've been here before. I know this.

She staggered, then dropped to her knees, stirring the ash.

It's over. It's done.

But of course, nothing really ended. What of her old conclave now? Would they believe her story? Or were they a part of it? Had they conspired with Sinjan to allow all this to happen?

She had no idea what came next. And for once, the idea was pleasing.

Red light played on the white ash before her. She glanced up. Fitch, leaning haphazardly to one side, several of his mecha-dendrites broken and sparking, was hovering there, just above her left shoulder.

Sabbathiel laughed. 'Looks like the past just keeps on catching up with me,' she said.

Behind her, the cathedral roof collapsed as the building was utterly engulfed in flames.

CHAPTER THIRTY-FIVE

'There is no end; there is only the beginning of something new.'

– Solomon Thoth, *Deathbed Revisions*

Below, the water glistened like a blanket strewn with diamonds, as far as the distant horizon. Not a single land mass marred its pristine surface, not a single shore.

Sabbathiel peered out of the viewport in wonder. Here was a place unblemished by war, by the wants and needs of human or xenos kind. Here was a place at peace.

There was a time, not that long ago, when she'd wondered whether a world like this could even exist any more, but this moon was still new, unspoiled, *pure*. The very thought of it brought a smile to her lips.

There are still places worth fighting for, then.

She'd left her team, those who had survived, recuperating on Garabon. Brondel had suffered severe burns that would need time to heal – it was a miracle in itself that he was still walking – and Mercy was stable and awaiting repairs to her chest unit. Metik, in the meantime, was back at his sanctuary on Tistus, rebuilding himself with the help of his mind-slave and a small army of servitors.

Bledheim remained as curious as ever; his wounds, like her own, ran deeper than mere flesh and blood and bone, and would take far longer to heal. That she didn't yet understand the true nature of those wounds was a constant source of both frustration and fascination to her. She'd resolved to keep him close. If nothing else, he offered an interesting perspective on matters. And he wasn't without talent.

Of Mandreth and Nol there had been no sign. She'd searched for them on Hulth in the days immediately following events at the cathedral, but she could only presume they'd gone to ground, or else fled the planet to avoid the inevitable questions they would face in the aftermath. She could hardly blame them.

'Coming in to land now, ma'am.'

'Thank you, Fitch.' She eased back into her seat as the lander banked, then righted itself, before settling onto the landing platform with a whooshing sigh.

Outside, the sight of the facility stole her breath. It was a simple platform that rose high out of the ocean, its transparent floors and walls imparting a disconcerting sense that she was walking directly out across the ruffled water.

A small, domed building stood at one end of the platform, jutting out over the waves, away from the landing pad.

She stood beside the ship for a while, taking it all in, allowing the wind to whip up her hair, filling her nostrils with the rich, salty tang of the water.

Waves again. And so, we come full circle.

We make our own shores.

She set out towards the building.

She found the door open.

She knew this place. She'd seen it before, in her visions; seen the dark-skinned man inside, standing before the tall plate windows, looking out upon the foaming water, watching huge aquatic beasts cavort and play, leaping up out of the waves, only to crash back down moments later, sending whirling tornadoes of spray back up into the air.

Jherek.

The final piece of the puzzle. The final player in this strange game.

He had not been an easy man to find, but then, Sabbathiel was resourceful.

She cleared her throat.

The man turned and smiled. His face was careworn and creased. In appearance he was probably close to sixty human years, but of course, he was most likely far older. He was wearing a black thigh-length coat and tarnished silver armour, and his hair – once comprised of tight black curls – was now flecked with grey. 'Welcome, Astor Sabbathiel,' he said, and gestured for her to join him by the window. She did.

'I must say – I'm impressed.'

Sabbathiel smiled. 'Yes, they are rather impressive beasts, aren't they?'

Jherek laughed, and it was a genuine, throaty laugh that seemed to boom throughout the room. 'Oh, they said I'd like you.'

Sabbathiel felt a spike of annoyance. She had little time for more games. 'They?'

Jherek waved a hand dismissively. 'You know how it is.' He rubbed the side of his nose with his finger. 'You did well, Sabbathiel. Heldren would have been proud.'

'You knew Heldren?'

'Of course. He and I were... well, let us just say that we were working together.'

'To investigate Hulth?'

Jherek nodded. 'And the rest. We knew there was a problem at the heart of the Palmarian Conclave. But we didn't know what, or who. Heldren was simply too close, too mired in old friendships to see it clearly. You, however – your re-emergence presented a unique opportunity. A fresh perspective. Not to mention your legendary talent for weeding out corruption.' He smiled. 'Plus, as Heldren intimated, it was an excellent test of your loyalty.'

'He said Balthos was the test.'

Jherek chuckled. 'The sly dog. Balthos wasn't the test. Hulth was.' He glanced at her, as if gauging her reaction, and then turned back to the view when he saw that she wasn't going to give anything away. 'Weeding out the corruption, choosing to stand against your former conclave rather than join it. Picking sides.'

Sabbathiel's annoyance flared into anger. 'You *used* me,' she said. 'You tossed me into the lion's den without a second thought.'

Jherek seemed to consider this for a moment. 'And you survived. Indeed, you far surpassed all expectations. You uncovered the web of corruption that had evaded Heldren and I so successfully.'

'How *dare* you.'

Jherek sighed. 'I sent help. And besides, I was busy attempting to round up the scattered remnants of your former conclave. Most of whom have fled or are already dead, by the way.'

'Help? You sent a Sister of Silence and the inquisitor who pulled me out of a warp storm.'

Jherek reached out, placed his palm against the window before him, as if trying to touch that bright, unforgiving landscape beyond, to drink of its purity. 'This Mandreth – where is he now?'

'Gone,' said Sabbathiel. 'He disappeared after Hulth. I've heard nothing. I looked, but presumed he'd made a swift exit to avoid having to deal with the aftermath.'

'Interesting,' said Jherek.

'So, you *didn't* send him?'

Jherek turned to regard her. His eyes, despite his jovial attitude, were hard. 'No. I did not. I am not familiar with the man.'

'I see.' Sabbathiel nodded, distracted.

Who, then, was this man who had pulled her out of the warp storm and coaxed her back to life, who had fought by her side against her enemies on Hulth? Who had demonstrated not just his interest in her, but his loyalty to her, too? Where had he come from, and why had he chosen to involve himself in her life?

I shall find you, Mandreth. And I shall learn the truth.

This I vow.

Sabbathiel watched the beasts tumbling in and out of the water; playful, peaceful. Her own reflection seemed superimposed over the view, looking back at her from the other side of the glass, faint and ghostly.

After a moment, she turned to Jherek. 'What next? With my old conclave gone…' She trailed off. There was nothing more to be said. She did not like the idea of being beholden to this man that she did not know, but for now, he was the last connection she had left to her former life. She would have to tread very carefully indeed.

'Next?' Jherek chuckled. He nodded, satisfied. 'There are four remaining survivors of Sinjan's coterie from within the conclave. Next, Astor Sabbathiel, you become a conclave of one.'

CODA

'To mourn for the dead is to carry the memory of all those we have lost. It is our moral obligation, a necessity of being human. To mourn for the living... well, that is a heavier burden still, for it serves to remind us of our own mistakes.'
— Warris Hildenkhar, extracted from the treatise
On the Cost of Humanity

'It's just... it doesn't feel right, leaving them behind like that.'

The ogryn's voice was plaintive, tinged with genuine sorrow. Mandreth's heart almost went out to him.

Almost.

But then it *had* been over a week since they'd fled Hulth in the aftermath of the battle beneath the cathedral, and Nol had talked of little else. It was, Mandreth had to admit, becoming somewhat wearisome.

'Why is that, Nol? They're quite capable of looking after themselves. You saw that with your own eyes.'

The ogryn shook his head. 'It's not that,' he said. He was sitting against the bulkhead in the rear of the ship, stripping and rebuilding his ripper gun like a jigsaw puzzle, just as he had every day since Mandreth had woken from his brief injury-induced coma.

Click-clunk. Click-clunk.

Over and over and...

Mandreth took a measured breath. His chest flared in pain. His body was still battered and bruised, and several ribs had been broken, but he'd dosed himself with analgesics from the medical supplies on the ship, and there didn't appear to be any permanent damage. Except to his patience, perhaps.

'Well?' he prompted. 'If not that, what?'

Nol placed his weapon down on the plasteel panel beside him. 'It's because I miss them.' His shoulders visibly drooped with the admission. 'Especially the little one with the beard.'

Mandreth sighed. He dropped to his haunches before the slumped ogryn. 'You'll see them again soon, Nol.'

Nol looked up, his forehead wrinkling in confusion. His dark eyes shone. 'I will?'

Mandreth nodded. 'Of course. Hulth was just the beginning.' He stood, smoothing the front of his coat. 'Inquisitor Sabbathiel is marked for great things. But she'll be needing our help along the way. Have no doubt of that.'

Nol's frown broadened into a bright grin. 'Soon?'

Mandreth nodded. 'Now, I must prepare for landing.' He offered Nol his most reassuring smile, and then turned his back on his sole remaining acolyte and made a beeline for his quarters.

Once inside the small room, he closed the door behind him, filled his nostrils with the rich, musty scent of the stacked tomes lining the walls, and crossed to the modest dressing table by the far wall. He placed both palms upon its worn and pitted surface, leaning forward to peer at himself in the small, wood-framed mirror. His reflection stared back at him, pale and implacable.

'Marked for great things,' he said, the curl of a smile forming on his thin lips. 'Wouldn't you agree, Inquisitor Mandreth?'

For a moment, the reflection stared out at him blankly.

And then it flickered, as if the quality of the light had changed, and the visage in the looking glass contorted, so that Mandreth's face became fretful, desperate, twisted into a terrible, soundless scream.

The true face of the man.

Pathetic.

A shadow passed across the silvered glass, and as swiftly as it had changed, the reflection was restored – pale and implacable, just as before.

Mandreth, or the thing inhabiting his shell, straightened his collar and turned away from the dressing table. 'Right, then,' he sighed. 'What's next?'

ABOUT THE AUTHOR

George Mann is an author and editor based in the
East Midlands. For Black Library, he is best known
for his stories featuring the Raven Guard, which
include the audio dramas *Helion Rain* and *Labyrinth
of Sorrows*, the novella *The Unkindness of Ravens*, plus
a number of short stories.

YOUR NEXT READ

EISENHORN: THE OMNIBUS
by Dan Abnett

Charting the career of Inquisitor Gregor Eisenhorn as he transitions from zealous upholder of the truth to collaborating with the very powers he once swore to destroy, this omnibus brings together the novels *Xenos*, *Malleus*, *Hereticus* and *The Magos*, as well as four short stories.